FIRST AMERICAN POPE

Pontifex Maximus

BY:
ANGELO PAGNOTTI, SR.

PublishAmerica

Baltimore

© 2000 by Angelo Pagnotti, Sr..
All rights reserved. No part of this book may be reproduced, stored in a retrieval system, or transmitted in any form or by any means without the prior written permission of the publishers, except by a reviewer who may quote brief passages in a review to be printed in a newspaper, magazine, or journal.

First printing

ISBN: 1-4137-2788-3
PUBLISHED BY PUBLISHAMERICA, LLLP
www.publishamerica.com
Baltimore

Printed in the United States of America

Dedication

*Smitty, your constant encouragement kept me on track and your furry friend, Sandy, kept me company while I wrote.
To my biggest supporter, and toughest critic, my love, Elisa. Your inspiration and encouragement made all the difference in my life and this book.*

FOREWORD

Everyone lives with a degree of superstition. This peculiar gene has been passed through successive generations since man stood upright. Anthony Pavelli had a life-long superstition of the number twenty-nine; he considered it an unlucky number.

Prologue

From every point on the compass an elite group of men gathered in the ancient hall. They were entrusted with the most secret of Catholic ceremonies—electing a new Pontifex Maximus. On the fifteenth day of the conclave, at exactly noon, princes of the Church cast another secret ballot.

Recently elevated from bishop, Anthony Cardinal Pavelli considered himself unworthy to hold his new rank or participate in the Papal conclave. He felt self-conscious placing his handwritten ballot into the ornate antique black box. Would his peers notice the anxiety wracking his body, hear the wheeze as he struggled for air, or sense his erratic heartbeat? Could they smell the fear rising from his skin? After submitting his vote he felt reluctant to mingle with his peers, so he retreated to the hard wooden bench in the dimly lit area.

Waiting for the official tally, the junior Cardinal distracted himself by surveying his surroundings. The Sistine Chapel was undergoing renovations so the Papal Conclave convened in an adjoining hall designed over 500 years ago specifically for Papal elections. The huge hall was sparse and intentionally void of all modern comforts, to remind participants of their solemn duty. Like his Church, the handcrafted twenty-foot ceilings latticed with sturdy wood beams were built to last. Uneven plaster walls, once stark white, looked dreary and stained by ceremonial oil lamps that illuminated the room. The only aesthetic feature, a cracked and faded fresco, depicted men in red casting secret ballots.

Eminence Pavelli's thoughts returned to the circumstances at hand. Ten days in a sequestered conclave took a toll on men accustomed to comfort and control of their lives. Nerves, his included, felt raw and tender. Politeness had vanished. The slightest misstep caused an argument. Intuition guided his daily interactions and this sixth sense warned him to remain distant and aloof from the various cliques.

Before the conclave began, the Vatican rumor mill focused on his personal choice and friend, Dominic Cardinal Marconi. The other leading candidate, Vatican Secretariat of State, Walter Cardinal Wronowski, remained the most powerful and influential man in the Vatican—a tyrant feared and despised. If the voting had been an open ballot, Wronowski would have undoubtedly swayed the election; few would openly deny him their vote.

Clearly none of the nominees had enough votes to win. Distancing himself from the power brokers was a means of self-preservation. At the same time, he couldn't help speculating why in the last few days he'd been excluded from all private caucus gatherings. Although this made life easier, it limited his ability to politic for Dominic. He also caught strange looks and sideways glances from certain cardinals, especially Eminence Wronowski. It made him shudder. The simple sight of *that* man prompted him to make the sign of the cross. Tongue in cheek, he asked God's forgiveness for such unchristian thoughts.

Sitting alone, the anxiety finally under control, his breathing and heart rate returned to normal. Within minutes activity in the hall increased, followed by a churning deep in his gut. Something felt off kilter. Scanning the hall, far too many cardinals looked in his direction. Some openly pointed, sending shivers along his old tired spine.

The simple toll of the ceremonial bell silenced the noisy conversations. With the count tallied, the chamberlain of the Papal conclave, Marco Cardinal Grazelli, called the session to order with an invocation to the Holy Spirit. Without preamble, Eminence Grazelli announced the results of the twenty-ninth vote; Anthony Cardinal Pavelli had received exactly two-thirds plus one—the minimum number of votes required for election to the highest position in the Roman Catholic Church.

The hall remained unnaturally subdued. Trying to hide the human vices of envy and jealousy, princes of the Church watched the virtually unknown Pavelli for his decision. Would the Papal chimney cough white or black smoke? More importantly, they speculated about Anthony Cardinal Pavelli. Was he Papabile? Did he truly have the makings of a Pope?

Stunned, Eminence Pavelli's senses fought to stop the numbing overload;

his mind demanded *absoluta tranquilita* in order to think clearly. He asked the conclaves' indulgence, lowered his head to avoid eye contact, and retreated to the chapel on unsteady legs. During the short walk his thoughts centered on controlling the anxiety that was beginning to overwhelm his entire body. He desperately needed solitude to calm his fear in order to consider the second most difficult decision of his seventy-two years.

One knee at a time, he descended on hued marble, inhaled deeply until he calmed his erratic breathing. His eyes lifted up and locked onto the life-size crucifix suspended above the altar while his mind slipped back twenty-five years. Time could never erode this haunting and compelling memory. He began to relive his first life altering decision, and the sacrifices he made to follow the Lord's calling. His mind repeated the words he had spoken to his loved ones, explaining his decision to abandon a business career, leave his children and the woman he cherished beyond love. Until this day he had never regretted the decision, only the pain it caused.

This Papal election was the direct result of that never forgotten choice. Deep down Cardinal Pavelli already knew his answer. A loud, agitated voice echoed through the small chapel. "Dear Lord, what decision? Was there ever a choice? If I really have a choice, send me to a small parish so I can reach out and help Your people. I thought that's why You called me."

Startled by the unrestrained rancor in his own voice, he paused for an answer he knew would never be spoken aloud.

Bowing in deep repentance, Pavelli knew with utmost certainty he was plucked from among the most talented and worthy Catholic leaders for a purpose. He knew accepting this mantle would, without a doubt, change the remaining years of his earthly life; as well as the one billion Christians he was handpicked to lead.

From that moment, Anthony Cardinal Pavelli became Alex IX, the first American Pope.

Chapter One

Pope Alex IX called an emergency meeting with the directors of the Vatican administration, the Curia. Cardinals and bishops generally managed the Curia departments. Appointments were at the Pontiff's discretion and the directors considered under his direct control. The directors had been in their positions for many years, every man appointed by previous Pontiffs.

The Holy Father was initially reluctant to make hasty changes until he understood the inner workings of the "Vatican Club," as he sarcastically referred to the Curia. The reticence continued when his credibility as a qualified Pontiff came under fire. Now that he had an imminent plan to clear his tattered image and reputation, it was time to take control. Once he began he had no doubt his personal imprint would forever change the role of the Curia.

"Holy Father, the directors are assembled, except for Archbishop Walford. I understand that he's not attending," said Brother Jacomo.

"Thank you, brother. I will join them in a moment." The Pope shook off any lingering doubt as he rose and stretched. Time to piss off a few princes.

The directors stood to greet their Pontiff as he entered the meeting room adjacent to his living quarters.

"Welcome everyone; please be seated."

As they obeyed, Pope Alex remained standing at the head of the oblong walnut conference table. He glanced across the room before starting. He felt ready, in total command of the room and his emotions. His naturally olive face appeared void of any expression, while beneath the surface emotions raged beyond the simmering stage.

The directors sat comfortably around the conference table and although they knew that the Pope rarely called an emergency meeting they exuded a smug business-as-usual confidence. What a huge error in judgment.

"Gentlemen. Since my election nine months ago, our meetings have been one-on-one sessions to discuss your department's progress or review difficult issues that required my attention. During that period I haven't interfered with the Curia's activities. However, I have formulated my opinion of the Curia in general. Getting right to the point, I don't like what I see and hear!"

Caught off guard, the directors shifted uneasily in their seats, shaken by both the unexpected attack and the inflection in the Pope's voice. They quickly understood this was serious; this Pontiff wasn't a man prone to humor.

The sharp jab jolting his audience brought him a sense of control that amplified his determination. "Effective today, we will begin monthly joint meetings in addition to individual sessions, as they become necessary. Every director *will* become familiar with the issues and complexities that your Curia peers are experiencing. You will have an opportunity to suggest possible solutions. It may be advisable to reassign directors to new responsibilities. One of the lessons I learned during my twenty-five years in business was experience has its benefits, but often new blood re-energizes outlook and efforts."

The meeting room fell absolutely silent, except for the rigid body language, which spoke volumes. Instantly the air had a charge of hostile energy, focused directly at the Pontiff. The Church leaders had managed their departments for years without the slightest oversight. These proud men considered the Pope's comments and interference as a vote of no confidence. The directors tried to avoid him. Instead they looked at each other or stared down at the table. Some men turned pale while others' faces flushed, tempers held in check before they flared in an open forum.

"I have also discovered that it has been some years since consultants and outside auditors have evaluated the various Curia departments. An independent review of staff, policy and procedures is long overdue. Please notify your respective team members to expect a visit from outside consultants in the next thirty days. I expect every member of the Curia to provide complete, full and open cooperation."

Looking directly at each individual, his confidence masked behind an expression that wasn't stern or irritated, but lacked the slightest warmth. "Some of you may have noticed that Archbishop Walford did not join us.

He's been reassigned to a diocese in Austria, his homeland. While I certainly appreciate the Archbishop efforts during his five years of service to the Vatican, I felt a reassignment would best serve our Church. Bishop Newhart, seated to my left, is from Great Britain. He has accepted Archbishop Walford's position as Curia Director for Vatican Media and Communications, including the Vatican radio, effective immediately."

Both hands held behind his back, the Pope began to slowly circle the table and waited for hushed murmurs to subside. The more this group squirmed, the higher his confidence grew. He neared a perfect stride. "Media and communication far beyond our traditional radio broadcasts will be an integral part of focusing Catholics and all Christians on God's commandments and solidifying our resolve to spread the word of Jesus Christ. It's my firm belief that as Church leaders we can no longer direct our flock from a perfect vacuum behind the Vatican walls. We must take an active role, set an example…be accessible to our flock."

Pope Alex stopped moving while he emphasized the next point. "The Church is confronted with a magnitude of social and financial issues. We *must*, and I repeat *must*, resolve the financial shortage caused by lower contributions. Recently there's been a marked decline in contributions earmarked for mission work. These funds are needed for social programs, which help mankind's material needs while teaching God's Word."

Completing the circle, the Holy Father shifted his pacing to the front of the conference room, all the while making individual eye contact with each director. He made a mental note of any man who diverted his eyes or those that didn't look at him. "The Vatican cannot…I repeat, cannot, continue to function under the cloak of medieval secrecy. Starting today, communications will be open and forthright. I want all financial statements open to the public." Muffled gasps echoed around the table.

He purposely slowed his delivery to properly enunciate this next point. "This means… anyone and everyone can review the expenses to run the Vatican and the amount we contribute to social and missionary programs. In my experience, people are reluctant to donate to organizations that withhold financial information."

After this last remark, it was apparent the directors were eager for the berating to end. Each man wished he could somehow become impervious to the Papal eyes that bored through layers of thin skin and boiled their princely blood. Powerful men such as these were not accustomed to being on the receiving end of a berating.

His criticism was direct and relentless. His brown eyes spewed venom down the long conference table. The final blow was delivered with enthusiasm. "I have scheduled our first full meeting for next week. You will each receive a complete agenda by noon tomorrow. I'm frequently pained and disappointed with some clergy in this room. You should be setting the example by identifying monumental issues and giving advice on how to approach resolutions. Instead, some sitting around this table have taken the title of prince far too literally, overseeing Curia departments as personal fiefdoms."

Placing his hands on the end of the table, he leaned forward into his broad shoulders, "Before we adjourn, does anyone have any questions?"

A silent uneasiness emanated from every curve of the oblong table. "Good. Since there are no questions, we are adjourned until next week. Eminence Marconi, can you remain a few moments?"

Marconi bowed slightly, "I'm at your service, Holiness."

While the conference room quickly emptied, His Holiness studied Dominic Cardinal Marconi, his advisor and only close friend in the Vatican. Standing five foot, six inches tall, Cardinal Marconi was by no means a physically imposing man. However, his strong aura and aristocratic demeanor commanded attention. His always-searching blue eyes, the way they contrasted with his dark hair and skin were striking and the first thing people noticed.

"Well Dominic, how do you think they reacted to the meeting?"

Marconi looked deep into the Pope's demeanor for a sign, any sign of what he was thinking. No luck; the man remained immutable. He carefully worded his opinion. "Your Holiness, I am sure their initial reaction was negative. I could literally feel the tension swell as you hammered home each point. By the end, some directors wanted to crawl under the table. I'm sure many are grumbling and licking their wounds as we speak. Those devoted to the Church will eventually see the benefits of change, and of course, there will always be a handful that will never accept change. Those directors must be weeded out and replaced. It may take time to identify the devious ones that offer passive resistance."

"Then we are in agreement! This is the beginning. We have our work ahead of us. I intend to maintain constant pressure on each director and his whole department until they see the light, or we replace the bulb."

The Pontiff moved to the closest window overlooking St. Peter's Square. He loved to watch the faithful milling about. No matter how often people traversed the square they were as awed by the grandeur as he was every day. He thoughtfully fingered the pectoral cross that hung from his neck, not quite sure how to broach the next order of business. The timing seemed perfect; however, he wanted to be sure that Dominic would accept. In his heart he knew his trusted friend would never refuse due to loyalty.

Cardinal Dominic stood waiting patiently to be excused. As the Pope's Chief of Staff, he had numerous activities scheduled. As the Holy Father turned and walked towards his friend, Dominic sensed something wasn't quite right and that somehow it involved him. Pope Alex placed his right hand on his friend's shoulder and guided him toward the conference table. This unusual gesture confirmed Dominic's suspicion.

"My friend, please have a seat. There is one more item on my mind."

They sat on the same side of the table, facing each other; inches separated their crossed legs. The physical contrast between the two men was striking. The Holy Father's full frame glistened in white from head to toe, while Cardinal Dominic's black cassock adorned with the red piping of his office covered his slight physique. Since birth, every aspect of their existence differed, except for what truly mattered: Their love of the Almighty and His Church.

Dominic didn't speak a word, permitting the Holy Father to work through his visible angst until he was ready to talk. The waiting exasperated Dominic.

The Pontiff looked at Dominic, ready but not eager to place his friend in a tough situation. "This morning I had another eventful meeting with our Secretariat of State, Wronowski. I tried to reopen discussions about laicized priests returning to the priesthood. It's no secret that we desperately need more practicing priests. He's vehemently opposed...refuses to discuss the issue."

The Pontiff stopped when Dominic raised an eyebrow but continued when he failed to speak. "Our meeting almost disintegrated into a shouting match. The man's a pompous ass...has no respect for the Papal office. So arrogant that he makes no attempt to even hide his disdain. Unfortunately, he's smart enough not to do so in public. That would give me the opportunity to chop him off at the knees. How can I continue to seek guidance from a chief advisor who's so...so vehemently against my ideas? If the timing was right I'd immediately remove him as Secretariat of State."

Dominic offered a simple nod, not quite sure where the Pontiff was going with this tirade.

Nearing the delicate part of the conversation was always difficult. The

Pope slowed in order to take deeper breaths to calm the thumping in his chest that signaled an angina attack. Once the topic was on the table, and the initial shock over with, his heart would begin to relax.

"This brings me to what's on my mind. Although I'm not officially ready to castrate Wronowski in public by stripping him of his title, I'd like you to begin taking over the majority of the Secretariat's responsibilities. You will become the official Papal Consigliore. When the time's right, I will announce your appointment as Vatican Secretariat of State. I intend to minimize interaction with Wronowski. He'll gradually understand he's being squeezed out, losing his power base and access to the Pope. It'll be interesting to see if he's astute enough to resign.

"So, I come to you, my trusted friend, to ask if you will take the burden of this office without the title." Pope Alex instinctively raised a hand. "Before you answer I have one last thing."

Dominic leaned forward, curious as to what information the Pontiff wanted to share.

"I'm not sure who he despises more, you or me. Once he realizes what's happening he'll try to crush you at every turn."

Dominic's insides churned, acid heaved up his esophagus. He wouldn't permit his friend and Pontiff to see the disgust he felt toward that arrogant pig. Clearly the Polish Cardinal hated the Italian Magrestrum that Marconi represented. Dominic stopped himself from moistening his dry lips lest he betray any concern before giving his answer.

"I'll gladly accept the assignment because my Pontiff asked; however, if a side benefit is removing Wronowski from power, so much the better."

Dominic had always suspected that Wronowski and his followers blocked his opportunity to become Pope. He also firmly believed that the Holy Spirit worked in mysterious ways, and perhaps, Pope Alex was chosen for a reason, a higher purpose.

Chapter Two

Henry Cardinal Belfonte exited through the back door to avoid a Wronowski tantrum. During the meeting he felt trapped between two powerful locomotives about to collide. Belfonte's ears stung from the Pope's berating, at the same time Wronowski's stern glare penetrated every fiber of his being. The Secretariat of State never let Belfonte forget he was beholding to him, obligated for life. On bad days Belfonte's disgust about Wronowski prompted his recollection of the most degrading day of his life. A day he would never forget; a reminder to remain vigilant against that monster posing as a cleric. Belfonte forced his memory to recall every aspect of that awful day.

The caucus room was sparse and cramped. Far too small for Wronowski's bulky six foot four, three hundred and fifty pound frame along with a small table encircled by mismatched chairs. The Cardinal paced the windowless cube like a trapped animal, trying to exhaust his volcanic rage. It was hot and stuffy. Sweat trickled from his baldhead, down a round, bloated face into deep-set fierce eyes. Children expected to see those eyes looking down from an evil gargoyle.

Walter Cardinal Wronowski's unbuttoned black cassock clung against his massive body, held in place by perspiration and the red sash that signified his rank. A single thought drilled his skull over and over; losing wasn't an option. He would not permit failure, to simply walk away when he could almost touch and taste the pinnacle of power. He'd fought, groveled, bribed, intimidated, lied and clawed his way to this opportunity. Powerful Polish fists hammered the table again and again, as he released pent-up rage. The pain didn't help; nothing did.

Recently appointed Director of Vatican Security, Henry Cardinal Belfonte tried to please the boss, his mentor. Accompanied by Father Borgotta, Cardinal Wronowski's aide, they cautiously cracked the door and eased into the small room.

Anger echoed around the small cube. "Belfonte, where have you been? Do you know how long I've been waiting in this box? And where are the other chicken-shit cardinals?"

"I am sorry...*your Eminence*. We were unavoidably detained."

"Belfonte...you've grin-fucked me for the last time. You smiled...assured me I would be elected POPE! I should fire your skinny ass and send you back to that rat-infested French village."

"But your Eminence—"

"No buts. I made you a Cardinal...handpicked you for the Vatican. I own your ass. Got it?"

Like a supplicant, Belfonte was petrified of the Vatican's Secretariat of State, a man who yielded absolute power in the Church. Responding to the outbursts would only fuel his rage. Belfonte and Father Borgotta avoided eye contact and waited like sheep ready to be sheered.

Wronowski raised his fat arm and pointed a chubby finger at Borgotta, "And you, Father Asshole, all you do is nod that ugly head."

"Ah, sorry...*your Eminence*."

He pounded the table several more times before focusing his venom back on his lackeys. "After twenty ballots it's obvious I haven't secured enough votes to win. A Pontiff must be elected by two-thirds plus one vote, by the twenty-ninth vote. Otherwise on the thirtieth vote the rules change and the election is based on a simple majority. Cardinal Marconi had the majority on the last five ballots. I may lose this election but damn it, I can assure you that pompous runt Marconi will not—I repeat will *not* be elected Pope. Do you *hear* me?"

The sweating supplicants nodded in unison. "If that sixty-year-old bastard's elected, all our plans are shot to hell. By the next election, I'll be dead or over eighty...too old to qualify."

Belfonte meekly held up a hand. "Your Eminence, acting as the conclaves' Devil's advocate, I may have found a short term solution."

"Well, the mouse has something to say. Speak up man!"

"My sources have identified a candidate who has the makings of a Pope...at least for our purposes. He's also an American, which means he'll be overshadowed by suspicion in many parts of the world. Every decision will be suspect. This junior Cardinal's relatively unknown, with no political affiliations. He's seventy-two years old and in declining health. Most significantly, his private life is potentially ripe for a scandal. If we elect him you can pull his strings; control him like a puppet master. That gives us a year, maybe two, before he dies, to gather enough votes for the next election."

Cardinal Wronowski pulled in all outstanding markers to elect Pope Alex on the twenty-ninth vote. At the Curia meeting, Wronowski's eyes blamed Belfonte for not doing his homework. They elected a leader, not a puppet.

Belfonte pacified his searing anger by reciting his mother's favorite antidote: "What goes around comes around." He closed his eyes and mumbled, "Some day Wronowski, you'll get your due. Some day!"

As members of the Curia disbursed, Cardinal Wronowski touched Cardinal Capaldo's elbow, a signal for Capaldo to follow him into his private office. This was an unlikely meeting of adversaries. His countryman, Pope John Paul II, appointed the ultra-conservative Polish Prince, Vatican Secretatiat of State. As Secretariat of State, Cardinal Wronowski held a powerful and influential position. Until Pope Alex's election, he held the position of chief Papal advisor and second-in-command.

John Cardinal Capaldo's life-long friend, Pope Andrew IV, appointed the middle-of-the-road moderate Director of the Institute of Religious Works, the Vatican Bank. Both men represented their respective political factions, and were normally at odds concerning Church issues.

Wronowski's mind whirled. He wanted to stop this Papal madman before things got beyond his control. What satisfaction it would give him to bring that American bastard to his knees! Deep in thought, Wronowski barely noticed Capaldo standing beside him.

"Eminence, what do you think about today's meeting?" asked Wronowski.

"I think the lion is stirring from his den."

"So it seems, Eminence Capaldo. So it seems."

Standing at arm's length, both cautiously eyed each other while deciding how to proceed. Each realized they could be venturing into an adversary's trap. Once their contempt was divulged, there was no turning back. Wronowski had his doubts and wondered; is it wise to trust a man who conjured the image of a short, squat Italian peasant? Unfortunately, there weren't many choices; he needed Capaldo and his group of moderates. Instinct urged

Wronowski to forge ahead.

"Eminence Capaldo, it's common knowledge that our positions on many Church issues have been at different points of the compass. Despite our differences I believe it's time we join forces. I have information that shortly both the conservatives and moderates will be under siege by this Pope. Today's meeting all but confirmed this information."

Capaldo raised a hand to interrupt. A bit uneasy with this topic, he knew the Vatican walls had ears. "Eminence Wronowski, I think we need privacy. Would you care to join me for a walk through the east gardens?"

With that suggestion, Wronowski couldn't wait to reach the garden, and if all went well to recruit Capaldo. The big man picked up speed, his huge body wobbled through the long corridors and down the stairs to the garden. Slightly winded and looking a bit disheveled he could hardly contain the urgency in his voice. "Let me catch my breath. You... you have heard the rumors about this Pope's private life. The stories are running rampant. He must be stopped. We must stop him before he gets out of hand. The conduct...his actions are intolerable! I can't stand being in the same room with the man."

Wronowski's ears tingled as he talked about his nemesis. "As Church leaders, it's our solemn duty to protect our Mother Church. We must use whatever pressure we can to stop this renegade, this usurper, this, this...American prick from destroying everything we consider hallowed."

Feeling the heat of the midday sun, Capaldo led them under a large shade tree and turned to face Wronowski. "I'm aware of many things. I've done my homework as well and it confirms the Pope's private life since he became a priest is unblemished. Someone is taking great liberties in spreading rumors about his background and moral conduct.

A vile grin spread across Wronowski's lips.

"As Director of the Vatican Bank my trusted position gives me access to private documents. Through my contacts I've heard that the Pope is on the verge of a major announcement which somewhat confirms your information. We moderates gave our tacit approval by not interfering with certain subversive actions, namely, the rumors spread about the Pope." He caught the change in Wronowski's expression. "Son of a bitch—you know all about these lies!"

Wronowski's grin grew larger as Capaldo rambled on. Capaldo decided to play Wronowski to gauge his reaction. "Now you're asking for our direct support against him? Eminence, this is a matter of grave conscience. Should we oppose God's chosen leader because we mortals do not agree with him and the changes he wants to make? Isn't it our belief that the Pope's infallible? It's a very complex ethical issue."

Wronowski wiped the moisture off his bald head. Growing impatient with the hollow rhetoric, his eyes darted left to right. He wished Capaldo would get to the point.

"This isn't something I can simply give you an answer on and become your standard bearer. I have the same doubts about this man's ability and agenda. However, I won't make this decision based on differences in personalities."

Wronowski's expression sagged as he hastened to end the conversation. Yet he held back his frustration, allowing Capaldo to finish.

"I need to pray on this matter and confer with my closest advisors before I can give the conservatives my support."

The giant towered over Capaldo, glared down at this runt of a man with his practiced menacing stare and summoned a vile tone filled with rancor. "Your allegiance is to God and the Church, not this American Pope. As a matter of conscience we must join forces to save the Holy Church."

"You may be right, but as I said, I must think and pray on the matter. Eminence Wronowski, I must ask you this one question: If I should decide to join you in this venture, just what did you have in mind for the American?"

Stepping closer, Wronowski's girth invaded Capaldo's personal space. His voice low and guttural, more vile that moments ago, he said, "When I have your oath we'll discuss the options. I need your decision in the next few days. Time is of the essence. We must move quickly to stop this bastard."

With that, Wronowski turned and walked at a quick pace through the gardens and back to his office.

Meanwhile, the spark of ambition ignited in Capaldo. He too had plans. With the unwitting help of Wronowski's resources he'd whittle this Polish giant down to a stub and garner his power before casting Wronowski aside.

CHAPTER THREE

After celebrating morning Mass, Eminence Capaldo entered his office and found a voice mail message from Cardinal Wronowski. Capaldo had been expecting, dreading this call. Time to make a decision that could irrevocably change the Catholic Church or destroy his career, possibly both. Wronowski wanted an answer this morning or he would proceed without Capaldo and his group of moderates.

Capaldo had an answer but was reluctant to say the words out loud. He feared starting a chain reaction that would not stop until he reached his ultimate goal. Whatever the cost in ruined careers, or if need be, actual body count, once the door swung open he'd prevail.

Capaldo knew something about Wronowski's background, but not enough to feel comfortable about forming a partnership. So his staff had been assigned to gather intelligence. Just as he suspected they differed in background as well as philosophy.

Wronowski's mother Nada, and her brother, Stanley, raised Walter in Communist-controlled Poland. His father died in an auto accident when Walter was five years old and his sister Olga a mere toddler. Before World War II, his mother's family belonged to the Polish aristocracy. The family squandered their wealth long before the Communists took control. Uncle Stanley resented the family's decline and the fact that former friends and relatives snubbed them. This resentment of the wealthy class drew him into the Communist party where he eventually reached a middle level position of power and influence. Uncle Stanley never married and was the only father figure Walter ever knew. His uncle was rumored to be a tyrant who controlled the entire family with the same forceful hand he used to control the subjected Polish people.

There was one crucial battle where mother Nada eventually prevailed. Walter, against his uncle's wishes, wanted to enter the seminary. The family was in turmoil until Uncle Stanley relented and helped Walter obtain a travel visa to attend a seminary in Austria. The rest of Wronowski's career was public knowledge. He returned to Poland an ordained priest before Communism fell and was instrumental in rebuilding the Polish Roman Catholic Church, eventually following his friend Pope John Paul II to the Vatican.

This background information didn't push Capaldo's decision in either direction. He better understood Wronowski's previous stance on Church issues, his tyrannical method of gaining influence and abuse of power. *No point in delaying further*, he thought. He dialed the Polish Prince.

The private line picked up on the second ring. "Pronto, Cardinal Wronowski, speaking."

"Your Eminence, this is Cardinal Capaldo. I received your message. After considerable thought and prayer, the decision is 'yes'; we will join you. Since we spoke, I cautiously approached only my most trusted friends. Three other cardinals and I will join. Six others will support us only if we are successful. All are sworn to secrecy."

"Good, very good. That means our group has nine active members willing to take action and twelve others in reserve to support us after we are in control." Capaldo considered the disdain he had for his so-called peer. After a few short minutes on the phone he wanted to pound the arrogance out of Wronowski.

"Eminence, what's our next step?" asked Capaldo.

"My sources confirmed the rumor you heard about a major announcement being imminent, but no hard facts. My intuition says the rumors are true and we must move as fast as humanly possible. This is short notice but can we assemble the group to meet in two hours?"

"I can make that happen. No one is traveling. Where do you suggest meeting?"

"The Vatican Bank. As a director you have access, and a meeting of cardinals will not appear unusual. Notify your people we meet in two hours, and Eminence Capaldo, can you arrive a half-hour earlier?"

"Yes, I'll be there." *This felt right*, Capaldo thought, *very right*. He sneered,

In due time I'll have a few surprises for that big Polock.

Capaldo arrived at the Bank an hour early to prepare the meeting room. Cardinal John, as his friends and family referred to him, was extremely proud of this conference room. In fact, it was his favorite room in the Vatican Bank. Entering it reminded him of his first victory over the Vatican administration. Shortly after his appointment as Director General of the Vatican Bank, he decided the conference room needed renovation. Architecture was a hobby, so he designed a bright modern room with muted walls, plush carpet and a lowered ceiling. He ordered modern art for the walls and a smoked glass conference table with chrome chairs. The Vatican renaissance motif had its place but this was his world and he wanted to make an imprint. In addition, it was a play to exercise his political clout.

The construction design was submitted to the architectural antiquity committee and immediately rejected by Fredrico Giovanetti as not conforming to Vatican architecture. Capaldo resubmitted the request with a glowing explanation for the new design. The committee sat on the second request for two months without an answer, obviously hoping the request would die from lack of interest. Not so, Capaldo requested a private meeting with Signor Giovanetti in an attempt to convince the head of the committee to approve the request so they could fund the project and begin construction. The Cardinal reminded the architect that it was one interior conference room utilized by Vatican personnel; the public did not have access to the area. Giovanetti's gave a simple answer, "no." So the battle began.

The architects had approval on design while the Vatican Bank appropriated funding for new projects. Coincidentally, funds for all major projects were delayed by the Vatican Bank for various and sundry reasons, never denied, simply relegated to a drawer for months, and then returned to the antiquity committee requesting additional information or clarification. Although many projects sat six months behind schedule, Signor Giovanetti would not budge; nor would Capaldo. The entire Vatican community watched the Mexican stand-off. The first man that blinked lost.

Eventually a young architect's assistant submitted an idea, simple but clever, that satisfied both men and the conference room renovation proceeded using the Cardinal's design. The plan was simple but brilliant. The room was quite large, twenty-five feet wide and thirty feet long, more than adequate for a small conference room. The proposal suggested building new plaster walls a half-meter from the existing walls, and a drop ceiling at a height of three meters. This met the Cardinal's design. Equally as important, Signor

Giovanetti approved because the original walls and ceiling remained intact. In the future, if need be, the room could be returned to its original condition. Signor Giovanetti approved without losing face and Capaldo achieved his objective.

The community knew Capaldo won. However, the new design wasn't common knowledge. The Curia directors saw another side of Capaldo. From that time he rose as a leader, a man of strong will. The young assistant moved up rapidly and recently transferred to the Vatican Bank staff.

As Capaldo re-lived his victory, he thought about the side benefit of the room's design. The space between the old and new wall allowed him to observe and overhear conversations in the conference room. He installed hidden cameras and microphones to record meetings that proved beneficial to his various political intrigues.

A juicy videotape staring his new partner sat tucked away in his private vault. Wronowski was definitely a snake that had to be watched. While the former Pope lay near death, the Vatican hosted an ecumenical council of all the Catholic sects, including Russian and Greek Orthodox. As Vatican Secretariat of State, Wronowski acted as the official host. Late one afternoon, after the main session adjourned, Wronowski had a private meeting with Russian Orthodox Archbishop Rosonov, nicknamed the Red Bishop because he supported the Communists when they controlled Russia. No real surprise that when Communism evaporated, at least on the surface, the Russian Orthodox religion became the official religion of Mother Russia. The only sanctioned religion owed its existence to the Russian politicians.

The Russian leaders still had their sights on expanding their sphere of influence—this time by using Russian Orthodox missionaries to pave the way into parts of Africa and South East Asia. They selected prosperous nations or those rich in natural resources that they wished to eventually control. The video recorded Wronowski and Archbishop Rosonov discussing how they would partition parts of the world so as not to interfere with each other's expansion plans in those areas. They agreed there was no point in competing. Wronowski was confident that when the last Pope died he'd be elected Supreme Pontiff. Wronowski would be ruined if the video ever leaked to the Pope or College of Cardinals. Whoever had the tape owned the big Polski.

Wronowski strolled in with a king-of-the-hill attitude. Capaldo contemplated the pompous ass, but controlled his personal feelings in order to achieve a higher purpose.

"Good morning Eminence Wronowski. How are you this momentous day?"

Such a pleasant man, his reply sounded like a cross between a grunt and moan.

"The room is prepared. Considering the delicate issues, the staff's been instructed to give us complete privacy." Wronowski paced the room, had yet to give him eye contact. This irritated Capaldo. "You asked me to arrive early."

He remained standing while Wronowski finally sat, selecting the head of the conference table; already posturing for control.

Wronowski finally looked at his new junior partner. "Eminence, you are the leader of the moderates and as we discussed we've been at odds for some years. Once this group meets and discusses possible strategies there's no turning back. Everyone in this meeting must fully understand. Our careers and positions in the Church are at risk. I must be certain that everyone…especially you are fully committed to stopping this Pope by any and all means before he destroys our Church. One weak member reluctant to do what's necessary and we fail. Then we're all screwed!" He rose and moved within arm's length of his quarry. "How can we confirm your allegiance and commitment?"

Taking a deep breath, Capaldo steadied his resolve not to strangle this jackass, assuming he could reach up to his neck. "Initially I had the same concerns about you. I asked myself, 'Is this a set-up, a way to discredit the moderates?' However, I discovered you're a fanatic about this Pope."

Wronowski didn't respond so Capaldo continued. "To directly answer your concern, as a Director General of the Vatican Bank, I have access to private financial information. I've known for some months that your Curia department has been under-reporting contributions. You're trying to make it appear that Catholics are protesting with their wallets. All along the unreported funds have been deposited into a secret account. I could have divulged this information openly or covertly to Eminence Marconi. By not acting on this information, I gave tacit approval."

For a moment, Wronowski remained motionless, taken aback by information that was supposed to be top secret. He abruptly turned, placed both hands behind his back and paced while deliberating this new information. A sly grin slowly emerged across his puffy lips. "Well, *Eminence*, welcome to the modern crusade. Shall we open the door for our comrades?"

The other members entered the room, poured coffee or tea and selected seats at the long glass table. Two cardinals joined the meeting via video telephone, using secure phone lines.

Opening the session, Wronowski stood to address what might be the most important meeting of his career. "Fellow cardinals, welcome to an exclusive group of clergy dedicated to preserving the true religion founded by Jesus Christ. We are beginning a grave journey that will affect the rest of our lives, whether or not we are successful. A few moments ago, I referred to our quest as a crusade. It is indeed a modern day crusade to save the Catholic Religion from a leader who has lost the respect of the clergy and lay people." He waited for a reaction. Nothing. They waited, willing to hear more.

"We cannot proceed with this lightly. Everyone who chooses to join us must first take a holy oath of allegiance to God, the Holy Church and the Crusade. Anyone not prepared to risk everything…and I mean everything we hold dear…can leave this meeting now, before taking the oath."

Each prince scanned the room. No one moved or breathed for seconds, waiting for a possible dissenter. To a man they remain seated and the two-video connections continued live. The energy in the room continued to build as they waited for Wronowski's next pronouncement.

Wronowski felt energized, and needed to pace. He controlled himself and continued to take advantage of the momentum. "Good. I was counting on everyone's support. Our adversary is in a powerful position. Many—actually the majority—of weak, gutless Church leaders are reluctant to oppose him. Once his power is broken—and it will be—those same people will shift their support to us. Please stand and swear a holy oath."

Every member repeated in unison: "I swear on the body and blood of Jesus Christ our Lord and Savior to act in the best interests of the Holy Church to maintain and preserve Catholic traditions. I will not discuss our meetings or plans with anyone not party to this crusade, and I will never divulge any member of this group. Amen."

Wronowski held the floor. "Please be seated. Everyone is familiar with Eminence Capaldo and me, so there's no need for formal introductions. Can each member address the group giving your name and country and if you are holding a position in the Vatican or are on special assignment for the Vatican. Let's begin from left to right, the video participants can go last."

Eminence Pasquale began. People noticed his thin gaunt face and wild, bushy white eyebrows and the way his robe hung loosely over a wiry frame. He had a powerful influence on the Spanish Church, a country that was over ninety percent Catholic. He was a distant cousin and confidant to General Franco, Spain's former dictator. His power base was unchallenged.

"Most of you know me. I am currently on a finance committee tasked with restructuring the Vatican budget process. The assignment should last three months. I spend one week each month in the Vatican. It's an honor to be part of this."

The second member, Henry Cardinal Belfonte, was born in France, raised in Belgium. His lanky frame and bright hazel eyes were overshadowed by a somber personality. He had a reputation for a quick temper and long memory. He didn't waste time with a lengthy resume, simply stated his name, country and position as Director of Vatican security. Wronowski was instrumental in Belfonte's elevation to Cardinal and appointment to head of Vatican security. Capaldo's prior misgivings about Belfonte moved to the back burner. Security would be instrumental in gathering information and monitoring the Pope's activities.

"Eminence, tell us about what you're doing to keep tabs on our friends," said Wronowski.

"Well, first recording telephone conversations; Alex, Marconi, Brother Jacomo and Cardinal Tornetta. Although, so far nothing of any substance. All the Vatican computers are connected to our network. We intercept and review all e-mails, and determine what web sites they query. We also have receivers to capture cell phone conversations. That's getting tricky because Marconi has a new handheld cell/computer. This unit garbles voices. It also condenses e-mail text and transmits in high-speed packets. We intercept the data, but haven't been able to break the code."

Wronowski wanted the group to understand what's been going on behind the scenes, "Keep working on it. You have the best computer people at your disposal. What about listening devices in the papal quarters and Marconi's office?"

"That's a problem. Marconi uses an outside security company to sweep those areas on a regular basis. I volunteered to use Vatican security people. He claims he can't break a two-year contract."

MacRay asked, "Why Tornetta?"

"Let me answer that," said Wronowski, "He is the Vatican Nuncio to Italy. We're applying pressure to Roman and central government politicians. How the politicians respond to Vatican requests tells us how they are leaning."

The next member stood. "Kurt Bechtold, from Germany. It's a privilege to join this prestigious group. I'm relatively new to the Vatican's internal politics, but I share your views about protecting the Church against this renegade Pope. I'm on the international mission committee and expect to be in the Vatican for another three weeks."

The group welcomed their German brother. Wronowski recruited Kurt; therefore he was considered beyond reproach.

Daniel Cardinal MacRay spoke more to hear himself than impart useful information. "Distinguished cardinals, I'm Canadian, and have accepted a special assignment to investigate and prepare recommendations on increasing religious vocations. I feel like an army or navy recruiter. Vocations are from God …and should not be viewed as an advertising blitz," he chuckled at his own joke.

A large man with broad shoulders, he had the physique of a former athlete. His pure white complexion and longish uncombed thick brown hair gave him a wild man look. He was often compared to a bull in a china shop; tact wasn't his strong point.

The next Cardinal's introduction came across as smooth and cosmopolitan. He and Capaldo had a long history of colluding on Church issues. "Fellow clergymen, I'm Frank Gonzalez from Argentina…the pride of South America. I plan to visit the Vatican next month for the annual overview of my diocese. I expect to complete my business in three days. I will lend whatever support I can from my home country or I can travel back to Rome if required."

Capaldo nodded and gave his friend a welcome smile.

"The distinguished Eminence from England is joining us on video," said Wronowski.

"It's unfortunate that I can't attend in person. I'm Timothy Hildabrand from Manchester, England. I have no current projects associated with the Vatican. However, if you need on-site support I can arrange to visit my old friend, Eminence Wronowski."

"Thank you, Timothy," said Wronowski. He then requested the last member provide an introduction.

"My pleasure. I'm Cardinal Raj Patel from New Deli, India. I have been summoned to the Vatican next month for my annual review of the New Deli Diocese. I, too, can arrive sooner if needed."

Wronowski responded, "Thank you Eminence Patel. At this time there's no need to join us; however, your distant support is appreciated. I suggest that each of us be available twenty-four hours a day, via cell phone or pager. Your assistants must always know your location in case we need to contact each other. This brings us to the substance of our meeting: How do we stop the Pope from changing dogma, precepts and traditions, not to mention reorganizing the Church structure? Does anyone have any thoughts or ideas?"

After a long silence, Wronowski, the self-appointed leader, felt drawn to again take the floor. "I suggest that two or three cardinals meet with Pope Alex and discuss the extreme lack of confidence the College of Cardinals and lay members of the global Roman Catholic community have in his performance, reputation and new ideas. We convince him that he has lost support and is an embarrassment to the Church and his high office. For the good of the Church we encourage retirement. He can save face by claiming health reasons. It's unprecedented for a Pope, but cardinals do retire for health reasons. Church leaders will reluctantly understand and accept his decision. If he refuses we threaten to force a schism with powerful cardinals establishing a new Pope and Papal administration. The Pope knows a modern schism will devastate the Church for hundreds of years and that the Catholic faith might never fully recover." Wronowski looked at his cohorts for a reaction. Two were shaking their heads in agreement; the other faces were hard as granite. He had no option but to continue with the shaky idea put forth.

"We convince him the schism will be far worse than the breakaway of the Russian and Greek Orthodox Churches, the Avignon schism in the thirteen century, and the Protestant reformations. He must be made to understand, sixty to seventy percent of the cardinals will separate from his leadership."

"Do you believe this approach will convince the Pope to resign?" Pasquale interrupted. "He's headstrong, absolutely sure he is God's chosen instrument. The short bit of time I spent with him convinced me of that much."

"Very unlikely that he'll immediately resign. We need to plant the seed," Wronowski replied. "He may think we are bluffing or that if some cardinals do secede the majority of officials, clergy and lay people will not follow the splinter group."

MacRay didn't wait for Wronowski's response to register. "Your approach is risky. Once we announce our intentions, Pope Alex could try to limit our power by intimidation, banishment or excommunication. Are we actually prepared to break from the Vatican? The aftermath could be worse than living with Alex for a few years. He's almost seventy-three years old and in poor health. If he makes changes, we can always push to reverse them after he dies, claiming mental incapacity or something of that nature."

Disjointed side conversations sprang up. Capaldo raised his hand to gain attention. "Eminences, we know how easily history can repeat itself. Similar to our current Pontiff, Pope John XXIII was an Italian farm boy, a political nobody and elected in his early seventies as a compromise candidate. The College of Cardinals counted on him keeping the status quo and dying in a few years. May I remind everyone…the reforms he enacted through Vatican

II dramatically changed our Church, and haven't been rescinded! I tell you this Pope is a carbon copy!"

Facial expressions that only moments before appeared upbeat, rapidly turned acerbic and expressing doubt in the group's ability to pull off this intricate maneuver without destroying them individually or splitting the Church. The group, unsure of how to proceed, fell back into disjointed conversations.

"Can I have your attention please!" shouted Hildabrand. Everyone turned to face him. "Thank you. We are not politically or tactically prepared, nor do we have enough time to plan a successful schism. We have financial slush funds at our disposal; however, time is the enemy. Walter and I have struggled with this issue for months. I believe the best way to shake Alex's Papacy is by continuing the rumor campaign. A sexual episode or even better, a financial debacle is the best course of action. Sex people can forgive as a human weakness. Financial malfeasance is never overlooked. The right scandal will surely force Alex to consider resigning but under the guise of health, of course."

"Pardon me, Eminence Hildabrand," interrupted Gonzalez, who had followed his friend Capaldo's lead in joining this group and already had misgivings, "is this an idea or have you a definitive plan?"

"We have been spreading rumors about his personal life and they appear to be taking hold. This can be expanded into a full-blown scandal. The one sexual dalliance that is never ever overlooked is pedophilia, especially in the United States. His name was in the news during the American pedophile scandal. We should push that rumor full tilt!" Hildabrand replied.

"Any other suggestions? Eminence Gonzalez, do you have anything, suggestions, thoughts?" asked his friend Capaldo.

"Yes. I agree with Eminence Hildabrand. We leak a scandal, or several small stories combining sex and finances; that hits everyone's hot button. Once he's under pressure we plant the idea of retirement then slowly squeeze him in that direction. I don't know about this pedophilia thing; it took years to white wash that ugly issue. Does anyone want to risk dredging that up again? We do have another option. Once all the rumors have fully saturated the Catholic community we threaten to file charges against the Pope with the Sacra Romana Rota-Vatican Court unless he voluntarily resigns. Eminence Capaldo, you have some close friends presiding on the court, no?"

"Of course. But ruling against the Pope, I don't know if any member will stick their necks out that far. In fact, the Pope controls the Vatican Court and could insist that the charges be removed from their docket."

Not sure how to proceed, the members remained silent for a few uncomfortable moments. Other workable ideas just didn't flow. They had much to consider yet no definitive plan of action. Some members felt overwhelmed by the suggestions and the possible repercussions if they failed. They previously heard the harsh prospects if they failed, but this was their first taste of playing for keeps. If this crusade exploded in their faces there was no hiding behind the red sash or sanctuary behind the Vatican walls. They were vulnerable, exposed on the field of battle in a conflict they initiated.

Wronowski rose to take the floor. "My friends and comrades, this is disappointing. I was positive this group would quickly develop and deploy a strong strategy. I guess we all need time to consider alternatives and to pray for guidance. I feel and see the frustration around the table. Let's adjourn and meet in a few days to review these, and hopefully, additional options. Does anyone disagree or have anything else?" The silence was deafening. Waiting a moment, Wronowski continued, "Thank you all for joining us on short notice."

The cardinals departed one by one, until only Capaldo and Wronowski remained. Wronowski plopped in a chair looking dejected. His cohort felt energized, pulling his chair close to the Polish Prince. "You realize this is a support group. Any real action will have to come from both of us; these so-called leaders are pansies."

"I'm afraid you're right. They all have good intentions but not the guts to handle this. Even that MacRay is nothing but a big jackass!"

"Okay then, we're on the same page. I have a plan to eliminate the American. It's drastic! No way the pansies can handle even discussing this."

Head lowered, Wronowski felt gloomy about the lack of progress. "Yes, after today's meeting, I'm open to options."

Capaldo wanted to test this arrogant blowhard's determination. "Basically, we kidnap Alex and whisk him into seclusion. Tell the world he's gravely ill. In two or three weeks announce his death, followed by a closed casket funeral."

The words felt like a wasp sting. Wronowski instinctively raised his head, and jumped to his feet with such agility it surprised both men. His first thought—pure disgust; Capaldo was a certifiable. A high-pitched shout parted his dry lips. "Are you out of your mind? I'm dealing with a lunatic!"

Jumping up, Capaldo moved toward his new partner. "Calm Walter, calm down! The Pope's not really dead. He'll be a prisoner for life."

"I expected more from you, Capaldo! This is a far fetched, harebrained scheme."

"Oh, not a scheme, a plan. And it will succeed with a minimal number of people."

Raising a large fist, Wronowski yelled, "Stop right there; this is nonsense! Fucking insane!"

"You established the rules. Now you listen!"

Wronowski lowered his fist and backed away from Capaldo, prepared but not eager to listen. "Colonel Tearsue, head of the Swiss Guard will never join us but his second in command, Major Bordeau, is ripe. We'll arrange for your man Belfonte to send the loyal Colonel on a business trip. While the major's in charge he and two Swiss Guards will wake Pope Alex in the early morning, tell him he's in danger and they're escorting him to safe house. Once in the vehicle, they drug him and drive to the Papal summer residence in Gandolfo. The Gandolfo staff, everyone loyal to me, announces his grave illness and subsequent death. After the announcement my friends will move the Pope to a remote villa in Sicily, where he'll remain a prisoner for life."

Wronowski's mind reeled, his senses assaulted by the plan's audacity. He looked closely into Capaldo's eyes; there wasn't a hint of mirth. His mind screamed, *This idiot is serious*! "Who are these friends? Why would they get involved with Church matters?"

"My friends owe me for past business favors conducted through the Vatican Bank. My friends also believe that Pope Alex is conducting a bank audit and as long as he is in charge we can't continue business. At least that's what I've led them to believe." Capaldo walked over and gently held Wronowski's arm, guiding him to the glass table. "Please sit, we need to talk."

"Well, you do have big balls."

Capaldo bowed his head slightly, accepting the vulgar recognition.

"The plan is risky," said Wronowski, "it sounds clear-cut. What about the loose ends? The two Swiss Guards, the major and my biggest concern, Marconi. He'll be suspicious about Pope Alex leaving for Gandolfo without notifying him...he'll insist on visiting the Pontiff with medical experts."

"All good questions. The Swiss guards will be my friends in disguise. After the mock funeral, Belfonte will promote Major Bordeau. The major's marital indiscretions along with his part in our plan will insure his silence. Marconi's the unknown element. During our conversations he hedged his bets but favored having a new Pope; however, that ass may be working me. But, we have options: keep Marconi away from Gandolfo with emergency issues, or bribe him with votes for the coming Papal election. If he becomes a large thorn in our side my friends will take care of him. They're very persuasive or when necessary, they eliminate problems."

A chill permeated Wronowski's bones; his blood turned cold. He wondered if this would turn ugly, possibly bloody. He's the one that said success at all costs and Capaldo was pushing it to the max. He figured if he walked away now, Capaldo would take charge. His plan to become Pope lost forever to a borderline lunatic. Trapped by his own connivance he felt the clerical collar ever so slowly choking his windpipe.

The Italian's face brightened. This maneuver proved that he had resources and guile. This put him one step closer to leapfrogging Wronowski to become the group's leader.

Wronowski grumbled while keeping his head turned, unwilling to make eye contact as though his eyes could seal the deal with this devil. After a long silence he stood to leave. "A masterful plan worthy of Prince Machiavelli. You have given me much to think about. I need some time to consider the plan…see if there's an alternative."

Wronowski was hooked, twisting on his string. Both men understood if they truly wished to succeed that their choices were limited. This Polish dupe would agree to take decisive action.

Capaldo stayed in his favorite room and speculated how long it would be before he could take full advantage of the crusaders and oust the Pope. He'd manipulate those donkeys any way he wanted to.

Looking around the room he dwelled on his life and questioned what he had really accomplished. He held the exalted position of Cardinal, and had a hefty bank account from laundered Mafia money. This room was a visible symbol of his power and determination. He never wanted to join the priesthood; it turned out to be an unlucky quirk of fate. However, this fate was far preferable to the alternative.

His mother relentlessly pushed him toward the priesthood. His dream had always been to become a businessman or if lucky, follow his brother into a powerful crime family. Young and over-eager to prove his worth, he and a friend robbed a number of small businesses. Reeling in the invincibility of youth they decided to raise the bar and hit a warehouse. They botched the robbery. With nothing of value inside, they had fun vandalizing the building. The warehouse belonged to the mob, and a few days later his friend's mangled body turned up in a narrow alley. His brother Roberto saved him by pleading with his boss, the local capo. Roberto promised that his younger brother would enroll in the seminary. Not having much choice, their father consented to the agreement. It thrilled his mother, although she never understood why her husband changed his mind about their youngest son entering the priesthood.

Some days, his whole existence depressed him. Each day he rolled out of bed and with great difficulty faced his chubby reflection in the mirror. He swore that would change and soon. This is his life and he would make the best of it now that he had a worthwhile goal, a purpose. He contemplated that when the dust settled, Wronowski and the Pope would be history. Marconi and Belfonte would serve under the Capaldo Papal banner…or else. He saw himself reach out and grab the brass ring. He had what it took, and he had a plan to become Pontiff of the Roman Catholic Church.

CHAPTER FOUR

"Flight attendants, please prepare for landing. Please return all seats to their upright position, secure tray tables and stow carry-on bags under your seat. Flight 393 is arriving on schedule."

The cockpit crew began descent procedures and activated the hydraulic landing systems. Each procedure generated a mechanical whine that vibrated through the entire cabin. The landing gears descended and banged home, locking into open position. The cabin shuddered as the pilot raised the wing flaps while throttling back the powerful jet engines, gradually easing the ship lower and lower toward the runway.

The flight attendant strolled up the first class aisle checking landing preparations and noticed Kate Murphy wrapped in a blanket still dozing. She'd been restless, sleeping on and off for the past three hours. The attendant gently touched Kate's arm. "I'm sorry to disturb you Miss, we're making our final approach and the Captain has asked all passengers to prepare for landing."

Kate managed a slight smile while arching her slim back and adjusting her seat. Half-gazing out the window she noticed the tell tale signs of spring approaching while earth tones of land, rocks and buildings overshadowed the patchy green. Still groggy, her mind was already churning. Kate's fourth trip to Rome in five months. Thankfully, she finally convinced her editor to spring for first class, which seemed a rather small perk considering all the personal time she devoted to this assignment. Ironically, Ted Blake had initially considered this project futile.

Since her first visit to Rome, every free moment had been fixated on securing this assignment. It was absolutely critical to her success as an international journalist. The mere thought of this trophy assignment jolted her adrenalin and quickened her pulse. An opportunity of this magnitude might never come along again. Without a big break she was destined to remain just another second string player. Securing an exclusive interview with the controversial and much maligned Pope would propel her career, and there's no room for error in the final stages of negotiation. Failure wasn't a consideration. She wanted this badly, her pulse beat even faster as she dwelt on stopping at nothing to capture the dream.

Unfortunately, life has its share of trade-offs. Pursuing her dream came with a down side, and a twinge of guilt surfaced as she gauged the strain it placed on her relationship with Matt Janson, her live-in boyfriend. It was beginning to take a toll on her, on Matt, on their relationship.

How quickly three years slipped by, life was good. So good in fact, that Matt began hinting about a more permanent commitment. The word *marriage* crept into his conversations and Kate admitted that her head would have spun with anticipation had it not been for this assignment. After five months and four trips, the subject of marriage brought more indigestion than exhilaration.

The plane neared the tarmac and stationary objects became a blur. Kate closed her eyes and speculated about why the negotiations were taking months rather than weeks. Like many motivated young people impatience was a flaw. Not quite thirty one-years old, this was the beginning of her career. Many co-workers considered her young and doubted that she had truly "paid her dues" that come over time. A scream echoed through her brain every time people mentioned experience, age and hard knocks in the same sentence. *What bull!* she thought.

Her employer, Global News Network, broadcasted up-to-date news via television, radio and Internet magazine, the hottest news mediums. GNN was a vast entity in a powerful industry. Aware of her competition in GNN's talent pool, Kate considered herself fortunate to be handpicked to cover this high profile project.

The 747 hit the runway and gently jolted the passengers forward. Kate offered a silent thanksgiving for the safe arrival. After docking at the jetway the door unsealed, and the attendant announced that passengers could begin exiting. They had finally arrived.

First class had several advantages, least of all being the first to deplane.

First stop, immigration. Displaying a passport and press pass, Kate was ushered directly through the line to baggage claim and spotted her luggage almost immediately. "My luggage gets heavier every trip," Kate muttered to herself while struggling to lift the heavy bags from the revolving carousel. At customs she again presented the press pass. *Almost home free*, Kate thought as she waited while her bags were given a thorough search.

"Buon Giorno," offered Kate. The customs agent looked her up and down without a reply. She couldn't help thinking, *Here we go again*; another set of sweaty hands pawing my undies!

Eventually clearing customs, she hastened through the crowded foot traffic in Leonardo Da Vinci Airport. The clean and modern airport had wide concourses to handle the large volume of passengers. Remnants of power from the ancient empire still exuded an undercurrent through Rome, and she felt the emanating energy.

Kate appeared to glide through the concourse, as her pleated skirt accentuated the provocative sway of her hips. Despite the jostling crowds, a tall, thin, attractive woman with fair coloring stood out. Giorgio, her GNN driver, spotted Kate almost immediately and tried to attract her attention with an easy wave. Making his way through the crowds he caught those sparkling hazel eyes, and saw a smile appear on her oval face.

Ah, if only I were a younger man and she was not a client—his thoughts interrupted by Kate's outstretched arms. They embraced Italian style and pecked each other on both cheeks.

Their relationship had grown over the past months and Kate felt comfortable with Giorgio. In the preceding months he became a guide, an interpreter, and a friend.

"Giorgio, *come sta?*" she asked. "It's so good to see you, my friend."

"*Bene*. Welcome back, Miss Kate. Good to see you as well."

Standing beside the illegally parked limo, an airport policia and Giorgio exchanged rapid-fire Italian accompanied by numerous unfriendly hand motions. Fortunately, Giorgio managed to escape without a ticket. Tour buses loading and unloading passengers snarled traffic around the terminal. Insistent honking and exaggerated hand gestures were skills needed to navigate the crowded roads around Rome and Giorgio used every perfected skill to maneuver his Alfa Romeo to an open lane. Out of the gridlock, they slowly inched toward the express road leading into the Eternal City.

Settled into her position in the right corner of the back seat made it easier to see the driver. Extremely concerned about pitching the Vatican people, she preferred to be left alone with her thoughts of what lay ahead.

It was imperative that she arrive at her best, well rested for the next round of tedious negotiations. Kate had an uneasy suspicion about this whole deal. High profile leaders don't volunteer for an interview unless they are trying to sell something or defend themselves by setting the record straight. Based on the circulating stories, Pope Alex IX had a lot to explain.

Not wanting to appear rude, she asked, "Giorgio, do you mind if I rest my eyes? It still takes me a while to adjust to the jet lag, and today I'm feeling especially pooped!"

"*Si, Signorina*. Rest; I will wake you when we arrive at the hotel."

Entering the express road, the hectic traffic started to flow. Drifting into twilight, not quite awake or asleep, Kate's mind couldn't rest. Fragments of Matt, the assignment and her career all fused together.

In just over thirty minutes, Giorgio called, "Signorina Kate, we are here."

"Some how I realized that, Giorgio," she answered. By the sounds of the screeching brakes it's a wonder she hadn't fallen off the seat.

The eight-story Michaelangelo hotel was reasonably modern and quite functional. Not to mention the hotel's best feature—location, four blocks from the Holy See, the center of religious power. Above the fourth floor, deluxe rooms overlooked St. Peter's Duomo.

The trip had been seamless up to this point and Kate felt a bit more relaxed. "Giorgio, I do love Vatican City. Tell me; living in Rome, do you visit the Vatican often?"

"Signorina Kate, when I was young, I too, had a fascination with the magnificent Vatican—in particular the splendor of St. Peter's. Like everything else, time passes; we grow older and our lives are very busy. We spend less time in church. Even the magnificent Vatican does not draw us closer to our religion. Especially since this foreign Pope's election. The second foreigner during my lifetime and I tell you *Signornia*, the crowds in St. Peter's Square seem to get thinner each month. Something is not right with this Pope Alex IX. You note my words. I think the cardinals made a big mistake or the election was fixed!"

Attempting to end an uncomfortable conversation, he popped the trunk and exited the car to gather the luggage.

Kate followed the driver, ready to continue the discussion, "Oh come on, Giorgio, why do you say these things? Maybe your Italian pride has been hurt a little. Don't you think?"

Turning to Kate, his arms were tightly folded across his broad chest.

"*Signorina*, it's possible, we will see. What I do know is Vatican City may seem large with thousands of workers, clergy and those who live there, but they are like a family. They may have their problems, but they are loyal to their Church. This man does not belong. He is a foreigner and to make things worse, an American. There's talk of his past marriage and annulment, his lifestyle and dare I say, God forgive me, his lovers. Even rumors of illegitimate children and grandchildren! Mama mia, can you imagine? He has been Pope for less than a year and many in the Holy City are uneasy about the rumored changes he plans to make."

This subject was obviously a hot button for Italians, and Giorgio sensed he had gone too far expressing his thoughts. His position at GNN required discretion, but he also knew his opinion was shared by many. His arms reached out in an imploring motion. "*Oh Signorina*! Please excuse my remark about the Pope being American! I meant no disrespect to you."

"None taken, my friend. No need to worry. I'm a Canadian citizen living at least for now in New York City. Canadian since birth, raised in Toronto, aye!" With the awkwardness of the moment defused, Kate flashed a coy smile. Yet in some way she did find Giorgio's comments a little unsettling.

The hotel's General Manager, Giuseppi Panichelli, bowed politely to his guest, "Miss Murphy, so good of you to return to the Michelangelo. We have reserved your favorite room with a view of St. Peter's Duomo. We are also holding a message for you. It arrived about two hours ago."

"Thank you Mr. Panichelli, you know I adore visiting your hotel." Giuseppi was easy on the eyes, quite a hunk, almost worth the long flight…almost.

Kate unfolded the message from Aldo Fumo, Managing Director of Rome's GNN office. It read: Please call me after you're settled. Discussions are progressing at a quicker pace.

The good omen brightened her outlook and she quickly headed for her room. The bags would be delivered in due time. Romans work at their own pace, even for a special guest.

Dialing Aldo Fumo's number, she looked across the four short blocks to St. Peter's; the magnificent structure filled the window and never ceased to inspire her with awe.

"Pronto. Aldo here."

"Hello, Aldo! This is Kate Murphy. How are you?"

"Welcome back to Italia and Roma. It is so good to hear your voice and have you back with us."

"Well thank you, Aldo. I always feel at home here." She couldn't decide what appealed to her more, the men, excitement or the architecture.

"I wish it were my city, such changes I would make. The city belongs to the unions; they control everything, all aspect of daily life and existence. Oh, how they torture their citizens. Unions...what a scourge to human kind. Not even His Holiness can control the unions!"

Her eyes rolled as she waved her hand in a let's-move-on motion. "Aldo, how soon can we get a final answer about this project? Headquarters is bugging the hell out of me. I barely landed when an e-mail popped up on my cell phone. Help! Do we have an exclusive or still in blasted negotiations?"

"Kate, one item at a time. Things in Italy move slower than New York but we do succeed in good time, in good Italian fashion. One final meeting with the Pope and his staff, they'll make the final decision this evening at an 8 o'clock meeting. I am sure you remember Signor Zuto from last month's short meeting. The decision will be heavily weighted on his recommendation. The interviewer is a major factor in their decision. As GNN's main contact with the Vatican, I handpicked you for the interview based on their profile. You concentrate on landing this assignment...I'll keep your boss, and the corporate office in the loop."

Not knowing about the profile blind-sided Kate. Her first instinct—scream bloody murder and lay into Aldo. She quickly cooled down, suspecting he had a reason for not telling her. She carefully gathered control before speaking. "What profile? This is the first I heard of a profile. Can you give me the details? It might have been useful when I met Mr. Zuto."

"You know the Vatican is looking for a major network. The next crucial element in their decision is the interviewer; he or she can't be an American or a Catholic, and certainly not a high power media figure. There can't be a hint of manipulation. You fit their profile along with some of your competition."

Time to end the conversation and scream in private. "Okay. Thanks for the update, but I should have known about a profile long before today. I'll wait by the phone. Call me if you hear anything, anything at all. Wish us luck! Ciao."

Aldo had been a GNN director and respected media icon for three decades. He consistently prodded Kate to continue her efforts and not give up on this assignment and she latched on to every nugget of advice that he offered.

The big meeting was in three hours and she needed to call Matt. Their personal issues had to be addressed. The last thing she needed was business and personal pressure's colliding, especially during precarious negotiations.

She needed a clear mind in case the Vatican called requesting additional information.

How did things with Matt become so complicated? She wondered. No doubt they could work through their differences and build a lasting relationship, that's what she really wanted, but under her terms. Outside of work, Matt was the center of her life. Her heart ached whenever their harmony vibrated out of kilter, and recently it ached often. The physical distance proved far easier to handle than the coolness that had slowly eked into their lives. What was it about this man? Why did he make her love and care about him so much? An important element in any relationship is physical attraction. Their strong chemistry was compelling, approaching animal magnetism. The observation jolted her. Yes, she was sure the relationship was far more than physical. She needed him, if only to hear his voice and suck in the reassurance.

Calculating the time difference, Matt must be in his New York office. Three rings, Kate prayed that he would answer before the voice mail picked up. *What the hell, where are you, Matt?* She needed to speak with him, to clear the air and draw on his strength, to share the news and her excitement.

"Hello, you have reached Matt Janson. Sorry I can't answer your call. Please leave a brief message after the beep and I will return the call promptly."

Feeling dejected she muttered, "Damn answering machine. Why can't people be where we expect them to be?" This aggravation made her hot and sweaty, she hated it. Now she had to decide to leave a message or call back in a few minutes. "Hi Matt, this is Kate," she finally said. "I arrived safely. Missing you very much and I need desperately to speak to you, wish-"

"Hi honey, I just walked into the office and ran to the phone when I heard your voice. I'm glad you called. I was just thinking about you."

The short telephone cord was annoying; it confined her pacing into a small semi-circle next to the night table. "Matt, let me say something, just bear with me a moment. I haven't been able to get this off my mind. You know that I deeply care about you. But I also want you, no, need you to understand how important this assignment is to GNN, not to mention my career."

To hell with GNN's directive about confidentiality, she thought. *It's time to include Matt.* "It's not finalized yet but it looks like I'll have the opportunity to interview the Pope. Can you believe it? Me interview the Pope!"

"Kate honey, that's wonderful. I'm excited for you; this is something you've worked for...dreamed about. Wow, that's great! I never understood the magnitude! When will you know for sure?"

"I'm hoping in the next twenty-four hours or less."

He paused, waited for Kate to continue. This was not at all like Kate; she vacillated, tentative about the right way to broach her concerns. Sensing the reluctance, Matt jumped in to fill the void. "This explains your recent preoccupation. You know, babe, we also need to talk about us. I hate the way we left things last night…so unsettled. I need to know where we're heading."

"I know. It's been on my mind and that's why I called. I hoped we could talk through some things and I want to thank you for your patience. I've been thinking about us since yesterday. Most of all, I want you to know I love you the most in the world. We are two adults that love each other; it can't be that complicated. Other couples mix love and their careers. I was thinking we should use this time apart to come up with answers. Give us some time, please. Besides, since I plan on spending 'quality' time in the Vatican, maybe I can get some expert advice."

"Okay," he laughed, "you always know how to work a room and me in particular. Okay babe, you can have the time you need. We'll work things out. I just need assurance that we're both working toward the same thing."

Simply hearing Matt's voice confirming his love and willingness to give her the time she needed lifted her spirits and confidence. "Trust me, we are. Our relationship is very important to me. I couldn't work on this project without talking to you first. I haven't been able to fully concentrate. All I think about is you and how to bring us closer together." She sensed Matt's warm smile from three thousand miles away. "Matt, you have my love and promise. Now I really hate to make-up and run but as usual I am tight on time. I love you and miss you already. Bye."

"Be careful and call me with the decision! Come home soon." The line went dead. "Kate, I miss you, too."

CHAPTER FIVE

Tired, elated, the emotional pressure drained, Kate could concentrate on the assignment since Matt was pacified, at least for the time being. She had a few hours before the final meeting. Leaving the room Kate ignored the elevator, preferring the stairs to the slow claustrophobic box. Not only were the stairs faster, the exercise pumped her adrenaline. Approaching the car she saw Giorgio's outline waiting in the driver's seat. Aldo had recommended dinner at Franzone's, a small family trattoria. Fortunately, the restaurant was only seven or eight blocks from the hotel. Traffic cooperated and they arrived in a few minutes.

Before leaving the car she checked her make-up in the mirror. Satisfied, she approached the entrance to the restaurant. The last time this place was redecorated had to be the 1970s, she thought. The restaurant was one large room with a black and white checkered ceramic floor, a tin ceiling, slowly circling ceiling fans and faded white paint. The bar area looked like a converted soda fountain. The evening rush hadn't started, and Kate was quickly escorted to a table. "*Signornia*, welcome. Table for one this evening?"

Kate nodded yes. She wanted to finish dinner and be back at the hotel by 8:30, even though the Papal meeting might take hours.

Kate ordered an espresso, wondering how she ever got hooked on the strong pungent drink. She recalled her last meeting with Vincenzo Zuto, thinking, hoping she made a positive impression that would influence tonight's decision.

Kate remembered being impressed with his command of the English language. "Vincenzo, you speak English very well. Do you get a chance to speak it often?"

"Almost every day, out of necessity I'm afraid. However, I must tell you it doesn't roll off the tongue like Italian."

She remembered overcoming her upside-down stomach and jumping in with both feet. "Vincenzo, I don't wish to seem impatient, but I would like to know if your client is close to making a decision." Kate hoped he didn't hear her heart thumping as she searched his face for an indication of his answer. The question hung in mid-air for what seemed to be an eternity before Zuto replied.

"Ah, an impatient North American…how unusual." Zuto laughed at his own joke. "An impatient people. Our entire staff is experiencing this impatience first hand. To answer your question, the list has been narrowed to two finalists. By your next visit to Rome we will likely have a decision. My client is also eager to begin, as is my direct supervisor Cardinal Marconi."

Kate recalled the end of their meeting when she slowed down a bit to catch her breath. The proverbial line was pulled taught, the hook in deep; she wanted to reel Vincenzo in with her closing. "I will do everything I can within ethical guidelines to present your client in the best possible light. My ultimate goal is to earn a reputation as an honest journalist capable of interacting with world leaders. And that is why, Vincenzo, I want and need this interview!"

In retrospect, since that meeting she wondered if she hooked Vincenzo or was he simply being a gentlemen? Oh God, how she hated second-guessing herself.

Vincenzo Zuto was ready to make his recommendation. He entered the Vatican grounds through a rear employee gate and proceeded past the Swiss Guard to Marconi's private office. His Eminence decided to work late while waiting to hear Vincenzo's media recommendation.

They had a comfortable working relationship that allowed Vincenzo to get right to the point. "Your Excellency, I am ready. After considering various media candidates I'm confident that GNN will best represent the Papacy and the Vatican."

"Excellent, Vincenzo! The Holy Father's eager to get started on this project. He'll be pleased to have a final recommendation. Please have a seat while I confirm our meeting with the Pontiff."

A few minutes later they left the office and walked down a long hallway to the Pope's private quarters. Vincenzo rarely saw the Pope. Once he briefly spoke with the Pontiff after Mass, but he had never entered his private quarters. Elated, a bit on edge, Vincenzo felt awed by the prospect of a face-to-face conversation with His Holiness. Approaching the private quarters they passed through two security checks manned by Swiss Guards. In addition to standard side arms, the guards carried stun guns and Mace. Guards located in the central security room followed their progress in the corridors via closed circuit TV. After entering the quarters they were ushered to a small meeting room. Without a word, Vincenzo knelt and kissed the Papal ring.

"Gentlemen, please take a seat. Since you are together we must be close to a recommendation on our upcoming media event, yes?"

A slightly pale Vincenzo looked toward Marconi to answer. "Yes, your Holiness. Vincenzo's here to give his recommendation and based on the information accumulated over the past months, I fully support his conclusion."

Gripping the arms of the chair, Vincenzo sat up straight, turned to face the Pontiff, and swallowed to clear his throat. "Your Holiness, the full details of the interview have not been arranged; however, I am recommending GNN. Miss Kate Murphy will conduct the actual interview. Are you familiar with her work, Holiness?"

Pope Alex held his favorite Mont Blanc fountain pen, snapping the cap on and off as he listened. The Pope's peripheral vision caught Marconi nodding agreement. He carefully placed the fine writing instrument on the antique desk while partially reclining in the leather high back chair. "Gentlemen, I have reviewed the background on each company; GNN is a well-known organization. What I do know about Miss Murphy is that she is a youngster, a virtual unknown. So why select this combination?"

"Holiness, GNN's reputation is impeccable; the organization speaks for itself so I will go directly to my selection of Miss Murphy. She's young, talented, attractive and most critical to our plan, ethical...unlike some of the more jaded veteran journalists. There's an innocence about her that inspires trust. Another important difference is she's a Canadian national and an Episcopalian. An American or Catholic journalist might be considered prejudiced. Plus, we have Miss Murphy's personal commitment that she will work with us to present the best possible image of the Vatican, the Catholic religion and your Holiness...of course, all within ethical guidelines. When you meet her you'll understand. She wants to succeed and this is a huge opportunity for her."

"I see. Thank you, Vincenzo." A slight smile raised the Pope's lips. GNN was his front-runner from the beginning. Marconi and Vincenzo returned his smile. "Gentleman, we are in agreement. Make it so! Excellent job! Thanks to both of you for the diligent effort on this long assignment." Pope Alex looked directly at Vincenzo. "Now tell me, what's the next step, what's the time line?"

Vincenzo, the behind-the-scenes man, was getting recognition. Feeling a tad more at ease and pleased with himself, he crossed his legs. "Your Holiness, in order to prepare for the interview, Miss Murphy needs some private time with you. Time to gather information about your life, interests, family, etc. From these meetings we will develop a series of interview questions, which you will have the right to approve in advance. This will also allow the two of you to become acquainted. Once you meet with Miss Murphy you can set up the final timetable."

"Clearly an excellent idea. I'll schedule time for several short meetings with Miss Murphy. Gentlemen, if we don't have any other items to discuss?" The Pope looked at each man.

"No, your Holiness."

"I suggest we retire for the evening." The Pope's swivel back chair bolted forward, he stood and offered his hand to Vincenzo. "On your way out, please ask Brother Jacomo to see me. Again, bless you and thank you for the perseverance."

The door closed and immediately swung open. "Your Holiness wishes something?"

"Yes, Brother Jacomo. Please cancel my morning meeting with Cardinal Tornetta. Then telephone Miss Kate Murphy and invite her to join me for coffee at 10:00 a.m. tomorrow. Mr. Zuto mentioned she's staying at the Michaelangelo Hotel. As usual, ask Miss Murphy to use the private entrance. Keep this as confidential as possible. I know it's almost impossible with the local gossipmongers, but try your best to be discreet. Brother, I am counting on you!"

"Yes, your Holiness, I will do my best. Can I be of any additional service this evening?"

"No, after you reach Miss Murphy you can retire. Good night. Oh...Brother, thank you for working late. God bless you."

Lowering his eyes, Brother Jacomo's expression conveyed that it was part of the job.

The Pope wished he were closer to Brother Jacomo. Walking to his bedroom, Pope Alex considered his assistant. What an interesting character...mid-forties, short even for a Sicilian. Tightly cropped light brown hair, hazy blue-green eyes. An intelligent linguist, he spoke five languages and kept his personal life ultra-private. Maybe the brother was just quiet, probably waiting for him to open up and build a rapport, not wishing to overstep his bounds. While the Pope needed trusted friends and allies, he had to be cautious at least for the near future. Brother Jacomo accepted his position before the Papal election. He wondered if the brother was a plant from the old guard or a qualified assistant who could be molded and trusted. Time would eventually answer that question.

Meanwhile, he had faith in God's intended purpose. Pope Alex prayed quietly, "Dear Lord, I know you placed me in this position to serve you and your flock. Guide me with helping hands and protect us from the Philistines."

Sitting up in bed, pillows propped against his back, he scanned satellite TV searching for the latest results on the 76ers. Sometimes he wished for less formality, more open feeling and honesty from the staff and clergy, some social interaction at a personal level. *Laughter, fun, and children never echoed through these walls, this place needs life, excitement.* Completely alone, every day he felt the heavy weight of isolation. This new station in life made it so and he realized the loneliness would continue until God called him to his final assignment.

Leigh and her life-long friends Denise, Diane, Patty and Eileen, certainly know how to liven up a place, he smiled to himself. Soon, if all went well, he'd request a command visit. His thoughts brought a chuckle. *Like anyone could ever command those women to do anything!*

Confident that his plans were about to fall into place he relaxed and his eyelids fluttered.

Chapter Six

After dinner Kate was eager to return to the hotel and wait for the important call. Crossing the hotel lobby, the front desk clerk motioned her to approach.

"Hello, Giovani," she smiled, "how are you this evening?"

"*Molto bene, Signorina* Kate. I have a message for you, from a Brother Jacomo. Please call him as soon as possible. Lateness of the hour is not important."

Kate's heart leapt. *This is it*, she thought, *the assignment is mine*! Bounding up the stairs her heart raced at full throttle, breath sucked out from the excitement. Trembling fingers dialed the number. Without a moment's hesitation she accepted the Pope's invitation.

She'd finally done it! GNN was the winner! Kate's mind shifted into overdrive, immediately planning the next move. The first call would be to Aldo Fumo, giving him the good news. The second call to Ted, her boss. This was a feather in his cap as well and she knew Ted wouldn't hesitate to pass the good news along to GNN's president, Mr. Convery.

Her immediate reaction was to call Matt but she thought better of it and decided to wait until morning when he was fully awake, and after it all sank in. *Time for sleep*, she told herself. Hopefully sleep would come. Her body ached from the six-hour time difference and she needed to be fully rested for tomorrow's challenge—meeting the headman.

Unfortunately, Kate's body clock didn't cooperate. She lay half-awake as golden rays peeked through the green drapes. Before her eyes could fully focus, reality hit her square in the face. Running on pure adrenalin she rolled out of bed, raring to go.

After completing the calls and accepting verbal high-fives, it was time to prepare for the first meeting with the Pontiff. Kate had difficulty organizing her thoughts and staying focused. She wondered what does one wear when meeting the Pope? She chided herself for not packing more clothes. No matter how much she packed, the selection laid out before her seemed all wrong. Her mind flashed between meeting the Pope, and wanting to squeeze in a call to her parents. She also admitted that she was a little scared about how Matt would react. Even though he sounded thrilled, they were both aware of the time this would consume. Inhaling deeply, she forced herself to concentrate on the simple task at hand—dressing.

The telephone rang once—Giorgio's signal that he was waiting out front. From the Michaelangelo Hotel it's an easy stroll to St. Peter's Square, the gateway into the Vatican public areas.

Kate grumbled as she finished combing her hair, "Okay, Giorgio, keep your shirt on. I'll be down in three minutes." She grabbed her purse, checked in the mirror one last time and locked the door. Descending the steps two at a time she cut across the main lobby, zigzagging through milling tourists.

"Good morning, Signorina."

"And good morning to you, Giorgio. Our drive will be a short one today. Take me to the Vatican, and please use the private entrance. My meeting should last about ninety minutes or so."

"Certainly, Signorina, I'm at your disposal until at least midnight…longer if you wish."

"In that case, while you're waiting think about somewhere interesting you can take me this afternoon."

Seated at the antique roll top desk the bright sun illuminated the Pope's work area while he tried to collect his thoughts before meeting Ms. Murphy. This outwardly routine meeting signaled the first salvo in a declaration of war against the still unknown internal enemies. Once the media offensive began he expected passive resistance to become direct confrontation. His concentration waned. Thoughts flitted between the struggle for survival, his firm belief that God chose him to refocus the Church, and the feeling of loneliness away from family, especially the two women dearest to him.

With the time difference, it was early morning in Philadelphia and he could call Leigh right after the meeting with Ms. Murphy. Marie, however, he could not telephone, although he sensed her presence day and night. This belief was his only consolation since her passing away a quarter century ago, along with his memory of the beautiful vibrant woman. He wondered how the years would have treated her if she were still alive. Certainly her inner beauty would've continued to blossom. His memories would always recall a truly kind and gentle woman.

Regardless of his titles and worldly accomplishments, inside he was still Anthony, with human doubts, frailties and needs. At that moment he felt incredibly needy and turned to Marie for solace. Most days he chatted, simply talking to her. Believing she watched and listened brought him great comfort. This day in particular he asked her to stay near.

Although the Vatican walls were only a few blocks from the hotel, traffic and one-way streets lengthened the trip to twenty minutes. The drive provided time to collect her thoughts and control the butterflies circling around in her stomach. Feeling overheated she asked Giorgio to turn on the air-conditioner. As the car approached the entrance, two Carabiniere officers with Uzi automatic rifles halted the vehicle. The officers checked the vehicle and waved them through. Inside the gate they stopped and spoke with a Swiss Guard.

The Swiss have protected the Pontiff for hundreds of years. Each guard takes a personal oath of loyalty to the Pontiff. In addition to protecting the Holy Father, they were a tourist attraction in the Vatican, easily recognizable by their colorful thirteenth century uniforms with horizontal stripes. The guard, a stern looking youth, acknowledged Kate's name on the visitor's list and directed Giorgio to park in a designated area. The guard radioed ahead and a member of Brother Jacomo's staff approached the car. Introductions were not exchanged; no idle chitchat. He simply led her to the waiting area.

The receptionist, a cheerful middle-aged woman, offered refreshments. Kate politely declined. In her jittery state the last thing she needed was spilling a drink on her outfit. The clock handle moved, twenty minutes to 10:00. Arriving early, she anticipated a lengthy wait, *Something like waiting for a doctor*, she thought. Patients rush to the appointment then wonder why, since the doctors are usually late.

An intense looking man in dark brown clerical robes approached. "I am Brother Jacomo. It's my pleasure to meet you, Miss Murphy." Keeping his hands clasped together in front of him sent a clear signal that he didn't wish to shake hands.

"Brother Jacomo, I am honored by this invitation and pleased to meet you."

Brother Jacomo's eyes demurred, then reviewed her attire. The Vatican had strict rules on exposed shoulders, necklines and length of skirts, all of which Kate adhered to. "Shall we go?" asked the brother. Without waiting for a reply he turned and quickly moved, almost trotting down a long, wide, dimly lit hallway. Knocking on a huge hand carved door, he opened the wide door without waiting for an acknowledgement and ushered the guest into the Pontiff's private library.

"Please be seated Miss Murphy. May I offer some refreshments?"

Suddenly her mouth felt parched. "Yes, thank you. Some water would be nice."

"Miss Murphy, since this is your first meeting with the Holy Father, I would like to go over normal protocol. You may address the Pontiff as Your Holiness, Holy Father or Pope Alex. When introduced, it is customary to kneel and kiss the Papal ring. Since this is a private session, typically the Holy Father will be less formal. Do you have any questions?"

Kate's mind reeled. *Questions? You've godda be kidding*, she thought. Her whole body went numb. Exhaling deeply she managed to blurt out, "No, Brother, not right now."

Brother Jacomo had a nervous habit of rubbing the palms of his hands together when he made eye contact. Kate wondered if he did this with everyone or if women put him on edge.

"His Holiness will be with you shortly; please make yourself comfortable."

Watching the door slowly close she suddenly understood the phrase, "Be careful what you wish for."

She needed to calm down, try to take everything in and use her skills as a journalist, what she trained for. A large window overlooked the grounds. Kate studied the garden spread over a large area, one of several on the property. Spring was on the brink, and flower buds darted out to absorb the sunlight. Her attention returned to the library. The room was definitely masculine, thick wood paneling, probably mahogany, and intricately hand carved. Oversized hand carved crown molding bordered the ceiling. Bookshelves reached ten feet high on one wall and six feet on the opposite side. The exquisite gas fireplace was designed to ease the chill during cold spells. Six Queen Anne burgundy chairs were placed in a semi-circle around a dark wood coffee table. The leather looked soft and supple. The antique tabletop was protected by thick glass etched with the Papal seal. There was perfectly directed lighting so each chair's occupant could read comfortably.

Mildly startled from her concentration, she heard a firm but gentle male voice say, "Hello, Miss Murphy, welcome to the Vatican."

Kate turned to face the kind voice that greeted her. "Holy Father, I am so honored to meet you." Regaining composure, she thought, *How handsome for an older man.*

This felt very awkward, being expected to kiss the Papal ring, but this gentleman dressed in casual clothes and looked more like her image of a typical grandfather. After the slightest hesitation, she managed to bend down and kiss his ring.

"Please rise, Miss Murphy. Although kissing the ring is customary, I try to limit the ceremony to public meetings. To be honest, I sometimes get embarrassed during the ceremony. So when we meet in private, shaking hands will do fine. Please be seated…make yourself comfortable. Refreshments are on the way."

She headed for the nearest burgundy chair before her wobbly legs went completely weak. "Thank you, Holy Father." It was difficult to concentrate after being taken completely off guard by the Pontiff's appearance and friendly mannerisms. Kate didn't know exactly what to expect, but it wasn't this.

As though he could read her mind, the Holy Father began, "Please excuse the casual clothes. When possible I prefer civilian gear. I thought this was a perfect opportunity to help keep our meeting relaxed. I'm sure we will meet more than once. I realize the selection process has been slow and tedious, but it was of the utmost importance that we chose the right combination of network and interviewer. Now, I am quite eager to move forward. Can GNN work with a five-week deadline for the live telecast? I would prefer it be aired on a Sunday, early evening. It's critical that we reach the European audience. Certainly a much smaller congregation than North America, where I already have strong support, however, Europe is still a very powerful element in Church politics. The goal is to improve this backing while gathering support from the European, Asian, South American and the African Churches. Do you think five weeks is a realistic time frame or are we pushing the envelope?"

Good Lord, no pun intended, this man doesn't waste any time on preliminaries! Kate mused. Following his lead, she jumped right in. "Holiness, as of today, this project is GNN's top priority. The only thing that could delay five weeks is a major disaster that requires extensive news coverage or a delay in your schedule to meet and prepare for the interview."

"I understand emergency issues may disrupt our schedules, but with the

Lord's help this won't be an issue. I'm counting on HIS cooperation!" The Pope looked up at the ceiling. "As for my schedule, this project will take precedence. I'll be counting on your commitment as well, Miss Murphy."

"Holy Father, the Vatican's request for an interview is a first, and a highly unusual one. I know I discussed this with Mr. Zuto, but before we proceed I want to clarify this main question. What are you trying to accomplish with this interview?"

Pope Alex looked out the window at the opaque sky and dwelled on the question before answering. "Miss Murphy, do you mind if I call you Kate?"

"Please do, Your Holiness." Relieved that he acted like a normal person, after all, the butterflies weren't fluttering quite so much anymore. *God, I need that water*, she thought.

"Thank you, Kate. It's much easier to explain what's at risk if we don't change the public's perception about me. I firmly believe the Church has been declining for some years. The evidence is compelling: A lack of religious vocations, both priests and nuns...the loss of Catholics due to controversy about birth control and women priests...the list is extensive. I truly believe I was selected, handpicked by God to help correct this situation. My goal is to increase the number of faithful members in the Church. In order to accomplish this I need to drag the Church, kicking and screaming, into the twenty-first century. The Church needs to embrace changes in tradition. I can't fathom any other reason in God's plan for me to be elected Pope.

"However, a leader can only be fully effective when followers have confidence in him and the direction he is leading. So the reason for this interview is to reestablish confidence in the Papacy and me as Pope. I would like to defer discussion about the specific changes until we are closer to the interview date. Have I given you a clear picture of my objectives?"

It took a moment to digest the statement: "handpicked by God." *This man was either headed for the psycho ward or was indeed a holy man*, she mused. "Yes, your Holiness, I believe I have the whole picture. I have another question though. How do you anticipate media coverage will help and not hurt you?"

The Pontiff stood to stretch his weak back muscles and moved to the bookshelves near the section marked "poetry," and fingered the spine of an old book. "The old adage, 'the truth shall set you free!' We must overcome the rumors and disinformation surrounding Anthony Pavelli, aka Pope Alex IX. What I do hope to achieve is a reverence for the Papal office held in God's name. The Pontiff's position must retain leadership, and along with it respect and confidence. Otherwise, I'm afraid the Church will splinter and stray from God's prescribed path."

"As a non-Catholic, I find it interesting that the leader of the Catholic Church has many titles: Pope, Pontiff, Holiness and Holy Father. Can you shed some light on that?"

"Catholics take all these names for granted. They all refer to God's appointed head of the Roman Catholic Church. The official title is Pontifex Maximus, the Supreme Pontiff or Highest Priest. The title came from the early days of the Roman Empire. In ancient Rome, Pontus were priests elected to their position. Pontifex Maximus was the head priest and responsible to conduct state religious ceremonies."

"Holy Father, can you help me understand the Church's belief in the Pope's infallibility?"

"One day you will come to realize that's a prophetic question. Catholics believe that Popes are infallible in regard to establishing Church doctrine. Many religious groups splintered from the Catholic Church because they would not accept this tenet. However, there are many areas other than doctrine not covered by infallibility that Popes have the ability to influence…things that require updating for today's faithful. This brings us back to garnering support; some background may help you to understand."

Pope Alex returned to his seat, ready to tell Kate about his election. "My election could easily be perceived as a fluke. Neither conservatives nor moderates had enough electoral votes to elect their candidate. I was a new Cardinal with no personal agenda or political affiliation, or so they thought. After numerous votes, the College of Cardinals stood at an impasse. No cardinal was even close to the two-thirds plus one majority required for election, so they shifted votes to me as a compromise candidate. Due to my advanced age and presumed lack of political agenda, I was a perfect short-term fill in; an acceptable figurehead until the next Pope is elected."

There was a soft knock on the massive door. Sister Martha entered with Diet Coke and lemon for the Pontiff and sparkling mineral water for Kate. The sister appeared to be a jolly woman, short and best described as roly-poly with a smooth face. However, her light gray eyes portrayed a much more serious nature.

"Sister Martha, before you leave, may I introduce you to Miss Kate Murphy? She will be visiting us from time to time. Please make her feel at home. Sister, now if you could please see that we are not disturbed."

Extending her hand, the sister welcomed Kate, nodded slightly then turned and rapidly left the room. "Sister Martha has been with me since I was elected and understands my idiosyncrasies," he explained. He took a sip of Coke. "Ah good! Well, back to my short saga. When my name was announced, I wavered on whether to accept. That's when it struck me that it was God's will. He chose me for a divine purpose. It didn't take long for the cardinals representing both liberal and conservative factions to realize I refused to be a figurehead. I spoke openly about making sweeping changes in the status quo. So began the campaign of rumors, half-truths and misinformation about my personal life. All designed to keep me on the defensive and retain the status quo."

Kate was familiar with the ugly rumors; now she heard the Pope's side. A big part of her quest would be searching out the truth; there is often a third side to a story. "Holy Father, in order to present a creditable interview, I need to know about your past. I intend to develop a mini-biography. How do you feel about that?"

Placing his right hand on his jaw, he contemplated the idea, knowing that he couldn't let his sense of privacy or modesty stand in the way. This whole process was far bigger than his personal wants. "Clearly an excellent idea."

Over the anxiety about meeting the "big guy," Kate felt confident now that the Pope had agreed to her idea. "Good. I am pleased you agree. Now where's the best place to begin? What are your thoughts on gathering personal background...who are the best sources?"

With the slightest smile, Pope Alex crossed his legs. "During the last seventy-two years, my life has changed several times, and I have been influenced by many special people. Of course, all of this gives my adversaries plenty of ammunition. Speak first to the people who helped me live those lives. Then we'll meet again and I can fill in missing pieces. My earnest hope is that the lay parishioners will strongly identify with the first forty-eight years and my ecclesiastical brethren will identify with my years in the priesthood. Yes, the more I think about the biography the more excited I am." *Vincenzo was right*, thought the Pontiff, *this young woman has a spark, a zest hidden under the-girl-next-door image.*

The Holy Father let out his first hardy chuckle in days. "I'll prepare a short list, with addresses and telephone numbers. Also, suggestions on whom would be most helpful discussing different time periods. I'll contact each person and ask them to cooperate...answer you're questions, no holds barred. Will that meet your needs?"

As the Pope spoke, Kate leaned forward to make distinct eye contact. The man didn't flinch. She wondered, *A forthright man or great actor?* "It sounds like a start, as long as we can talk between the interviews. I may need clarification."

"I'll be available directly or through Brother Jacomo." His Holiness glanced at his watch and frowned. "Time doesn't stop for any of us. Now, if you have no further questions please excuse me. I have appointments waiting and I need to change clothes before meeting a group of Northern Italian businessmen. They might faint if I greet them like this." As the Pope rose to leave, Kate jumped to her feet. "Kate, please give Brother Jacomo a weekly status on your progress. He'll keep Cardinal Marconi and me up to speed. As the date gets closer I suspect we will speak and or meet as needed."

"Your Holiness, I am honored and can only say both personally and on behalf of GNN, *thank you*, you won't be disappointed. Holy Father, as you know, I am not Catholic, but may I ask for your blessing?"

"Certainly my child."

With a solemn face, he placed his left hand on Kate's head, raised his right hand making the sign of the cross. "*In nominee Patris, et Filii, et Spiritu Sancti*. I pray that the Holy Trinity guides you to the truth and keeps love and compassion in your heart. Amen. Now, I must leave. During your next visit if you wish, Brother Jacomo can arrange for a guided tour of the private areas in the Vatican."

"Thank you, I will speak to him about it." Under any other circumstance Kate would lunge at the opportunity, but with the bio hanging over her head that was all she could focus on. She needed time to clear her mind. It had been a whirlwind since landing. *God*, she thought, *it was just yesterday, it seems like days ago.*

Before the door closed, the triumphant journalist let out a deep breath of relief and jerked her arm upward in an "I won" motion. The mission she planned to embark on was, in many ways, uncharted territory. Her head spun with excitement. It would take every ounce of concentration and the outcome would drastically alter her career and the Pope's image, hopefully for the better, if he was in fact what he purported to be. Her inner being felt somehow that the Pope's blessing would help. In any event, it certainly couldn't hurt.

CHAPTER SEVEN

Not far from the VIP visitors' parking area, Giorgio stood in deep animated conversation with a bony gardener, who appeared to be upset. The short man wore a straw hat that looked battered and stained from years of sweat and grimy hands.

"*Ciao,* Signorina Kate. May I introduce my cousin, Vito Vichelli...a second cousin on my mother's side. We grew up together. As children, during the hot Roman summers, Vito often visited my family in Calabria."

"*Ciao,* Signor Vichelli, so nice to meet you." She was reluctant to offer her hand in Italy, allowing men to make that gesture. "Your gardens are beautiful. No, they are magnificent, living works of art. If I had this talent, I would love coming to work every day."

Vito nodded and removed his trademark straw hat, exposing a large bald spot to the strong sun. "*Grazie,* Signorina Kate. So nice to meet you, please forgive my English. I am but a humble gardener. Yes, each day is a joy, fair or foul weather. I've tended these gardens for thirty years...but how much longer is a question."

"Signore, surely you're too young to retire?"

"Signorina, I and others in the Vatican community are concerned, deeply concerned. There's talk of the Holy Father moving his residence and the Curia to New York City, near the United Nations. Our lives are connected to Vatican City. The enclosed world as we know it will vanish. This can't happen."

"Signor Vichelli, as a journalist from New York, I would have heard about such plans. I am sure the Vatican will remain the Papal residence for many years, if not forever."

Vito fidgeted, looked down at his feet and moved the straw hat through his hands. "Signorina, I have said too much, overstepped my position. Please forgive the ramblings of a tired old man."

"I think we should allow Vito to continue with his gardening. He has much work to do."

"Signore, it was a pleasure meeting you and looking at your splendid garden. Next time we meet I hope you can teach me something about flowers. *Ciao.*"

Walking toward the car, Kate tried to get Giorgio to open up about the Vatican community. "You are fortunate to have access to the Vatican private areas. This explains how you know so much about the Vatican administration and rumors. You could be of great help to me, Giorgio. I am working on a new assignment. Would you consider being a personal advisor?"

"Miss Kate, I'm not so sure I would be good at such things. However, I'll consider your kind offer." Giorgio responded too quickly—an act of self-preservation. He felt he couldn't afford to become involved in whatever this woman was up to. In many ways, although an outsider, his life was tied to people deep in the Vatican.

The imploring look on her face made him change the subject. "We Italians are very emotional, caring people. Our relatives' concerns become our concerns! Vito will worry that he spoke in haste. Can I…what is the word…assure Vito that his conversation will be kept quiet?"

"Of course. Assure him that our meeting will be kept confidential. Also, mention that I'd appreciate hearing about any rumors circulating through Vatican City."

"Thank you, Signorina. Please enjoy the beautiful flowers. I'll return soon."

While enjoying the blooming flowers and shrubs, Kate's thoughts returned to the assignment. Any information from Vito or Giorgio would be helpful to understand the intrigue swirling through St. Peter's. There must be other rumors that have not reached the Pope's ears, some so vulgar no one would dare repeat them to his Holiness. Time was so short, GNN would have to pool its resources to pull this off.

Although the calendar showed early spring, the vegetation neared full bloom. More than the beauty, the peace and tranquility mesmerized. Looking at the bougainvillea hanging down from one of the nearby residential apartment buildings, Kate noticed someone looking down at the gardens. As the figure turned to leave she saw a flash of red, a cardinal. Could it be Cardinal Marconi, the Holy Father's closest advisor? More importantly, was Marconi one of the good guys?

Giorgio found Kate sitting on a bench enjoying the sunshine. "Thank you for the time to speak with my cousin, Signorina. He feels much better."

His body language told Kate that Vito would never be a source of information but she needed Giorgio to feel comfortable and relaxed so she thanked him for the help. "I believe you, Mister Driver, promised me a shopping tour. Let's go back to the hotel, so I can change clothes and call Mr. Fumo. I can't wait to see the wedding cake you told me about. How can it be the biggest cake in the world? I'll bet you're fibbing!"

Giorgio hesitated, not knowing if Kate was serious. "Miss Kate, I would never.... how do you say, fib. It *is* the biggest cake in the world. You will see."

At the hotel Kate endured another slow elevator ride, and speculated on how management could renovate a hotel without improving the elevators. Kate had to remind herself, *This is Italia!* She dialed Mr. Fumo's private number; the telephone chirped once. "Pronto."

"*Ciao*, Aldo. I am pleased to confirm the GNN eagle has indeed landed. There are no words to express my feeling except, maybe, *fabulous*!"

"Kate, this is wonderful...a first in journalism. Congratulations! I can see it now; Kate Murphy...a household name. Give me the details on proceeding, where, when and how."

"Aldo, I'm thrilled but filled with mixed emotions that I don't understand. I should be yelling and hooting. Instead I'm in a funk, feeling disoriented and searching for true north. I am good, but am I good enough to pull this frigging thing off? We are talking about the Pope and worldwide exposure. What have I gotten into? What's wrong with me?" She held the phone in her left hand while she twirled her hair with the other. No matter how hard she tried to break the habit there were times when it was the only thing that calmed her.

"This is an amazing accomplishment for anyone but especially for… shall I say a young person. You are discovering some of life's strange twists. Sometimes climbing the mountain brings more emotional rewards than actually scaling the top…reaching the summit. Right now you are only on the second plateau and nowhere near the top. Once you begin the interviewing your confidence and emotional high will return with a vengeance." Kate turned and looked at St. Peter's dome, her mountain. "Kate, details please, my heart can't take this."

"The 'where,' is the Holy Father's private chambers in the Vatican. Millions will tune in just to see his private living space. The 'when' is in five weeks, a tight schedule but, Aldo, you and GNN can make it happen from a technical stand point."

"Ha, with the unions I will need God the Father's help!"

"Aldo, stop with the union crap. This is serious. The 'how,' is a one-hour biography that will be broadcast three or four times during a week, followed by a live interview with Pope Alex broadcast worldwide."

Fumo's mind started processing the logistics. "While we Italians are working on the technical aspects, what's your agenda, when will you be back in Rome?"

"My schedule is aggressive. His Holiness is essentially a quiet and very private person. His early life will be a key issue during the interview. We decided that I should visit some relatives and close friends to gather background for a biography. It will also provide some objective insights into our Pope. I know GNN and the Pontiff will both expect to benefit from this venture. However, I need to be sure there won't be any surprises. GNN can't afford to be manipulated. Before we proceed I have to make sure His Holiness is '*uomi di fiducia*,' what you Italians call a 'man of trust.' Aldo, I need your assistance to determine if our Pope is really trustworthy. Use your resources around the world, especially in the States, to dig deep…check him out…very low key, of course."

Revved, Aldo paced his overcrowded office. He excitedly waved for his assistant to come into his office. "I'll begin immediately. New York has given us a large budget to complete this project."

"Great! Once I finalize the research and interviews, I'll dedicate time to compile and edit the biography."

"We need you back in Rome for at least one week prior to the interview. That leaves you four weeks or so to complete your end. You'll be one busy journalist."

"Just over three weeks should be enough time. I have a list of five to seven people, most on the East Coast. The interviews have to be completed before GNN starts advertising. Aldo, I also need some personal time with Matt. You know, the man I love…and rarely see."

"Life's never easy. Always choices...the need to juggle. I know you can hold it all together. But we'll talk. I'm sure we can arrange some time for you and Matt. Well, Kate, as usual, excellent work. My assistant Amelia will make arrangements for your return flight to New York. It's a tight schedule. I don't need to tell you how important this is, but I also trust your instincts. If you need a couple of days for personal issues, so be it. Come back rested and keep me posted."

"Please ask Amelia to contact the New York office and let them know when I'm returning but not to expect me in the office for a few days. I have a few days before the interviews begin. *Arrivederci* for now and thanks for the advice. I have to run."

Kate rushed to meet Giorgio in exactly thirty minutes. She was fond of Giorgio. His barrel chest reminded her more of an aging burly bodyguard than a driver. The salt-and-pepper hair over his ears needed a trim.

"Where are we going?"

"We go to Venice Piazza, Signorina. Splendid shopping, sightseeing and just for you, a giant wedding cake."

Giorgio was a very capable driver; he had driven tour buses for twenty-five years until forced into mandatory retirement at age fifty-five. Like most Italians he drove like a maniac, from the hotel to the Piazza in twenty minutes. Familiar with the city, he found convenient parking on a side street.

"Miss Kate, please walk one block, turn right and you will be in the Piazza. You will not have any problems. Enjoy."

"Why don't you join me to point out the interesting spots and tell me some of the wonderful history? You must get bored waiting in the car. I'd love the company."

"It would be my pleasure to join you. It's been some years since I walked the Piazza. Where would you like to start...shopping or touring antiquities?"

"Lead the way, Giorgio. Since it's a square, how about we start at one corner and walk around? We can decide as we go."

They walked along a side street that would be considered a wide alley in the States. Kate thought about how many thousands, possibly hundreds of thousands of people walked this street before Christ was born. How many great and ordinary people shaped this street and the city of Rome? Through all those centuries, only a small number of people left their lasting stamp on humanity. Would she become a small cog, helping the Holy Father take his place in history? Giorgio's baritone voice penetrated her thoughts.

"Sorry, my mind was elsewhere. I missed what you said."

"Look, there is the giant wedding cake at the end of the Piazza."

A wide smile melted across Kate's face. At the far end of the Piazza, covering one whole side of the square, was a pure-white marble monument. The multi-tiered structure looked like a wedding cake. The candles were mammoth statues on each tier. The monument's height and girth was amazing. "You old fox, this is great! Tell me about the cake."

"This monument was dedicated to the soldiers that fought in World War I. It was built while Mussolini was Fascist dictator. Rumor is, he helped design it to remind citizens of Italian military power and victories during the war. Rome is a city filled with marble. From the day it was unveiled, Romans considered the marble to be 'too white,' because of how it looks it was quickly dubbed 'the wedding cake.'" His voice lowered, "However, no one would dare say this while Mussolini could overhear. If it weren't for the size and tourist attraction, it probably would have been torn down years ago."

Pointing off at an angle he continued,"That's Mussolini's former palace. We can't tour it because it's a private residence. From the outside it looks like a large hotel with a very plain brick façade. The interior is said to be spectacular. The original furnishings, of course, were paid for by the taxpayers."

At the far right of the monument, an ancient basilica stood on a high hill overlooking the wedding cake. The steep climb appeared daunting and their time limited. To the left of the monument was a small park and rest area under shady trees where locals could eat or enjoyed the pleasant weather. At the rear of the park stood a Roman obelisk. Approaching the tall stone needle, Kate noticed the base of the sphere was in a hole twenty meters below where they stood. At the rim of the hole visitors were level with the middle of the stone needle, the top half reached another twenty meters above them.

"Signorina, look at the carvings. According to local myth, Julius Caesar brought this giant stone to Rome. Some of the carvings appear to be Egyptian while others are Latin. It's solid stone. We don't know how the ancients transported the stone. Just as curious is how the stone survived over two thousand years of barbarian invasions, revolutions and earthquakes."

"Your city is a marvel. How fortunate Romans are to live in such beauty and history. I guess it's true, we North Americans are still the new kids on the block when it comes to history."

"Romans are indeed blessed. If only I was more educated and could, how do you say… explain our ancient works, especially statues and art."

"You can be my tour guide anytime, Giorgio. This was very informative and fun, but now it's time to shop. I only have a few hours before my flight to New York. Let's start with that shop on the corner and work our way back to the car. I know you men hate shopping for clothes, so you can wait outside if you prefer."

"Miss Kate, if you don't mind I will enjoy the spring sunshine."

Kate loved shopping in Rome. The clothes were chic, in style and very expensive. After today's success, she deserved to indulge herself. Besides, she needed good outfits for the interviews and broadcast. The store she selected was very upscale and catered to professional women. The selection of styles, fabric and colors went beyond the every day shopping experience. The clerk's spoke perfect English, while Kate's Italian was almost non-existent, so bad she often resorted to hand motions.

Selecting two appropriate business suits for her meetings and interviews, she decided to splurge on a Versace handbag and matching shoes. The items were way out of her price range, which she ignored. Today was a celebration, she reasoned. It wasn't every day a journalist met with the Holy Father to begin his biography. Running late, Kate headed out to meet Giorgio.

"Ah, you were easy to find. Did you enjoy the spring sun and that nasty cigarette?"

Giorgio stubbed out the butt and shrugged his shoulders.

"Thank you Mr. Tour Guide, the whole day has been wonderful, pure abundance. This might be the best day of my life."

He bowed slightly. "As always, I am at your service to drive and tell you about Italy. Please, Miss Kate, zip your purse and keep your bags under your arm. Remember last trip, I warned you about the gypsies. I noticed several of them working the Piazza. They're expert thieves and pickpockets. Whole families, young and old, work the streets, especially in crowded areas. These gypsies are very clever, trained as small children to lie, cheat and steal. They are human street rats."

"What an awful comment! It's such a shame children must grow up in the streets." She was disturbed by his comment and without further conversation they headed back to the hotel.

Within half an hour Kate sat in her room packing. The first order of business was to call Matt and let him know she was on her way home. Unfortunately, no one answered so she left a sweet and sexy message. Before closing, she asked Matt to call her parents and tell them she'd be in touch over the weekend.

The departure area at Leonardo Da Vinci airport overflowed with people, more hectic than usual. After the red cap accepted the bags, Kate and Giorgio hugged. She waved as he pulled away from the unloading area.

While merging onto the busy highway, Giorgio pressed the speed dial on his cellular telephone, dialing a private number in the Vatican. The telephone answered on the first ring. "Pronto."

"Eminenzia, this is Giorgio. She is at the airport...in route back to New York."

"Is all going as planned or should we be worried?"

"For now all is well, Eminenzia. I will keep you informed of all her activities."

"Thank you Giorgio. Call me when you know of Miss Murphy's return."

Success did have its rewards! For once she was booked in first class without having to ask her boss. Kate planned to sleep during most of the flight without one moment of guilt. She'd earned the perk. An hour after takeoff, Kate had settled into her travel routine: feet up, second glass of white wine in hand, finished the mandatory small talk with the woman seated next to her. Deciding what to read, the flight attendant interrupted and asked if she would accept a telephone call. Kate grinned, "Of course," thinking it had to be Matt. "Hello, this is Kate."

"How good to hear your voice. This is Ted Blake. Again, congratulations on a marvelous job, another coup for GNN."

Kate sat up straight, more than surprised. It was very unlike her editor to call since she had spoken to him earlier in the day. "Well thank you, I'm ecstatic about GNN being chosen. Only the first step, still much to complete."

"Charles Convery is sitting next to me and he would like to speak with you, if you have a minute."

"For Mr. Convery, I have all the time he needs." She covered the phone and cleared her throat.

"Hello Kate, congratulations. For this level of accomplishment, congratulations seems so shallow. It doesn't fully express my professional respect and GNN's gratitude for a job well done. When you're back in the office, please call my secretary for an appointment. I would love to discuss the details."

"Why, thank you, Mr. Convery." Her voice raised an octave and her face beamed with pride—the president of GNN was speaking to her, personally.

"You have a bright future with GNN. See you soon...have a safe trip home." The call disconnected. Kate held the phone, not believing the president called her on an international flight. Things were truly looking up. Mr. Convery was so high up in the corporation that people practically got nosebleeds taking the elevator to his floor.

The second glass of wine empty, dinner was about to be served. Kate needed sleep, and hoped to dream of Matt and their next few days together.

Exiting from first class proved to be painless as usual. Amazing how quickly Kate consistently cleared immigration with her press pass, yet received close scrutiny by customs.

With any luck Matt would be waiting at the gate with roses and a physical hunger. He was nowhere to be found. Kate did receive a nice surprise, though; she was met by the GNN car service—an upgrade from previous trips. The drive home was tediously slow, hampered by snarled traffic on the Long Island Expressway. If Matt got her message and couldn't make it to the airport, Kate hoped he was at home waiting. She wasn't sure what she missed more—romance or wild abandoned sex. Probably both in equal proportions, she figured.

Entering the dark apartment, her only greeting was the persistent buzzing of the burglar alarm. The noise wouldn't stop until the access code was entered within the allotted forty-five seconds. This temporarily distracted her about no Matt.

Looking around, the apartment looked spotless, cleaner than she remembered leaving it. "Good work Matt," she said to an empty room. *What a let down*, she thought. *No Matt...no messages on the machine or on the refrigerator*. At least she had time to freshen up and take a quick shower before he came home.

The warm water felt refreshing; she could have stayed in this soothing cocoon for hours. The tingle reminded her of a mild massage, something she and Matt shared often. Regrettably, it was quite some time since they had enjoyed this intimacy. Kate's mind drifted to their last shower. The arousal building, she visualized Matt, remembering how she pushed his wet sandy blond hair away from his slender face, and green eyes. Embracing the steamy water she closed her eyes and let the tension ease. So good to be home, in a matter of minutes her lover, friend and emotional guidepost would enter the apartment.

Soap in her eyes blurred her vision. Just beyond the clear shower door he stood, visibly happy to see her. Matt's six-foot one-inch frame moved into the shower stall and gently leaned down, devouring Kate's mouth. One hand held her buttock; the other gently stroked a slippery breast. His lips slowly kissed their way to a soft, warm, circular nipple.

"Welcome home, lady; I've missed you."

She grabbed his firm ass with both hands. "Me too, baby. It's been way… too long."

They lingered in the shower, enjoying the warm comfortable reunion until both were almost waterlogged. "Turn around; let me get your back," said Matt.

Gently drying each other with soft Turkish towels, Kate shared the good news—three whole days together. "Possibly four, if you can arrange some time off, Matt."

"Babe, of course we need some time together; it's a matter of our sanity. No interruptions, no distractions. Good as done! I'll call the boss tomorrow. Now come here woman!" They kissed as he playfully pushed her into the bedroom.

Wrapped in a comfortable summer robe, Kate started back to the bathroom. Matt took her hand, leading the way. In the dim candle lit room she found a dinner table set for two with a centerpiece of budding red roses.

She threw her arms around his neck, and nuzzled her face in his chest. "When did you do this? Oh Hon!"

"It was a choice of picking you up at the airport or arranging romance. A tough choice, hope I picked the right one."

"You're the best, Mr. Janson. Now, get over here so I can thank you properly."

Arms entwined, they moved toward the bedroom. Halfway down the hall Matt spun her around, pushed her back against the wall, the robe slipped off in one smooth motion. Instinctively her back arched. They joined together in a fever-pitched rhythm. There was a lot of lost time to make up for and this was a good time to start.

CHAPTER EIGHT

After hours of passionate sex that lasted into the early morning, Kate and Matt slept late on Saturday. They decided to stay in bed and catch up on what was happening in their respective lives. Gathering coffee and bagels, they jumped back in bed to eat, snuggle, laugh and simply enjoy each other. A luxury they hadn't experienced in months.

"Before I tell you about the Rome assignment, I have other great news. I really have managed to clear my schedule for three or four days, so we can run away together. Just us, no work, no pagers or video cell phones. I promise. What do you say? Can we get away? Can we, can we?" Kate asked coyly, knowing all the while her strategically placed hand would help get her way.

"I can check with work hon, but I don't see a problem. It's mid-month and we're slow at the moment. In fact, I'll make a few calls to wrap things up, and maybe we can leave later today." Matt was not going to pass up on this opportunity. It was the chance he'd been waiting for to bring them closer. "Sounds like a plan. Let's do it!"

Organizing the bedroom, Kate considered where to spend a few days. Matt was in bed working up enough energy to call his office while he watched Kate flit around the room happier than she'd been in a long time.

Matt thought back to when they first met. At first he was mildly attracted. She was pretty, but not a knockout. Almost his height, although very thin, at times so thin she looked frail. Kate's face tended to be more round than oval, accentuated by vibrant hazel eyes. Ultimately, Kate's sweet personality and goodness attracted him. On the flip side, she could also be headstrong and relentless after identifying a goal.

Making a quick phone call Matt had everything set. "Any idea where you would like to spend the next few days, my Lady? Your wish will be granted."

"I'm thinking about the Pocono Mountains. A few of my interviews are in North Eastern Pennsylvania, near the Poconos. Early Wednesday morning I can drop you on a commuter bus back to the City then drive the rental car to north of Scranton. What do you think?"

"Sounds good to me. Don't you remember, Denise and Mike went skiing and stayed in a lodge very near the Mt. Pocono turnpike exit? They talked about that resort for weeks. I'll call them for the name of the lodge and hopefully, make reservations for tonight. Spring is off-season; we should be able to get our choice of rooms. Mike really enjoyed the sunken tub. I guess he's into indoor water sports!"

"You won't hear any complaints from me." She dragged him out of bed. "Up and at em', fella."

The cool morning made it more difficult than normal to rouse out of bed. The couple, half awake for some time, refused to acknowledge it was time to get up. Neither was willing to break away from the warmth and security of each other's arms.

After an extended weekend in the mountains Matt couldn't miss the bus to New York. If he did, his boss would be furious. He hadn't checked with the office since leaving a voice mail telling them about his short holiday.

Gently touching Kate's shoulder, Matt said, "Honey, I hate to say this but it's time to get up."

"I know, just two more minutes. I promise, I will get myself together fast."

Beginning to fret, in exactly two minutes he kissed Kate on the forehead and rolled them both out of bed. They showered together to save time, savoring a few more intimate moments together. Lathering his chest she gradually worked her way down and lingered on his manhood. No reaction, he was already in his work mode. *Your loss, lover!* she thought.

They dressed, packed and were standing at the checkout counter in thirty minutes, an all time record. The drive to nearby Stroudsburg was relatively quick. They hit light traffic until turning onto Main Street, where commuters jockeyed for limited parking spaces. Matt hoped for a few minutes together in the parking area, until he saw the bus loading and he still had to buy a ticket. He hugged Kate and mussed her hair, whispering, "I love you and will miss you, babe. Come home soon…call me every night with an update on your progress. Say 'hi' to the Pope. Tell him I'm a big fan." He could feel her energy and knew she was ready for action. The best thing he could do to help was to give her the space and time she needed.

"I really love you, Mr. Matt. Think about me during the day. I'll call you as soon as I'm settled in the hotel. And thanks for the long weekend!"

Kate waited until he boarded the bus and it rounded the corner heading for the Big Apple. In recent years the Poconos had become the outer edge of commuting for people working in North Jersey and New York City.

It was time for coffee. The local 7-11 was near the bus station and did a brisk early morning business. Local contractors quickly replaced commuters in line for coffee and cigarettes. Kate treated herself to a cup of special Kona blend and a French Cruller. The coffee smelled good and the cup warmed her hands. The clerk, although not her type, was cute. He thanked her for the purchase and offered a friendly smile. As an afterthought, she turned and asked directions for Clark Summit, a town north of Scranton. Within seconds, two burley construction workers offered personal assistance.

Primed for the ninety-minute ride, she headed north. Since the appointment was at 10:00 a.m., she had plenty of time to enjoy the ride and popped in a favorite CD, mentally preparing for the hectic day ahead. She hoped her videographer, Jay Collins, checked his voice mail and had the correct address and time. The first interview had to begin on an up note.

The last few days Kate had reconnected with Matt. She understood the glue was still fragile, it would take time and resolve to strengthen their bond. This long weekend should hold them together at least until the Papal assignment ended.

The first interview was with Mrs. Pavelli, the Pope's mother, and his youngest brother, Louis, who volunteered to join them and help his 93-year-old mother. This saved time for both parties since Kate had planned on meeting with Louis some time during the interviewing process. During the ride north she fussed over the best way to approach the session. At this early stage, no one could know about the live Papal interview, so she'd only discuss the biography.

The drive through rolling green hills with sparse population was pleasant and relaxing. Traffic was almost non-existent until she reached the outskirts of Scranton, where commuter volume slowed her progress for ten miles. Once traffic disbursed her speed returned to just above the legal limit and the exit for Clark Summit came up rapidly.

The town and nursing home were not far off I-81 and easy to find. Clark Summit was not a typical northeastern Pennsylvania town; this was definitely an upscale community. One imagined the residents as business owners and professionals; the well-manicured lawns and expensive cars screamed wealth. The nursing home sat in a gated community set back about a quarter mile from the main road. The guard asked Kate for an I.D. and whom she was visiting. Supplying the information, Kate was passed through. A GNN camera truck was already parked in the visitors' lot. Jay waved as Kate made a sharp right into a parking space.

"Kate, how are you? How long has it been?" Jay kissed her on the cheek.

"Seven…maybe eight months. Doing great. How about you?"

"Never better," he smiled, "Richard finally moved in a few months ago. His father had a fit. Thinks his neighbors will find out Richard's gay. Like they don't already know!"

The receptionist asked them to be seated and notified the floor nurse. They were fifteen minutes early and Kate craved another cup of strong coffee. Before she could ask for directions to the coffee machine, a tall, good looking man with light brown hair and hazel eyes, early fifties stepped into the waiting area. "Miss Murphy?"

"Yes, and this is Jay Collins."

"Hello, I am Louis Pavelli. It's so nice to meet you." He extended his hand to Kate, then Jay. "Mom has been eagerly waiting. She's been up and dressed since 8:30. Asks every ten minutes, 'Is she here yet?' Since Tony called last week, Mom's curiosity has been piqued. He didn't give us any details, only to meet with you and answer all your questions, no matter how intimate or personal. Quite honestly, I'm a bit curious myself. What's the story?" For a few seconds their eyes locked. Kate sensed Louis was a kind man with a short temper.

"There's no secret; I'm a historian preparing a video biography for the Vatican library. Mr. Pavelli, if I can ask you to be patient for a few minutes longer, when we meet your mother I will explain why we are here. And please, call me Kate."

"Okay, Kate. We better get to Mom's room before she comes looking for us."

"Before I meet your mother, tell me about her physical and mental condition. What should we expect, is there anything I should be cautious about so I don't upset her?"

"That's very considerate. Mentally she is very alert, has excellent recall. However, at ninety-three, she has some physical limitations that require managed care. She's mobile but cooking and cleaning are out of the question. Mom is very happy here and enjoys visitors. She's somewhat of a celebrity in this area, so we try to be careful about who meets with her."

"Well, Louis, we're ready if you are. No wait…I need a good cup of coffee."

"Taken care of, Mom's already ordered coffee and tea."

Moving through the corridors, Kate noticed it was obviously a Catholic nursing home as well as a first class facility. Nice size rooms, each similar, except for the individual décor selected by the residents. Every room had two windows facing either the expansive manicured lawn or garden areas. They were bright and cheery; not exactly home sweet home but very livable. Entering Mrs. Pavelli's room, Kate noticed the bureau and shelf filled with family pictures spanning Mrs. Pavelli's adult life.

"Mom, this is Miss Kate Murphy, the journalist that Tony asked us to meet with."

"Miss Murphy, welcome. I've been waiting for you. Oh, you are so young and pretty. A are you really a journalist? I have great grandchildren older than you."

"Please don't get up, Mrs. Pavelli. That rocking chair looks so comfy." Kate suppressed chuckling about the age comment and extended her hand to Mrs. Pavelli. "A pleasure to meet you, Mrs. Pavelli. Yes, I am a journalist for GNN. We are sorry to keep you waiting; our plan was to arrive exactly at ten so we didn't rush your morning activities. May I introduce Jay Collins? He handles the equipment end of the interview."

Mrs. Pavelli offered her pure white hand. "Hello, Jay. I can tell by all this special equipment that you must be very capable."

"Well, thank you, Mrs. Pavelli, I do my best."

"Please call me June. I am just eager to hear news about my son."

Before meeting the Pope's mother, Kate didn't know what to expect, after a few short moments she was pleasantly surprised. "I had the opportunity to have a private meeting with the Holy Father last week. He's in good health and excellent spirits. He sends his love. Mrs. Pavelli, the reason we are here is because the Vatican has assigned GNN, my company, to complete the Holy Father's biography for the Vatican Library. It's quite an honor to be selected for this assignment and we intend to do our best."

"Is he as handsome as ever? How is his weight? Are those Italians taking care of my son?"

Sitting across from Mrs. Pavelli, Kate couldn't help smiling, not only at the questions but her intensity. "He's a very attractive man, Mrs. Pavelli, but I try not to think about that, considering he is not only a priest but also the Pope. He's trim and it looks like he probably exercises when time permits. Don't worry, the Italian staff is taking excellent care of your son." She didn't add, *except for the cardinals stabbing him in the back*, cautious not to reveal anything about the internal intrigue.

"Thank you, Kate. It's been some time since I saw Tony. Although he calls frequently, it's not the same as seeing him. Now, how can we help you?"

"The Vatican library is pushing to have the biography completed as quickly as possible. I'd like to start at the beginning. Tell me about you, your husband and family, especially while your son was young."

Mrs. Pavelli sat in the rocking chair, her left hand instinctively reached for her crystal rosary beads. "Folks, get comfortable. This could make for a long day, so start thinking about lunch. Young man, you can start that recording machine. Okay, here we go."

"My name is June Pavelli. I am ninety-three years old and live at the Holy Mother Home in Clark Summit, Pennsylvania. I am proud to say my son, Anthony Pavelli, is Pontiff of the Roman Catholic Church. Somehow, saying that always makes me smile.

"I was barely seventeen when I met my husband, Joseph. He was still in the Army. I worked in the local drug store and we met while I was working the soda fountain. Tall and handsome he was. There were few Italians in Shamokin; the town was mostly Eastern European, Polish, Slovak, Russian and Ukrainian. Mother was Ukrainian and my father Austrian and Ukrainian.

"Soon after we met, Joe was discharged and he moved back to this area to live with his family. Angelo and Mary emigrated from Italy in their early twenties. They had eight children—five boys and three girls—all living at home when Joe moved back. He loved cars and became an auto mechanic, opened his own repair shop after his discharge from the service."

Mrs. Pavelli paused to study the journalists. "I often think we were ahead of our time, having a long distance relationship. Back then Shamokin was a three-hour drive, but Joe found his way to my town almost every weekend. I know this sounds strange, considering how things have changed in the past seventy years, but at the time we moved fast. My family accepted him, although they were usually suspicious of Italians. I also had a large family, with seven surviving children: three boys and four girls. I'm number six, the second youngest. I'm the only one left. For some reason, all my brothers died young…cancer and heart problems.

"We were married two months after my eighteenth birthday, seventy-five years ago. I know it sounds silly, but thinking real hard it often seems not so long ago. Folks, it's a function of life; time slips by. So know what you want and make it happen. Don't have regrets when you're fifty. Am I rambling?"

Kate understood the message from a woman who had no regrets. Even so, Kate wanted everything on her terms and timetable, knowing life almost never works that way. "No, you're doing fine," smiled Kate. "This is just what I was hoping for. Anytime you are tired let us know…we can take a break."

The rosary beads never left Mrs. Pavelli's hand. Even when she became animated, or raised her arm to emphasize a point, the beads swung back and forth. "Well, back to my memories…Where am I? Oh yes, married at eighteen. I was still very young and naive, rarely traveled more than fifty miles from my hometown.

"My dad was a tall man, always lanky, never put on any weight. A hard, hard man. Worked his whole life in the coal mines. Hard on the family, especially on Mom. Drank hard liquor every day, and no one bucked the master of the house…could be a mean bastard. My parents owned a local bar room, first floor was the bar and we lived on the second and third floors. All day Mom cooked for the bar. Us kids helped by cleaning and making beer and moonshine in big vats in the damp basement. With the bar and mine wages, the family should have been in good shape, even though it was the middle of the Depression. We lost everything, the building and the bar. The bank foreclosed. Mom was beside herself, lost heart. Although still young, she looked and moved like an old woman."

Louis helped his mother slowly get up. She moved toward the window to loosen stiff joints and check her bird feeder hanging just outside. "Don't mind saying I was scared and excited at the same time, but my happiness about a life with Joe overcame the other feelings. We were young and ready for what lay ahead. I never once looked back and thought 'what if,' even during those tough times we all deal with."

There was a quiet knock on the door. "Come in…I hope this is the coffee and cakes. Oh thank you, Darlene. Just leave those on the side table. You know my son, Louis, and this is Miss Murphy, and this nice young man is Jay. They are journalists from the Vatican."

"Nice to meet you. June, if you need me just ring. Lunch will be served at 11:30. Should I arrange for Louis and your guests to join you?"

"Yes, thank you. Please call to remind us. Everyone, please help yourself to coffee and cake."

Kate said quizzically, "The description of your hometown is different, although interesting."

Louis chimed in, "Central Pennsylvania is coal country and certainly different. If you want an idea of what the town was like, watch the movie *Deer Hunter*."

"I did see that old movie some years ago," Kate replied.

Mrs. Pavelli returned to the rocker, gliding back and forth. "My new home was still in the Pennsylvania coal belt, about 100 miles away, just north of Scranton. Newly married, new business, and cash was short, so we moved in with Joe's parents. We lived in tight quarters; two brothers and two sisters still lived at home. Joe's parents, Angelo and Mary, were wonderful people and accepted me as part of the family. Mary was a homemaker and ruled the roost, warm but you didn't cross her. Angelo and Mary spoke English with thick accents. The children's first language was English but they could all speak Italian. The children are first generation Americans, good citizens, every son spent four-plus years in the armed services.

"In a few months I was pregnant...told you we were moving fast. I became very close with my sister-in-law, Louise. She was a big part of our lives for the next fifty years until her death. There were times we were as close as sisters. Sometimes we fought like hell, especially as we got older. Our boys, all three, considered her a second mother. Oh yes... back to my pregnancy. Anthony was born eleven months after the wedding. God bless him, he was a strong and healthy baby, with thick black hair.

"Joe got itchy. He needed more privacy and American cooking...was tired of spaghetti, so we moved to our own place. The big move was across the street about 300 feet away. Speaking of near by...Joe's auto repair shop stood next door to the family house, so he saw his parents every day. We lived in a small world.

"Kate, every morning I take my daily constitution and putter around in the garden. Do you mind if we enjoy the outside?"

Kate looked at Jay. Because of the video equipment the ball was in his court. Jay gave an Okay signal. "Mrs. Pavelli, if you're ready, we can move to the garden."

Mother Pavelli continued her saga as she slowly, with the help of a walker, waddled for the outdoors. "We rented a very small single house, one story. No central heating, coal stoves in the kitchen and living room. Money was tight. We had essentials, but no luxuries other than a car. My little family survived and most importantly we were all happy. Anthony was a beautiful baby with bright eyes and curly black hair. Did I mention his photo won honorable mention in a national contest? I just happen to have the picture with me. Would you like to see it?"

"Thank you, Mrs. Pavelli. I'm sure we can use it in the biography."

"Three years later I gave birth to Dom, son number two. Anthony was growing and before I knew it he was in kindergarten, then first grade. "

As the group walked through the side door, a dapper old gent waved his cane while saying hello to Mrs. Pavelli. "Ignore that old goat. He's always pestering me. I'm too old for his romantic nonsense." Kate grinned and Jay made a note to erase that section of videotape.

"He seems like a nice old guy," Louis teased.

"This is more important than that old goat! Louis, you walk ahead; you're making me nervous back there." She waved a hand shushing him ahead.

"We finally saved enough money to build our own house. I lived in that house until two years ago, when I moved in here. It's still in the family... won't sell it.

"In fourth grade Anthony became an altar boy. What a thrill. Between that and the influence of Catholic school, he began to talk about becoming a priest. Of course half the kids in his class talked about becoming nuns or priests. This was before the big drop in vocations. Jay, is your machine getting all of this?"

Jay waved. "Yes, Mrs. Pavelli, the machine is working just fine."

With that assurance, Mrs. Pavelli switched the rosary beads to her other hand and continued. "On a Sunday morning, while getting ready for Mass, Grandmom Mary died from a massive cerebral hemorrhage. A loss of a mother is terrible...the family crumbles. That's exactly what happened to the Pavellis. They drifted apart.

"See that bench in the sun? That's my spot. Let's sit over there. Watch the grass; it's still damp from the rain."

Kate felt relaxed with the Pavellis and comfortable with how the interview was progressing. Mrs. Pavelli reminded her of a great aunt that she visited some years ago. The two women had much in common—strong, determined and reared during the Great Depression. Everyone sat and waited while Jay changed batteries on his camera.

Mother Pavelli looked at Kate to make sure they were ready. "A year or so before high school, Anthony grew tall and thin, so handsome. He also hung around with six or seven friends that lived in the neighborhood. He and Dom often worked at their father's auto shop after school and on Saturdays, mostly cleaning up and helping their Dad with small repair jobs. His brother usually found a way to avoid the after-school work. Anthony decided that if he was going to work he should make some money and took a part-time job."

This background was good filler, but Kate needed to delve into the part of the Pope's life that was fueling the rumors. She intended to ease Mrs. Pavelli in that direction. "Mrs. Pavelli, can you tell me about his friends in high school?"

"Let me think, yes, that small group of six or seven close friends that I mentioned, he palled around with...Bob, Harvey, two Jim's, Eugene and Dick...I can't remember the other, maybe Tom? Their hangout was a pool hall down the street. I am sure they picked up some bad habits at that ratty place. I know it's where he started smoking and cursing. Anthony loved that damn joint."

"What else do you remember about high school?"

"Anthony liked his little Catholic high school, especially the last two years. He was a star business pupil and the teacher's pet; she encouraged him to pursue a career in business. You know he was very good at accounting and economics. There was no more discussion about the priesthood. He had the college bug; moving on to college became fashionable. Some kids wanted an education, while others needed draft deferments. That awful war in Vietnam took our young men. Anthony wanted to become an accountant and CPA... the first Pavelli to attend college." Kate heard a mother's pride.

As a mother, Mrs. Pavelli was always concerned about feeding someone, especially guests. "It's eleven-fifteen. Is anyone hungry?"

With the mere mention of lunch, Mrs. Pavelli hopped up, ready to mosey along with her walker. They all needed a break before heading for lunch so they scattered to the washrooms.

The dining facility was large and open, although nicely decorated in pastel colors; it could easily pass for a modest hotel restaurant. The hostess directed the group to a reserved private table. Jay set up the camera on a tri-pod and sat next to Kate. Everyone took Mrs. Pavelli's advice and ordered the chicken. Their salads were served in minutes; the main course arrived quickly, in fact before the salads were consumed.

Kate turned her attention to Louis. "You've been very quiet. What do you recall about Anthony's high school days?"

"I'm thirteen years younger. I was only four years old, so I don't remember his high school days. My memories really don't start until after he was married."

"Okay, we can cover that later. I prefer to go through this in chronological sequence. Did Anthony have any girlfriends in high school?"

"Anthony was shy. He had the usual dates to the sophomore hop and junior prom. By their senior year, Anthony and his friends all drove and went to other schools' activities. That's how he met Vicky. She attended West Valley High. A pretty girl with pitch-black hair, her mother was Hispanic and father Irish, just off the potato boat. Vicky was outgoing, could talk your ear off. I had an instant dislike for her because I knew what she really was."

The mere thought of Vicky agitated Mrs. Pavelli, souring her mood. "Can you tell us?" prompted Kate.

"A mean, rotten, self centered...I better stop right there. At least that's my opinion."

Wow! Kate sat back, taken a bit off guard. Mother Pavelli's face reddened but didn't veer away from the camera lens. "As it turned out, I had her pegged. After graduating high school, Anthony started at a local college. He worked all summer to pay the first semester of college. Through bits and pieces of conversation, I could tell she was a very unhappy girl, and I hoped my son could see through her manipulations. College during the day and working nights and weekends was rough; he was tired and his grades were lower than he wanted.

"After the first semester ended Joe and I got hit with a bombshell." She needed to compose herself and stopped briefly. Before continuing, Mrs. Pavelli flashed a contrived smile to hide her feelings. "Anthony wanted to get married. We knew...the girl...was pregnant."

"How did you and your husband handle that?"

"We were sick...so many things on our minds at the same time. Where will they live? He can't go back to college and support a family. Too young to get married, this will ruin his life.

"We had family meetings with our pastor to convince them to put the baby up for adoption. Anthony's sense of right and wrong, his Catholic upbringing, wouldn't allow him to walk away from his responsibility."

Kate looked around at the nearby tables. Every table sat quiet, turned in their direction. "Let's finish eating; I think it would be better to discuss this in private."

After lunch, Kate checked her video voice mail before returning to Mrs. Pavelli's room. There was a brief message from Brother Jacomo, asking her to call him on his private number between 3:00 and 4:00 p.m.

"Mrs. Pavelli, do you need a few moments to rest or should we continue?"

"I can rest when we're finished...plenty of time for rest. It's not often I can talk about the old days and my family. My best days."

"Mrs. Pavelli, you must be experienced at these interviews; you are doing very well. But if you need to rest just let us know." That bit of praise encouraged the old woman. She raised her hand with a motion to continue as the rosary beads swung.

"What happened with Anthony and Vicky?"

"Against our wishes they got in the Scranton Basilica. Naturally, he quit college and accepted a full time job with National Shoes and moved near Philadelphia. My boy was just eighteen and already married, a father-to-be and moving over a hundred miles away. Our hearts...dreams were shattered; I was sure they were on a downhill road. Once he left home our relationship was strained for many years. Of course we visited, but Joe and I were no longer part of his daily life....and...all of a sudden, Kate, I'm tired." Mother Pavelli stopped rocking, and pulled a shawl over her legs.

"I understand. Thank you, Mrs. Pavelli, you've been wonderful. You relax while I talk to Louis. Can you add anything?"

Shifting the focus to Louis made him a bit nervous. He spoke slowly, carefully selecting his words. "I was still a toddler when Anthony moved out. Years later I asked him what happened and how he survived marriage, fatherhood and being on his own at eighteen. I can tell you the little that I remember. Financially things were tight living on a shoe clerk's salary. Thomas was born five months after they were married. With new responsibilities, Anthony found a better job working for a major corporation as a clerk. That fall he started night school at Villanova University."

He folded both arms over his chest, signifying discomfort as he broached a very personal period in his brother's life. "Anthony worked days and attended college three nights a week—a busy schedule. His wife quit high school.

"After three years of marriage, Anthony knew the marriage was in trouble; they barely saw each other, no intimacy at all. Shortly after trying to discuss these issues with his wife he was blindsided. She wanted out, it was over."

"What happened after she dropped that message?"

Louis glanced at his mom. She'd fallen asleep. Kate could tell he disliked dredging up embarrassing events and kept his eyes diverted toward the window. He probably felt this whole episode was better left in the past. Rising, Louis moved close to the windowsill before continuing. "Depressed, angry, his whole world in shreds. He tried to convince her to stop and rebuild the marriage."

Sensing his rudeness, Louis returned to his chair. "She realized that marriage was just another trap. She wanted her freedom, to take control of her own life. Vicky left and took Tom. A few months' later, things were not going well, she had a new friend…know what I mean? Anthony convinced her to give him custody. Anthony filed for divorce soon after. He became a single parent working full time and attending night-college. His ex-wife really showed her true colors, making his life miserable about visitation and interfering with Tom's routine. Vicky gave Tom the good times like movies, ice cream…while his dad made him go to bed early, eat his vegetables and go to day care. At that point his mother flitted in and out of Tom's life.

"I should probably stop at this point. Other people, especially Tony's children, are in a better position to discuss his second marriage and that part of his life."

"Louis, your mother is still napping. Poor soul, we tired her out. I think we covered a lot today. We really appreciate your time and cooperation. I will be speaking to your brother Anthony in the next few days. Can I tell him you're all fine?"

"Yes, we're all great. Send him our love. Thank you and Jay for working on Anthony's biography, I can't wait to see it."

"Jay and I will pack as quietly as possible."

Packing took a few minutes; they were ready to leave when Louis recalled something. "I just remembered, Mom wanted you to meet her friends down the hall. They have been anxiously waiting all day. Would you take a moment to say hello? It'll really make their day."

The journalists exchanged glances. They wanted to leave as soon as possible. *What the hell*, Kate thought, *a few minutes to give the old people a brighter day would be nice.*

"Sure we'd love to meet her friends."

Meanwhile, Kate's mind rattled with confusion about piecing together a biography. She looked forward to the next two interviews, hoping they would help construct a cohesive documentary. She also wanted to respond to Brother Jacomo's message.

Chapter Nine

Before leaving the nursing home, Louis gave them directions to I-81. Kate preferred to rely on the dashboard direction finder. The directions were convenient, accurate and provided a printed hard copy. If the driver went off course the computer beeped, indicating they strayed.

Just after entering I-81, Kate turned on her combination video cell phone and pager and was immediately notified of one new and one saved message. The old message was Brother Jacomo. She called the voice mail and heard a sweet poem from Matt, extolling his love and reminding her to call from the hotel. With light traffic she estimated arriving in time to call Brother Jacomo, who was probably looking for an update. At the halfway mark she called the GNN office in New York and spoke with her assistant, Joan.

"Hello Joan, anything hot I should know about?"

"How nice to hear from you. My day is going well, thanks. Actually, the whole office is in high gear about some big project. Top secret—nobody's talking."

Joan really knew how to bust chops. "Sorry for being curt. I am glad you're having a good day. Anything directly for me?"

"Nothing you should be concerned about. If anything comes up, I'll call your cell phone."

"Thanks, Joan. I am staying at the Sheraton in Valley Forge, Pennsylvania, tonight. I will check in tomorrow. Goodbye."

Driving south, the mountains seemed endless, crisp and spring fresh, turning a deep lush green. As the miles rolled by she tuned into satellite radio and relaxed to the background music. This first session gave Kate an entirely different slant on the Holy Father. The assignment was taking on a whole new twist. Kate was becoming confident the man wearing the white hat was in fact the good guy. Checked-in and unpacked, she immediately called Brother Jacomo's private number. The phone answered on the second ring.

"Pronto, Brother Jacomo."

"Hello, this is Kate Murphy returning your call."

"Are you using a video phone and is it a secure line?"

"It's an unsecured hotel line. If you wish I can turn on the video phone?"

"Please do while I place you on hold."

In less than thirty seconds the Holy Father appeared on the video screen. "Hello, Kate. How was your meeting with two of my favorite people?"

"Everything went better than I expected. Your mother is charming and brother Louis refreshing."

"Excellent, a good start. I have contacted everyone on the list. They are expecting to hear from you...promised to be open and cooperative. Who are you contacting next?"

"I have an appointment with your sister-in-law, Chris, early tomorrow morning. I'm staying a few miles from her house."

"Very good. Can I be of any assistance at this point?"

"Actually, yes. I am curious about a few things. How did you manage as a single parent working and going to college without a family support-structure near by?"

"That was so long ago. I was young, twenty-one or twenty-two, didn't know any better and did what had to be done. Quite simply, I had no alternative."

She heard the slight hesitation in his voice. Trying to downplay raising his son as a single parent. She didn't understand why. "Holy Father, you had alternatives. You could have given up child custody or moved back to live near your family."

"At that time, Tom's mother was, ah...let's say, 'unsettled,' and turning over custody wasn't an option. Don't forget, Vicky voluntarily gave up Tom. I liked the Philadelphia area and had a good job. I could see opportunities that were not available in my small hometown. I never even considered moving back."

This was obviously a sore spot from his youth. Kate noticed his cringe just talking about it. He wanted to move on, change the subject.

"Holy Father, now I need to discuss a very touchy subject." The Pope's brow wrinkled, suspicious of what she might ask. This early in the process he preferred to err on the side of caution concerning Kate and GNN.

"I'm sure you realize that part and parcel of your biography is a thorough investigation by GNN."

The Pope waited with anticipation for the punch line, wondered what they uncovered. "During our investigation of the various rumors we discovered that your name is connected with the pedophilia scandal in the United States. Is there anything we need to discuss before proceeding with your bio?"

"Oh! That's one of the ugly rumors that I haven't heard. I wonder how many other vicious half-truths are whirling about. Kate, I had involvement in that situation. It was unfortunate for everyone—the young victims, the Church officials and the priests that were affected. I had just transferred to the diocesan staff. The Cardinal needed a representative, in his words, that was 'above reproach' to interface with the victims, their families and the authorities.

"As a parent with children and grandchildren, I fit the bill. My experience as a parish priest, although limited, carried some weight. I could empathize with all concerned parties, and I spent the better part of two years working with victims and some very disturbed priests. I also participated in the committee of priests and laity parishioners searching for solutions. So yes, I was intimately involved with the scandal, as a counselor though, not a pedophile. There's a clear trail in the newspapers and courts for anyone wishing to complete even a cursory investigation."

As the Pope discussed his involvement in the scandal that tarnished the Catholic Church in the United States creating a crisis of confidence, she felt the weight of concern evaporate. "I am sorry for opening that old chapter in your career. Regrettably, we have to confront all the issues in order to clear your reputation."

"I understand. Kate, the video signal is breaking up. I'll sign off for now. Call Brother Jacomo at least every other day. Oh, I almost forgot, my people have not received any instructions from GNN. I'm a bit concerned."

"GNN will contact your media people by next week; we haven't forgotten. This is important to all of us." The picture faded before Kate could say goodbye.

The Holy Father soft peddled the comments about his ex-wife. Based on fragments she picked up from Mrs. Pavelli, Vicky was difficult at best. Kate was more than pleased about the progress of her mission. This call was a small preview of the coming interview. The picture was a bit fuzzy, it didn't matter—the Holy Father held a commanding camera presence.

Kate decided to treat herself to a hot bath, followed by an early dinner in the hotel. By 7:30 p.m. she felt relaxed, well fed and ready to call Matt. The phone rang several times before a female voice answered. It was Bunny, Matt's dotting mother.

"Hello Bunny, how are you and that lovable husband, Tim?" Kate started to pace, feeling a bit irritated. Bunny had a way of putting her on edge. Kate figured it was a "mother thing".

"Just fine, Kate. Tim is spending a few days at the shore house to get it ready for the summer season. And you?"

"Rested and well fed. It's nice that you spend some time with Matt while I'm away. I know he enjoys your visits." *As long as they don't go beyond two hours*, she said to herself. "I have been thinking about dinner and an off-Broadway play. Are you and Tim interested in joining us?"

"Sure, ah…let me know when you will be in town next and I'll order tickets. Do you or Matt have a play in mind?"

"Not really. You pick one; you know what's hot. If Matt's nearby, can I speak with him?" Bunny said goodbye and handed the telephone to Matt.

"Hello. How's my best girl after her long day in mountain country?"

Kate plopped her body sideways on the bed, one smoothly shaved leg dangled over the end. "Your best and only girl couldn't wait to hear your voice. Thank you for the poem on my voice mail, lots of romance points."

"How was the interview? Did it go well?"

"Actually turned out better than I expected. They are lovely everyday people. I hope all the interviews go that well. Has your mother fed you? She's always *worried* about her son's nutrition."

Matt picked up on the sarcasm in her tone. "Oh yes, Mom whipped up some homemade cooking, delicious as usual. She's trying to turn me into a gourmet…it's not working. When will I see you?"

"Based on our agenda, I should be home Saturday afternoon. At which time I can demonstrate my female talents, some of which may or may not be cooking!"

"Can't wait. I miss you hot stuff."

"I know it's hard to talk with Mom hovering near by, so goodbye for now. Matt, I love you."

"Good. I love you!"

Rolling out of bed at sunrise, Kate felt chipper, ready to start the day. Last night she left the Pope's sister-in-law Chris a message confirming their appointment at 9:30 a.m. It was early so she decided to take a long walk through Valley Forge National Park located a short distance from the hotel.

This was her first visit to the park so she drove around and through the park before starting her walk. She pictured Valley Forge as a fortress with battlefield monuments scattered through out the park, possibly an old military cemetery. Instead, the park was a natural setting with open rolling countryside, dotted with park benches and paths for walking, jogging or cycling.

A beautiful, non-denominational chapel located along the main road was a focal point in the park. The chapel was open to the public and not far from the recently renovated visitors' center. The Arch of Triumph built in the middle of nowhere at the far end of the park caught most visitors by surprise, a grand monument to all the soldiers and sailors who fought for freedom from Mother England.

The park map highlighted the five-mile walking trail that meandered through the park then circled back to the visitor's center. The clear sky had a hint of clouds, a perfect spring day. Along the walkway and scattered through the fields dogwood trees reached full bloom, the vibrantly colored buds a pleasing contrast to the green fields and light blue sky. She walked for one hour then headed back to the hotel to dress for the interview.

Back in the room, Kate showered before noticing the voice mail flashing. Two messages; the first was a disappointment. Aunt Chris rescheduled to 4:00 p.m. There was one benefit; Kate and Jay were invited to a home-cooked dinner. The second was a message forwarded from her office. The Pope's brother, Dom, canceled Saturday's interview; he had to leave Friday for a two-week business trip. He suggested conferencing on his office videophone before 7:00 p.m. This might work to her benefit, saving a ten-hour round trip drive to Richmond. Although she preferred face-to-face meetings, timing didn't permit a two-week delay.

Checking with the office she received a confirmation that GNN's tech people had contacted the Vatican. The boss was tied up on a corporate conference call and his secretary sent a message: "Keep me informed of your progress."

Kate dialed Dom's videophone, hoping to schedule a meeting before 2:30 p.m. so she could keep her appointment with Chris Draga. He answered, and fortunately had some free time before his next commitment. He turned on the videophone.

A pleasant surprise, Dom was quite handsome. His thick black hair had a hint of light gray streaks. In contrast, his older brother's hair was pure white. While still handsome, the white hair added years to his age. Dom's facial features and voice were similar to Pope Alex's. As a businessman and short for time, Kate suspected a brief and to-the-point conversation.

"Miss Murphy, thank you for understanding my schedule change. I hope it's not a great inconvenience."

"Please, call me Kate. No inconvenience, this actually helps my interviewing schedule. I had factored a ten-hour round trip to Richmond."

"I'm glad it worked out for both of us. This is my last project before retiring. And please call me Dom, everyone does."

"Okay, Dom."

"I was briefed by Louis, so I know you are working on Anthony's biography. Where should we start?"

"I am sure this is a secure telephone line, but let's use first names in case someone can over hear this conversation. What is the age difference between you and your brother?"

"I am three years younger, the middle child."

"After his divorce, you were what, eighteen or nineteen? Were you close enough to your brother to tell how this affected his life?"

"Yes, I can shed some light on that. At first he was sad and very much embarrassed. At that time, divorce wasn't common, especially in a Catholic family. Shy and intense, the divorce shook him up. He had to rethink his life. It drove him to succeed in business so he could meet his financial obligations and provide stability for his young son. In short, he became a tight ass. Excuse the French. For a time after his split he seldom communicated."

"Then what happened?"

"As reality settled in, it was time to move on with life. He started dating a girl from work. The relationship didn't go very far; her parents weren't thrilled about a divorced man with a young son. It ended after six or seven months. Shortly after this breakup he met Marie, who also worked at the same company. Anthony went nuts about her. Excuse me a second please."

A phone rang in the background and Kate heard a faint voice for a few seconds.

"Kate, I am sorry about the interruption. My boss…he needs me right away. I have about ten minutes before an emergency session. Getting back to your question. My career required moving to different parts of the country. Over the next twenty years we didn't spend much time together, mostly holidays. With the whole family always around trying to catch up on events, it's tough to get into personal issues, difficult to know what's really going on? Sorry, I can't be of much help during this period of his life.

"I hate to cut you short, but I have to run, my boss is buzzing the damn intercom. If there are any questions covering the last twenty years--we were much closer during that period--call me and I will try to fill in the missing pieces. Good luck and God speed."

"Thank you, Dom."

The video screen went blank. This was a very small piece, but every little bit added to the puzzle.

Kate called Jay to inform him of their dinner invitation, then called the office and finalized some old correspondence before ordering a light lunch. The afternoon evaporated answering e-mails.

Arriving a few minutes early, the GNN van parked in front of the two-story Victorian house on a quiet suburban street in Wayne, Pennsylvania. The house and grounds appeared neat and well maintained. The front yard's centerpiece, a massive oak tree reaching forty feet into the air, branches extending well above the roof line, providing shade and an overall sense that the tree protected the house and inhabitants. Chris and her husband, Gene, waited on the porch for the visitors.

The journalists received a friendly welcome. Following the introductions, they moved into the house. Chris offered cold and hot drinks. While Jay set up his equipment, Chris gave Kate a brief tour of the house they had lived in for the past thirty-five years, longer than Kate was alive. During the tour it became clear that the Draga family took pride in their lovely home.

Just as they settled down to begin, the doorbell rang, quickly followed by the front door swinging open. A tall, dark haired, very attractive woman about Kate's age entered with a teenage boy, possibly thirteen or fourteen years old. Chris jumped up with a smile, kissed the boy and hugged the woman.

There were immediate introductions. Julia was Chris' daughter and the Holy Father's niece. The boy, Peter, was Julia's son. Peter was clearly Gene's grandson; the facial features and physical build were unmistakable.

During the introductions, Kate had an opportunity to study Chris. Not just her physical appearance, although appealing for a woman close to seventy, more so the warmth and nurturing that she exuded. All instincts shouted a loving woman who people liked and admired.

"Miss Murphy, I wanted to meet you so I invited myself. Since I'm here I've been elected to finish dinner. I'll take care of kitchen duties and join the group afterward."

Jay signaled, ready. Chris settled everyone in the living room. Gene excused himself to watch a basketball game. Peter looked bored sitting in the corner.

"We can start anytime you wish. Dinner should be ready around 5:00," said Chris.

Kate sat at the edge of the soft comfy sofa, and took a deep breath. "Thank you for meeting with us on such short notice; it's very important that we finish the interviews as quickly as possible. The Vatican library has commissioned GNN to complete Pope Alex's biography. The interview format is very informal. We want viewers to relate to the Holy Father, seeing him through the eyes of his family and close friends. So, if there are no questions, let's start. Chris, what is your relationship with the Holy Father?"

"Anthony is my brother-in-law. He was married to my sister, Marie. I've known Tony for over forty years. He still manages to spring surprises."

"I gather you met him through your sister, Marie. How'd they meet and become a couple?"

"They both worked at a large company. During lunch, Tony played cards near an office window facing the parking lot. When Marie passed the window, Tony began to wave. It became a ritual, although they didn't speak for months. Finally, Tony had enough nerve to make the first move and visit Marie in her office. A few weeks more of lunchtime waves, and he asked for a date. Meanwhile, Marie found out all she could about him through the company grapevine. A nice guy…quiet…divorced…single parent…and just happened to live in the same town."

"Tell us about Marie. What was she like?"

"Marie and I still lived at home with our parents. She was single, had a great personality. People took an instant liking to her…sensing her kindness, not to mention a knock-out beauty. Shiny, long black hair falling to the middle of her back, contrasted against crystal blue eyes. Best legs in town, they made her look taller than five-feet-seven.

"After a few dates Marie liked Tony, but they almost broke up when she found out he was five years younger. Somehow he convinced Marie that he was actually much older because of his maturity. In many ways he was older. Marie was young and spirited, while Anthony, for a young guy, was somewhat stodgy and ultra-serious."

"Then what happened?"

"They became pretty serious, he wanted as much of Marie's time as possible. She held him off. Marie had a long relationship that ended badly. And she worried about his son...what strain he might have on their relationship. After Tony's divorce was final he proposed. She accepted, but I knew she had reservations.

"Our parents were dysfunctional. They had a very unhappy marriage. Mom stayed with Dad and hated it and Marie didn't want that kind of life. Single and happy, so why look for heartache? However, Marie's biological clock ticked away and she loved Tony. They finally set the date and were married by a Protestant minister. By the way, Gene and I were dating at the same time and married a month later. We just made forty-eight years." Chris quietly applauded their accomplishment.

"That's great! What a wonderful achievement!" Kate wondered if she and Matt would even make ten.

"Thank you, and happily married, I can add. Getting back to Marie, she was pregnant in three months and the new little family in their first house in six months. Marie tried to treat Tom as a son...it didn't work. Tension continued because of his mother's meddling.

"While Tom was in first grade, his mother had weekend visitation, and during one visit she kept him. Tony had legal custody, but the laws at that time didn't consider taking a child and breaking a custody order as kidnapping. Tony and Marie worried sick for three months. Back then, the authorities considered it a domestic matter...wouldn't help...not even file a missing person's report. A concerned old friend let Tony know where his ex-wife was living. They found his son's school and took him home.

"However, the turmoil didn't end. The mother continued to make everyone's life...well, difficult. Ultimately for the child's sake, Tony and Marie gave up custody. Tom's mother had remarried and it appeared she had some stability; however, custody and visitation continued to be a constant sore spot."

Kate could only guess how Vicky, who had since died, would feel about Anthony's election to Pope.

Julia peeked in the room. "Five-minute warning for dinner."

"That's my Julia." Chris shrugged. "Gina was born almost a year after their marriage. A lovely child, with terrible colic that lasted, oh, it seemed forever.

"After seven long years of night school, Anthony graduated college with a B. S. in Finance. Ah Kate, is this what you want? Am I going too fast?"

"It's perfect. Tell us in your own words."

"Works for me. Let's see. Oh, with diploma in hand, he changed jobs and was quickly promoted. About the same time, he received his annulment from the Church. They were married again, this time in a private Catholic ceremony.

"Our family's close. Saturday was family visit time. My sister Peg, Mom and I would visit Marie, drink coffee, and catch up. Everyone has issues; but overall Anthony and Marie were a happy normal family... in some ways the American dream. Tony used his Saturdays to develop handyman skills. He loved to tinker, and woodworking became a passion."

Kate held up a hand. "Are we ready to break?"

"In a few seconds. Julia will call. Oh yes, their first house was a small Cape Cod handyman special. After three years of renovating they decided to move. Well, the second house was a gem, two-story Williamsburg colonial—three bedrooms and all. Tony loved the two car detached garage with a workshop.

"Have you heard the old saying 'New house, new baby'? Yes, Marie became pregnant. Unfortunately, she had a miscarriage in her third month. Years later she still talked about that child; just knew the baby was a boy. God can be good. He closes a door and opens a window. Not long after, Marie was pregnant again, with Steve."

A loud yell echoed from the kitchen, "Let's go gang, dinner's ready."

Julia set a lovely table and directed everyone to a seat.

Gene asked, "Kate and Jay, have you ever eaten pigs-in-the-blanket? It's a traditional Polish meal."

Both replied no, looked quizzically at the meal set in front of them. Specially prepared ground meat and rice rolled in cooked cabbage, simmered in a light red sauce. The side dishes were familiar fare, and smelled delicious. Conversation during dinner was intentionally light. Chris picked at her meal, contributing little to the banter about Peter's school and Gene's plans for a long overdue retirement. Chris appeared to be deep in thought. Kate wondered how she was holding up, reliving old and sometimes painful memories.

They elected to postpone dessert and coffee. Everyone was stuffed. The pigs-in-the-blanket, although different, were delicious and Kate asked for the recipe. Chris just happened to have the recipe in her cabinet as they walked through the kitchen. Julia, the chief bottle washer, started to clear the table, and suddenly changed her mind. It could wait; she was interested in joining the interview. Gene flicked on the TV in the den. Everyone else headed back into the living room.

Chris appeared more relaxed, hands folded on her lap.

"Your information is exactly what we are looking for. Can you tell us a bit more about Anthony, the man, at this time in his life? What was he like?"

"Simple and complex at the same time. What you saw was what you got. Tony was straightforward, quiet, loved his family and would do anything for them. Deep down, few people understood his thoughts or motivation. I know Marie did, and often chided him about more open communication… telling his children and parents how much he loved them. Tony found opening up his emotions very difficult. Over time and with prodding, he began to crack open the door. Marie and the children were his whole life. That's all he needed."

"Before I forget, can you give Jay the addresses of their houses so we can film from the outside?"

"Actually they owned three houses."

Once into the story, Chris appeared to be beyond the pain of her loss and ready to discuss her sister. The doorbell chimed. Kate glanced at Chris. "Another surprise visitor?"

Gene opened the door to a middle-aged couple accompanied by a striking young woman, twenty-four or -five years old. She held Kate's attention until the hugs and kisses were over and they were into the introductions: Tom, his wife Beth, and their daughter, Ashley. Tom looked in his early fifties, a younger version of his father. The only real difference was Tom's light brown hair, while Beth looked a few years younger than her husband. Ashley, their daughter, looked like a model. Giving Kate a faint smile, Ashley snuggled next to Peter in the corner, pulling her legs up under her chin. The room was certainly getting crowded.

Over the preceding years, Chris had evolved into the family matriarch, so she graciously took the lead.

"During the holidays or whenever we can, the family gets together to visit, play cards or whatever. The more people we have the memories become sharper, easier to recall. So, we decided to do a group interview…so you and Jay could meet the whole or at least most of us. We are also expecting Gina and Andy, Tony's daughter and son-in-law. We think this will be more of what really happens when this family gets together. Hope you don't mind?"

Kate tried to quell an anxious stomach while maintaining a cheerful façade. "It's different, that much I can say. I think I like the idea. If everyone's comfortable, let's continue. You were about to tell us about the third house."

"Marie loved the second house, never wanted to move. Unfortunately, the neighborhood was changing, and not for the better."

Tom spoke up. "I should chime in at this point." He glanced around, there were no objections. "During my second year in high school my mother and I fought like hell, couldn't get along. Thinking back, I guess…yah, I was a typical teenager…a real ass, with poor grades, a party animal. Drinking was my favorite sport. A fifteen-year-old rock star wanna be, ah… I wanted to control my own life. Mom pushed me out of the sunny Florida nest and I landed in Pennsylvania in November! Moving from a dysfunctional household to living with Donna Reed and family. What a shock to my system! Of course, I only thought about myself and how my life was screwed.

"Now you asked about the third house. Transplanting a teenager into a family with young children creates all kinds of issues. Within a month or so, it was obvious that the old three bedroom house was too small. Gina and Steve would eventually need their own rooms. Although Marie hated to move, she found her dream house. After that, Marie said she would never move again, which proved to be true."

"Tom, what happened after you began living with Marie and your dad?"

Tom was third generation Italian, and articulated with his hands and torso; his left hand was especially mobile. "Marie tried to be a mom without forcing the mom stuff. Dad was Dad; he tried…lots of tension. I felt trapped…had to have full control of my life! I often yelled at them, 'It's my life.' The answer was always, 'Not while you live under this roof!' I had nothing in common with my five-year-old brother, Steve, and eight-year-old sister. They bugged me constantly, worse than my brother and sister in Florida.

"The more I resisted family life, the more I was expected to be part of the family. No matter how much everyone tried, I just felt like a black sheep. It was time to change my strategy. First, a part-time job to earn money and a good excuse to be out of the house. Next, gradually join the family so I could get them off my back so they didn't watch my every move."

As Tom spoke, Beth looked bored. This was old news. Ashley paid close attention, interested to learn more about the family's inner workings, absorbing some things hidden from her when she was a child.

Chris excused herself to gather coffee and dessert. Kate drifted, thinking about the family's interaction and how GNN could tie all this information into a homespun biography. She forced herself to refocus on Tom, who looked so like a younger Pontiff.

"A year goes by and Dad's career improved. He took a new job with heavy travel, usually Monday through Friday. It was great. Dad's away, and Marie worked part-time. Party time baby…party I did. My friends and I had six great months until Marie found cigarettes and a bottle of vodka in my room. Friday, when Dad came home, we had a come-to-Jesus meeting. Dad did most of the talking, but the words came straight from Marie. In a nutshell, I was a bad example for the younger kids. Stop smoking and drinking, especially in the house or I was out. They called it tough love; I called it um…something else.

"I purchased an old used car, and didn't want to leave but I could deal with it if I had to. I just wanted them off my back."

Tom slouched, with an arm across the back of the sofa. Kate noticed that as the story progressed, he sat up straight. The easy animation gradually slowed until his hands were folded on his lap—a sure sign he was less comfortable as his story unfolded. "Appears that things went from tense to ugly. How'd you react?"

Red blotches on Tom's neck and cheeks betrayed his tension. The memories, although they appeared to be healed, hit a tender nerve. "Dad still traveled, leaving Marie in total control. Amazing how full responsibility for a family can strengthen one's self-image and confidence. Always a strong personality, but with her new confidence Marie became formidable. I played it careful for four or five months. Then some friends and I cut class and partied in the den. We left the vodka bottle under the sofa. Friday Dad came home and I get the word: Graduation in two months then I was out. It was done. I started looking for a place." He looked down at his hands, "Tough love; no reprieve and no third chance."

Chris carried in coffee and cake. Kate suggested everyone take ten minutes. Between the equipment and people, the room was warm. Kate mentioned the heat to Gene, so he turned on the air conditioner. Cups and saucers clanked as cake and coffee were passed around.

The doorbell chimed, in came Gina and Andy. Kate hoped they were the last surprise guests; the room was already crowded. Everyone hugged and kissed. Gina stood close to six-feet tall, with a well-proportioned figure. Longish curly brown hair fell off narrow shoulders and partially obscured a wide smile. Andy looked a tad shorter with glasses. His round face made him look academic rather than a professional accountant. The couple had been married more than twenty years. Both retained a youthful appearance. They had two children, Cara Marie, twelve, and Andy Jr., ten.

During the introductions Gina appeared stiff, while Andy came across as relaxed, prone to a retro-collegiate dry sense of humor. He quickly excused himself, joining Gene to watch the 76er's.

Gina sat next to Chris on the love seat. Her favorite aunt patted her knee. Chris tried to relax Gina, soothe the anxiety that already turned her smile into a pasted-on version. Gina's emotions were very close to the surface, she couldn't hide the red blotches on her neck and chest. Everyone found a place, a hush settled over the room as Jay turned on his equipment.

Tom looked around to make sure everyone appeared okay. "I was pushed out after graduation. My relationship with Dad, Marie, Gina and Steve remained strained for years. Deep scars take a long time to heal; having my own teenagers helped me to understand their decision and how difficult it must have been."

Kate wondered how well the scars healed. If this interview centered on Tom, she'd probe by asking if he'd make the same decision under similar circumstances. Then again, no one really knows until faced with the tough decision, especially concerning their children.

"Can I comment?" asked Gina, feeling this was the right moment to join in.

Kate answered, "Go ahead,"

Gina turned to Tom for approval. He didn't object. "Tom, Steve and I have worked through these issues long ago, but I would like to clarify things. Steve and I did treat Tom as a second-class brother because of the way he treated us when he was the older brother living at home. He was a true asshole; we responded in kind. I know he wonders about how Dad and Mom, ah...Marie, felt about him. Their relationship with Tom was also strained, but they loved him. We're very proud of Tom's personal, family and business accomplishments. Very proud that Tom and Beth are part of the family. He should also consider that if our parents didn't take the tough love route, Tom might not be the man he is today. I just needed to say that."

Scanning the room, Kate could see everyone was quite aware of their history. Aunt Chris leaned over to squeeze Tom's hand. A faint smile parted his lips, his nod a thank you. The wounds healed, but memories were not far below the surface.

"Gina, you were about eleven when Tom left. Can you take us through major family events during the years that followed?"

Trying to bubble over with enthusiasm, Gina sat on the edge of the cushion and leaned into the circle of people. "Sure, Kate. Dad's travel finally stopped and his career moved along. We seemed to have less financial concerns, finally started to take nice vacations. Tom and Beth were married very young. He was nineteen and Beth seventeen. Our parents were disappointed that they married so young. Statistically their chance of success was slim…but they beat the odds."

Gina looked at Tom then Beth, gave them the briefest of applause. "Time moved quickly. I started college and Steve moved into high school. I went through my hate/love thing…I usually fight change. No matter what, Mom and Dad were supportive, even though I drove them crazy, looking for reassurances at every turn.

"As a whole, life was good, flowing smoothly. Then a massive earthquake shook the family; at least it felt like an earthquake. That year will always be unforgettable. I was a senior, Steve a freshman in college. Tom had his own business. Dad worked in a senior management position, and Mom ran the household and had a part–time job." Her deep sigh overtook the room. Gina closed her eyes to hold back the sobs ready to overcome her deflated body. "And Mom…Mom had cancer."

Even though the family knew it was coming, they were overwhelmed by the loss. "Over twenty-five years and I still get upset discussing ah, the… whole thing…you know, her illness and passing."

Gina cupped her hands together to keep them from shaking; the pink hue that colored her neck and face grew brighter. Her lowered eyes glanced at Aunt Chris, her rock, her maternal replacement.

"Gina, do you need a few minutes to compose yourself?" asked Kate.

"No…I'm fine." Gina's left hand began to squeeze the life out of a crumpled tissue. "During Mom's illness, only a few of us were close to the day-to-day events: me, Aunt Chris and Dad, so I'd like to finish."

"Okay, but if you need a moment just signal…Jay 'ill stop the video."

Looking away, Gina blinked several times to dry faint tears. She leaned toward Kate, blinking rapidly, struggled to look at Kate. Gina somehow felt leaning closer transmitted the depth of hurt and pain this interview forced her to relive. "For months, Mom was tired and losing weight. Dad was concerned, pushed her to see the doctor. Early diagnosis was cancer, but it took a month of tests before confirmation and the full extent of the damage was known. They broke the bad news to the family. From that point…Dad became a mother hen, kept involved with all of the treatments."

Beth handed Gina more tissues to wipe her eyes and nose. "What an awful time. Damn...it still hurts!"

"Gina, everyone who has experienced a loss understands," said Kate. "Can you continue?"

She wiped her eyes, and nodded, yes.

"What was the general atmosphere in the household?"

"My college was in commuting distance so I came home at least two days a week. Both parents were in good spirits and confident they could beat it. Weekly chemo treatments started in late May. At first they seemed harmless. A month later, Mom's hair started falling out in clumps; in two weeks she was bald. That had to be the worst. She always had thick, beautiful hair, was very meticulous about her grooming. From that day she wore a wig outside or a baseball cap in the house.

"I graduated and started my first job. Steve was home for the summer and having us around lifted Mom's spirits. As the treatments continued, Mom became thinner and weaker. The doctors told us chemo takes people to the brink of death in order to kill the cancer cells. Over time the body recovers and rebuilds itself as the chemo flushes out.

"Mom and Dad tried to shelter us. They didn't talk about the illness or doctor visits, and that disturbed me, especially when I heard my parents talk quietly and sometimes cry together."

"Did the chemo help?"

"At the time it was hard to tell. Later we discovered that the treatments didn't work, other than reducing the quality of life during Mom's final months. New ailments appeared...pain in her hip, headaches, temporary loss of speech... this terrified everyone. I can still see Mom at the dinner table trying to speak and no *sound* coming out." Gina's head snapped back. "Do you understand...no sound came out! Oh God."

Unable to hold back the tears, her eyes filled. She burst out sobbing, touched Aunt Chris's arm, and rushed for the powder room.

Aunt Chris expelled a hard breath. She counted on Gina discussing Marie's illness, because recalling the memories still stung deep. "Every time Gina discusses her Mom's illness...well she can't really deal with it.

"The doctors weren't open and honest about the prognosis. One month before Marie's death the doctors told Tony that the cancer had spread, it was hopeless. Before that, they were led to believe the treatments would at least prolong her life, if not put the disease in remission. If they knew this in the beginning or at least the odds of success, their decision might have been not to have chemo. At least, to have some quality of life for the final months."

Chris looked over her shoulder to see if Gina was returning to take over, then looked at Tom and Beth; neither volunteered, so she continued, "The last month was sad and ugly. An experience I never want to relive. The whole family understood the prognosis...Tony couldn't bring himself to tell Marie. She knew. Had known long before the final diagnosis. The family decided to stop treatments and placed Marie in home hospice care."

While Chris spoke, Kate observed the young peoples' reactions. They were frozen, concentrated on every word. Ashley's eyes closed in deep concentration. Peter sat up straight, mouth gaping. The young folks never knew Marie as their grandmother or great aunt. They understood how important she was to the family, how deeply she was loved.

Even Jay, an old hand at interviews, was engrossed. Kate felt herself drifting into thoughts about the inevitable loss of a parent, her parent. She couldn't think about that now. With super woman effort, she forced her attention back to the conversation.

"Marie slipped quickly, her movements slow, pitifully weak. All her siblings jumped in to help set up the den as a hospital room. Steve came home from college. The whole family was notified it was a matter of...days."

Chris's deep-set memories flashed back. Her eyes moistened. Tom reached over to hold her hand. She squeezed it tightly without taking her eyes off Kate. "Friday afternoon the family set up a vigil. Early Saturday Marie slipped into a coma. The family sat at her bedside every moment, saying goodbye, each in their own way. Saturday night the family slept on the floor near Marie's bedside. Sunday afternoon at 2:00 p.m., our Marie passed into God's hands."

Looking around the room, everyone was crying or on the verge of tears. They couldn't look at each other, afraid to see, maybe feel each other's exposed pain.

Kate waited for the right moment and broke the awkward silence. "Beth, you were a relatively new family member and could be objective. How did the family unit recover from this tragic loss?"

"Well, as a family they never really recovered. The cohesion was gone. They are family, but each went off in their own direction. The death changed everything. I think Dad is an example of someone who learned from life's lessons and acted on that insight. I also believe the world will be better because of his efforts."

Beth's restless movements distracted Kate a number of times. While speaking, she had a nervous habit of extending her index finger and running it under the tip of her nose as though it was itchy.

The room remained uncomfortably still. They could faintly hear the TV commentator yelling the final score from the next room. The questions exhausted, Kate asked if anyone had any further memories or comments they wished to share. Almost in unison the family turned to Aunt Chris, who with a throaty voice offered a closing comment.

Trying to smile, Chris began to finalize her story. "Life is too short and full of surprises, some mundane, others huge. Anthony becoming a priest was a big surprise, his election as the Pope huge. He changed his life to help Catholic Christians and mankind. He's in our daily thoughts."

Kate searched the room. Everyone had recovered. The tempo decidedly upbeat, focused back to the main reason for the interview, supporting their Pope. "Thank you all for taking the time to meet and discuss very private, personal and family matters. It's getting late and I'm sure you all want to go home and relax for the remainder of the evening. Again, thank you…a pleasure meeting each of you. When the biography is completed I'll send a CD-ROM to each family."

Chris took Kate's hand. "Take care. Call me if you need anything else…I mean it!"

Entering the vehicle, Kate left the dome light on to see Jay's reaction. Looking straight ahead he said, "I hope the remaining interviews aren't this…you know!" After tonight he wasn't ready to dwell on tomorrow. He put the vehicle in gear and pulled away from the curb.

Kate began to see a clearer picture of the Pontiff and knew he had enough stamina to forge ahead through his current adversities.

Chapter Ten

Eminence Capaldo basked in glory as he celebrated High Mass at the Papal Altar in St. Peter's Cathedral. Reaching high above his head he held the Communion Host with both hands while standing under the magnificent Baldacchino, the grand canopy designed by Bernini. As his Eminence completed the consecration of the Host, Martino stood at the outer edge of the worshipers, waiting for mass to end.

Immediately following, "Peace be with you, the mass is ended," Cardinal Capaldo with the aid of his assistant, Father Nuccio, removed his vestments and proceeded toward the confessional booth, adjacent to the Papal altar.

His black cassock was adorned with red: piping, buttons, sash and the zucchetto that covered the crown of his head signified the rank of his office. A group of elderly Italian women timidly approached and asked for his blessing, which he graciously proffered. He entered a confessional booth. The sign above the solid oak door read 'English'.

The Cardinal slid open the confessional window separating priests from penitents. Martino knelt inches from the black screen. His dark eyes and twisted grin focused directly on his Vatican contact. "Bless me father, for I have sinned. It's been two weeks since my last confession."

"Yes, my son, and it may be many months before I can again hear your confession."

"I don't understand, Your Eminence. Our agreement is to meet every two weeks to discuss the transfers."

"And I wish to continue our business, my son. Unfortunately, the American

Pope has scheduled a bank audit and it's too risky to continue, at least for the time being. I suggest we make this the last transfer until things are under control. Now my son, what do you have to tell me?"

Only into the conversation a few seconds, Martino began sweating profusely, soaking his shirt. He worried about telling his capo that the Vatican connection halted their money laundering activities. His job was to make sure things ran smoothly without a hiccup. His capo must understand this was beyond his control. Yes, beyond his control. Since this transaction was already in motion the Cardinal had no choice but to continue.

"Eminence, the transfers will take place this afternoon from two Brazilian banks and one Trinidad bank. Reroute the funds no later than Monday morning to our three accounts in Vienna."

"As always my son, your sins are forgiven. As a penance, I want you to carry a message to your capo. Remind him confession is good for the soul. He hasn't received the sacrament of penance in a long time. I hold confession every Friday. We can pray together and ask for a way to reinstate our business partnership. Now, my son, go in peace."

The confessional window slid shut with a resounding thud of finality.

Pope Alex's son, Steve, hadn't attended the family interview. Kate managed to reach him early the next day. He didn't usually start work until noon and had a few hours available. They met in the hotel lobby. Like his brother, Steve was another big guy, at least six-foot three-inches, and looked very much like his father, although with short cropped jet-black hair. Kate guessed his age to be early forties, those piercing eyes—almost black liquid. GNN researchers provided Kate a brief background: He married Tiffany fifteen years ago, no children, a car enthusiast, and an expert in home and car audio electronics. He held a number of patents in audio systems. According to Gina and Aunt Chris, Steve rarely talked about his parents, especially to non-family members.

Standing very close to shake hands, Kate had to look up at his face. "Hello, Mr. Pavelli. It's so nice to meet you."

"Hi…everyone calls me Steve."

"All right, if you call me Kate. I reserved a private meeting room. I know you're pressed for time so if you follow me, I will introduce you to Jay, my associate and video specialist."

Jay waited in the room. Coffee, tea and pastries sat on a side table. Daylight was sparse because of light rain and an overcast sky.

"Steve, I am sure you know we interviewed members of your family last night. Did you receive any feedback?"

"No, I'm usually last on the communication chain. By the time I get home tonight my wife, Tiffany, will have several versions from different relatives. Ah… before we start I have some questions. When the family gets together, the women are a loud bunch. Was the information you gathered useful, will the family have an opportunity to review the tapes before the segment is submitted to the Vatican Library?"

"Due to the time limitations to produce the biography, the Holy Father—I mean your dad—and his media experts are the only people who will be able to review and edit the tapes prior to finalizing. Are you concerned about that?"

"No, I trust that my father won't embarrass the family. I am only guessing, but people don't rush to place videos in a vault. Feels like a deadline for a national broadcast."

Kate hesitated. Her eyebrows lifted, realizing she had to be candid. "Steve, you're absolutely correct, except the broadcast is global. I trust you will keep this confidential. We can't go public for another few weeks. This whole process is very important to your father." She gauged his reaction, "Now, if you are ready?"

Maintaining that intractable expression, Steve reluctantly agreed to proceed.

"Try to recall the period right after your mother's untimely death. Tell us about family life."

Steve settled in with one arm hung over the back of the sofa, in easy reach of a fresh cup of tea. "The first week is a blur. Family, friends, the wake, funeral, all melded together. During one short week Mom was gone. By the next Monday the family was back to life's routines. The old cliché is true. Life does goes on, but it's never the same. Gina was working and living at home. I went back to college to finish the fall semester. Dad tried to maintain the household routine: Kept the house exactly the way Mom liked it. It's no surprise to anyone who has experienced a loss; things are never quite the same—never would or could be.

"Dad and I had a difficult time talking about Mom without getting emotional. Some days it was very difficult listening to Gina chatter about Mom this, and Mom that. Some days just listening hurt."

"Did family life eventually return to normal?"

"Ha! The age-old question, what's normal? We lived together, but the family was fragmented. That January I quit college and found a job in electronics. Everyone mourns and grieves in their individual way, at their own speed. Four years after Mom's death Gina started counseling to deal with her issues. I buried feelings of grief for years. Dad grieved hard. He was also the first one to get his life together.

"One night at dinner Dad made an announcement. Saying, 'Kid's, I loved your mother deeply. We must learn from life's hard lessons and I learned life is short and fragile. It's as positive or negative as we decide to make it. I have made a decision to continue living.'"

Kate interrupted, "Well, we know his path led to the priesthood and Rome."

"Yes, eventually. The path took some twists and turns before heading in the final direction."

"Would you guide us along that path?"

His dark eyes darted to Jay, back to Kate. His ingrained instincts about family privacy were in conflict with his father's request to be open and cooperative. "I can share as an observer rather than a guide. Dad started dating not long after that dinner announcement, just several months after Mom's passing. Gina was appalled, disapproved…made sure Dad absolutely understood her feelings. She thought he was being disloyal to Mom. Dad explained his feelings, then continued to live his life as he saw fit. Gina boiled every time the subject came up. He dated now and then. Within a short time he met Leigh on a blind date. They picked up steam very fast. Soon they were inseparable."

Steve calmed down, slouched on the sofa. At the beginning of the session he repeatedly removed his baseball cap and ran his left hand through his short thick hair. Sometime during the discussion the hat came off and sat next to him on the sofa.

"How did Gina and the rest of the family react?"

"Lots of whispers…who is this woman. 'Dad should be careful; he could be on a rebound.' Eventually Gina and I, then the whole family, met Leigh. Another time at dinner, Dad asked us how we felt about their relationship. I supported his decisions. Gina went ballistic. Not about Leigh in particular…any serious involvement. A few months went by and it became obvious that Dad and Leigh were sleeping together. That really made the situation between Dad and Gina tumultuous. It didn't bother me…Gina went off the deep end and moved out."

"Just the two of you living in that big house. How did you get along?"

"Another change. Dad's work began to heat up. His company was sold. That kept him busy consolidating operations and reassigning employees. His social life consumed a lot of his time. Actually, we saw very little of each other. I worked nights and weekends; Dad worked days. Most of the time it felt like we were roommates. Occasionally he put his 'Dad hat' on, usually when I didn't finish chores."

"Steve, you're giving me background, but I sense there is substance that you glossed over. Very few comments about Leigh, little about the new life's path that your father talked about."

Slouching further in the soft sofa, he crossed a very long leg. "Okay, I do recall some of the obvious changes. Initially there were subtle changes in Dad... things like washing his car was less important. His circle of friends widened. He began to bowl...lessons in ballroom dancing...went to the Jersey shore every weekend during the summer. As months went by, the changes became obvious...to the point that even every relative commented about Dad. He certainly had fun and laughed often. Frugal Dad could at times be down right cheap. That changed as well. He began to spend money, taking exotic trips to the islands and Europe. He and Leigh purchased a vacation house at the shore, a new car, and better clothes. All in all positive changes, except everything was different.

"A few years back I came to realize Gina and I were getting older, had less time for him. However, when we wanted him he wasn't always around. Clearly, Leigh was a major influence, especially on his social life. She had hundreds of friends and family. And he became part of this large social group. Leigh is a partner in a travel agency and they took advantage of her discounts and special incentives. She was obviously a catalyst for change."

"I don't mean to interrupt, but I can tell you are struggling with this. The change, was it good or not?"

His defenses surfaced again. He sat up straight, arms tightly folded across his chest, eyelids fluttered as he looked at the camera. "Deep down I knew it was change for the better. It's just difficult, ah...to see someone you love and depend on change so drastically. I began to wonder if he was happier with his new life. The thoughts children dwell on, but are afraid to ask...tricky subject because we may not like the answer. One afternoon Gina finally got up enough nerve to ask in a roundabout way. Dad responded that he was extremely happy with his married life. He loved us kids and Mom. If Mom were still alive he'd be perfectly content. He said, 'Some events are beyond anyone's control but we all have choices on how to handle change. It's also possible to love many people during a lifetime.' The answer made me feel better. Gina was skeptical."

"Wow, that's some answer. How did it affect your relationship with Leigh?"

"Our relationship was…is dynamic. The first few months, my attitude was to wait and see. I tried to keep distant, not knowing if she was a friend or not. Over time, Leigh wears people down with her friendly manner, wit and openness. It's hard work not to like her. After three years of dating, Dad and Leigh decided to live together and she moved into our house. I still lived at home. There were some rough spots, but we worked through them. I still see her often at family functions and around the holidays." Steve glanced at his watch for the third time.

"I know you are tight on time," said Kate, "do you have any other thoughts or observations you wish to share?"

There was a quick hesitation before his final comments. "I'm glad that Dad was strong enough to make the choices that were right for him," he said and placed the baseball cap on his head.

"Steve, I can understand you and the family missing him. I know how difficult it is to be separated from parents and loved ones. Thank you for the frank and helpful insights. Jay, you can close up while I walk Steve to the lobby."

On their short walk to the lobby she wondered if Steve would talk about issues that he was reluctant to discuss in front of the camera. The walk was quiet until they reached the lobby. Suddenly he turned and stood close to Kate, looked down into her eyes. "Kate, I trusted you and opened up." His pupil's narrowed, dark eyes turned hard, harder than flint. "Don't hurt my family, any of us." The threat was implied but evident. "Tell my dad we love him…and, good luck with your biography."

Although Kate heard he was a very private person, she had hoped for some personal insight into Steve's thoughts. She never came close to cracking his shell. Kate wasn't sure why she lingered to watch him walk across the parking lot to his pristine, vintage yellow sports car that had to be at least thirty years old. Returning to the room, her thoughts were muddled. The three days had flown by, although it seemed like a week since she and Matt were together.

"Jay, let's pack up. If we get on the road by noon, with any luck we can be in New York by 2:30 p.m. Both head straight home, forget the office until Monday."

Jay took the lead in the GNN van. Kate followed at a safe distance. Traffic was light and flowed at a steady sixty-five miles per hour clip. The Pennsylvania Turnpike and southern part of the New Jersey Turnpike offered scenic views of woodlands and flat open country. As they approached North Jersey and New York, traffic grew heavier and the view deteriorated to rows of grimy industrial parks and manufacturing facilities. Jay waved as he exited at the Lincoln Tunnel, heading for mid-town Manhattan. Kate continued to the end of the turnpike, exiting for the George Washington Bridge. The approach to the bridge was backed up as usual. She called Matt at 2:45 p.m. and his voice mail answered. She left a message that she'd be waiting for him at home. The next call was to the office, checking her voice and video mail. She punched her assistant's extension.

"GNN, Joan speaking."

"Hi Joan, it's Kate. Anything hot I should know about?"

"Nothing super hot. Mr. Blake would like you to give him an update on Monday or Tuesday at the latest. Preferably in person, by video phone if necessary."

For once the boss' timing was perfect. She planned to be in the office on Monday. "Tell Mr. Blake we can meet any time after 10:00 a.m., better yet, for lunch. Joan, how is your little boy Luke, is he recovering from his leg surgery?"

"Luke's great, hobbling on his crutch. You know how kids spring back fast. Thanks for asking."

"I know we have a lot to catch up on. Next time I'm in the office for a few days we will have lunch. Also, if you need any time off to care for Luke, take whatever you need."

"Okay. Looking forward to it! See you Monday, have a nice weekend…say hello to that lovable Matt."

After turning in the rental car, Kate grabbed a taxi to her apartment. Normally she enjoyed walking through the local neighborhood and stopping at the various specialty stores. She eagerly headed home to nestle in for the weekend. No matter what happened during the day, home was the best place to relax and recharge. A home shared with loved ones was the absolute best. That's how Kate felt about the home she shared with Matt. When the assignment's completed, their relationship would take first priority. Her mood turned upbeat with a determination to make it happen. Their apartment was neat and tidy, although it could use a good spring-cleaning. Three glorious hours of solitude before Matt came home. Time to scan the mail, catch up on calling her sister, Ginny, and Laura, her best and oldest friend. Didn't think she'd have a chance to see either any time soon.

Around five o'clock, Matt called. "Babe, what a great surprise. I didn't expect to see you until late tonight."

"I came home as quick as I could. Broke every speed limit in three states just to be in your arms before the weekend starts. When can I caress those kissable lips?"

"Very soon woman, no later than 6:30. Is dinner in, out or take out?"

Six a.m. on Mondays feel like the middle of the night. Time to get up and begin all over, another day, starting another week. Weekends, never enough time to rest and catch up. Fortunately, Kate liked her job more than sleep. Time to shower, then head for her Manhattan office. She remembered that Mr. Blake wanted to have lunch. This was a big one; GNN couldn't risk losing this big fish.

Kate hopped the subway to mid-town, then walked three long blocks to the GNN Corporate headquarters. The whole sixth floor was a buzz. Navigating the bullpen area, fellow workers offered congratulations and mock high-fives. Her pulse and mind raced; obviously the news was out. In three weeks, the live Papal interview would be announced. The clock was ticking, the intense pressure like a five hundred-pound gorilla sitting on her chest. She needed air. A group of co-workers stood near her office so she diverted to the rest room and occupied the farthest stall, inhaling several deep breaths to regain her composure.

After the mandatory chatting, Kate summoned Joan into her office and closed the door. "Joan, before you start to pout, this assignment was top secret. I didn't even tell Matt."

Joan knew a white lie when she heard one, and offered an "ah ha" smile.

"Do me a favor, as you come and go please keep the office door closed. I need privacy to think." Kate began a rapid-fire list of items for Joan to handle. "Please notify Mr. Blake that I'm available for lunch at noon. Bring in the mail that has stacked up and ask Jay to see me as soon as he arrives. Order a one-way Amtrak ticket to Philadelphia. Reserve two hotel rooms for three nights in Center City. Call the four names on this list and confirm the interview appointments."

Stopping to take a breath, she slowed the pace. "I promise we'll get together and catch up as soon as this Papal thing is over."

"I understand. Our lunch date can wait. Just promise me you will slow down and take this one issue at a time."

"I truly miss you, Joan. Now let's get to work. Leave all the confirmations on my desk. I'm going to leave work early. Oh, and please close the blinds on this fish bowl."

Jay strolled in about thirty minutes later, looking fresh and full of vigor. He rarely spoke about Richard, his life partner, unless people asked. Jay was in an exceptionally good mood so after discussing that the Papal assignment was out of the bag, Kate inquired about Richard.

"Kate, I'm sure you noticed my glow. Well it's all due to Richard. We've decided to make a major commitment and buy a house together. It's a small rancher just over the river in North Jersey. This could lead to the big decision. We window shopped for partner rings Sunday afternoon."

"That's wonderful. Congratulations! I pray everything works for you and Richard. You're both very fortunate to find partners that understand the time and demands of your careers. My best to the happy couple! And make sure we're invited to the house warming."

She wasted no time transitioning into business. "Jay, we're a bit pressed on time. Duty calls, so unfortunately it's back to work. Please start editing the video. I'll join you in an hour or so. Also, see Joan about our interview schedule for the rest of the week. You can give me all the details about you and Richard during dinner in Philly."

Jay and Kate worked on editing the video and made substantial progress. After three hours of machines and recording devices, Kate couldn't listen to the whine of one more DVR recorder. Leaving around four o'clock, she told Joan she had to complete some research at the library. Instead, she headed straight home. Jay copied the work and sent it to the Vatican via overnight express.

It felt wonderful arriving home at a decent hour while the sun was still out. *Time to chill out, put on jammies and plan a light dinner*, Kate thought. Packing for the three- or four-day trip to Philadelphia could wait.

Matt arrived later than usual, well past 7:00 p.m. He stormed through the front door in a miserable mood. The boss was on his back to complete a three-week assignment in one week. Giving Kate a light kiss he went straight to the bedroom and changed into jeans and a golf shirt. Kate heard muttering and "that bastard" repeated a number of times, followed by slammed doors. Matt moped his way into the kitchen, head down, clearly dejected. Kate gave him a little hug. "What's the matter, my honey?"

"The same old problem; the mother humpen' boss makes unrealistic demands."

"Have you discussed this with him?"

Tense muscles began to respond and relax as Kate rubbed and stroked his neck.

"I try, babe. The humper claims to be busy...blows me off, just keeps walking away."

"Matt, you're a talented man. Stop playing his game. Confront and resolve the issue. If he's unreasonable tell him to go screw himself. Your business skills are in demand. Go find another job."

"You're right, but it's easier said than done. I have time invested in this company and I can't let this duffus drive me out. Anyway, I can handle it! Can you just rub my lower back again? Feels great. That's the spot, so... good!" Stretching he asked, "So babe, what's for dinner?"

Kate growled. "Men are so basic. Food, sleep, sex and not necessarily in that order." Now that Matt had settled down, she began concentrating on her next trip to Philadelphia. These interviews should be the most perilous and revealing. Some instinct warned her to wear steel undies.

Chapter Eleven

Kate rode the early train to Philadelphia, arriving at 30th Street station by 8:30 a.m. Jay had driven the van to Philadelphia the night before and waited for her at the station. It was a short drive to 22nd Street, if one was familiar with the traffic flow and one-way streets. Center City Philadelphia was famous for historical preservation and museums and the center of commerce in Eastern Pennsylvania. Skyscrapers and historical buildings were often located in the same city block, an unusual mixture of old and new, but it worked for the city of Brotherly Love. Kate made a mental note to schedule a three-day weekend with Matt to visit and explore this urban gem, sandwiched between the Big Apple and the rotten capital. They drove by the cathedral, an imposing structure. No competition for the Italian Domos, but impressive by colonial standards. By comparison the diocesan administration building appeared bland, which described the administration in general. Bishop Dunbar's office was located on the second floor. The receptionist took Kate's name and asked her to please wait. About fifteen minutes later the Bishop entered the reception area, extending a pale hand.

"Miss Kate Murphy, I presume."

Kate picked up on the hostility and cautiously accepted his clammy hand. "Yes, Bishop. Thank you for seeing me on short notice."

No response. Bishop Dunbar walked away, expecting her to follow him down the narrow off white hallway to his office. Instantly annoyed, Kate was put on guard by his gruff behavior.

The Bishop sat behind a large desk, arms limply folded across his chest.

"Please be seated, Miss Murphy." He gestured for Kate to select a seat in front of his desk. A typical power play, he wanted her to know who's in charge. A man accustomed to raw power and authority. Very different from Pope Alex, who tried to make Kate comfortable by sitting side-by-side; two powerful men, close friends yet so obviously different! The Bishop offered coffee. Sensing a perfunctory offer, she declined because she felt uncomfortable even drinking morning coffee in front of the Bishop.

"I know this is important and I cleared time on my calendar. There's a chance we may be interrupted due to an unfolding emergency."

Gently probing, Kate asked, "Bishop, I hope it isn't a personal emergency?"

"Thanks for your concern, but no, it's a diocesan matter. Since Anthony called I have been eager to meet you and unravel the mystery. Cardinal Gates and I have speculated about your visit."

"My mission is fairly mundane. As I mentioned to your secretary, GNN is compiling a biography on the Holy Father for the Vatican library."

"Miss Murphy, since I'm a former mentor, Anthony still keeps in touch. I spoke to him yesterday. So I will ask again! What…is GNN's purpose for gathering this information?"

Taken back by his unvarnished gruffness, Kate's eyebrows involuntarily lifted, displaying wide eyes. The tone and inflection bordered on outright rude. This could be a bluff to obtain information, or simply testing her candor. Less than three minutes with this cleric and Kate felt beyond annoyed. Acting as somewhat of a Papal representative, she didn't expect shabby treatment. It took all of her professional training and patience to avoid an ugly confrontation. *Oh, the temptation to slice and dice this creep.* Realizing her answer was likely to set the tone for the remainder of their session, she chose to maintain her cool, at least for the moment. Confiding in the Bishop wasn't likely to make a difference; by now the story must have leaked in the Vatican and the media community.

Under duress, she softly answered, "The biography will be housed in the Vatican library and we also plan to broadcast the biography worldwide."

"Thank you." The smile of authority spread across the turned up corners of his small mouth. "As I suspected, Anthony is planning a very aggressive offensive tactic. I hope he thoroughly considered his overall strategy. Tactics and political intrigue were never his strong suite. He only knows one way, plow straight ahead." With that comment, his chair leaned back as far as possible. The Bishop had openly baited her.

"Discussing the video brings me to Jay, my technical associate who's waiting in the parking lot. Can he join us to record the interview?"

The Bishop's eyes glazed over, his mind calculating. A sense of privacy struggled against an ego boost from international broadcast exposure. After a longer than normal pause, he finally answered, "Please ask him to join us. While we wait, can I offer you a cup of coffee?"

"Actually, I would prefer a Diet Coke. Thank you."

They both smiled, sensing a breakthrough, now that the bullshit was behind them. While they waited for Jay, the Bishop placed a few short telephone calls. Kate volunteered to leave the room, but the bishop motioned her to stay. Ever the journalist she used this opportunity to assess the office. A stereotypical academic's office, with plenty of clutter and piles of dusty old books and outdated magazines. The office needed updating, a fresh coat of paint. The cream color looked bland and faded. The office also needed new furniture, and, at the very least, organization. Trying not to be obvious, she also studied Bishop Peter Dunbar. He was a good-looking older man with an aristocratic bearing, possibly a few years younger than the Holy Father. Kate thought he had above average sex appeal, if he was your type. From head to toe, his speech, posture, the quality of fabric, reminded her of a Philadelphia mainliner. The diplomas scattered around the wall were designed to impress—a Masters in Theology and Ph.D. in Philosophy.

Jay instantly surveyed the cluttered room and dim lighting. He preferred using the small table near the window overlooking 22nd Street. The street noises were louder near the window but Jay could edit out background noise. Just as the Bishop hung up the telephone, Jay was ready.

After introducing himself, Jay suggested moving near the window. Once they were settled Kate began, "Bishop Dunbar, how and when did you meet the Holy Father?"

"I was a professor of Theology at St. Charles Barromeo Seminary. The campus grapevine was buzzing about an old guy accepted into the seminary as a first year student. As a priest and theologian, my curiosity was piqued. The unknown student was not assigned to any of my classes, so I went looking to meet him. He turned out to be Anthony Pavelli. I introduced myself while he was taking a coffee break in the cafeteria. During the first short conversation we began to build a rapport. I liked Anthony. He's four years older." She made a mental note, *Shot number two.*

"Over the semester we compared personal backgrounds. During the prior twenty years I pursued theology and philosophy while his career choice was middle manager in large corporations. It was clear that outside the classroom we could help each other to learn new disciplines. Although I liked Anthony, naturally there was a question about his commitment to the priesthood. Can an old dog learn new tricks, a leopard change his spots?

"Outside the classroom we were peers and began to spend a great deal of time together. Anthony needed help with theology and background on life as a clergyman. He was a sponge—absorbed everything. My involvement wasn't strictly altruistic. I wanted to learn about finance and administration. Without this knowledge I could be confined to teaching at the seminary for years, possibly life. Not a bad life, but the opportunity to move up in the Church was limited."

"Bishop, with your credentials surely you had other career paths?"

Both elbows on the armrests, his hands were steepled in a mock gesture of prayer. "Many moons ago, I spent two years as a parish priest before turning to the academic life. Not to sound snobbish…my talents were wasted in suburbia or the ghetto. My best opportunity out of the seminary was moving to the diocesan staff, which required learning business fundamentals."

"I gather your relationship continued to develop?"

"Yes. Yes it did. Anthony liked to be a loner. Along with the other students' age difference, he only had a few friends at the seminary. I had a similar situation, students too young and the professor's old or stuffy. We were drawn together by mutual need and confinement of the seminary. During the first year summer break, Anthony continued to live in the dorm taking a few classes and spending much of his time doing social work in poor areas. During the second year he struggled with academic assignments. I felt he would be an excellent parish priest or diocesan administrator. Gradually, I shifted from advisor to mentor."

The Bishop felt in his element: Relaxed, slouching a bit, hands still steepled. His self-confident arrogant half-smile nettled Kate, almost to the point of disgust.

"Bishop, as a mentor, what did you hope to accomplish?"

"No specific agenda. I handled each issue as it came up. Actually the Archbishop helped set our direction, and gave Anthony exposure to the Church hierarchy. During the second year in the seminary the diocese wanted to increase contributions and enrollment in the seminary. The same lack of vocations we struggle with today. The public relations people stumbled on using Anthony as a poster boy for vocations and funding. I made sure he took every opportunity to make the circuit of local churches, speaking to parishioners about the need to support the seminary with funding and prayers. He spoke to young people about religious vocations and urged family men to become deacons. Our deacons are one step below priesthood without giving up family and career. He became a frequent guest on local radio and TV programs."

"Did your relationship remain as mentor and pupil?"

The chair rocked forward as though he was ready to stand. Instead he leaned forward and glanced out the window. "Our relationship turned into a close friendship…very close. Close enough to be invited to family functions, especially during the holidays. Christmas is my favorite. I became a regular at Roe Di Marco's fabulous Christmas brunch. Many of Anthony's friends and family are now my friends. When Roe's daughter and Anthony's son married I performed the ceremony."

"That certainly says a lot. Did the Holy Father continue to struggle with academics?"

"His grades steadily improved, but in his third year he struggled with other demons, guilt about leaving his children. Why I don't understand? The kids were all over twenty-one and lived relatively close, maybe a thirty-minute drive. He also vacillated about leaving his former, ah… significant other. Her business was only five miles from the seminary and they often met at family gatherings. You see, Leigh is Ro Di Marco's best friend and godmother to Ro's daughter Tiffany. Their lives are intertwined. Frequently seeing Leigh kept him wobbling about his decision."

"Bishop, you are saying the Holy Father is a man with human frailties."

Turning his gaze back to Kate, his eyes narrowed into slits. "Yes, like all of us, with his share of faults and weakness."

"Can we fast forward to the priesthood?"

"Certainly. Anthony graduated on schedule, in the lowest thirty percent of his class." Kate noted, *Shot number three*. "He was ordained the following Saturday, said his first Mass on Sunday. His first assignment was a cluster parish in Southwest Philadelphia, a blue-collar neighborhood. The parishioners loved him; he could relate to them at a very basic level, understood their way of life." The Bishop lightened up, actually cracked a smile.

"It's a long way from a poor parish in Philadelphia to the Vatican in less than twenty years. As the British say, how did he end up on the other side of the pond?"

Some memory disturbed him, his broad smile turned contemplative. As he started to reply, his torso rocketed back into a straight back position, arms folded tightly across his chest. "I opened opportunity's door. If I hadn't recommended him for a position working for Cardinal Gates, he would still be in some poor parish calling out bingo and serving burrito dinners."

Kate was thrown completely off balance by the comment and his inflection. *This was shot number four*. Puss just erupted out of a raw, exposed sore.

The Bishop jumped to answer the phone on the first ring. "Yes Michele, I was expecting this; tell the Cardinal I'll see him immediately." He turned to his guests, "Please excuse me, I should be back in ten or fifteen minutes. Rest rooms are down the hall. I'll ask my secretary to refill your drinks."

Jay looked flabbergasted with his jaw-hung open. "What the hell...what was that all about? Sounds like their friendship is in the dumper, shot to hell. I don't like or trust this guy."

Kate stretched and moved closer to Jay. "That may be true, but the feeling is one-sided; Holy Father sure speaks highly of Bishop Dunbar. This guy is a creepy bastard. I can't wait to get out of here. In fact, if this wasn't such an important project I'd cut this guy off at the knees on camera."

When the Bishop returned he acted like a transformed man. His arrogant in control demeanor replaced by a sheepish deportment that didn't quite fit his persona. He needed to tell a deep secret. "Ms. Murphy, let's take this off the record. I must apologize for my behavior during this meeting. The last two days I've struggled with how to handle this interview. One part of me loves Anthony; the other knows he's not Papal material. I introduced him to the Cardinal and he became Anthony's new mentor, the rest of his career is public history. This is not easy to admit...I don't understand and I'm jealous of his inconceivable supersonic rise in the Church. It's beyond my comprehension that he's the Pope!

"He's in trouble. Asked me to join him at the Vatican. I turned him down. I can't support his Papacy or the changes I suspec— Of course, I didn't...just couldn't...tell him why. Deep down he knows. The worst part is, he wants to continue our friendship and insisted on recommending me for this interview."

This self-serving confession pushed Kate off balance for a moment until she realized his tell-all made her despise him all the more. "Bishop, the Holy Father has final approval on the biography. Something tells me he will leave it intact. He knows many of the clergy have your same festering concerns. He may want them to confront those feelings head on. Searching those feelings, are they justified or jealousy? I am going way out of my area of expertise but this reminds me of certain Bible passages that I am sure you are familiar with. God called Moses; he had no religious training. King David was a young shepherd. St. Peter a poor fisherman. A prophet is never accepted in his village."

Bowing his head in an exaggerated act of contrition, the fastidious, arrogant, self-centered Bishop admitted, "I know, oh how I know. However, I'm human and can't shake the way I feel. It's a sin I confess often."

"I suggest we leave your off-the-record comments as part of the draft and let the Holy Father make the decision on how to present the interview."

His vacant eyes lifted, "I have a huge problem with Anthony knowing my real feelings." Breaking eye contact, he took a moment to absently move papers around his cluttered desk. Looking up he offered the camera a lazy shrug of acceptance. "I guess your suggestion makes the most sense; let's leave the interview intact."

Abruptly he extended his hand to Kate then reached over to Jay. "If those are all your questions, please excuse me. I must attend to an important issue. Have a safe journey." He walked out of the office without another word.

They both thought what a strange interview. They didn't know how it would play when Pope Alex and the Vatican people reviewed the tape. It certainly wouldn't build his confidence. This was the first real indication that the man wearing the white miter had the same human flaws as everyone else.

CHAPTER TWELVE

Just before dusk, a dark blue four-door Mercedes slowed as it approached the Vatican VIP entrance. The rear passenger window descended, the occupant displayed a Vatican visitor's badge. Leigh Stevens owned a tour company and every so often she escorted twenty or so clients on a seven-day Italian holiday, culminating with a guided tour of St Peter's and the Vatican Museums. Leigh had a standing invitation for dinner with the Pope anytime she was in Rome. The Swiss Guard recognized her as a frequent visitor, and rumored to be the Holy Father's mistress. The Guard couldn't care less. He figured, *Let the old man have his fun.*

The Holy Father and Leigh realized his enemies used these visits as an example of his moral turpitude. Yet, their relationship and quality time together outweighed the vicious rumors. They had not been intimate since Anthony entered the seminary two decades ago. The Pope considered Leigh a member of his immediate family, as well as a trusted advisor, often soliciting her advice and council. Even before becoming a priest, the Holy Father always sought a woman's view on important issues. Women have a way of sifting through clutter.

The Pope stood on his veranda and looked across the rear Vatican grounds at the sunset with its spectrum of florid red, blue and white coloring the evening sky. The sunset brought back memories of the Jersey shore and leisurely summer nights he spent with Leigh. He often thought the Jersey sunsets rivaled the famous Florida Keys. Those extraordinary days and nights were some of his fondest memories. Most evenings the shore house was full of friends and relatives, especially Leigh's Dad, Smitty, and his everyday companion and man's best furry friend, Sandy.

In the distance he could barely make out the figure of a woman walking towards the Papal Palace, accompanied by a Swiss Guard. Probably Leigh. He expected her any minute for their dinner date. Long before Anthony was Pope, Leigh's tour business brought her to Rome at least once each month. As the figures came closer he recognized her. She waved and he returned an enthusiastic wave with both arms.

The Swiss Guard escorted her to the entrance door; she touched his arm while thanking him. He blushed and executed a crisp military salute. As usual, Leigh made a grand entrance into the reception area. Greeting Brother Jacomo with a warm smile and a hug, she immediately asked for Sister Martha, who heard her voice and hurried into the reception area. The two women embraced, and whispered. The staff enjoyed Leigh's visits. They were a break from the usual Palace solitude.

The Pope eagerly waited to see her, but when he was present the staff became stiff and formal, so he held back a few minutes. Not able to wait any longer, he entered the room, Leigh gave him a big hug, with a kiss on the left cheek then the right. She stepped back to study his face. "You are looking good. I can see your friends, Brother Jacomo and Sister Martha, are taking good care of you." She turned to the staff. "And Mr. Pope, you better be taking good care of them. If I find out otherwise, you *will* answer to me!"

The first time the staff met Leigh Stevens they grimaced, appalled at the way she spoke to the Holy Father. Gradually they grew accustomed to her open and somewhat boisterous antics. This woman was the only one who dared speak so dismissively to the Holy Father. The staff believed every word; if the Pope failed to care for his people she would have no qualms about promptly rectifying the situation.

"Holiness, dinner will be ready in thirty minutes. Do you wish to eat in the dining room?" asked Sister Martha.

"Thank you. Ah, I prefer the library, if it's not an inconvenience. Can you find a bottle of Tuscany Merlot for Ms. Stevens and Diet Coke with lemon for me?"

"Yes, Holiness. I'll make preparations."

They retreated into the library, closing the massive hand carved door. The way the heavy door glided gracefully on ancient hinges fascinated the Pope, a throwback to his woodworking hobby. Once inside, the Holy Father transformed into Anthony and couldn't wait to give Leigh a powerful hug and long kiss on the forehead. They nestled in the burgundy leather chairs. each waiting for the other to begin.

Anthony broke the short silence. "You just missed the sunset. It reminds me of the great times we had at the shore. I miss it more every year. Doubtful I'll ever see it again. Can you remember to e-mail recent photos when you have a minute?"

"I'll send new pictures. Missing the shore is understandable, but I imagine the Papal summer palace in Gandolfo, high in the Alban mountains, is certainly more than a match for New Jersey. Hardly slumming, your Holiness."

When they first met, he had difficulty recognizing her dry sense of humor, which frustrated Leigh to no end.

"Yes, wise ass…Gandolfo is magnificent. You're playing with me. My comment is not about the house, it's the atmosphere and people. Living in luxury doesn't guarantee happiness."

"Just testing…you passed this time, kiddo! By the way, this room is way too masculine. When are you going to add some female touches, like a little color? Wood—and dark wood at that—everywhere in the room."

Faking a stern pout he thought, *She never changes*. "Here less than an hour and starting already. I will let the first female Pope handle the decorating. Now, if you've finished heckling, can you talk to me about my family? How are Steve and Tiffany?"

"Both are doing just fine. They are considering a larger house. A four-car garage and workshop have turned Steve's head."

"Any more talk about children? Steve is getting older and Tiffany's biological clock must be running up hill."

"Tiffany talks about children at times but Steve is adamant about no kids. He says it will change their lifestyle. They are very comfortable in their Generation X way of life. With more toys than most kids have."

"Too bad, I was hoping to be a grandfather again. They'd have beautiful children and you'd spoil them the way you spoil Ashley." Crossing his legs, he gave Leigh a "got ya" half smile.

"Don't start. I love spoilen' Ashley, and she loves her 'Lee Lee.' We've been close since she was all of four years old, so let me have fun with my pseudo-grandchild. You're just trying to push my buttons."

He always loved to push those great buttons. "Tom and Beth…how are they?"

"They're just fine. You could call them once in a while. Tom's business is growing…he's considering buying a company and combining it with his current business. I always told you he's a chip off the old block. They are still crazy about each other. It warms my heart."

Shifting in his chair, the Holy Father ignored the comment about calling the kids. "What's up with Gina?"

"Not much news. Doesn't keep in touch as often as the others. Last time I saw her she looked good."

"How about you and the travel business?"

"Business is good, very good! My partner Bill, your buddy, is considering retiring. We want to sell the travel business and split the proceeds, but keep the tour operation."

"And you, personally, are the tours and traveling wearing you down?"

"The frequent tours are starting to wear at me, but the perks are great. Who else has a standing dinner invite with El Popo!"

He chuckled. El Popo, he liked that. Getting hungry, he looked at the grandfather clock about to chime. Almost an hour had passed. It seemed like only a few minutes. As if right on cue, there was a knock on the door and Sister Martha came in carrying a large silver dinner tray. The meal smelled delicious, tender chicken cutlets cooked in a wine sauce, green garden salad, in-season mixed vegetables and baked sweet potato. During dinner Leigh continued her animated conversation, chatted about this and that until the coffee arrived.

Following a long silence, Leigh felt compelled to ask, "Okay, what's going on? I know you; something's wrong. You're pensive, more quiet than usual, which is almost mute. What's on your mind?"

Anthony flashed an impish smile; she could always read him. "Before we get deep into my psyche, a few days ago I heard from Eileen. The big day is around the corner. Christine is marrying her 'Mister Perfect'. Unfortunately, I can't attend. As Christine's godmother I know you will be there. Can you deliver a gift and a special Papal blessing?"

"My pleasure, Mr. Pope."

"Now to answer your question…the same problems as last time. My Papacy's in trouble; I'm losing credibility. The rumors are out of control to the point where they've taken on a life of their own. If some of them were true, I would be a wealthy and sexually satisfied man."

Leigh moved her chair closer, and touched his hand. "Okay then, I understand. But you're taking steps to resolve that by working with GNN…what else is bothering you? By the way, my interview is scheduled in a few days, and if you think you have problems now buddy, wait until I'm finished!"

"Woman, are you finished? This is serious." Breaking away from her expectant gaze, he stood and walked to the window overlooking the dark garden. "The GNN biography and interview will be successful; I'm sure of it. My concern goes beyond that. Within the Vatican I don't know whom I can trust. Earlier today I viewed a video of my 'friend' Bishop Dunbar. That turncoat's been feeding personal information to my enemies. Very few people know the details of my personal life that have surfaced in the rumors. That's the issue."

He turned back to look at his closest friend. "Dunbar's the leak; at the same time I wonder if Marconi can be trusted. He may be involved in this as well. It's awfully convenient that Marconi's been my sidekick since I came to the Vatican. He has supported me at every turn and because of that support I appointed him chief of staff. What if he's a mole?"

"Please come and sit," she patted the chair, "you know the answer as well as I do, Dunbar is no good; I warned you years ago not to trust that stuck-up aristocratic bastard. He struts around like a grand Pasha. But oh, you wouldn't listen; his fast talk clouded your judgment. The man is cold blooded and weaseled his way into our family. As far as Marconi, goes there's no option. He is your closest advisor and the only person you've developed a relationship with. You need him on your team. No choice but to take him fully into your confidence. You need Marconi because of his influence and circle of friends. Anthony, you are not a stupid man. You know the answers; get your act in gear and settle this."

He gave her an imploring look and lightened up a bit, one problem about to be solved. "As always you're on the money. This is an important decision...I just ah, needed your opinion. This Papacy will likely stand or fall based on trusting Marconi."

"Well then, let's chat about Marconi and why he is your only ally. You are hardly an open book. People can't read you, find it difficult to get close. Only forceful people with determination break through that thick shell. We've discussed this God knows how many times. Will you ever truly learn? You improve for a while, then revert back to your old stoic self."

"Okay, okay, good God!" His olive face turned a light shade of pink as his blood pressure surged. He hated this same old conversation because she was always right. Throwing his arms into the air, he said, "You worked me over for the last time on this subject! I *will* truly make an effort to do better at opening myself to people. Okay?"

"Remember, Anthony, people know you are a good man but you must meet them at least part way."

He had enough and changed the topic. "Listen, soon Sister Martha will bring more coffee and dessert. When she's finished, excuse her for the night. I'll be right back. I have plans and I don't want to place the sister in a difficult dilemma."

Leigh tried to speak, "What—"

"No questions. I'll explain when I get back."

Sister Martha delivered and served fresh coffee along with a rich chocolate cake smothered in raspberry filling. The curious mother hen wondered but didn't ask where the Pope was. Leigh assured her that dinner was exceptional and volunteered the Pope was in the bathroom. Otherwise, sister would have waited until he returned.

"It's so nice when you visit, Ms. Stevens. The weight seems to lift off the Holy Father's shoulders. Except for you and an occasional family visitor, the Holy Father frequently dines alone and has few personal visitors."

"I know, Sister, we're working on that. The Holy Father creates his own roadblocks. If people make the first move he does open up, so you, Brother Jacomo and the staff need to make an extra effort and his Holiness will respond. Don't be afraid, he's really a big teddy bear."

"Thank you, Miss Stevens."

"Sister, how is the Holy Father's health?"

"Not the best. The doctor is worried about his heart. His blood pressure is erratic and he recently had two angina attacks. He claims they were mild. The doctor recommends slowing down, but of course he doesn't listen."

"Thank you, Sister. I know you take excellent care of him. His Holiness said you could retire for the night. Pleasant dreams and I will see you next trip."

After the nun left, the Pope came back into the library.

"When the hell did you buy a fedora?"

"Well, thanks for the compliment. This hat is my disguise, part of tonight's plan." He turned, so Leigh could see the full outfit. She sat with arms folded, giving him a dismissive stare.

"Listen...I have cabin fever. Haven't been outside these walls in months. You're my out of jail card, at least for one night. No assistants or security guards...just you and me. Let's take your car for one night of freedom. Come on...don't be chicken, let's do it."

His extended hand helped her up. Leigh moved close to adjust his collar.

"I really don't think this is such a good idea. What if someone recognizes you and people start to gather? If we're discovered, your enemies will use this as more ammunition."

"I don't give a damn. Let's sneak out and have some fun for a few hours. I haven't been back to Piazza Navona since we visited Rome together eons ago. It's dark. In civilian clothes and this hat, I'm just another *Amerigan touristo*."

So they started on their secret adventure. The Pope wore his white robe over civilian clothes, his fedora rolled into Leigh's travel bag. Leaving his quarters, the Pontiff told the guards he didn't need an escort to stroll through the gardens to the Fontana dell' Aqualine, his favorite fountain with a bronze eagle, the Borghese family symbol, then taking Miss Stevens to her car. Changing of the guard was scheduled in an hour. He counted on the new guards thinking that he was safe inside. Laughing to himself he thought, *If discovered, what can the security people do, fire me?*

The evening looked overcast, a thin sliver of a moon hung in the night sky surrounded by distant twinkles. The stars winked encouragement as they strolled arm-in-arm toward the VIP parking area. Opening the rear door for Leigh, he took off his robe and slid in alongside her, slouching low in the seat. The driver followed instructions and ignored the passenger, proceeding directly to Piazza Navona. Since the vehicle was leaving the Vatican, the Swiss Guard performed a cursory check and passed the vehicle through the security gate. The driver spoke passable English, so the pair remained silent until being dropped off at the entrance to the Piazza.

Walking into the Piazza, Leigh could see Anthony's broad smile even though the fedora was pulled down low across his forehead. A slight hesitation then he turned backward while walking. When he turned to the front he had a fake mustache. Ridiculous as it looked, he insisted on the disguise.

Seconds after stepping into the piazza he was calm, his mind free of the constant jealousy, intrigue and painful hurt he endured from the relentless rumors. This might be his last night of physical and mental freedom. He planned on enjoying this precious night and who better to share it with than his Leigh.

The Piazza hadn't changed since his last visit, no real surprise; changes in Rome are counted in centuries, not years. Just as he recalled, it was a giant square full of locals and tourists enjoying the pleasant evening and Roman entertainment. Specialty shops and restaurants were located on the first floor of three- and four-story stone buildings weathered by centuries of use. The pitted stone facades contributed to the piazza's Romanesque charm. Monuments, statues and artwork from various eras stood indiscriminately placed in the middle and edges of the park. Thick flagstone covered the entire center of the piazza. Groups of people gathered around vendor tables piled with unique handmade or imported items. The largest gatherings were around street performers: dancers, mimes, and Anthony's favorite jugglers. He couldn't juggle one orange so this talent fascinated him. Small flocks of pigeons constantly swooped up and down landing near easy pickings. Leigh was deathly afraid of birds, so her protector stood guard to shield her from the pesky but harmless creatures. No surprise, gypsies worked the crowd for handouts or whatever they could easily lift.

Leigh had visited Navona probably a hundred times; it was a regular stop on her tours. Tonight she concentrated on watching Anthony enjoy the evening. With youthful anticipation they held hands and moved from performer to performer. The best entertainers received extra donations for their hard work and homespun talent. Eventually they made their way to the specialty shops. Spotting a quaint item, Anthony purchased an old-fashioned mood ring from the 1960's. She accepted the trinket, as a reminder of this night alone, no chaperone, no guards. Saving the best for last, they had to hurry before her favorite ice cream shop closed.

The owner said "No," and tried to shush them away. "*Signore, Buona sera*, good night. We are closed." Leigh whispered something in her ear. The old woman looked at Anthony and laughed, waved them in and locked the door. The ice cream tasted thick and smooth; they enjoyed every lick as they slowly strolled to the entrance. The crowd had thinned; Leigh glanced at her watch. "Oh damn, it's 1:00 a.m.! Where did the night go?"

Anthony gave her his "ladies should watch their language" expression.

"Sorry I forgot. I'm with El Popo."

"And I'm sorry. I thought we'd be back by 11:30 or so. I know you have an early flight tomorrow and a meeting the following day with Kate Murphy...but what a wonderful time. Thanks for being my co-conspirator. Some day you can write a magazine article about how you and the Pope snuck out of the Vatican for a wild night in Rome!"

The contented, tired friends continued through the narrow street to the main boulevard. The driver saw them and made a U–turn, pulling up to the curb. On the ride back Leigh thanked the driver for patiently waiting. Anthony handed the driver a generous tip.

At that late hour the return trip was short. The vehicle slowly rolled up to the VIP gate and Leigh presented her Vatican visitor's badge. On the ball, the Swiss Guard considered it strange for a visitor to arrive this late without being on the visitor's list. The guard asked the driver to turn off the engine and the occupants to step out of the vehicle for a physical inspection.

The jig was up; Cardinal Belfonte would hear about his adventure by morning. Marconi would know a few minutes after. He could already hear the long boring lecture.

Without the fedora and mustache, the guard immediately recognized the Pope and saluted. They reentered the Mercedes and passed through the gate to the VIP parking area. They said goodbye outside the car in the dimly lit parking area.

He gently caressed Leigh's back and hugged her close to his chest. He couldn't express his pent up emotions, except to say, "I miss you, can't wait for our next time together. This has been the best night. Thank you, babe." He kissed her forehead and gave her one last hug. She always cherished the endearment.

"You'll solve these problems. The BIG guy is on your side. During the next visit I will see Alex IX, victorious El Popo. Goodbye and keep well." Her hand slowly slipped from his as she moved toward the car.

Anthony was almost ready to return to his responsibilities but desperately need to watch the vehicle pass through the security gate. Leigh waved, knowing it was too dark for Anthony to see her farewell. He was still on a high from eluding security and spending the evening as a normal person, no fuss, pomp or frills. He felt tired, in fact overtired, the type of keyed up energy that made it difficult to sleep. If sleep didn't come he'd use the time to pray for God's guidance.

Leigh slumped in the back seat. As much as she needed time with her Anthony, afterward she felt an emotional dip. Stopping or cutting back on the visits wasn't an option.

Chapter Thirteen

The sun was cresting the seven Roman hills about to create the morning twilight, a time of half sleep, and vivid dreams. Alex the Pontiff's favorite time of day, drifting peacefully in and out of twilight sleep, normally relaxed and refreshed, his thoughts clear and unhurried.

This morning was different; his twilight drowsiness sharply interrupted by a sense of foreboding, an overpowering feeling of dread that he couldn't shake. As he aged his psychic receptors grew more acute. In the last twenty years he noticed the change. From never remembering his dreams, he now vividly recalled nightly dreams and at times experienced brief paralyzing premonitions. As a youth, he wondered why others, especially women, had these powerful gifts. These disturbing powers that uncontrollably invaded his life were no longer considered gifts; rather they were a troubling, unwanted burden.

His brain wouldn't accept twilight sleep so he rolled out of the thirteenth century four-poster bed. Following his morning ritual, he took a few minutes to stretch and limber arthritic joints. The dread continued to hang over him like a thick fog. He opened the French doors to the veranda that overlooked the courtyard and garden. Usually he rang for breakfast. Instead the Pontiff threw on casual cloths for a short stroll in the morning chill to clear his head and watch the glorious sunrise. One never knows how many sunrises remain. Taking a page from Leigh's book of living, he tried to seek and experience life's abundance.

Recently his deepest thoughts had lingered on mortality in general, and specifically his remaining days. He speculated on how the recording angel had documented his life in the Book of Judgment, wondered if he had a balance in the plus or minus column.

Leaving the Palace so early surprised the two Swiss Guards stationed at the entrance door. Addressing them by name, the guards executed a crisp salute, their eyes cloudy in the pre-dawn light. The story about last night's adventure had been puffed up and circulated among the staff. One guard followed at a short distance. Normally the Pope preferred privacy in the gardens; this morning the corporal following close behind felt comforting.

He headed directly to the garden below his veranda. At ground level the garden appeared massive; he could only see a small portion of it from any location. The veranda provided an expansive view of the entire garden. Regrettably, it was too far away to focus on a single flower or smell the delicate floral scents. Instinct drew him to ground level to better appreciate God's handiwork. A heavy layer of dew lingered on the cobblestone walkways and grass. In some sections, waist high ornamental hedges lined the worn walkways, creating a wall of shrubs that obscured large sections of the garden. Other areas remained open so visitors could enjoy the assortment of seasonal flowers.

Vito, the preoccupied gardener, slowly maneuvered his wheelbarrow along the path. "Good morning, Vito."

Vito looked up, briefly startled. Regaining his composure he bowed ever so slightly. "Holy Father, good morning. You surprised me. I wasn't expecting visitors this early."

Pope Alex moved closer to the gardener. "Vito, it's so good to see you again. I have walked this lovely garden many times. Ah…I would like to thank you for helping nature create such beauty."

"Holiness, these are my adopted children. They always need love and caring. It gives me pleasure that you enjoy them."

Vito looked uncomfortable so the Pope continued to walk a short distance then thought better of it, and turned back to the gardener wearing his trademark floppy straw hat.

"Vito, when I was a Cardinal I often spoke with you and your friends. I enjoyed our talks about your children, grandchildren, and even the weather. I never see my old friends; I miss the old days."

Embarrassed, the gardener reached for his rake in order to divert his eyes, reluctant to answer and carefully composed his thoughts. "Holy Father, you are a busy man with much weight on your shoulders. Old friends do not want to, how do you say, consume your time."

"Old friends don't waste my time. You are all important to me, and I want to make time for everyone. Each week on Wednesday one hour is set aside for special visitors. I will take a second hour to visit with members of our Vatican family. Tell everyone they are welcome to visit me on that day. Anyone on the staff can call Brother Jacomo to make arrangements."

"Thank you for the kind offer."

"Goodbye, Vito. I hope to see you some time Wednesday." Vito offered the Pope a pensive smile as he lifted the wheelbarrow.

At 6:30 the Pope returned to his quarters to dress and prepare for another long day, starting with joining Marconi for breakfast. He frequently prayed for wisdom and guidance and at the end of his prayers always placed his fate in God's hands. The rumors creating the lack of confidence started almost immediately after his election; he didn't even have a honeymoon. Who could he trust? Who knew the intimate details of his personal life? Who knew his private thoughts concerning Church reforms? Only three people knew him well enough and had the high level Church contacts to perpetuate this negative campaign so quickly. He thought about Bishop Branducci, a Vatican theologian. On many occasions they discussed the Pope's latitude to make and change Church doctrine. *However, the Bishop died before I was elected. Could Branducci have branded me a heretic? If so, I'd never be remotely considered.*

Cardinal Marconi sought my friendship soon after I joined the Vatican staff. Dominic knows more about me than anyone in the Vatican. It's incomprehensible that Marconi's part of this plot. Yes, "plot," the only word that accurately described the campaign of rumors. Then there is Dunbar, old friend and mentor. He knows every minute detail, including my musings about drastic changes to Church doctrine and contempt for the leadership status quo. Dunbar's interview proved to be an eye-opener. Friend, adopted family member turned Judas.

He sighed at losing a trusted friend.

Brother Jacomo entered quickly after knocking. "Holiness, Eminence Marconi is waiting in the dining room."

"Thank you. I'll be there in a moment." Without being impertinent, the brother gave him that "I know what you did last night" smile.

The Cardinal sat at the corner of the sixteenth century mahogany table for twelve, symbolic of the twelve apostles. With leaves, the table extended to seat twenty-two.

"Good morning, Dominic, early as usual."

"Good morning, Holiness. I've already ordered your usual breakfast, eggs and toast, plenty of grape jelly."

Sister Martha followed the Pope into the dining room, placed a pitcher of Italian orange juice, the color more red than orange, on the table and poured hot coffee for both men.

"Thank you, Sister. Please give us privacy until breakfast is ready." Sister avoided eye contact. She also heard about last night's adventure.

"Holiness, we have important developments."

"Finally, I've been counting on your sources. Before you start, I need to get something off my chest. But first, I don't need a lecture about last night and security precautions. Understood?"

Dominic fought to hold a smile in check. "Yes. Last night never happened."

Dominic sat with hands on his lap, impatient as always for the Pontiff to continue. He worried about his friend; the strain showed on his face. Doctor Bruno Bananni was also concerned about the Pope's heart and elevated blood pressure. The Doctor wasn't sure how the Pope's health would hold up under the daily pressure of his position combined with the strain of constantly coping with rumors and intrigue.

The Pope didn't practice what he needed to say; it had to come from the heart. The pulse in his forehead pounded like a drum as he wondered if Dominic would tell him to go to hell. If that happened, it was all over, he'd be one step closer to resigning. "I don't often bare my soul." The Pontiff pushed his chair back from the table for a full view of the Cardinal's reaction. "Ah…Dominic, we have known each other for what…three years? Three years can be a lifetime. Some days I feel we are close. I seek and respect your advice. You were my first and only choice for Consigliore and Chief of Staff."

"During the last election you were also the most likely candidate to become Pope, until fate intervened." Holy Father reached for a sip of coffee to wet dry lips. "I suspect that some person or persons who know me very well are the source of personal information that my enemies are using against me. After watching the video interview I'm positive Bishop Dunbar, my old friend, is a traitor. My confession is, until yesterday I suspected everyone…including you! Please…please accept my apology for doubting you. From this moment, my full trust is placed in your capable hands. No doubts… nothing held back."

Dominic's face softened as an expression of relief spread across his tan face. "Holiness, suspicions and secrecy are normal, even natural. After all this is Italy, home of Prince Machiavelli and the Vatican's notorious Byzantine politics. I'd worry about your leadership if you weren't cautious. That said, it's good to know all doubts are behind us."

The Pope placed his left hand on the Cardinal's shoulder while extending his right hand to seal their partnership. "Thank you, my friend."

Sister Martha carried in the Cardinal's traditional Italian breakfast: cold cuts, cheese, hard bread and biscottis. The Holy Father still preferred a typical American meal. Two powerful and determined men from different cultures enjoyed breakfast while contemplating what surprises they'd need to trump in the near future.

Sister Martha fussed around the table refilling coffee and juice as they dined in silence. When Sister left, Dominic moved his chair closer to the Pontiff. He leaned forward, hand cupping his face, virtually whispering in the Pontiff's ear.

"Holiness, I'm concerned about your welfare. Some cardinals recently met in the Vatican Bank. I believe this is the group creating our problems. I have a few names and some suspicions, but no hard information on their plans."

"This is a disappointment. By now I thought you'd have specifics on our enemies. Not knowing who they are and only some idea of their plans is causing me to delay changes that need to be implemented immediately. How many members are in the group…what names do you know for certain?"

"The group is at least six, and as many as twelve. Some attended via videophone so I can't be absolutely sure of the group's size. I know Cardinal Capaldo hosted the meeting. Wronowski and Pasquale attended. Capaldo and Wronowski are strange bedfellows and usually at odds. Their alliance is troubling; both are powerful and have numerous allies."

"When can we expect hard reliable information?"

"Very soon, Holiness. I am sure you're familiar with the story about Cardinal Capaldo's battle of wills to renovate his conference room. Well, the young assistant that helped him has accepted a transfer to Capaldo's staff at the bank. He's my second cousin and will provide whatever information he can, including any suspicious activities at the bank."

"Excellent…excellent. We need that information—yesterday!" Pope Alex paused and leaned back, "Now on another important matter…its time to discuss plans to visit Africa. I think the best choice is Somalia and on the return trip stop for a few days in United Ireland."

Dominic moved back from the table and stood. He counted on not dealing with this for a few months. "Holiness, I know part of the Vatican outreach program is visiting troubled countries; as I previously advised, Somalia is a huge security risk. The country is just now recovering from revolution and the rebels still control a large section of the countryside. You have Bishop Tobua's report on his recent visit. The country is unstable, the leaders can't guarantee your safety."

The Pope's posture was perfectly aligned with the back of his chair, arms tightly folded across his chest. He spoke slowly, enunciating perfectly, "I fully understand the situation and your issues about safety. Now please understand my position. As Church leaders, we cannot in good conscience ask missionaries to live and work in countries or areas that we're afraid to visit for a few short days. I need to see and hear first hand the conditions. This area's been unstable for decades, and I don't expect it will improve without direct help—and not just cash that politicians divert into their personal bank accounts. These people need food, clothing and training on basic subsistence skills. Are the leaders refusing our request to visit or just reiterating they cannot guarantee our safety?"

"Holiness, they'll permit a visit at our own risk. The leaders actually encourage diplomatic visits because they often bring media coverage, which keeps their plight public and helps fund assistance programs. I'm the one concerned about the potential risks. Can we at least limit the visit to the capital and the large cities?"

Expecting continued resistance, the Pope rose to make his point clear. "No. I need at least two days visiting villages and the last day in the capital to meet with the leaders. Please make arrangements to leave ten or twelve days from today."

Dominic moved close, stood toe-to-toe looking up at the Pontiff, his voice raised an octave, the tone almost impertinent, "Holy Father, you can't be serious. That schedule is…is *impossible*. The logistics are enormous: security, travel, hotels, shipping the Popemobile…and the list goes on and on. So many minute details no one thinks about. We need at least a month to plan a trip of this magnitude!"

The Pope casually glanced at his wristwatch, stared out the window, and waited. During the long silence Dominic's eyes bore into his friend, tried to comprehend his bullheaded compulsion about this trip. The Pope turned to face Dominic. Both men stared each other down. The Pope was adamant and knew the first man to speak lost the argument. Dominic broke first. He wasn't swayed by the Pope's arguments, but respected his wishes. "I'll do my best."

Pope Alex placed his arm on Dominic's shoulder as they walked to the reception area. "My friend, that's all anyone can ask. Go in peace knowing you are doing the Lord's work. Keep me informed about the trip and our friends."

Cardinal Dominic left the meeting shaking his head, upset about proper security and the difficult logistics of arranging group travel in a third-world country. Diplomatic approval, moving people and equipment to Africa then transferring everything to United Ireland, all had to be coordinated in a short time. His over-wrought mind turned to prayer. *Dear Lord*, he silently prayed, *help me to become a miracle man or magician, whatever works best. Lord, you chose a good man as Pope, but he has become my cross*!

Reaching his office, his first call was to Cardinal Kilgannon in Dublin, the second to Bishop Abodda in Somalia. During both conversations he explained the general plan for the Pope's pending visit and requested their assistance in obtaining official approval and visas. They would also take responsibility for hotel accommodations and local travel within the country, once the number of people in the group and dates were firm. Reluctantly, the third call was to Cardinal Belfonte. Dominic's stomach flipped every time he had to deal with the man, but as the head of security, Belfonte's involvement was vital. Speaking with Belfonte's secretary, he requested a meeting within the hour.

Belfonte quickly finished his morning espresso and walked to Marconi's office in an adjoining building. The Cardinals had been at odds for years and Belfonte took every possible opportunity to berate or irritate Marconi. The chief of staff never let anyone see him sweat, gave the perception of being in total control at all times.

"Eminence Belfonte, thank you for joining me so quickly. This is an urgent matter and we have very little time."

"I am always available to serve his Holiness. However, I would prefer to meet in my office. Your work area is so…so…I hate to say it, um…drab and dated. Won't the Pontiff allow his chief advisor to improve his office?"

Reaching into a drawer for a pen and a note pad, Dominic replied, "Actually my staff refers to the motif as a 'retro' look. When I have time to work on updating the office I will be sure to ask for your expert decorating advice. We have much more important issues to tackle. If you recall, during the Holy Father's last Curia meeting he mentioned visits to troubled countries."

"Yes I remember wondering how the Pope can think about traveling at a time when the Church and his administration are near crisis! As chief advisor, I'm sure you tried to dissuade him from such foolishness! Excuse me. I didn't mean to interrupt. Please continue."

Dominic had already reached maximum tolerance of this ass. "The Holy Father has decided to begin his visits sooner than expected. He plans to visit Somalia and United Ireland. Our problem is...he wishes to begin the trip in ten to twelve days!"

Marconi waited for a reaction. Belfonte raised both eyebrows and shrugged his shoulders, indicating so what, another unrealistic deadline.

Belfonte's reaction was out of character, but Dominic ignored it for the moment. "*Eminence*, I need you involved in coordinating security with the local authorities. Also, contact Interpole and request information about Somalia and United Ireland. Especially a current update on terrorists. Somalia needs special care; it's very unstable. I understand the rebels control portions of the countryside and warlords exert influence on all the transportation in and out of the country. After speaking with the Somolian authorities, if you don't feel comfortable with the security arrangements, it may be advisable to request assistance from the Italian government. We have a standing offer from Dell' Ufficio Centrale Viliganza, the national police, to assist with security. Try to arrange for an anti-terrorist team."

A quick nod indicated Belfonte understood, "As head of security I'm also leery of the situation in United Ireland; terrorist attacks are on the rise. High profile targets like the Pontiff are hard to protect, especially when he wants high visibility. Of course, we will maintain our standard security precautions. The Popemobile will be shipped in advance with security personnel. I expect the Pontiff will wear the latest bulletproof clothing. Each security person and the Pope will wear a special tracking device that allows the security control center to monitor each person's exact location. The device can also determine if the person is alive or dead. If a guard is killed, we know immediately and declare a code red." He paused to gauge Marconi's understanding of the grave issues. Belfonte felt compelled to ask the question, "Can you guarantee that the Pope will cooperate with our security measures?"

Controlling a short-fuse Italian temper, Marconi placed folded hands on his desk, leaned forward and bored directly into Belfonte's arrogant eyes. "I will handle the Holy Father; just make sure you hold up your end."

Belfonte's eyes narrowed into slits, his voice resonating with the slightest quiver as venom neared the surface. "Keep in mind, *Eminence*, we all know some methods of attack are difficult...if not impossible, to prevent such as bombs. Or some person in a crowd gets close enough to shoot at point blank range, God forbid!"

Dominic immediately shifted the monkey back to the head of security. "Thanks for the security update. Ultimately it all comes down to people and planning. That's why we are counting on you and Colonel Tearsue to find the right people and organize the necessary precautions. If you need my help just ask. I'll personally remove any roadblocks. I don't need to stress time is of the essence, so please move *rapido*! You only need to focus on security; all other logistics will be assigned to others. Again, if any issues or questions arise contact me any hour of the day or night. Do you need anything further at this moment?"

"No, but questions and issues are inevitable."

"Thank you, Eminence Belfonte. God speed."

Unsettled, Henry Cardinal Belfonte opted for a short walk before heading back to his office. The warm sun accompanied by a gentle breeze mussed his thinning gray hair. His thoughts disturbed him. He had sworn an oath to remove the Pope from office or at least minimize his power to reform the Church. Now he had accepted an assignment to protect the Pope in foreign lands. Certainly he knew a mishap eliminating the man would solve the crusaders' problem—not a Christian thought. His dilemma was: Could, or would he assist in creating a mishap by intentional action or inaction? His oath, no matter how important to the crusade, did not extend to injury or possibly murder. Breaking the fifth commandment would place his immortal soul at risk. He wouldn't even consider it, no matter how much he disagreed with the Pope's plans to change the Church. Solving his moral dilemma, he realized this impromptu trip was important news; he had to notify Wronowski.

Hearing about the Papal trip, Cardinals Wronowski and Capaldo called an emergency meeting. All members of the crusade in the Vatican were summoned to attend within the hour. Remote cardinals would be brought up to date after the gathering. The meeting was held in Wronowski's office—not a very secretive move. Wronowski was livid, not thinking clearly, yelling at his assistant, throwing papers, slamming down the telephone. Capaldo arrived within minutes and poured himself a drink of Polish vodka while Wronowski worked through his maniacal tantrum, oblivious to Capaldo's presence.

Finally Wronowski turned his large bald head and deep-set blue eyes directly at Capaldo. "That son of a bitch must know we are after his ass. This whole trip thing…is… is a plan to improve his image. I wonder if Marconi is the brain behind this move; if so, he's working you big time. So what are you going to do about Marconi? We need an answer. Is Marconi with us or not? And we need the answer now!"

"Yes, this could be serious. It could also be the opportunity we've been waiting for. After the meeting we need a few minutes alone to work out real options. Meanwhile, calm down until the others arrive."

Due to short notice, only Cardinals MacRay, Belfonte, and Pasquale attended. Wronowski sat still fuming, tossing papers and mumbling obscenities, as the others took seats around the small conference table. Capaldo opened the meeting with a short prayer. Wronowski quickly grabbed control of the meeting, providing a brief overview of the upcoming Papal visits. He explained that if this trip were successful it would set back their plan to pressure the Pontiff into retirement. The Pontiff had also announced a live interview with GNN after the trip and right before Easter, the season with the greatest focus on Christianity. Any improvement in the Pope's image would be a set back for the crusade.

Wronowski's hoarse voice tried to speak louder, "That's the latest information we have. The old fox is sharper than we gave him credit for; these maneuvers can mean disaster. It's very possible that Marconi is orchestrating everything. Capaldo, you are closest to him; how soon will we know where he stands?"

Capaldo couldn't wait to take over as the real and decisive leader, seizing control from the boisterous blowhard Wronowski. "I have a dinner meeting with Marconi this evening. I'll massage him until I have an answer. Meanwhile, we need to discuss options. Do we confront the Pope before his trip, pressure him to step down immediately? Or wait until afterward, hoping the trip is a flop and his credibility further tarnished, which improves our position?"

"If I may comment?" said Cardinal Pasquale. The men nodded consent. "The Pope's obviously trying to improve his image. If we confront him now, he's likely to rebuff our demands. At best, he'll take our demand under consideration. My opinion is that he won't retire until he at least takes the trip and gages public reaction. Once we come forward, he'll have time to consider various alternatives. I think we should wait until after his trip, but confront him before his GNN interview. At that time, if he doesn't cooperate, we must consider physically removing him from office." Pasquale stood and walked to the bar, and continued speaking while pouring a stiff drink. "It's drastic but necessary. That's why knowing where Marconi stands is crucial. Belfonte, you control the Swiss Guards and Vatican police. You must determine which officers and men will support us if we remove him from office."

Belfonte scowled. "I'll begin working on the guards and police. We haven't talked about the Italian government. If we act and don't take control quickly they could step in to restore order. Walter, you need to pull some strings and get a read from the Prime Minister. But make sure Cardinal Tornetta doesn't get wind of your activity."

MacRay interjected, "If we find out about Marconi tonight and quickly assess the Security personnel, why can't we confront the Pope before the trip and if he refuses, physically remove him right then and there? Time is slipping by—why delay?"

"I wish we could move quicker on the guards," replied Belfonte. "I can't call a meeting and simply ask for a show of hands. This must be handled delicately; the same serious moral questions we all had to confront. We're closer to the Pope's defects; it was a much easier decision for us. No, gentlemen, we can't rush. This could boomerang."

They began squabbling. Capaldo stood and clapped his hands like a strict grade school teacher. "Cardinals, *please*! The overt actions you're considering will never be accepted by the Catholic world. The Pope can't be detained against his will indefinitely. When he's released, there'll be a tidal wave of support for the man the masses believe is their legitimate leader. He could establish his Papacy in Europe or the United States. This is exactly the schism we are trying to avoid." Capaldo pounded a fist against the palm of his hand. "No, no, no! As much as I understand your fervor and frustration, this is not acceptable. Convincing the Pope to voluntarily retire is our best option."

Capaldo slumped into his chair while the men mulled over his comments. Each silently acknowledged that Capaldo was correct; a coup was no good, at least right now. There had to be a better way to remove their renegade. These were intelligent men; with enough time they'd find a solution. Time was their big enemy.

Reluctantly, Belfonte stood with arms behind his back. "We all agree a coup can't work. Regardless, we still need to know about Marconi and security. It may be necessary to neutralize them once we develop a final solution."

The room shrank into a claustrophobic cell. Every cardinal except Capaldo wanted to bolt and leave this mess for another day. Although his left eyebrow had a noticeable tick, Wronowski looked a bit calmer. Noticing the group's frustration level, Wronowski decided to end the meeting. "I truly share your frustration. Have faith…as Princes of the Church we *will* prevail. I'll contact the members that didn't attend. This is absolutely the most important issue in all our lives. Be available; we may need to meet at a moment's notice." He turned to look directly at Belfonte, who he considered to be the group's weakest link. "Capaldo and Belfonte, keep me informed of your progress."

The others quickly departed the office. Wronowski and Capaldo stayed behind, waiting for privacy while sipping espresso.

"Walter, I hope you're calm enough to discuss a real plan."

The bald giant slouched in the chair, extending both arms in a gesture that said "tell me, I can handle it." Capaldo held in the smirk that tried to slither across his pudgy olive face. Ever so slowly, he began to describe the first part of his master plan: eliminating the Pontiff. "My original plan to kidnap the Pope may not be necessary. Somolia and Ireland are both fermenting. What a golden opportunity; tragedy happens every day. In Somalia, security will be extremely tight, although, accidents do happen."

With pursed lips, Wronowski glanced at him. "Which means you don't have any influence in Somalia."

Capaldo smiled on one side of his mouth thinking, *As usual this Polack is sharp as a tack.* "That's correct. United Ireland is a different story. My Palermo Family sold weapons to the IRA for years. Since Ireland's been united and the south in control, the Protestants are the minority. Roles are reversed and the Ulstermen are buying weapons to fight the southern oppressors. Factions of the old IRA can have a field day blaming the Ulsters for harming or if we fail, which is unlikely, attempting to harm the Pope."

"I don't understand? What are you trying to say?"

"With some help from my Palermo friends and the IRA, our problem can be eliminated and the Protestants will take the blame. All three partners benefit by eliminating our common problem."

"What if the plan doesn't work? Can this be traced back to us?"

"No, never. We're fully insulated. Any investigation would never uncover the crime family, much less the Vatican connection. For years the Ulster's and IRA groups will point fingers at each other. Just another muddled and unsolved mess."

Wronowski couldn't even say the word "Mafia." "Explain to me again why this criminal organization would be willing to help you and the crusade?"

"I told you, they believe the Pope is sniffing around the Vatican Bank. My business associates can't afford to have certain financial activities investigated."

"Are we trading one problem for another? What will these...people expect from the Vatican once a new Pope is elected?"

"Walter, don't sweat it; they just want business as usual. They aren't interested in Church matters. Pure and simple, they want access to the bank. Trust me; I know them."

"Security in United Ireland will be tight. What are the odds for success?"

Holding back a smile while discussing the raw outline of his plan was impossible. "I'll arrange for Major Bordeau to head internal security during the trip, and coordinate security precautions with the Irish police. We only need one lapse in security. An assassin will take care of the rest. And if the Irish fail, we fall back to the old plan: Kidnap the Pontiff and keep him in seclusion until we announce his death."

"I almost wish I didn't know the extent of your plan or your relationship with these people." Bending forward, Wronowski placed his elbows on his knees, hands cupping the sides of his head. "God help me. I'm in this neck deep."

"We both are, comrade; it's too late to turn back. My friends don't tolerate indecision. Only one option, move forward or ...I'd rather not say it."

"What time are you meeting with that other asshole, Marconi?"

"My apartment at 8:00 p.m. Should be very interesting. I'll call you after the meeting. Now I must get back to bank business. *Ciao*, your Eminence."

CHAPTER FOURTEEN

Ro Di Marco sat in her small office at PZ Plus, a prominent Main Line physical therapy facility where she worked for the past twenty-four years. Divorced after twenty plus years of marriage, she put herself through college and earned a degree in physical therapy. Ro had immersed herself in her work since the divorce, rebuilding a new life now that her two girls were grown and on their own.

She had fifteen minutes before her appointment with Kate Murphy and trying to concentrate on the file before her proved next to impossible. Ro hated not being in control and this meeting was something she couldn't control nor anticipate what the outcome would mean for her best friend and confidant. Lee Lee and Ro often joked they should have married each other since their friendship lasted longer than their marriages. They never had a fight in all those years; although, that's not to say they always agreed. In fact, they were about as different as two friends could be. Leigh had the knack of befriending anyone in need, whereas Ro acted far more cautious. If she thought that anything she revealed to Kate Murphy would harm Leigh, she'd rather cut off her arm first. Ro knew one thing for certain, if Kate Murphy wanted information on Ms. Leigh Stevens, she was Kate's ace in the hole.

"Ro, Ms. Murphy is on her way back...good luck, Rosie. You'll do just fine," assured her co-worker, Ann.

Kate found Ro Di Marco waiting in the doorway of her office. Both women extended their hands in a formal greeting and Ro invited her into the office.

"Thank you for agreeing to meet with me, Ms. Di Marco. This is my associate and video expert, Jay Collins. Do you mind if we video the interview?"

Ro welcomed Jay and consented to videoing the session, although the office was small and space for the equipment limited.

Kate continued as Jay surveyed the pale green windowless room and the best spot to set up. "As I explained to you on the phone, I am gathering information for a biography on His Holiness, Pope Alex IX. He suggested that I contact you to shed some light on certain aspects of his secular life."

"Sure. Can I offer you something to drink first?"

"No thanks; I've just finished lunch. I'm fine."

Concentrating on his work, Jay shook his head no.

Ro gave a half-smile. "Well then, fire away. This could take awhile."

In her early sixties, Ro looked much younger. Her face had few if any wrinkles and her thick hair only a hint of gray. Large solid breasts helped accentuate her short solid physique.

"Can you tell me how Anthony—I mean His Holiness—first met Ms. Stevens?"

Ro began to answer the question, recalling the telephone conversation the day Leigh's brother told Leigh about a potential blind date. "Joseph is Leigh's younger brother, who she raised with my support after both parents died. Joseph stopped by her office to give her the big news—she might actually have a date! He gave his boss her number, feeling she would be a good first date. His wife of twenty-three years had passed away. Leigh being Leigh immediately said 'I'm game' but not before asking, 'Hey Joe, what can I expect on a scale from one to ten?' Joe jokingly replied, 'No sneak previews. Have fun Leigh.'

"Joe was barely out the door when she phoned me. 'Who knows', she said, 'he may or may not call, but at least I have something to look forward to. Except then you always have to worry if they're going to call back. Maybe I shouldn't go. What do you think Rosie?'

"Leigh always seeks my approval for whatever reason, and always feels better when I give her the green light. So I told her, It's only a drink, and besides you're right, he still has to call you. Call me.

"We always end our conversations that way, even though it's understood we'd check in every day even if it is to say, Call me." Ro added this last part so Kate could better understand the unspoken bond that existed between them.

Kate knew the answer and said, "Of course he called!"

"He did," Ro explained, "not only did he make the first call, but he kept calling back."

Kate gave a half-smile. As a single woman, she knew what a rarity a call back could be. The air in the room seemed to lighten a bit. Ro relaxed, sitting back in her plush ergonomic chair. "Leigh and Anthony became quite an item. They spent all their free time together. Think nothing of jetting off to an island for a long weekend or flying to the coast for a friend's wedding. Leigh's career as the owner of a travel agency afforded them many travel opportunities, which they both jumped at. Leigh never had children of her own and Anthony's kids were grown, so they were footloose and fancy free. They were a real envy to most of us. At that point Leigh's friends still struggled with college tuition and car insurance."

Cautiously, Ro weaved her friend's story, while occasionally looking at Kate's reaction. Sensing approval, she continued between sips of homemade ice tea.

"Long before Anthony, Leigh found out she couldn't get pregnant. She tried the whole nine yards, the fertility route and all, but after years of emotional stress and enormous financial burden, Leigh resigned herself to 'God just said no,' and pretty much got on with her life and career. Her and her ex-husband Bill own the travel agency where Leigh worked since high school, so it affords her many opportunities to experience things the rest of us only dream of. When we turned forty—our birthdays are only a week apart—Leigh had just separated from Bill. I arranged a surprise trip to Chicago to see the taping of a TV show she liked. Plus I had her two sisters and a few close girlfriends join us. She was thrilled and so surprised! She's a pretty hard one to surprise…has to know everything: Where this one is, what that one's doing, when is she going to call the other one…way too much work for me, but that's what keeps her going. She's happiest being with the people she loves and making us all laugh. You just can't help yourself from laughing.

"Anyway, in return for planning her fortieth in Chicago, she had an opportunity to take a week-long cruise to the Mediterranean and bring a companion. Well, there we were traipsing through Italy together—friends since we were ten years old and now all grown up and cruising our way through the Med. Who'd a thunk it!"

Pausing for a moment, Ro reflected on the fond memories shared with a girlfriend over half a lifetime and also to see if the information she offered was useful. "Am I giving you what you need?"

"Yes. You're giving me a feel for your friend. I think it's safe to assume that Leigh is a loving individual with many friends and a successful career."

"Pretty much, though that's really the Readers' Digest version. There's so much more to this woman. I could tell you stories that would make you laugh till your sides hurt. Then relay a story of how her mother passed away when Leigh was twenty-five after a bout with lung cancer. Two years later her stepfather died in his sleep, leaving her younger brother and sister orphans. She didn't hesitate for a second to assume the responsibility of raising the kids. Did all she could to make their lives as normal as possible, right down to imposing curfews on her sixteen-year-old brother and making him pay the consequences when he didn't abide, to being the proud mother of the bride when her younger sister got married. The kids adore her. They always joked that even though Joe gave her a run for her money when he was growing up, he's the one who found a man when she needed one most. Little did we know that he'd go on to become the first American Pope! Looking back, we should have suspected. Nothing in her life is ever ordinary. Take the fact that she and Anthony still remain friends."

"Ro, if you know, please explain how the Holy Father told Leigh about his decision to become a priest."

Both of Ro's eyes opened wide. "Know, I will never forget. What a blow when Anthony first dropped the bomb. In shock, none of us knew what to say or do. Things seemed to be going so well for the two of them. Marriage seemed like the next natural step. When Leigh first told me, I thought she was kidding. What do you say to your best friend when she tells you that her lover has a higher calling?"

Kate thought about what Ro Di Marco just said. Kate had been *dumped* before, and recalled at twenty-five what it felt like hearing, 'I'm just not ready for commitment' after a year-and-a-half relationship. Once your heart's been broken, you can't forget the feelings of total disbelief, emptiness, abandonment and asking yourself that infamous question "WHY?" a thousand times in an instant. She could only vaguely imagine what it was like for Leigh Stevens, at forty-five, to hear that the man she had trusted her heart with for three years was contemplating a life of celibacy and devotion to a higher authority.

Ro offered Kate and Jay a bottle of spring water and this time they gladly accepted. The women both looked at each other, sharing a common bond of women whose hearts had once been broken; Kate motioned for Ro to continue.

"Leigh and Anthony had been away in Jamaica on travel agency business. When they returned, the first call Leigh made was to me. This was a little ritual we still share. I could always hear Leigh smiling over the phone and in usual fashion she would spill her guts to me about all those things that girlfriends share, even at our age. This time I could immediately sense something. I knew Leigh's PMS moods and hormone swings almost as good, if not better, than Anthony did. So when she said we needed to talk, I knew things weren't good.

"We met for lunch the next day and she dropped the bomb. She explained how they attended Mass in Jamaica celebrated by the local bishop. It was a small congregation, and Anthony felt the Bishop's words were spoken directly to him. Apparently they touched his soul. After Mass they went back to the hotel to get ready for the beach and Leigh started 'fooling around' with Anthony. He didn't respond. The first red flag...certainly wasn't like him. She let it go, figured he was just tired. At the beach, he seemed distant. Finally as they floated on a raft, she questioned his mood. He reluctantly, at first, went on to explain that the Bishop's sermon truly touched him and as unreal as it may seem, he felt the Bishop was a messenger from God speaking directly to him, clarifying religious callings that he ignored at various times in his life. He couldn't really explain it much better than that but that he needed to think, alone and that he hoped she'd understand. 'Understand!' Leigh yelled, and almost tipped the raft. Actually knowing Leigh, I'm sure she wanted to drown him.

"The rest of the trip turned into a nightmare. When they got home, Leigh gave Anthony an ultimatum. She needed to know where they stood. As an independent woman, she shied away from marriage. She didn't need him to support her. Just really loved him, believed he loved her and assumed they would spend their lives together either as a couple or husband and wife. Well, we all know what happens when we assume! The unthinkable happens. He dumped her, plain and simple. I could have killed him with my bare hands. The news devastated all of us.

"Leigh is a devout Catholic. Thank God, because her faith must have been what pulled her through. How can you argue with a man that believes God called him? I guess she knew in her heart Anthony was not the kind of guy who would jerk her around. He must have experienced a pretty strong calling to give up the life they shared, if you know what I mean. They had it all—money, independence, a true love and respect for each other. They also shared a very satisfying intimate life. That's how Leigh knew he meant business; he told her they needed to refrain from ah...intimate contact. They both had very healthy appetites. At forty-nine, that ol' Anthony was still going strong and she was one happy woman! When it ended, we all paid the price! We have a very close-knit group of friends and we all took turns checking on Leigh and just being there for her.

"It took some time but eventually she got on with her life. She really threw herself into building the business and bottom-lining it, she never gave her heart to any other man. He was her last true love. I wanted to hate him, but it was kind of hard for me to carry a grudge with Leigh telling me that only a brave and honest man like Anthony follows his conscious. But between you and me Kate, I could have killed the bastard."

Kate believed her, saw the lingering pain Ro Di Marco felt for her friend after so many years. It made Kate wonder what or who it was that hardened Ro's heart so that she couldn't find it in herself to forgive and let go the way Leigh had obviously done. What made these two women so different, yet so bound to each other? Kate found herself envious of the relationship that spanned more years than Kate was alive.

Shifting nervously in her chair, Ro asked, "Was I too honest? I mean…uh, I don't mean any disrespect to the Holy Father or anything. It's just that I honestly don't understand how she found it in her heart to remain friends with *him* after the breakup…let alone keep seeing him on a fairly regular basis. She's a far better woman than I."

"How often does Leigh see the Holy Father?" Kate's curiosity got the better of her.

Ro thought a minute before reluctantly answering. "Well, you will find the more you get to know this group there is never an easy answer. You see, Anthony's younger son is my son-in-law. Steve is married to my daughter Tiffany. Leigh is Tiffany's godmother, so of course any family affair when Anthony is in town, they run in to each other. Besides that, when Anthony became a Cardinal he encouraged Leigh to conduct tours to Rome. They could see each other frequently and she could expand her business. Now that he's the Pope, her tours have become extremely popular because she can arrange a private meeting with the Pontiff. Maybe Anthony feels this is the least he can do for her. It's a definite plus that attracts clients. The tours are in demand. It also makes it easier for them to maintain a friendship. Leigh always feels better after she sees that Anthony is happy and doing fine. It gives her a feeling of contentment and validates that the decision he made is apparently the right one. She truly finds comfort in it. Well, to each his own as they say. Whatever gets you through the night."

Just then Connie buzzed on the video intercom. "Excuse me, Ro. Barbara

Ristano is here for her treatment. Would you like me to have Karl treat her?"

Ro held up three fingers, indicating she'd see Barbara in a few minutes. Kate checked the time, amazed to see that over two hours had passed.

"Ms. Di Marco—I mean Ro—I had no idea I'd taken up so much of your time. Please, see to your appointment. I'll send you a copy of what we discussed today. As I mentioned, His Holiness will review the material before it's published, so don't worry; anything he doesn't feel is appropriate or the public's business will be cut. Thank you so much for your candor. It's been a real pleasure meeting you." Kate got up to leave the tiny office.

Extending both hands, Ro firmly grasped Kate's hand and elbow. "Your quite welcome Kate. I hope it helps. Oh, and Kate, please do my friend justice when you weave her into the biography. She is a very special lady, as you will soon find out for yourself. Don't give me another reason to wish His Holiness ill will. He's getting a little too close to the 'Big Guy' for me to put the evil eye on. But, if push came to shove, I'd take my chances. Jay, a pleasure."

While Jay loaded equipment into the van, Kate considered the interview. They were really getting into the meat of this biography. Initially she worried about finding the real man while interviewing the Pontiff's friends and former lover. After this interview she couldn't wait to meet and interview Leigh Stevens. No matter the outcome, it would be the flash point of the biography.

"Excuse me, Eminence Marconi is on the phone. Says it's important."

Cardinal Tornetta raised the handset. "*Pronto*. What's so important, Dominic?"

"The National Police won't assign an anti-terrorist team for the Papal tour of Somilia and United Ireland!"

"What? Impossible!"

"According to the minister of defense, his people are scheduled for maneuvers or some such thing. My sources tell me that the Prime Minister is reluctant to become involved with Vatican activities."

"I'll handle this. *Ciao*." Tornetta thought, *What bullshit! Wronowski got to the Prime Minister. We'll see about this.* "Carmella, please connect me to Defense Minister Marcelo De Medici on the videophone."

"Eminence Tornetta, it's been how long? Good to see you."

"It's been a while. We're both busy, but that's no excuse for not keeping in touch with old friends. Your mother and brother—they are well?"

"Yes, Eminence. Mom will be seventy-five this month. My brother and his family are doing fine."

"Good. I always enjoy your mother's visits to the Vatican. She makes me laugh...some of those outrageous stories about you boys. Listen, the reason I'm calling is His Holiness is about to make his first tour, of all places...Somalia and Ireland. Our director of security requested assistance from your anti-terrorist people. He was told no men were available. I know there must be a mistake so I decided to call you."

"Ah...I'm afraid that is correct. We had short notice and the men are all on duty or scheduled for special exercises. Of course if we had more notice—"

"Marcelo, please! We've known each other too many years. I know the Prime Minister doesn't want his administration involved with the Vatican at the present time. I won't even venture to guess his motivation. The Defense Ministry and the Vatican have always had a clear understanding and working relationship. The Pope needs Italy's help. Your help!"

"Eminence, you must understand this is a delicate situation."

"No, I understand Italy has an open offer of assistance since the Vatican became an independent state in 1929. I'd like you to reconsider our request. Remember, Italian Prime Ministers change at the drop of a hat! Oh, did I mention your mother sent me a beautiful letter thanking me for helping your nephew into the seminary?"

"No, you didn't mention that. We do appreciate your help. Um...I'll take your kindly advice and reconsider, your Eminence."

"God bless, my son. Say hello to your mother."

Chapter Fifteen

Just before 8:00 p.m., Cardinal John fussed around his apartment making sure everything looked neat and tidy. He double-checked with the chef; the meal had to be prepared exactly according to his directions. The chef scowled and ushered him out of the kitchen, mumbling a few crisp French adjectives. Everything appeared in order and ready for a guest known to be fastidious. Capaldo prepared his favorite meal, Italian opera playing in the background and bottles of aged Tuscany Chianti. They'd been associates for years, but in the past few months Cardinal Capaldo made overtures to develop a social friendship.

He studied Eminence Marconi, knew his every nuance and idiosyncrasy. Planned this meeting for months, practiced exactly how to approach the potential recruit. Dominic was old school traditional Italian; everything had a time and place. As an example, Italians eat dinner late in the evening, usually 9 p.m. or later, at times a light meal due to the late hour. Not tonight though. Capaldo prepared a gourmet meal. The host or guests don't discuss business until coffee's served. Since everyone knows the social etiquette, both guests and host enjoy the meal. Capaldo favored the American way of discussing business, starting with before-dinner drinks. This special night Capaldo would follow tradition and the evening wasn't expected to end until almost midnight.

Dominic's strong penchant for Catholic and especially Italian Old World traditions stemmed from a combination of heredity and environment. His grandfather, Christo, was a wealthy industrialist from Milan. During the

Fascist era he strongly supported his beloved dictator, Benito Mussolini, El Duce. And because of this support the Marconi factories received favorable military contracts. Following Benito's lead, he successfully kept the unions out of his factories until the war ended for Italy in 1944. The family's industrial power rapidly declined after the war. However, Christo Jr., Dominic's father, diversified the family interests into banking and finance, successfully husbanding the family assets and prestige. In the late 1970s, Christo, Jr. became active in politics and was eventually elected to several terms in the Italian Parliament.

The Marconi family claimed to trace their roots back to a Roman Centurion in 10 B.C. The money, power, political connections and their ancient heritage were a way of life, drilled into family members from an early age. They were required to live the family image and young Dominic was groomed for success, socially and in business. Because of Dominic's heritage, Capaldo judged and hoped that when Dominic was truly put to the test on Church tradition and precepts he'd stand firmly with the status quo.

John Cardinal Capaldo would have to learn the hard way never to draw conclusions from superficial information. Dominic Cardinal Marconi was much more complex than anyone imagined. Deep in the recesses of his being, there was a secret Dominic never discussed with anyone outside the confessional. A part of his life he rarely dwelled on, buried deep in his conscious. A biological urge that thankfully diminished with age and prayer, a secret hidden and controlled since his teenage years; Dominic was a homosexual. He never allowed himself to indulge in what he considered to be perverse sexual needs. In fact, he'd been celibate since birth, a virgin.

This hidden nature was almost a perfectly kept secret, except someone always knows or has a strong suspicion. Bettina, Dominic's mother, instinctively knew he was gay. By the age of fourteen she identified his sexual leaning, even before the young man acknowledged it to himself. Dominic was an only son of an only son. His father and grandfather expected their heir apparent to join the family business and propagate the Marconi clan. In their Italy, the fathers and grandfathers wishes were paramount. To make matters worse, both men were extremely homophobic, despising homosexuals beyond all reason, relegating them to a class of perverted sub-humans.

As Dominic reached mid-teens, the Marconi's began to seriously groom the youth for his eventual position in the family and society. The family men were on a course headed directly into disaster and turmoil, culminating with Dominic's total rejection. Bettina felt trapped; prayer the only possible hope for deliverance to save her son, husband and father-in-law. One sunny day the answer miraculously surfaced. On Dominic's sixteenth birthday, he announced a strong yearning to become a priest. Bettina saw this as a perfect solution. The Marconi men immediately rejected the idea; the only son and grandson must ultimately head the family. No other acceptable choice. Within seconds, his mother's emotions roller coastered from high elation to the depths of despair. The inevitable family conflict began. Again she turned to her only hope, prayer. The Lord had shown her the path; now she needed help in lighting the way.

The following week, Bettina's younger sister called to announce that she was pregnant with her third child. Of course both sisters giggled with elation. Later that day it struck Bettina that a second son was the answer to her prayers; everyone would be satisfied. With three children already, two girls and a boy, she thought her childbearing years were over. For her beloved son, she would do anything—including becoming pregnant. Bettina felt confident she'd birth a healthy son.

Punctual Dominic arrived exactly on time. Capaldo greeted his guest at the door with a firm handshake and a warm smile.

"Welcome Eminence. You honor my home with this visit."

"I hear you have a wonderful unique home. How long have you lived in this apartment?"

"Many years…since I earned the red hat. May I show you my home?"

"Please do. From this limited view I can see the decorating and art work is indeed beautiful."

Over the centuries, every apartment in the Vatican had been personalized and guests were often fascinated with the unique design and layout. Hosts were expected to offer a tour and guests appreciated the personal touch. In this instance, Marconi was extremely interested; he had heard rumors about Capaldo's antique furnishings and expensive art collection. He quickly realized the stories weren't exaggerated. The furnishings and artwork looked expensive and opulent. Capaldo graciously escorted his guest through each room, taking time to point out his favorite antiques and art pieces, which ranged from Roman statues to paintings that were modern as well as renaissance. One did not have to be an art expert to ascertain the collection was expensive. One painting appeared to be a small 8"X10" Ruben, but it couldn't be; Marconi was certain that all the known Rubens were accounted for in museums or private collections. He asked about the painting. Capaldo off-handedly claimed it was an old forgery, although it had some value due to its age, before he quickly flowed into the next room.

John Capaldo was born into a middle class farming family in the Calabria region of Southern Italy. He came from a farm family, Marconi wondered how Capaldo could afford these expensive items. Rumors about his association with the underworld could be true. Marconi was there to investigate and Capaldo generously provided information.

"And that, my friend, is the end of my tour. It's always a pleasure to share one's treasures. Do you agree?"

"Yes, I do. Your apartment and treasures are magnificent. I can tell you enjoy them. Hopefully, soon you will grant me the privilege of visiting my humble apartment in San Giovanni tower."

"My pleasure, Eminence Marconi; just name the day. Meanwhile, we've known each other a long time. In private I would consider it an act of friendship to use our Christian names."

"I agree, John."

"Wonderful. I just knew this would be a memorable evening. Dinner will be ready about 9 o'clock. Can I offer a light refreshment, a cocktail, possibly Amaretto?"

"Bourbon and soda, if it's no trouble."

"Dominic, I'm surprised, a very American drink."

"It's not my usual choice but I noticed the Bourbon as we passed the liquor cabinet and decided to give it a go."

They sat on an open balcony waiting for dinner, chatted small talk like old friends enjoying the balmy evening, which was quite unusual for the time of year. Dinner was fashionably late; the cook invited them to dine at 9:30. That annoyed Capaldo, but he didn't press the issue; he'd handle the cook tomorrow. The table setting appeared impeccable: fine China, gold tableware and a hand-embroidered tablecloth with matching napkins. The walls were smooth stucco painted a light mustard. An antique Italian chandelier with ten lights hung low over the center of the table.

The cook proudly described his creations for the evening: Light antipasto followed by cold shrimp cocktail, Italian wedding soup; the entrée Veal Roberto, thin fresh veal medallions cooked in a smooth brown sauce, a Northern Italian specialty. The meal would end with a small garden salad, espresso and a surprise dessert. Capaldo watched his guest beam and nod approval. The host began to feel confident as Marconi's usual reserve mellowed a bit more with each sip of wine. Things progressed better than his original plan. Eager to move the conversation into business, Capaldo held back until the proper time.

Looking across the table at his host, Marconi reminded himself that this superb evening was designed to gain his confidence and support. The proverbial lion's den, he had to remain open and friendly but ever so cautious. Once dinner was served, both men kept the conversation light and simply enjoyed the food. Capaldo constantly filled their wineglasses with aged Chianti. Between the espresso and special dessert, rice pudding, Marconi asked to speak with the chef to praise him for the exceptional meal and in particular, the Veal Roberto. The chef blushed and bowed, returned to the kitchen an appreciated artisan.

"Dominic, will you join me for an after dinner cordial and a fine Cuban cigar?"

"Yes to the cordial but I'll pass on the cigar. However, please enjoy yourself."

They retired to the comfortable parlor to relax and digest the meal. Both men chose Sambuca over ice. Capaldo reached into an antique humidor extracting a large Cuban cigar. Three deep puffs and the glowing tip outlined his face and full Cardinal regalia. Both men momentarily stared as the thin gray smoke whirled in the dimly lit room.

They sat in overstuffed armchairs facing each other at a slight angle. The only light came from pole lamps standing next to each chair, illuminating the occupants while the remainder of the room was in shadow. Marconi took a good look at the short fat man sitting across from him. Behind those thick jowls there was a devious intelligence and the willingness to use it for evil—the worst possible combination.

Suspecting the niceties were over, Marconi patiently waited for his host to lead the conversation. The host rested comfortably, legs extended straight out, toes pointed at the ceiling. It didn't take long to break his trance. After a few deep inhales he felt more than ready to transition into in a business mode and begin discussions about his guest's relationship with Pope Alex.

"Dominic, you undoubtedly have the hardest job in the Vatican. I certainly don't envy your position. In fact, I worry about you and what will happen with the Pope."

Marconi had steeled himself for the verbal chess match to begin. "Thank you for the concern, but I don't understand why you're worried."

"Dominic, Dominic ever too humble and loyal to his Pope. It's common knowledge that this Papacy is in deep trouble; things are not going well for *His Holiness*. Many, shall I say, unnamed, important and influential people believe Anthony Pavelli is not qualified to be Pope. Many, and I stress many, clergymen, including me, were sure you were the best choice for Pontiff."

Dominic's face slowly formed into a frown.

"I sense this conversation is making you uncomfortable. Please don't answer; hear me out. Because of your deep sense of loyalty and respect for authority you can't admit that other cardinals, including you, were a better choice than our American. You have to be torn between loyalty to your office and what you know is best for the Church."

Bending his legs and leaning forward, Capaldo raised his voice to make it emphatic. "Many other cardinals struggle with this same issue. I simply want you to know…you're not alone. Friend's are here to help. I worry in particular that when this Papacy collapses, you will be judged a loyalist to the American and your reputation will be tarred with the same brush, so to speak. Your position in the Vatican and possibility of becoming Pontiff may be ruined. Now, do you understand my concern?"

Casually sipping Sambuca, Marconi's eyes never veered from the predator. "I'm fully aware of the Papacy's precarious situation. I also know that Pope Alex is taking steps to strengthen his position in the Church with both the clergy and laity. I'm sure you are fully aware of his actions; there are few real secrets in the Vatican. I venture that even your chef knows the Pope's plans."

Both men chuckled, knowing that he was probably right.

Hackles began to rise on Marconi's neck. Capaldo freely admitting that a group of Church leaders were actively moving against the Pontiff—an unthinkable action on the part of cardinals who swore loyalty to the Pontiff.

The fine cigar extinguished from lack of attention and dangled from the Capaldo's fat stubby fingers. He took a second to relight the long tube. "My friends suspect you are aiding the Pope by providing schemes, such as his interview with GNN and the latest plan, Papal visits. If true, when the dust settles your future service at the Vatican will be in jeopardy. All I suggest, my friend…I hope you consider me to be a friend…is that you please reconsider your sense of loyalty to the American."

Marconi wondered how arrogant pigs became Princes of the Church. "I'm only following the boss' lead. He conceived and arranged the GNN interview and also planned the Papal visits. You are obviously underestimating him. Likewise, I didn't realize his naysayers were so many and powerful. He's in deeper trouble than he or I imagined."

"There in lies the problem: We don't consider him our boss or our spiritual leader. The man's in way over his head. The cardinals want him to retire for health reasons. Now you have a better understanding of the situation and more importantly have an alternative for your loyalty. It's almost time for each of us to choose. You can stand behind the Pope in the fight of his life—so to speak—or join a group of clergy dedicated to saving our Church."

Feigning surprise, Marconi uncrossed his legs and sat up straight. "You are correct on some points. My loyalty is torn and other leaders were better prepared to be Pope; however, I have to live with my actions. I cannot, at least at this point, join your group. Neither will I interfere with any actions you take to protect the Church. When the critical time comes, I hope to follow my conscience."

"For now that's all I ask. Just remember you have friends with, ah...let's say the same agenda. If you need us, we are here."

"John, it's getting late. Thanks for the hospitality and the concern. I'll take everything you said under advisement."

"Entirely my pleasure, Dominic."

He escorted his potential recruit to the door and firmly shook hands. "*Buona notte*, good night."

Both men were satisfied. Each believed he accomplished his goal. Capaldo felt reasonably secure that Marconi, if not helpful to the crusade, was at least neutralized. Marconi had a much better idea of what the Pope was up against and that his newfound friend had influential friends in and outside the Church.

While Marconi strolled to his apartment he tried to surmise what his enemies had up their sleeve.

Chapter Sixteen

After the Di Marco interview, Kate tried to reach Monsignor Haggerty to re-schedule his interview for late that afternoon rather than the next day. If they finished Monsignor today and Ms. Stevens's tomorrow morning, they could head back to New York early and focus on editing. No luck; Monsignor didn't answer. Kate left a message and her cell phone number. "Jay, do you have any suggestions on what we can work on while waiting for the Monsignor?"

"Um…we could use some video background and filler. Right now the biography is limited to interviews. We can video the seminary dorms and library. Let's also visit the Pope's first parish, video inside and outside and if time permits the diocese cathedral. The GNN video library already has great footage of St Peter's square and various parts of the Vatican property. Weaving the interviews with places where he worked and lived will create a flow."

The filming took less time than expected and they decided to return to the hotel. Jay looked and felt exhausted, his body craved a quick boost of energy so they stopped at a neighborhood store for an ice cream cone. While making the purchase Jay asked the middle age owner for directions to avoid the traffic headed toward Center City. Tossing back longish dyed blond hair, the friendly owner gave Jay a crooked "your cute" half-smile and suggested taking Belmont Ave. to Montgomery Ave. to the expressway. Jay instantly perked up and returned the smile.

The drive turned from urban row houses to quasi-suburban. They drove slowly through old neighborhoods with large brick and stone houses, stately three story colonials. The area had seen better days, although it appeared in the process of revitalization. Various houses were in stages of renovation, signs of fresh paint, additions or new roofs.

Kate mused, "I always wondered what it would be like to live in a big old house. My romantic side pictures quaint and charming, every room decorated with handpicked furnishings, some new but mostly old antiques. Miss Practical, however, assumes hot in the summer, cold in the winter...maintenance bills that rival Rhode Island's budget. When I become wealthy, Matt and I will find a big old house and spend our free time renovating room by room."

"You do that. Just don't invite me over until all the work's finished! Handy I'm not. Although, I'm great at decorating."

"Your taste is way too modern for me, all that glass and chrome. Old houses need rich wood, colorful floral fabrics and warm window treatments. Jay, what's with the cigarette? I asked you not to smoke while I'm in the van."

"Sorry, I forgot. Your frilly house put me over the edge. Anyway, that's not my style. Your house and your dream, do whatever makes your clock tick."

The cell phone chirped. "Hello, Kate Murphy speaking."

"This is Monsignor Haggerty. I just received your message. How can I help you?"

"Thank you for calling, Monsignor. Well...our schedule freed up and we're wondering if you're available to meet this afternoon?"

"Um...give me thirty minutes or so and come over."

"Thank you, Monsignor. Can you give me directions from Belmont Ave.? We're almost at the expressway entrance."

"Piece of cake, Ms. Murphy. Take the expressway west toward Valley Forge. Exit onto Roosevelt Blvd. Follow to the Fox Street exit. Make a left on Fox, go two blocks and you'll see St. Helena's. We have a small mission in the church basement; you'll find me there. Should I prepare anything for this meeting?"

"Just your memories. See you in a half-hour."

The church doors were open so they proceed to the basement. The basement was a beehive of activity. The mission helped AIDS patients with financial and legal assistance. Twenty cubicles lined the basement walls, each with a counselor and client. The receptionist asked, "You guys looken' for the Monsignor?"

Jay nodded yes.

She pointed to Monsignor Haggerty with a group of children. Monsignor noticed the strangers and came over.

"Hello, I am Monsignor Haggerty. You must be Ms. Murphy and Mr. Collins."

They both said hello and shook the Monsignor's thin, bony hand. Kate thanked him for meeting on such short notice. The thin man with grayish hair and a kind face matched the gentle voice.

"My pleasure. Can I offer you coffee or a soft drink before we begin?"

They declined and followed Monsignor to a makeshift office deep in the basement near the boiler room. He invited them to sit on metal folding chairs; he sat on the opposite side of a small gray metal desk. The outside cinderblock wall was painted a pale gray. Steam pipes and electrical wiring ran along the low ceiling at odd intervals. The room's only redeeming feature was its warmth and privacy. The quarters were tight. The lower half of the Monsignor's body was fully engulfed under the old metal desk, his elbows resting on the top.

"I don't mind admitting I've been nervous about this interview."

"You will do fine Monsignor, nothing to worry about; just be yourself."

He thought it was easy for Ms. Murphy to say, "Just be yourself"; she wouldn't have to live with the consequences of potentially damaging a friend and the best man he ever met. He intended to follow his brother, the attorney's advice. "Don't lie and do not volunteer information, only answer what you're asked."

"Okay, since the Pope asked, I will do my best. GNN has me for three hours. How do we begin?"

Kate spoke slowly and softly, hoping to ease the Monsignor into a relaxed state. "How long have you known the Holy Father?"

"I met him twenty-odd years ago at St. Charles Seminary. I was a second-year student; he had just entered the seminary. No one wanted to room with the old guy. In fact, that was his nickname for a long time. So we drew straws. I lost."

"How long were you roommates?"

"Only one semester. I had to move because of his snoring. It shook the walls and I couldn't sleep. However, during that semester we became friends of a sort; he's much older, so the relationship is closer to a Dutch uncle. Anthony was concerned about the age difference and tried to keep to himself. The other seminarians never really considered him part of the 'in group.'"

"What did you learn about the Holy Father during your time together?"

"As we grew to know each other, I learned Anthony's intriguing story. He was married over twenty years and raised three children. When we met he was divorced, first marriage was annulled, deceased wife, ex live-in girlfriend, three children and two grandchildren, and a rising career in middle management. The information is fairly common knowledge."

He hesitated a second, he'd already ventured into the Pontiff's private life, doing exactly what his brother told him not to do—volunteer.

"Monsignor, I understand your reluctance to discuss some areas of the Pontiff's life. Keep in mind he asked everyone to be open and forthcoming."

"I do understand. I'm just trying to word this properly. Keep in mind there are personal, as well as Church issues, involved."

"I didn't mean to rush you. Take all the time you need."

Monsignor finally cracked a smile and sat back as far as the tight space would permit. "When Anthony applied to the seminary the Church didn't think he was a good candidate and turned him down. They considered him too old; the Church wasn't going to invest in his seminary education. Naturally tenacious, he eventually got his way. The fact is, the Church had nothing to lose; the seminary had excess capacity and he paid for the seminary, including room and board."

"How did he manage to live without working?"

"I gather Anthony was frugal. He sold his house to his oldest son and cashed in stock options from his former employer. In the last year I could tell finances were tight, but he made it."

"Monsignor, were you comfortable hanging out with an older man?"

Leaning forward as far as possible, the Monsignor planted his elbows on the desk and gave Kate a slightly embarrassed smirk. "At first it was a bit unnerving. After a while it didn't matter. Some days he was one of the guys; other days he became big brother or uncle depending on what I needed that day. My friendship with Anthony helped me to better understand my dad, who was often a mystery. Also, I learned that older people are young at heart; they just have grown up responsibilities.

"He owned a house at the Jersey shore. One summer, Anthony, his grandson and I spent a week's vacation at the house. Under relaxed conditions he was fun and funny. He even broke into song now and then, even though he can't carry a tune. Great vacation, until one of the less popular professors from the seminary showed up for a few days. Fortunately, he had to cut his trip short."

Obviously, Monsignor was referring to Bishop Dunbar. Certainly no love lost between these two clerics. Kate knew Bishop Dunbar could never fully appreciate the work and contributions to society that people like the Monsignor made each day.

Jay had to back up as far as possible to video the priest. The camera picked up the monsignor's unnerving tension; he hadn't blinked in several minutes.

"So what was your relationship after you were ordained?"

"Well, I was ordained a year before Anthony and assigned to a poor parish in North Philly. He often did social work on the weekends and during summer break so he switched his work to my parish. He was a great help and I was able to give him some feel for the daily life and responsibilities of a newly ordained priest."

"And after the Holy Father was ordained?"

"He was also assigned to a poor parish that was consolidating into a cluster parish. A cluster is a pastor and assistant pastor spreading their ministry over several churches. He was assigned an assistant pastor position. One year later he became a pastor for a well-to-do parish in Villanova, not far from the university. That was a minor miracle—not only the short period as assistant but being assigned a wealthy parish in Villanova. We spoke often on the phone and during Church meetings and other social functions. He doesn't play golf like most priests, so we went fishing a few times a year."

Not realizing the room was in use, a worker casually opened the door. She graciously backed out, offering an apology. "Sorry, that was Ginny, my best social worker." The sudden interruption sparked a slight grin and helped dispel the Monsignor's tension.

"I must say I'm impressed with the type of services you offer and the large number of volunteers," said Kate.

"We try. It can be very rewarding work."

"I was wondering, with the shortage of priests how or why did the Holy Father quickly move from parish work to the Diocese staff?"

"That is the sixty-four thousand dollar question. Father Anthony became a master at seeking contributions for the parish and special charities. He took those funds and grew them through investments to the point where the proceeds from the principal almost fully funded the respective charities. This quickly came to the attention of Cardinal Gates, who wanted Anthony to work his magic at the Diocese level. The rest is pretty much history. Cardinal Gates took to Anthony and became his mentor, which eventually led to

Anthony's elevation to Bishop, quickly followed by an assignment in the Vatican."

Clearing her throat, Kate asked a serious question that she figured might give the Monsignor more angst than he was eager to deal with. In fact, after nearly twenty years, it was still a delicate subject that Church officials would rather not discuss, especially in front of the news media. "Monsignor, there is an ugly rumor about the Pope that continues to surface. It seems to have a life of it's own. I know you've heard it, and probably would prefer not to delve into the delicate matter of pedophilia."

Cringing, the Monsignor never expected that issue to surface. Once on the table, he had to deal with it since the Pope was part of the resolution—not the problem. He intended to answer cautiously and provide the Pope full vindication.

"Monsignor, this is a two-part question: Was the Pope ever accused of being a pedophile, and what was his involvement in the pedophile scandal?"

Bile lined the Monsignor's throat, leaving an acrid taste. His back to the wall, trapped behind the metal desk, trapped into discussing an ugly topic that just wouldn't go away—old scars he would rather not scrape. He intended to answer the same as always, with consideration for the victims and Holy Mother Church. "First let me say, the entire Catholic community was saddened by the events and especially the lack of appropriate action by our leadership at that time. The Church's procedures and attitudes have immeasurably improved since those terrible dark days.

"Now, to answer your specific questions. The Pope was never a pedophile or accused of being one. Because of his reputation and position, he was asked to represent the Philadelphia Archdiocese and coordinate with the victims, accused priests and authorities. In this position his name was associated with the situation, and of course he was often quoted in the newspapers and on TV. Period! End of story."

"Well said, Monsignor. Thank you. I know that was difficult." Kate smiled, trying to restore the rapport they were building before the "P" question. "You know the Holy Father and Bishop Dunbar are friends. Was the Bishop instrumental in the Holy Father's transfer to the Diocese staff?"

"The Bishop was on the Diocese staff when the Pope transferred, and it's possible that Dunbar influenced the decision. Let's just say it would be out of character for him."

"Are you surprised at how quickly the Holy Father progressed through the Catholic hierarchy?"

"He's very capable and should have moved rapidly. The surprise was that the 'old boys club' recognized his talent. Also, I don't think the other bishops or cardinals knew the real Anthony. He always had radical ideas that would never be accepted by the local leadership. Obviously he knew when to keep those ideas to himself."

"When did you last see His Holiness?"

"Oh, I remember it well," he replied, stroking his bushy left eyebrow. "It was four years ago before he left for his Vatican assignment. He invited us, that is Ron Bluefeld, a friend of ours, and me to a farewell lunch at the Italian American club. During lunch he congratulated me on my elevation to Monsignor. He didn't say so but I knew he pushed for my elevation. Ron Bluefeld worked with Anthony before he became a priest. He's a volunteer at the mission and is here today. I'm sure Ron could provide background on Anthony's business life if that would be any help to you?"

"Hum…Mr. Bluefeld isn't on the Holy Father's list, but if you think he can contribute I'll certainly meet with him if he's willing."

"Oh, by the way I mean no disrespect referring to the Holy Father as Anthony; it's just that during the period we are discussing he was 'Anthony'. Excuse me a moment while I check with Ron."

As soon as the monsignor left the room, Jay jumped on the comment about Bishop Dunbar. "I knew it, just knew it; Dunbar is a bragging, self-important pompous ass!"

"Why, Jay, how did you ever form that opinion? I'm sure he *is* everyone's favorite bishop!"

A few minutes later the monsignor returned with Ron, a well-dressed dapper gentleman possibly in his mid-sixties. He had short cropped salt-and-pepper hair, dark intelligent eyes and an impish smile.

"Kate Murphy and Jay Collins, meet my dear friend, Mr. Ron Bluefeld."

Ron eagerly extended his hand and welcomed them to the mission. He sat very close to Kate, crossed his legs and made instant eye contact, nodding that he was ready.

"I found him out back sneaking a smoke. Ron quit smoking at least twenty times since I've known him. If his wife finds out, he'll be one sad puppy!"

Ron gave them that same impish smile, displaying small straight teeth, confident his wife wouldn't catch him, again.

"Mr. Bluefeld, thanks for joining us on short notice. Do you mind if we videotape your interview?"

"It's okay, I don't mind."

"I understand you worked with the Holy Father. When did you meet Anthony Pavelli?"

"That's easy to remember. Thirty-two years ago, he was the manager of a large company that acquired the small outfit I worked for. I was ready to move on and Anthony convinced me to stay with the larger company. He said if the talented people remained we could make a difference and all become successful, not to mention make some serious money. I stayed, we grew the company and had some fun doing it."

"Where did both of you fit in the company structure?"

"He was the general manager, later a regional manager. I started as a sales representative, later promoted to senior sales rep. We worked together as a team for eight years. After that we worked for competing companies until Anthony packed it in to become a priest."

"Was he tired of the business world? Did he change careers to get away from the rat race?"

"I'd say 'no'. He enjoyed the thrill of the hunt and the emotional high that comes with winning."

"It's obvious you were friends in addition to work mates. Was he a good manager and businessman?"

"The best, a master at his trade, I'd work for him in a minute. I was there during his good times, when he won the General Manager of the Year award, and the rough part when his wife Marie died. He's the one that got me to volunteer at this mission, and I'm Jewish."

"Mr. Bluefeld, I would like to hear that story if you don't mind."

Ron adjusted his posture while re-crossing his legs. "My pleasure. A few months before moving to Rome he called me at work, he knew I was retiring. We talked about our families and then he went straight to the business on his mind. Neither of us wastes much time on idle chitchat. He asked a question, 'When are you going to give back?' I said, 'Give back what, I didn't borrow anything?' He said, 'Give back to the community, to society. Ron, you are a very fortunate man, with a wonderful healthy family, lovely home, and financial security. Many others are not as fortunate. So when are you going to start giving back to the community and your maker? With retirement around the corner it's a perfect time to begin helping others not so fortunate.' He suggested meeting the Monsignor, and I liked the way this mission helps people so I volunteer two days a week."

"So Bishop Anthony was good at networking!"

"More like using guilt; it's a Catholic tradition," Monsignor said, half kidding.

"Mr. Bluefeld, anything you wish to add?"

Ron looked at the Monsignor for approval or possibly guidance. The Monsignor raised his hand. "Go for it Ron; it's your interview."

"One observation, Ms. Murphy...as I mentioned, I'm Jewish and don't know much about the Catholic religion; however, Anthony's getting a bum rap. The rumors and stories about him and his family are just not true. He's one of the most respected and decent men I've ever known. I hope your story carries that message."

"Thank You, Mr. Bluefeld. Monsignor, do you have anything you'd like to add?"

"I agree with Ron. The Church community hasn't given Anthony an opportunity to prove himself. He's been on the ugly side of these rumors since the beginning. They are only focusing on his secular life and not seeing the overall good he has to offer. And Kate, that says it all."

"Thank you gentlemen. We appreciate your time and candor. I'm sure the Pope will be pleased with your contributions to his biography. I wish you success with your mission activities; it's a very worthwhile cause. Maybe I can convince my company there's a potential story about AIDS missions. I may be calling you.

"His Holiness will review the video prior to publication; he has the final approval. Now if you can give us directions to the Center City Marriott, we'll be on our way."

Settled in at the hotel, Kate checked her e-mail and received some background on Leigh Stevens and her involvement with the travel industry. The message began:

> GNN E-MAIL (private and confidential for use by GNN only)
> Two decades ago, small privately owned travel agencies were almost extinct. The airlines were squeezing them out of business by unilaterally reducing commissions. They squeezed slowly, allowing themselves time to build airline call centers and Internet order centers. Strong competition also came from dot.com companies offering discount travel on the Internet. For years the travel agencies and their associations were ineffectual in stopping the pressure that forced small owners to close up shop, something

similar to the slow demise of small main street businesses. Since the travel associations couldn't help, a grassroots movement was started, led by owners like Ms. Stevens. The plan was simple: Pick the airline that was most aggressive in cutting commissions and boycott selling any tickets for that airline for a one-week period. Only sell tickets on other airlines. When Brand "U" was the only airline available for a particular destination, tell customers that travel agencies are boycotting the airline and refer them to the airline call center. On the second day of the boycott, Brand U call centers and web sites were so jammed both systems crashed. Brand "U" was brought to their knees, so to speak, at least for that week. It turned out to be a hollow victory—the airlines didn't change strategy and many small agencies continued to go belly up. Savvy owners like Ms. Stevens diversified. Her agency selected Italian tours as their niche market.

Recently boutique travel agencies have made a strong comeback. People finally realize service has a value, and high caliber leisure vacation time is worth a premium.

She folded the e- mail and placed it in her briefcase, admiring Ms. Stevens for her resiliency.

CHAPTER SEVENTEEN

The Holy Father had a full schedule until early afternoon. Cardinal Marconi, eager as usual, poked around in his office waiting for his appointment. At the appointed time he walked to the Papal quarters and entering the reception area, he noticed the gardener Vito and two other members of the Vatican staff leaving the Pope's office. As a result of last night's dinner with Capaldo, he felt a shiver up his spine thinking about the Holy Father's interaction with clergy or Vatican staff. He wondered whom they could trust. At this point they had no idea of the depth or breadth of Capaldo's network. Exactly how many people were involved in the conspiracy or who might be unknowingly supporting the conspirators? For now, virtually everyone came under suspicion. Before Brother Jacomo could ask him to wait, the Cardinal proceeded into the office unannounced, and found Pope Alex on his videophone with Ms. Murphy.

She had just finished telling him about the interview with Monsignor Haggerty. In two weeks GNN would send a full rough draft of the biography for Vatican review and approval. Once approved and finalized, GNN would begin to advertise the hour broadcast that would be aired in three time spots during a week's period. If everything proceeded on schedule they planned on airing the live interview one-week after the biography.

Pope Alex played with his fountain pen, approved of GNN's progress so far. He thanked Ms. Murphy and ended the conversation by giving her a Papal blessing.

Turning, he rose to greet the Dominic. "Well, you heard we're making excellent traction on the GNN project. I expect you're here to tell me about last night's dinner or have you been recruited by the Capaldo connection?" The Pope still had the same broad smile from his telephone conversation.

"If he made me a better offer I might consider it. You know my boss is not the easiest person to work for." Dominic snickered as he eased into a high back leather chair facing the Pontiff's desk. Every time he sat in this office his eyes automatically focused on the two photos displayed at the edge of the Pope's desk: The Pope's wife sat on left corner and in the opposite corner stood Leigh Stevens. Both photos angled to face the Pontiff and visitors. He surmised that in addition to the saints, both women were tasked with watching over the Holy Father.

"What an informative evening. Capaldo rolled out the red carpet. All my favorites: music, wine, and veal. I must say he's a topnotch actor." While speaking, Marconi had a habit of fingering the large gold pectoral crucifix that hung around his neck and extended to his waist. "He claims a group of powerful cardinals are ready to force you into retirement or at least exert control over your Papacy. The short version is, he asked me to join or at least support the group. I declined to join for now, but told him I would not oppose any of their actions. If they think I'm neutralized they may be less cautious about their activities. Of course, my position on this issue will guarantee me additional votes during the next Papal election!"

Hearing the last comment, Pope Alex sat absolutely still, his natural olive complexion began to glow, his cheeks red as ripe tomatoes. "How generous of *his Eminence*." He slammed the desk drawer. "Now, do you know their time table or have additional names?"

"No exact time; he stressed that it's a number one priority. I gave you three members: Capaldo, Wronowski and Pasquale. Our communication records indicate Hildabrand from England and Patel from India participated in their meeting via videophone. That's five of a possible dozen active members. Capaldo claims double that number will support them once they are in control. Those people are less of a threat so I'll concentrate on the active members. My cousin, the mole in Capaldo's office, is making progress. I should have all the names in a week, possibly less."

The Pope scribbled with his fountain pen making larger and larger circles as though he had drifted off, then suddenly looked up. "Please be sure to thank your cousin for me. His assistance won't be forgotten."

"Holiness, based on this information, we have to be cautious of all unusual activities or requests. I don't mean to pry, but why were Vito and those men visiting?"

The Pope's color returned to normal. "I'm pleased to see that even you forget some things. Remember…I have an open invitation to the Vatican staff for one hour each week. I asked Vito to visit me and set an example. His two friends seemed very nervous. Eventually they asked a question. Any idea what they asked?"

"The exact question no, but I'm sure it was far-fetched."

"So far from reality it took me off guard: 'Do I plan on moving the Papacy to New York so it can be near the United Nations'? If they weren't so serious I was tempted to crack a joke and say 'Sure, the movers are coming next week.' Instead, with the most serious expression I could muster, I said 'Absolutely no—not while I'm making the decisions.' They had broad smiles, said, 'May God bless you,' and were ready to leave. Out of here in seconds."

Half chuckling the Pope sipped some coffee. "Changing the subject for a minute. Please give me some good news about the visit to Somalia and Ireland."

"The plan is well underway, so far so good, no major holdups. Cardinal Belfonte wasn't thrilled about the short notice. He assigned Major Bordeau to travel with the group and coordinate security forces."

Eminence Capaldo sat quietly in the back seat as the limousine wove through traffic heading to the Excelsior Hotel. The glass partition separating occupant and driver was tightly closed. He needed a few moments of solitude to steel himself for the coming meeting. He had been singularly preoccupied about this meeting since receiving a telephone call early that morning inviting him to lunch with Don Ricardo Pertruzzi. Capaldo liked to think of Don Ricardo as a friend and business associate. People in Don Ricardo's profession couldn't afford to have close friends—you were either Family or a business associate.

Growing up, Capaldo had two routes to success: Either the priesthood or follow his older brother and join the crime family. He screwed up his chance to join the Family and was literally forced into the priesthood, which of course pleased his mother to no end. How ironic, that his ecclesiastical success ultimately led to his involvement in the "Family" business.

He worried, grew increasingly nervous as they neared the hotel. Don Ricardo rarely traveled outside of Sicily. Only a matter of great importance could lure the Don from his beloved villa, his seat of power on the outskirts of Palermo. As the limousine drove under the Excelsior Hotel portico, his hands began to sweat. He made a mental note to wipe his palms on his robe before shaking hands with the Don. *Never give anyone an opportunity to capitalize on weak points*, he thought. He wasn't sure how to dress for the meeting, a low profile business suit or the robes of his office. Needing as much prestige as possible, he chose to display his rank with as much red as protocol dictated.

Two burley men in expensive business suits greeted him. Their silk Armanis were designed to minimize unsightly bulges. His driver was instructed to wait in the lobby while bodyguards escorted Capaldo into a waiting elevator. While not expecting to find anything, the bodyguards apologetically asked permission to check for weapons.

They escorted the Cardinal to the Emperor's suite on the eighth floor. In a show of respect, Don Ricardo stood and moved into the vestibule to greet his guest. Raising the Don's hand, the Cardinal bowed slightly to kiss his ring, both men embraced; the Don kissed his guest on the right then the left cheek. Each man stood five-feet five-inches, but that's where the resemblance stopped. The Don looked muscular and fit, tufts of white hair circled his bald dome. Outwardly his face appeared grandfatherly gentle, with dark intelligent eyes.

"Cardinal John, it's so good to see you. Why do we wait so long to see old dear friends, eh? We are together now, so welcome." The Don held his friend's elbow and guided him into an exquisite sitting area. "Please sit…sit old friend. Make yourself comfortable." The Don raised his hand. "Bruno, please bring his Eminence a glass of Anisette. The best in Sicily, you will like it!"

"Thank you Don Ricardo. I am honored that you take time from a busy schedule to visit an old friend. Your beautiful wife Florence, and your special grandchild Marco, how are they?"

"Florence is Florence; she will never change…attends Holy Mass every day praying for my soul. Marco, as you know, is a special child, my only grandson; he is well and growing like a Sicilian weed. Speaking of family…two weeks ago, I saw your brother Roberto at a business meeting. He spoke more about his brother the Cardinal than his own children. You are a man highly regarded by your family and all of Calabria."

In an act of humility, Capaldo humbly nodded, lifting both hands with palms up to indicate a reluctant acceptance.

"Because our time is limited I've taken the liberty of ordering lunch. For an appetizer, fried calamari and the hotel chef is preparing Florence's homemade ravioli with ricotta and spinach. Made especially for you."

"Your wife's ravioli," Capaldo kissed his fingers, "are the best in Sicily.

Please thank her and convey my best wishes. I'll say a special prayer for her."

A gracious host, Don Ricardo made sure his important guest was offered fine wine, exquisite delicacies and pleasant light conversation about old friends and local politics. Under normal circumstances, Capaldo would have enjoyed the food, companionship and the chance to catch up on events in Sicily and Calabria. Unfortunately, he was too keyed up to enjoy the food or conversation. His mind speculated about the various reasons why the Don requested this unusual meeting.

The Don was a traditionalist in the same mold as Marconi and followed the same Old World etiquette. He knew his guest preferred a much more direct approach to matters.

Much of what his host said was lost on Capaldo. His mind preoccupied thinking, guessing and worrying. His head automatically nodded to the beat of the sound bouncing off his ears. Finally, the meal was complete and the espresso served. The Don could discuss business at his leisure. The waiter cleared the table and the bodyguards retired to the adjoining room.

"Eminence, we have known each other since our misspent youth. You're not a patient man, so I thank you for indulging me." The seconds ago warm and friendly middle-aged face leaned forward, transforming into an expressionless mask. He wanted Capaldo to fully comprehend the seriousness of this matter.

"You asked the local capo for, shall we say, an accommodation to help you with a problem. He spoke with his superior Don Marcello, who contacted me to discuss your request. This favor has far reaching consequences to the Family in Italy and abroad. Don Marcello and I felt because this request came from a respected friend, it was due full consideration and we discussed it with the entire Family council. As your sponsor, I presented the request and it was discussed in great detail. As they say, we looked at the pros and cons. The council voted, and, my old friend, this is something we cannot do."

This powerful man, a Prince of the Church who exerted so much influence in the Vatican and through out Italy, suddenly felt used, belittled and betrayed. Inside he screamed *Fucking idiots*! Using all his will power to maintain composure, he asked, "Don Ricardo, with all due respect, does the council understand what will happen if the Vatican Bank ends our joint business venture?"

Maintaining eye contact, the Don leaned back into the soft cushion. "My friend, please allow me to explain. Our business has always survived; we will find other banks. The organization cannot permit a scandal involving death and assassins in the Vatican. Christians, especially Catholics, who look the other way about gambling, prostitution and money laundering, will quickly change their attitude. People rationalize our activities as business. The actions you contemplate can never be justified as simply business. The council's decision is final. No scandal involving the Pope's welfare can be traced back to the Family...we *will* protect our reputation! I hope old friend, we fully understand each other?"

This was the first time Capaldo truly comprehended this man was never a friend. He felt used and abused, cast out when he needed a friend the most. "Naturally I am disappointed. While I don't think it's the right decision, I accept the council's ruling. And appreciate you telling me in person."

"Now old friend, I've detained you from a busy schedule." The Don rose and buttoned his suit jacket, signaling the meeting had ended. "My associates will escort you to the lobby."

Clasping farewell, four hands intertwined, Capaldo maintained his exterior composure, while seething with anger at his rejection. He predicated his grand plan on assistance from Don Ricardo's people. Ever the optimist, he thought, *Ah just another minor setback, a short detour*; he wasn't about to give up. Descending to the lobby it dawned on him there was no real reason to discuss this with Wronowski. *Let him believe the Palermo Family is still backing the plan.*

Giorgio waited in the lobby smoking a crumbled stogie, talking on his cell phone. Seeing his boss walk toward the main entrance he quickly ended the conversation. Giorgio could tell by the cardinal's limp jowls this wasn't a good time for idle chit-chat. In route back to the Vatican, Capaldo asked when Ms. Murphy was scheduled to return. Giorgio didn't have an exact date but said definitely within two weeks.

Giorgio was an independent driver and worked for Cardinal Capaldo and others as needed. He knew the Cardinal through Roberto Capaldo, the cardinal's brother and Mafia capo. Although Giorgio liked Signorina Kate and would never intentionally do her harm, his first allegiance would always be to the Capaldo family.

Returning to the office, Capaldo canceled all appointments and instructed his secretary to hold all calls unless it was an emergency. He needed uninterrupted time to think around this obstacle. With a contact in the IRA he could by-pass the Family and negotiate directly with the Irish leaders.

Part of the unification treaty called for disbanding the IRA. In reality, the group simply went underground and changed their name. Past and present leaders of the subversive organization were kept ultra-confidential to avoid retaliation.

After the Don's warning, it wasn't prudent to even remotely ask for information from his other contacts in the Family, especially his brother. He thought about talking to Dublin's cardinal, and decided against it. He also doubted the Irish cardinal would acknowledge knowing IRA members, much less leaders. He vaguely recalled another source of information; he just had to remember from where. The telephone rang, interrupting his concentration when he specifically asked not to be disturbed.

"Pronto, what is it?"

"Eminence, I'm sorry to disturb you. Yesterday you asked me to remind you about a 3:30 meeting regarding the mission projects."

"Thank you, Ms. Liberto, I may have to cancel. If so, I will let you know."

He was sick of bullshit meetings conducted by the Pope's lackeys. *Mission contributions*, he thought sarcastically, *if they only knew how much money Wronowski diverted to his slush fund.* Hanging up the telephone his thoughts raced back to solving his dilemma. That's it, yes, yes, contributions to the IRA. He recalled that in the late 1990s, Bishop Dunbar helped the IRA with fundraising in the United States.

His fat lips parted while picking up the phone. "Ms. Liberto, please connect me via videophone with Bishop Dunbar, in Philadelphia, USA. Let him know it's urgent that I speak with him. Also, notify the committee that I can't attend the 3:30 session. Thank you."

Bishop Dunbar was pleased to hear from Capaldo. It had been some months since they last spoke. Cardinal Capaldo cut directly to the chase: Someone should warn the IRA about the Pope's plan to attack United Ireland's human rights record and specifically attack the IRA's influence on the campaign against Protestants.

So often the source of personal information about Pope Alex, Dunbar was more than willing to help and offered the name of an old friend, a low ranking member of the IRA. He also volunteered to call ahead and smooth the way for communication with a Vatican emissary.

Capaldo intentionally bypassed Cardinal Belfonte, and called Major Bordeau, requesting an immediate meeting. Belfonte was a lackey and expected to simply follow instructions without knowing the master plan; only Capaldo, Wronowski and Bordeau would be privy to the inner circle.

While giving the major guidance on negotiations with the IRA, he never mentioned Palermo's decision not to participate. The major was assigned to contact Kevin Donovan and schedule a two-day trip to Ireland, spending the first day with the Irish National Security people, the second day with Donovan.

Capaldo suggested flying into Dublin and departing from the more remote Shannon Airport. He also suggested the major meet with the IRA and outline the Pope's plan to attack Ireland's human rights issues and the IRA-backed politicians. "Major, when the time is right, discuss our common problem, namely the Pope and how he intends to make sweeping changes at the Vatican. Then lead into a conversation about our common business partners in Palermo. Drop Mafia names from this list. Remember to stress a common theme: Stop the Pope from causing trouble for the IRA, the Vatican and the Crime Family."

Capaldo became excited; hands and arms gesticulated in every direction as he stressed the final phase of negotiations. "The Pope's visit is a perfect opportunity for IRA experts to solve our common problem and place blame on the Protestants. After you have piqued their interest, play the cash card. If his people are willing to take the risk, our group and Palermo will fund the project. Make sure you and the headman are the only people discussing payment. This allows him to take his cut off the top. Offer $5 million for their participation for procuring the hit man and pay offs to police and politicians. You're authorized up to $ 9 million. Above that, Cardinal Wronowski or I need to approve the amount.

"While in Ireland only contact the Vatican if it's an emergency. I don't want a record of calls from Ireland. Details will just have to wait until your return. If you finalize negotiations start working on the actual plan. Do you have any questions?"

This was a huge undertaking and beads of sweat formed on Major Bordeau's forehead, the underarms of his shirt stained from perspiration. Keyed up didn't adequately express the way his body twitched inside and out. With super human effort he forced himself to sit still. At the same time he was flattered by the confidence Capaldo and the Vatican Secretariat of State placed in him. He shook his head. "No questions."

Capaldo offered a proverbial pat on the back. "Good, good. I have the utmost confidence you'll work through this. If you think of anything before leaving, contact me. Remember only you, Eminence Wronowski and I are cleared on this subject."

Escorting the major toward the door, he placed a pudgy hand on his shoulder. "Go with my blessing and report back to me as soon as you return."

Chapter Eighteen

Monsignor Haggerty's interview wrapped up, Kate and Jay returned to the downtown Marriott and grabbed a late lunch at Tony's famous cheese steak house. Although there's plenty of competition, Tony's promoted itself as the "best of the best" for cheese steaks and chicken cheese steaks. As first time visitors, they couldn't make a comparison but did agree the cheese steaks were worth a trip to Philadelphia.

Back at the hotel they video conferenced with headquarters to discuss options on how to compile and produce the video. By seven o'clock, Kate felt exhausted, rapidly losing interest. She felt it was better to stop and work on the project when they were both fresh. Because of the early quit, the night seemed to drag. Jay, on the other hand, was revved up and ready to scout some gay bars a few short blocks away on 13th Street.

Kate called her parents in Canada to update them on events in her life and catch up on family matters. She also had a lengthy conversation with Matt about his job and when they would see each other. If the interviews continued on track she'd be back in New York by late Thursday afternoon or early evening at the latest. Television didn't hold her interest so by 9 p.m. Kate lounged in bed reading a magazine, ready for sleep.

Just as she began to doze the telephone chirped. Reaching for the phone she cautiously wondered who could this be. She'd already spoken with work, Matt, her parents, and Jay was out. She answered in a deep voice, "Hello?"

"Is this Ms. Murphy?"

A man's voice. She instinctively sat up and pulled the covers to her neck.

"Who's calling?"

"Kate, this is Pope Alex. So glad I found you in the room. Can you speak privately?"

She expelled a sigh of relief. "Yes, Holy Father, it's so nice to hear your voice. I should have called Brother Jacomo with an update but we've been extremely busy."

A little white lie, the interviews were going well, better than expected. At the same time, progress on compiling and editing the video lagged behind schedule. The production team at GNN ran into difficulty on the approach and overall presentation. Until they nailed it down the video couldn't be completed. The Holy Father had enough to worry about.

"Brother Jacomo's resourceful and gets updates from your boss at GNN. I know you've been very busy meeting our schedule. The people you interviewed have complimented your professionalism. Thanks for making this process easier on everyone. I hear the video production is a bit behind."

Kate immediately thought, *Great, the Pope's playful tonight. He wants me to know he also has resources.* "You're welcome Holiness, it's my pleasure. Don't fret about the video, we'll make the deadline!"

"Excellent. Now, the other reason I called is to discuss your final, possibly most revealing interview. Leigh is very important to me, a link to my past and present. This could be difficult, maybe traumatic for her. Her mood may swing during the interview; stay with it. Deep down she's a good and caring person. Things may get a little hot, but the fire arrows won't be directed at you. If you're searching for the truth, go where she leads you. She can help tie up loose ends, especially if you need direction on how to tie the biography together.

"Oh, I almost forgot…the GNN advance team called. They set a date to meet with our Vatican media people. Well, that's my list of things to discuss. If we don't have any other items, it's late and I have big a day tomorrow. If you don't mind I'll say *buona notte*."

"I understand, Holy Father. Thanks for the advice…have a pleasant night."

Kate, the trained observer, latched on to the Pope's style. Polite and gracious, he also controlled the conversation, and minimized dialogue, when he chose to.

Earlier she spoke to Ms. Stevens confirming the appointment. Ms. Stevens requested a change in location from her travel agency office in Villanova to her home in Wayne, Pa. They decided on 9:30 a.m.

Kate and Jay finished breakfast and waited for the valet to deliver the van by 8:00. KYW traffic reported heavy volume heading west out of the city, so they opted for an early start. Jay drove the van while Kate navigated the unfamiliar streets. Though the in-vehicle direction finder provided specific directions, Kate watched for landmarks and street signs to help Jay find his way through the crowded city streets to the expressway—not always an easy feat in Philadelphia.

The smell of fresh brewed coffee filled the cozy kitchen as Leigh Stevens, a creature of habit, snuggled in her bed. Each morning at 6:15 the familiar radio sounds of B101 gently woke her. Hitting the snooze bar gave her precisely 15 more minutes. At 6:30 during the news and weather report, she mentally organized her day. This particular morning her mind ran rampant. She tried to fathom why she agreed to an interview with GNN; her entire life was about to become a public spectacle. Anthony had explained how important it was that the public had a clear understanding of their relationship. After all that's happened, she still couldn't refuse him. His position as Pope had little to do with it. Leigh wasn't one to be influenced by other peoples' opinion. At sixty-two years of age and a colorful life, why would she?

Lying in the security of the nice comfy bed she once shared with her former lover, Leigh's mind instantly replayed the past twenty years. Her memory was drawn back to the period right after Anthony revealed his wishes to end their four-year relationship. Where have the years gone? At the time all she could do was ask how could this happen to two people who were so very much in love? It was a mystery to her then and quite honestly, still somewhat of a mystery. Though, at this point in her life she tried not to dwell on mysteries too much. She'd rather deal in reality. Although it wasn't the road she would have naturally chosen, it was a road filled with twists and turns that made for a very memorable ride. The familiar sound of the day's forecast forced her back to the present and into the shower. The appointment with Kate and her videographer was less than two hours away and she wanted to look her best.

The journalists drove through the Main Line's beautifully landscaped streets and found themselves on a very busy highway facing one of the largest shopping malls in the country.

"We can't be too far now, Jay. I remember Joan telling me that if we can steal a few hours to shop, the King of Prussia Mall is practically around the corner from Ms. Stevens's home. We'll see how long this takes and if we can, I say you and I go on a little shopping spree. What do you think? Are you up for it?"

Kate glanced over to her sidekick and saw a broad grin appear. Jay had evolved shopping into an art form. Like an old married couple, they read each other's minds and understood the other's likes and dislikes. Intuitively she knew there would be no argument from Jay.

Making a left turn on to Knightsbridge Road, Kate recalled Rosemary Di Marco's take on Ms. Stevens and wondered how this meeting would play out. She wanted to meet this special woman who lost the love of her life to the most unlikely competition. Kate wondered how Ms. Stevens managed to remain a trusted friend to His Holiness after he broke her heart. Kate was ready to discover the answer to this and many other pressing questions very soon. Jay pointed and pulled up to the curb.

As Leigh Stevens welcomed Kate and Jay into her home the visitors felt like old friends. A warm and inviting home is a reflection of its owner. She decorated with overstuffed furniture in warm colors. Photographs of loved ones greeted everyone who entered the great room. Each photo told a story all its own. One couldn't help notice the prominently placed 8" x10" gold-framed photograph of Leigh and Pope Alex, taken on one of her pilgrimages to Rome. They made an attractive couple, there was no denying the chemistry between them. The average nosey person would definitely speculate about Ms. Steven's Vatican visits. Pictures don't lie and Kate could only imagine how they appeared together in public, regardless of how innocent their relationship is…or is it? Kate prepared to sort through those questions.

Leigh said, "Please, let's get settled in the living room. I'll pour some coffee and we'll have a bite to eat. Then we can get started…if that's all right with you. I'd feel a little better if we got to know each other before I bare my soul to you guys."

With that, Leigh Stevens winked and headed off to the kitchen before they could answer. Kate looked at Jay and thought, *Without a doubt Ms. Stevens is a take-charge kind of lady.*

Each selected a comfortable spot in the living room; Kate on the love seat, figuring Leigh would sit opposite her on the sofa. Jay selected an oversized chair and checked the lighting conditions. Two palladium windows at the far end of the great room filled the living area with sunshine. He placed the equipment to take advantage of the natural light. The room had a cozy feel. The sofa beckoned, grab a good book and curl under the warm afghan that was casually thrown over its back. She had positioned the loveseat to chat on the phone with feet propped up on the coffee table. Snickers and Reese's Peanut Butter cups sat in candy dishes within arms reach. The room was obviously filled with creature comforts to help people feel right at home. Jay sensed that on any given day he'd be very happy in this cozy setting.

Leigh returned with a tray of coffee, cream, sugar and a box of Suzy Jo's famous cream and jelly donuts. "You haven't lived until you've eaten one of these babies," she said placing the tray on the coffee table. "And I don't want to hear a word about fat calories, diets or any such nonsense. After all, it's not every day one gets to interview the Holy Father's former significant other! Now, please help yourself and then we'll get down to brass tacks." She gave the directive as if they were two small children being instructed to "Eat their veggies." They both reached for a fresh donut.

Leigh nodded. "They're incredible, aren't they? I knew you'd enjoy them. I always get them when the kids come by. It's kind of become a little ritual. They always know that 'Lee Lee' will have their favorite cream donuts and under no circumstances are they to tell their mom and dad about our secret. Little do they know that their parents grew up on the same special treat."

The "kids" that Leigh referred to belonged to her sister, Grace and brother, Joe…five nieces and one very spoiled nephew, who were the apples of her eye. From the looks of the photos around the room, the "kids" had been just about everywhere with their "Lee Lee." Anyone could see that it was very much a mutual admiration society. The love was clearly evident in the photos and it was hard to tell who was having more fun—Lee Lee or the kids.

"Okay, where do you want me to begin? It's been a while since I told the whole story and I'm kind of looking forward to it. It really is a great 'love story' and the ending sure beats the hell out of the usual, 'and they lived happily ever after'…so Kate, I'll let you do your job. Just ask me whatever it is you want to know. I promised Anthony that I'd be my normal honest self. He just smiled when I said that, because he knows that only God knows what's going to come out of this mouth next."

At that point Kate was near speechless. She didn't expect Ms. Stevens to be so candid so early on. *What an interview*, Kate thought. She hadn't been the one asking the questions so far. Leigh controlled the meeting. When the subject's cooperative, Kate let the person continue.

"Well, Ms. Steven's—"

Leigh excused herself once again, "Oh please, Kate, call me Leigh."

"Okay, Leigh, why don't you start from the beginning? I'm settled in here and Jay looks rather comfortable, so why not just begin."

That was all the encouragement she needed. There was nothing as important as telling her story. As Ms. Stevens began, Kate saw the sadness that crept into the sparkling brown eyes of this vibrant woman.

"Anthony and I met on a blind date arranged by my brother, of all people. Anthony was Joe's General Manager. Marie had passed away, and my brother told Anthony he had a sister he wanted him to meet when Anthony was ready. He thanked Joe, and told him when he was ready he'd ask for my telephone number. Well, not too long passed and Joe mentioned that his boss was going to call me. I hadn't had a date in many moons, and my only requirement for a man was to have a pulse and no nose hair, so I was thrilled! Actually, I figured I'd be a good first date for someone who hadn't been on a date in the twenty-three years. I was easy to talk to and open up if he needed to.

"I lost my mother and stepfather at about the same age as Marie when she passed. I raised two kids who were about the same age as his, so there was some common ground. I assumed that Joe, Anthony, and I would meet some night for drinks. It might be a little easier meeting me for the first time, but he didn't want that. He wanted to call me and go out alone. I remember thinking he sure did have 'balls'...oh excuse me, I didn't mean to offend you or anything, but I mean really, not having been out for twenty-three years and he'd rather do it cold turkey! This could be one special man." Leigh hesitated for a moment and then added, "Or one stupid man...back then, the jury was still out."

She continued on about never being apart after that first blind date. Her body never rested, her whole being fully animated from head to feet, some part of her continuously moving.

"Our happy hour drink turned into dinner, which led to a date for the weekend and so on and so on and so on. We were very comfortable being together. Just felt right. He was always up for anything I suggested. The man never said *No*. The relationship had a good balance. My life was always so hectic, running here, there and everywhere. I have lots of very good girlfriends and two wonderful sisters who had just began relationships. So it all jelled. And of course, my friends and sisters loved Anthony. A real 'keeper,' I believe the saying went.

"Every woman's dream. I always said he fell right from heaven. Little did I know at the time that those words would ring so true! Anyway, our life was very different from his former married life or mine for that matter. Anthony and Marie had a good marriage, from what I could determine. Otherwise, he'd never get involved so quickly after her death. But let's face it, a brand new relationship between two people who are old enough to stay out passed midnight without asking permission versus a relationship of twenty-some years and three kids, whew! Looking back, I'm sure we set everyone's tongues wagging! So damn happy and we looked it; we glowed."

Pausing for a second, she grinned. Kate could tell reliving her courtship wasn't a hardship. It was in her voice, she had genuine affection for this man who many years ago shattered her every dream. Kate wondered why Leigh wasn't bitter. How could she speak so gently about him?

Leigh must have been reading Kate's mind because the next words out of her mouth were, "I know...how can I speak so kindly about the man who, let's face it, dumped me?"

The words almost knocked Kate over. "Well...yes. That's exactly what I was thinking, if you must know."

Leigh laughed. "Believe me, you're not the first person to question my sanity. I'm sure you got a very different take on this whole situation when you interviewed my lovely Rosemary!" Kate couldn't help grin as she recalled how Ms. Di Marco wanted to "kill the bastard" after breaking her best friend's heart.

"You know that old saying: Hell hath no fury like a woman scorned? That's what everyone expected. But you see, it's much more difficult for those who love you to watch you in pain. All they see is the pain and the times you are sad. But I'm blessed with wonderful memories. Those memories I shared with this man will last a lifetime, and that's what helps me through to this day. No one, not even the BIG GUY upstairs can take them away from me." Leigh's eyes sparkled as she looked at the journalists trying to gauge their level of understanding.

"Kate, I presume you had an opportunity to spend some quality time with Anthony?" Kate shook her head yes. "Let me tell you folks, what you see is what you get. He's a very simple man. At times I'd call him simple minded, and he of course laughed. But seriously, I have never to this day met anyone quite like him. I always said there's a kind of innocence about him that helps him see the good in people or a situation. Don't get me wrong; he's no pushover, but he always manages to stay cool and level headed, look at all sides of a story before making any decision. He makes me see that *my way* is not the only way to view a situation, which also takes courage." Leigh half chuckled. "I guess I can sum it up very simply. He was and is fair... a man of the highest integrity. Now you tell me, how can I harbor any ill feelings after having been loved by a man of that caliber? It also helps that he didn't leave for another woman," Leigh added in her very dry way. Then in her usual fashion, smiled and added, "Anyone ready for a refill?"

Kate began to understand what she heard during previous interviews. Leigh Stevens was a very special lady. However, in Kate's opinion, "special" didn't even begin to cover this woman. Kate found herself drawn to Leigh's honesty and sensed that she had no regrets about the relationship. Perhaps a sadness, but definitely no regrets. No way is this woman a victim. Leigh Stevens held on to every bit of good that blessed her life and rid herself of the useless bitterness that made people ugly. Kate felt certain that's what made Leigh such a beautiful person. She was genuinely happy and so was her heart.

Leigh refilled Kate's cup, but Jay shook his head. A one cup limit; otherwise he'd be jittery all day. Leigh had half a cup and another half of cream donut. "Okay, what else do we need to cover? I don't want it getting back to the old Pope that I'm uncooperative."

Kate felt compelled to cover two more areas. One concerned the Pontiff's children and their relationship with Leigh. The other area, a delicate issue that was on everyone's mind--Leigh's and Anthony's intimate life. Kate was in a quandary, what to broach next, when once again Leigh made a flawless segue.

"I'd like to address one more area that is obviously on everyone's mind and that's our private life. Although I have no problem discussing *my* sex life, which at the present time is virtually non-existent, I do feel a loyalty to Anthony to have a level of decorum regarding *our* sex life. Did we share an intimate life? Yes, of course we did. We were in love. Was it wonderful? Beyond wonderful, because we were so much in love. Do I miss it? You bet your sweet life I do. Why, you might ask? Isn't it obvious, guys, because I still love him?" Leigh sank back into the sofa with a sparkle in her eyes, looked at Kate then Jay, their reaction predictable.

Jay visibly squirmed behind the camera, felt like he just read the most intimate details of a stranger's diary, yet there really were no details described. No sordid details that you wouldn't want your mother or children to hear— just pure emotion. The kind of emotion you hold in for people who don't return your love. In Leigh's case, her Anthony couldn't love her back. Years later there can still be an ache in the heart that never quite goes away, and at times still hurts like hell.

Leigh sensed she had just made both guests uncomfortable by her candor, and quickly tried to rebound. "Listen guys, please don't read any more into this than there is. Sure, I still love Anthony, but I'm not 'in love' with him. Those feelings went away a long time ago. Good thing you didn't interview me right after the break up. It wasn't pretty. I'm human, you know. Believe me, there would have been more bleeps in that interview than you could shake a stick at. But like I said before, time heals all wounds. I feel very blessed to have had a relationship with this wonderful man. Can you imagine how hard it was to tell me he was entering the priesthood?"

She actually laughed. "HA! If you only knew how ironic it was, given my past life. Not that I have a checkered past or anything…shall we say it's a memorable life and it almost stands to reason this would happen to me! Well, at least he wasn't gay!" Looking right at Jay and winked and added, "Not that there's anything wrong with that. This added drama of the priesthood put the finishing touches on my life story."

Leigh sat forward and turned serious as she continued to explain. "After a while, I knew that Anthony had to do what was in his heart. I respected his choice. To this day, I can honestly tell you that I have never tried to influence him otherwise.

"Certainly not the type of tidbit that sells novels, but it's God's honest truth. We built a new relationship based on respect and friendship. After all, we already had one built on tawdry cheap sex and that didn't work!"

Once again she caught Kate off-guard; however, Kate sensed this was Leigh's defense mechanism—always keep them off guard, and above all, always leave them laughing.

The rest of the interview progressed casually; touching on subjects that brought back many pleasant memories. Leigh shared stories of summers at the Jersey shore. They shared many cool summer nights on their deck with family and friends. She pulled out photo albums of their travels around Europe and also flipped through the family album that she treasured the most, pictures of Pope Alex's children and grandchildren.

"At first," she explained, "Gina and Steve had a hard time accepting me so soon after their mother's death. Having lost my mother at about the same age, I tried to be patient and wait for them to come around. Steve came around first. He and I established our own grounds for a relationship and it works well for the both of us. I never tried to be his mother, although I often pray to Marie to help guide my relationship with the kids. Gina's another story. She just had too many issues that stood in the way of establishing any sort of deep relationship. We still aren't as close as I'd like."

A deep regret lingered. Leigh actually felt sorry for Gina because she was missing out on a relationship that could be beneficial for both of them. Anthony's son, Tom, from his first marriage, and their children gave Leigh the most support after the break-up. She developed a very close bond with Ashley, the Pope's granddaughter. She and Ashley had a standing date twice a month to get together and catch up.

Jay tapped his watch, a signal for Kate to check the time. It was almost noon. The morning had flown by, and what a morning. Both hated to leave; they truly enjoyed the company of this remarkable woman and couldn't help speculating about what would become of her after the interview aired. They'd make sure that the biography did her justice, treating her segment with the same respect that she treated her relationship with the Holy Father.

Jay finished loading his equipment into the van when Leigh walked Kate to the car. She handed Jay the rest of the donuts and leaned over to kiss his cheek. "Make sure you only use the shots taken from the right; it's my better side. It's been a pleasure, Jay. I hope I didn't ramble on too much. I'll never hear the end of it from my kids."

"The pleasure has been all mine Ms. Stevens—Leigh—and thanks for the donuts! Stay well."

As the two women hugged each other Leigh pulled back, keeping her arms on Kate's shoulders and looked directly into her eyes. "Promise me you will do all you can to protect him." An emotional Kate tried to answer, when in typical Leigh Steven's fashion, she continued, "Because I wouldn't want to have to hurt you." With that she kissed Kate on the cheek and headed back to the solace of her home.

Chapter Nineteen

Cardinal Capaldo had twenty minutes to review his notes prior to the Curia Directors meeting. He thought, *Another meeting, what a damn colossal waste of time and energy.* Regardless, he'd use any opportunity to find flaws in the Pope, personally, with his ideas, programs or philosophy. While packing his briefcase, the computer chimed, signaling an e-mail from Major Bordeau. Capaldo opened it right away.

> To: Cardinal Belfonte
> Bcc: Cardinal Capaldo
> From: Major Bordeau
> Reason: Security for papal visit.
> I have scheduled a two-day trip to meet with the Irish Government to discuss security. I leave early tomorrow and will provide an update on my return. Arrangements have been made to ship the Popemobile. The Italian Anti-terrorist forces are providing five experts to support our security team.

The cardinal felt pleased with himself, thinking, *Excellent news!* After a successful contact, he hoped the major could close negotiations without direct assistance.

His smile lasted all the way to the meeting. The good mood evaporated as he entered the meeting room. The Pope scowled at his late arrival, while not commenting he stared the Cardinal down. Capaldo felt obligated to apologize for delaying the start and with a long puss selected a seat as far away from the Pontiff as possible.

The Pope stood beside the lectern facing the attendees. "Now that we are all present," he said somewhat sarcastically, "it's time to begin. Today's agenda will cover three topics: 1) Eminence Hildabrand, champion of the committee on vocations will present a status on the their preliminary recommendations. 2) I will discuss the upcoming Papal tour and 3) an open question and answer session to discuss any topics of interest. Eminence Hildabrand, will you please begin?"

Hildabrand stood and passed around copies of the full report before moving to the lectern.

"Holy Father and directors, you can read copies of the full document at your leisure. Today I will present a summary of findings to date and a list of recommendations for improving vocations."

He cleared his throat and looked at Capaldo, trying not to smile. "It's no surprise to any member of the Catholic Church that religious vocations have declined almost every year since the 1970s. The only exception is in the countries supported by our missionary activities. This is a very grave issue with far reaching implications on the Church's ability to sustain the religious well being of its members. Most industrial first-world countries have one priest and possibly a deacon ministering to three and four churches. This system is referred to as a 'cluster parish.'

"Although the clergy works long hours and are stretched to the limit, we often fail to meet the minimum expectations of our parishioners. The priests are aging and nuns are almost extinct. In some remote locations, Holy Mass and Communion are celebrated monthly instead of daily. At this rate of attrition our religion could be just a shell in fifty years. After an extensive study of the issues, the committee recommends considering the following reforms."

Hildabrand used slides to project the recommendations on an overhead screen. After highlighting each subject with a red laser pen he read the recommendation.

SISTERS
*There are too many orders to support the decreasing number of active sisters. Consolidate orders into three groups: teachers, health care and social work.
*Allow sisters to marry after making their vows

*Sisters must receive an adequate salary that permits them to live outside a convent.

*Permit sisters to become deacons

BROTHERS

*Allow brothers to marry after making their vows

*Brothers must make an adequate salary that permits supporting a family

*Expand training so they can have dual roles as Brothers and Deacons

PRIESTS

*Increase recruiting in third-world countries. Relocate young men to seminaries in countries that desperately need priests.

*Five years after ordination, permit relocation to other dioceses or countries.

*Recruit additional deacons, including sisters and brothers to support priests

DEACONS

*Expand the role of Deacons in the Church."

His voice came across monotone, dull and almost lifeless. As head of the committee he was obligated to present their recommendations, although he vehemently opposed most of them. "The committee recommends announcing the changes with a massive advertising/recruiting campaign. Send an emissary to each congregation asking for continued prayer for vocations, especially from their parish. These are preliminary recommendations; I suggest you read the entire study for discussion during our next meeting."

Pope Alex believed the committee was on the right track. At the same time he was extremely annoyed at Hildabrand's callous presentation and lack of enthusiasm. He quickly judged that the Cardinal didn't agree with any of the suggestions on the list and decided his Eminence would be excused from the committee the moment the meeting adjourned.

Hildabrand bowed slightly to the Pontiff and returned to his seat. Judging by their reaction, the directors did not appear to be impressed with the recommendations or presentation. The Holy Father took a second to steel himself before taking the floor to address a group that contained at least three enemies intent on his destruction. "Thank you, Eminence, for presenting the group's recommendations. I'm sure the directors will have much to discuss after reading the entire report. I suggest postponing questions until everyone reads and digests the document."

The Pontiff stood near the lectern with his back flat against the wall, symbolic of his present plight. His white robes blended with the pure white wall, and he appeared to be a head suspended without a body. He began, "Moving on to topic number two...I am personally excited about our visit to Somalia and United Ireland. Both countries are in turmoil. They need our support, daily prayers and in the case of Somalia, massive economic aid. Unfortunately, this morning we were notified that the Somalian government cancelled the visit because of rebel assaults on two cities and terrorist attacks in the capital. I hope to reschedule the visit when conditions improve. The food and clothing we planned to deliver and distribute during the trip will be shipped and distributed by Catholic relief. For the good news—plans for the Ireland visit have been finalized; we leave in a few days."

His reticence to address the meeting faded rapidly, confidence returned with a vengeance. Stepping away from the security of the wall, Pope Alex began slowly pacing in front of the audience. "Many people, including some in this room, wonder why I chose United Ireland. On the surface the country has stabilized its economic and social issues. I believe this is not the reality. The peace in Ireland is extremely fragile and about to implode on the government. An Anglican Church report confirmed the information presented by our Vatican emissary who recently returned from Ireland.

"After the Papal trip was announced, a journalist from GNN contacted the Vatican media office asking for a comment on the escalating social problems in United Ireland."

Pope Alex was on a roll. His strong voice emphatically echoed through out the room. "We declined to give a statement because the purpose of this trip is a first-hand evaluation. The journalist has been working on an expose, which is scheduled for broadcast within days. As a favor to our new media director, Bishop Newhart, the journalist provided a draft copy of the video. Our media people have edited and shortened the video for today's meeting. With your indulgence, and so we all have a better understanding of the situation, Bishop Newhart will play the abbreviated clip. Bishop, please start the video."

The bishop inserted the tape and hit play; the picture came into focus on a giant TV screen:

"Hello, this is Ken Stork reporting from United Ireland...... after months of investigation, this program will present a hard look at rumors of human rights violations and the resurgence of violence in six northern counties and terrorist activities in Dublin, the capital.... Before delving into the present realities, it may be helpful for some viewers, especially the younger generation, to look back into Ireland's history. As is so often the case, history repeats itself.... Ireland was one of England's first conquests and a Colony for over four hundred years. During that period there were numerous revolts and uprisings, which England resisted with an iron fist.... During this same period the English government encouraged immigration of English citizens, predominately Protestants, to Ireland. The English transplants were granted large tracts of Irish land....

"By the 1800s, the English controlled the farmland and businesses in the northern counties.... During the 'troubles,' that's how the Irish describe their struggle for independence, the IRA (Irish Republican Army) was born... The IRA fought back with guerilla tactics against the English government and the English colonists, eventually taking the fight to English soil...The IRA was responsible for numerous bombing deaths and political assassinations in England and Ireland.... England placed Ireland under a form of marshal law, and, often, suspected IRA members were jailed or executed without due process.... The IRA retaliated by executing English soldiers and politicians... and so the spiral continued, periods of peace and war....

"The 1916 uprising was widespread and violent. England was straining, contending with the 'troubles' in Ireland and World War I in Europe. It was time to negotiate a solution.... In 1921 Southern Ireland gained independence from England after signing the Anglo-Irish Treaty. The compromise allowed six northern counties to be excluded and remain part of the British Commonwealth, the counties heavily populated by Protestants of English decent....

"The new Irish Republic exploded in civil war over the six northern counties. In 1923, the civil war ended and Southern Ireland peacefully developed their country, while the "troubles" continued in the north: Catholics against Protestant or Irish against English, depending on how one defined the struggle. In the north, Catholics were second-class citizens socially and economically....

"...This situation continued for sixty years. Northern Ireland was heavily dependent on England for military support to protect them from the IRA and economic support to maintain their infrastructure.... Between IRA attacks on England and massive economic support the English Government sent to Northern Ireland, the English were ready to relinquish control

"...Late in the last century a peace treaty was signed and it held... Finally, three years ago England agreed to unite the six northern counties with the Republic of Ireland; the country was renamed United Ireland....The unification treaty outlined specific civil rights to protect the northern county Protestants and previous English supporters.

"That is the question under investigation. Has the treaty and the Protestants' civil rights been violated? The answer is an overwhelming 'yes,' and we will provide specific examples during this broadcast.... Three years after the unification, Catholics have systematically taken control of the local governments, police departments, public land and many business enterprises.... The Irish Army has troops stationed in the north to maintain the peace, which means to support the Catholic policies....This conflict has bred a new Protestant organization, the NIA (Northern Irish Army) for protection and to revenge civil rights violations.... History has indeed been repeated; however, with a complete role reversal. This time the Catholics are dominating and taking full advantage...."

"Bishop, please turn off the video." Pope Alex stood near his chair. "Before opening the general question and answer session, does anyone have any specific questions concerning the visit to United Ireland?"

Not one question was posed. He waited, scanning the room. He was a bit disappointed that no one openly supported the trip. "I hope no questions means you understand and agree that this is a necessary trip." He heard a few positive murmurs.

The weather outside changed rapidly. The mid-afternoon sky turned dark gray, almost black. Gale force winds shook the pine trees against the side of the stone façade. Pelting rain rattled the wooden windows and the antique French doors flew open, slamming against the inside walls. Wind and rain bellowed through the meeting room. The lights flashed off and on several times. Alex the Pontiff wondered if this was a harbinger of the storm to come in Ireland.

Returning to the podium, the Pontiff waited for the lights to come on before opening the general question-and-answer segment. The weather further dampened the directors' interest in the meeting. They asked a few questions, nothing of substance and no reference to Church doctrine. No one wanted to lift the lid on Pandora's box, certainly not in an open meeting.

ANGELO PAGNOTTI, SR.

After the meeting, Pope Alex and Cardinal Marconi spoke with Bishop Newhart and reviewed the status of GNN's progress. The bishop confirmed that the technical aspects were well under control. GNN equipment and manpower were scheduled. Once a room was selected, Vatican personnel would help clear the area so GNN could set up the equipment.

"Bishop, are you still joining the Papal group traveling to Ireland?" asked Pope Alex.

His front line public relations experience and enthusiasm fit perfectly into the Pope's short term and future plans. His sandy brown hair, easy smile and laughing gray eyes appealed to TV cameras. "Yes, Holiness. I am eager to join the group. It's my first visit to Ireland. It should prove fascinating."

"Glad to hear it. We need to make sure the trip is well documented, especially the stops in the north and our visit to the legislature."

"I understand, Holiness. Media people have been invited to travel with the Papal group with access to every segment of the trip. They will also provide a copy of any pictures or video footage. We can't edit their work, but we will have copies of the photos and video."

"Very good. Thank you. Again, welcome to the Vatican, this could very well be an experience of a lifetime. If there's nothing else, I would like a word with Eminence Marconi."

When the Bishop left, Pope Alex vigorously rubbed his hands together. "The Bishop is a find. The team is finally coming together. It's great working with qualified and eager people. Now to an important Church and personal matter: What to do about my old friend Bishop Dunbar. I think a promotion for his faithful service is in order."

Marconi involuntary flinched and his eyes narrowed. "How can you promote that snake?" Looking directly at the Pope, he realized the man was toying with him, a pleasant surprise. The Holy Father didn't often vocalize his sense of humor.

"Where is your Christian charity? Aren't we taught to turn the other cheek?" Playing along, Marconi nodded yes, curious to see where the Holy Father was taking this.

"Good, I'm so pleased you remember something from Bible school. Dunbar is currently an assistant to Cardinal Gates in Philadelphia. I want him to have his own diocese where he is in control, has full responsibility. The diocese in North Central New York State needs a bishop and it's a match made in the Vatican. My dear friend Dunbar enjoys the finer things in life— off-Broadway plays, the opera, fine dining and the upper crust Philadelphia social life. His new diocese is five hours from the nearest city even remotely offering similar amenities. It's an absolutely perfect diocese for the Bishop. He might even learn to yodel! Please ask Brother Jacomo to prepare the documents for my signature. Make the transfer effective immediately. The Bishop's earned his just rewards and the diocese will have a capable administrator. Do you agree?"

"Perfect Holiness," Marconi smiled, "absolutely perfect." Marconi had almost forgotten—Italian blood ran through the Pontiff's American veins.

Kate hated the feeling of running late, it put her on edge. Her catch up session with Matt lasted until the wee hours of the morning. Physically exhausted, she enjoyed every second of their vigorous lovemaking. Although running late, her thoughts flashed back to Matt. He liked to try different positions. Her whole body felt sore; he needed to realize they weren't acrobats, at least she wasn't.

Closing the apartment door, Matt cuddled under blankets trying to recover. In ten minutes Kate planned to call from her cell phone to make certain he got up. She didn't have to worry about catching the subway that morning. GNN had assigned a driver for the duration of the Papal assignment, certainly a welcomed perk. If Matt had been ready she would have given him a lift to mid-town. Oh well, his loss.

She arrived earlier than normal and the elevators were crowded, mostly with GNN employees. Kate knew many of the employees, some by name, others by sight. The elevator was quiet as a tomb until Marge, who worked down the hall in collections, couldn't contain her excitement and congratulated Kate on the Papal assignment. The biography broadcast was common knowledge so most of the riders ignored the conversation until Marge blurted out, "Well, Kate…is it true that the Holy Father is a womanizer, has a mistress and bastard children?"

Stunned, Kate hesitated for an instant. Everyone in the elevator heard the question, and human nature dictated they were all waiting to hear a reply. The ride would last at least another minute so Kate had to deal with the hanging question. Her mind raced. She could be non-committal and suggest that Marge watch the biography, or answer the question head on? In the coming months Kate would be asked this question a hundred times, possibly more, so she better get used to it.

Turning to look down at Marge, her hand squeezed into a tight fist. "The

Holy Father is a fortunate man who's been blessed with exceptional women in his life. However, none have been lovers since he became a priest. The children are from his marriages."

At first Marge seemed disappointed, had hoped for confirmation of the juicy rumors, but that was okay. She had fresh information for the secretarial pool and would play up what a fortunate man the Pope was. Knew it for a fact—heard it directly from the horse's mouth!

Kate fumed as she rushed out of the elevator, felt steam rising from singed hair. She wasn't just pissed at Marge but at all nosey and insensitive people. While cooling off, she realized this particular human trait kept journalists employed. Joan was occupied on the phone, Kate used hand gestures to mime "hello, need coffee and see me." While her computer booted up she checked voice mail. No urgent messages, just some items to resolve later in the week. Waiting for Joan, Kate's fingers nervously drummed the desk. *What's the hold up, Joan?* She wanted to yell. *I'm not in the office often, so get with the program.*

Joan peeked through the glass partition then opened the door while juggling two cups of coffee, a stack of mail and a note pad. Plopping in the old metal chair alongside the desk, she asked, "How is GNN's star journalist this morning?"

Moving a pile of old papers, Kate gave Joan an exaggerated smile. "Good but busy. How are you doing?"

"Just fine until my boss decided to come to work and disrupt morning nap time and probably the afternoon soap operas."

"I'm glad you still have a sense of humor, Joan. I plan to be here the rest of the week so get use to working for a change."

Both women smiled; each understood the other. Kate wanted immediate attention and Joan would comply as long as it didn't totally disrupt her work. Joan functioned as an administrative assistant for three journalists. Although Kate was the most demanding, she also liked and trusted her the most.

"Before getting too caught up in the day's events, how is my adopted godchild?"

Joan's face glowed whenever she thought about her only son. "He's recovering nicely from his accident. You know kids, way too full of juvenile spunk. Sends his love and thanks for the new video game."

"My pleasure. Some night I'll come over and he can teach me how to play. By the way, I haven't forgotten our lunch date. No matter how crazy the day becomes we will have lunch today. Call the caterer and speak directly to

Max. Order a top-of-the-line lunch and have it delivered. Let's eat in the small conference room. Just us with no interruptions."

"Consider it done, and thanks. Now, as you usually say, 'Down to business.' Jay's already working on the biography in editing room C. Here are three important memos that require your attention. I am sure you know the whole office is excited about the Papal assignment. Your competitors in and outside GNN are seething with jealousy...poor losers! Oh, the boss wants to see you at 10."

"When did Mr. Blake ask to see me?"

"Not Mr. Blake—the big boss, Convery."

Kate flashed a dismissive how-dare-you look. "Damn it! I...I should take back that lunch. You can really bust chops. That should've been my first message when I came into the office."

As a defense mechanism, Joan unconsciously tossed back her long hair. "Chill, woman. I was on the phone with his administrative assistant when you came in with that I'm-in-a-hurry look. Besides, he doesn't want to see you until 10 o'clock!"

"Okay...sorry. Didn't mean to fly off the handle."

"You're forgiven, almost."

"10 o'clock is good. Gives me time to see Jay and go over the editing." Kate abruptly stood, ending the discussion. "See you after my meeting with Mr. Convery."

She rode the elevator up to the technical staff area on the eighth floor. There was virtually no visible activity in the office area. Every "techie" was in a cubicle or editing room working, or playing on computers; surfing the net for information was a favorite pastime. Kate tried to open the editing room door; it was locked. She considered that strange. Jay should be in the room. A knock on the door brought no answer. "Damn it."

Frustrated, she dialed Jay's cell phone. "Hello Jay, where ARE you?"

"I'm in room C. Where are you?"

"Outside the room. I knocked no one answered. What gives?"

"Ah, this place has been like Grand Central Station with people taking a peek at the biography. I kicked them out and locked the door. Sorry, I didn't hear you knock."

The door opened and Kate crossed the threshold into a dark wonderland of electronic gadgets, a techie's dream. The gadgets held fascination and the technical staff enjoyed countless hours of editing and tweaking. Today, her main interest centered on the biography.

Within seconds Jay went back to work, totally engrossed in the high tech gear.

Kate hovered trying to get his attention. "One, two, three eyes on me."

Jay looked up very annoyed. "Yes, Ms. Murphy?"

"Jay, this is important. I need an update? I have a meeting with Mr. Convery and this project is sure to be first on his list. What's the time line, the estimated date of 100% completion."

"Give me a quick second. I just need to work this through." Ever so slowly and with patience he merged the information. "Okay, I will complete the cut and paste tomorrow. Together we can final edit and program background music in three full days. Management and legal have two days to review. At that point, assuming minor changes by the top dogs, we are good to go and the tape's off to Vaticanland."

"Great, that gives us a few days to spare just in case. Can you show me what's completed so far?"

At 9:50, Kate stepped onto the elevator and ascended to the executive floor to meet Mr. Convery, a pleasant, likable man in his mid-forties. In her industry, only sharks swim to the top floor, so although likable, continued and sustained top ratings were critical to his gainful employment. The express elevator opened directly into the executive reception area. Kate needed a moment to reorient. The enormous space had high ceilings and a wall of glass overlooking the city scape. The entire floor consisted of white Italian marble. Modern art and sculptures matched the décor. The receptionist smiled as she watched the visitor absorb the surroundings. People were usually wowed. "Ms. Murphy, Mr. Convery is expecting you. Please follow the hallway until you reach Grace, his executive assistant."

Evidenced by her palatial surroundings, Grace was a power broker in the organization. Her entire work area, just outside the big man's office, looked opulent. The desk, credenza and workstation were solid cherry. Modern art blended with the colors and design in the plush oriental rugs. A huge Waterford crystal vase overflowed with fresh cut flowers. Kate had once spoken to Grace at a company meeting. Their conversation was cordial and all business.

Grace saw Kate walk down the hall and, with a passive expression, greeted the visitor to her domain. "Hello, Kate, so nice to see you again. Mr. Convery is on the telephone; he should be free in a moment. Please have a seat."

Naturally, the visitor chairs faced Grace's work area. Toward the right, the windows overlooked the city and Central Park. Kate tried not to stare while Grace continued to work, although she couldn't help notice the collage of pictures on the credenza and the wall above. They were obviously family photos taken during vacations or holidays. She felt an urge to comment. "Excuse me Grace, what a wonderful collection of photos. You have a beautiful family." Kate rose and walked over to get a closer look.

Turning away from her voice-activated computer system, Grace offered a slight smile and replied in a much friendlier demeanor, "Why thank you. They are my children, husband and extended family. The list is endless. My favorites are Christmas and photos at the shore. We spend as much time as possible at the shore house. With all our friends and family, it's turned into an all-year resort."

"The picture on the left, the young girl with the mischievous smile sitting on the dock, is very pretty."

"Thanks. That's my daughter, Elisa. Beautiful but a real pip!"

"What shore, New Jersey or Long Island?"

"South Jersey, the small town of Tuckerton."

Hackles rose on the back of Kate's neck. She tried to control the flash of excitement. "Um…Someone recently mentioned Tuckerton. Yes, a person I just interviewed, Ms. Leigh Stevens. Do you happen to know her?"

Grace knew her—very well in fact. Leigh was related to Guy and Carmel, Grace's next-door neighbors. Reluctant to become embroiled in Kate's story, she responded with a vague answer. "Yes, I know Leigh, she's a casual acquaintance."

Kate contemplated pursuing the connection with Leigh Stevens when the intercom buzzed. "Mr. Convery is ready to see you. Good luck on your assignment!"

In the few seconds it took to enter the office, Mr. Convery was back on the telephone. He signaled Kate to be seated and put up one finger indicating he would be off in a minute.

Before selecting a seat she walked to the farthest corner of the office to look at the magnificent view of Central Park. Kate wasn't worried about this meeting. Although she felt confident in the progress to date and the final outcome of the assignment, she was somewhat anxious about why they were meeting alone. Normally her boss, Ted, would be present trying to suck up to Convery. She continued to scan the city scape until Mr. Convery hung up the telephone.

Easing around his desk, he offered his star journalist a formal handshake. "Kate, right on time. I've heard promptness is one of your hot buttons. How are you?"

"Very well, Mr. Convery, and my promptness is a phobia of sorts."

He moved to a cluster of easy chairs and sofa circling a modern wood and glass coffee table with no discernible style; simply there. Sitting in a straight back chair he motioned Kate to join him. She selected the sofa, a safe distance from the boss.

After the mandatory amount of small talk, Mr. Convery asked Kate for an update on Papal assignment. Once satisfied he had a clear understanding of the progress, he moved on to his next item.

"Good, appears everything is under control. This is an important project for GNN. If successful, which I'm sure it will be based on your update, our ratings will jump. Higher ratings give GNN an opportunity to increase market share, which translates into higher advertising rates. It also positions GNN to float additional company stock. If we can float additional stock every employee will receive company stock options. So you can imagine the employees have an interest in this project."

Touching an eyebrow to conceal an instant frown, Kate spoke in a controlled voice, "Not to be snide, Mr. Convery, but the last thing I need is more pressure, especially from peers."

Before answering he resorted to a nervous habit of smoothing out his hundred dollar silk tie. "I didn't tell you this to apply pressure, just that…ah…as a professional you need to know what events are in motion. You may notice an exceptional amount of camaraderie."

Still annoyed, Kate didn't back down from her comment. The silence made the boss uncomfortable. Staring across empty space neither spoke. Finally he looked away, breaking eye contact and offered Kate a drink. She politely declined and continued to wait, her breath shallow, unblinking, daring to glare at the boss. Mr. Convery squirmed under her direct gaze; he walked to the bar and poured seltzer water with a twist of lime. He wasn't looking forward to the next part of their conversation.

"The second reason I asked to see you is that another opportunity has been placed on GNN's door step and I want you to have first crack. The Vatican called; they are inviting GNN to travel with the Papal group touring United Ireland. They mentioned you because of the interview. However, they'll accept GNN's decision on the choice of journalists. Normally this assignment would go to Ken Stork, our British Isles expert, especially since he just completed an expose on Ireland. To be frank, he's *persona non grata* in some influential Irish circles. This is a great tie-in with the Papal project. Ireland's yours if you want it. I know it's short notice…they need an answer by the end of business today."

Expelling a short breath she blurted out, "This is out of the blue! I'd say the Pope's public relations efforts are shifting into high gear. On the surface it sounds great. You'll have my answer before end of business. Thanks for the vote of confidence."

Topping off the drink, he stood at his desk, flipping through a stack of paper, rubbing his chin as he mumbled to himself. Torn, he struggled with how to broach the subject. He abhorred mixing personal issues with business, especially asking a subordinate for a personal favor. Then again, this favor wasn't directly for him and he had promised to ask. "I'm sure you remember my wife, Monica. You met at last year's New Years Eve bash. You were in the lobby for half an hour talking about whatever it is women talk about when they first meet."

Still annoyed, she dug deep to switch on her charm, "Yes, I remember your lovely wife, and women never tell about first conversations."

Appreciating her humor, he snickered. "Well, Monica is a devout Catholic and is also fascinated with our American Pope. She asked me to ask you for a personal favor concerning the Holy Father." Kate's heart sank, expecting to be asked some impossible favor. "Ah…could you, would you, ask him, the Pope, to bless three gold crosses?"

So that's why I'm here, she said to herself. *That's the real reason for this little visit, a personal favor.* "My pleasure, Mr. Convery! I expect to meet his Holiness in two weeks or in a few days if I accept the Ireland assignment. I'll ask for his blessing on the crosses and a special Papal blessing for you and Monica."

Kate rose and accepted a black jewelry case. Mr. Convery took her hand, signaling the end of their meeting. "Thanks for the blessing and the update. If I can be of any assistance, don't hesitate to call me. My door is always open to valued associates."

Now he owes me one, ran through Kate's mind. "If need be, I will call you. Please say hello to Monica for me."

Lunch with Joan was an opportunity to catch up on things, mostly social friends and work gossip. Joan actually had to cut lunch short because of a rush deadline for another journalist. Back in the office, Kate mulled over the offer to join the tour. The assignment was definitely outside her normal expertise; however, versatility equaled experience. She had to discuss the offer with Matt—after all she promised him a full week at home. The trip didn't begin for three days; it wasn't like flying off within hours. *Matt can make this decision.* That way she lessened her feelings of guilt. Reaching for the phone, she said, "Call Matt," and the system dialed his number.

"Thanks for hearing me out. I did promise a full week at home. Ireland's not a must. I do have a choice. It's your decision, go or no go, no debate, no moaning. I need an answer in three hours, though…think it over and call me."

Feet up on the desk, he was calm and completely understanding. As long as Kate remained in the news business he had to maintain a level of flexibility. "It's not much of a decision. This is important to your career and Ireland has become a hot topic. If the stories are true, it needs as much spotlight coverage as possible. Besides, four days is about all I can take of togetherness. I have to ease into spending so much time together."

"You're wonderful. Thanks for being you."

"There's one condition. You can't under any circumstance miss dinner and the theater tonight. My mother is looking forward to the night out."

"Matt, I'm also looking forward to the evening with Bunny and Tim. See you at the restaurant. Love you!"

Chapter Twenty

Major Bordeau, in full dress uniform, more than a bit cocky and proud of his covert meeting, strutted into the office. He cut a rather dashing image, stood a tad under two meters tall with a lanky athletic build and longish black hair that often obscured his Germanic blue eyes.

"I counted on you breaking away from the office to give me an update," said Cardinal Capaldo. "Please have a seat and tell me everything that happened."

He sat at a small circular table, which forced the cardinal to leave his desk and sit at the table. "I spent the first day with a combination of security groups. The Dublin police will control security in the capital and Federal Security, a branch of the military, will manage security outside of Dublin.

"We reviewed the trip's itinerary hour by hour from landing to take off. Between the Swiss Guards and Italian anti-terrorist squad, we have eleven security people in our party. The federal and local police will work in unison and supply motorcade escorts, traffic and crowd control. As a precaution, the Popemobile and Italians will fly to Ireland in a military C-150 cargo plane arriving twenty-four hours before the main party.

"Security will be heaviest in the northern counties, especially Belfast. The head of security, Chief Inspector Black, is advising that the Pope limit his personal contact with the crowds. Emotions are running high since word spread about the upcoming GNN human rights broadc—"

"Cardinal Belfonte and Colonel Tearsue will be thrilled with the minute details, but I'm interested in the other meeting. Can you move to that please?"

This comment somewhat deflated the major. This first solo adventure was branded in his memory and he needed to recount every aspect of a journey that he could only discuss with Cardinals Capaldo and Wronowski. "Sorry, Eminence I just assumed you wanted an overview of the entire trip." The cardinal waved a hand as if to say "don't worry about it."

"Well, the second day was dark and damp and the ex-IRA people didn't make me feel warm and wonderful. The whole thing was eerie…yah, almost spooky. I met Donovan in a pub just outside Shannon on a desolate road; a good lookout can see anyone approaching for a kilometer up or down the pike. Donovan asked for my identification papers and a thumbprint. He offered a pint while we waited for confirmation of my identity. Once satisfied, he led me into the basement down a long musty tunnel into a large room with a single light bulb. I sat in the middle of the room, directly under the light. Reminded me of an old black and white police movie where suspects are quest—" Capaldo gave him a stern look but Bordeau ignored it continuing at his own pace.

"Anyway, there were three people in the room: the leader, Donovan and a bodyguard. The leader said the IRA disbanded about two years ago and they are a splinter unit, the Irish Retribution Group, IRG. He didn't offer his name and I knew better than to ask. Following your suggestions, I presented all the issues and players, suggested we work together to rectify the situation. They only asked a few questions so it was difficult to tell if they intended to cooperate. As I started to discuss eliminating the mutual problem, the leader asked his people to leave the room."

This was the most confidential part of the meeting and the major leaned closer. "When I completed the proposal he said, 'Ten million—six million up front in the next forty-eight-hours, wire transferred to two accounts. The other four million when the job is done, whether it is successful or not. I need an answer before you leave this room.'"

Taking a deep breath, the major looked for a reaction. The Cardinal's face looked hard as flint, so he continued. "Although the amount was above my approval limit, I agreed to the ten million. It was a yes or no situation." Proud of his decision, he leaned back in the chair with a wide grin. "I tried to negotiate the second payment of four million; if the job failed no final payment."

His voice sounded dry and raspy. "Hum, um… the leader wouldn't budge, so rather than queer our chance, I accepted the terms." He handed over a slip of paper. "Here are the two bank account numbers. Hum, ah…excuse me. If you want to move on this the funds have to be transferred by end of business tomorrow. Eminence, my throat is...can I bother you for a drink?"

Capaldo slumped in the chair, excited and giddy, hands intertwined behind his neck. "Help yourself, cold drinks in the fridge or liquor on the shelf. Excellent results, Major... excellent. Handled like a professional." He rubbed his chubby hands together. "So tell me... what happened next?"

Leaning on the bar sipping a single malt scotch over ice, the major continued with the end of his story. "The leader called Kevin Donovan into the room and instructed us to review the trip's itinerary and look for weak spots in security. The job has to be completed in the south before the Pope visits the Irish legislature. During the trip they'll give me instructions. I have to make sure there's a gap in security. That's all of it. Grabbed a flight late yesterday."

Still giddy, Capaldo clapped several times as he moved to the bar next to the day's hero. "We're going to move on this. Funds will be transferred early tomorrow. Our deepest thanks... you deserve a few days' rest, possibly a week's vacation on an island once the dust settles." Placing a hand on the center of the major's back, Capaldo tried to escort his conspirator to the door. "I don't mean to rush you but I have to tell the others."

The major held his ground and turned to face the architect of this ruthless plan. "Excellency, there is one other matter, if you don't mind. Ah...my part in this has escalated far beyond what I bargained for. Promotion to head of the Swiss Guards is small peanuts." He paused, watching for a reaction. Capaldo's face remained passive, impossible to read except for his eyes, they lingered on the major waiting for him to finish. "If you want my continued involvement, I expect two million U. S. dollars transferred into this account number." He handed over a folded paper with a Swiss Bank account number.

The Cardinal's imploring stare and slow articulation was meant to ruffle the puffed up officer. "I thought...hoped...you were part of the team working to protect the Church. This is a... a surprise I didn't expect."

The cold glass of Scotch camouflaged the major's sweaty palms; he didn't back down, waver or reduce his demands. Holding back a wince, the major's pasted-on smile faded. "I am part of the team but a star player expects his trophy, no?"

Feigning a deep sigh of disappointment, Capaldo thought, *This dupe has some spunk.* "Okay, consider this a one time bonus, a final payment. Once this is over if you implicate us you'll be condemning yourself. Do we understand each other?" The oversized peasant hand held the officer's right hand in a vice grip, the pressure slowly increased, sending an unmistakable message.

"Yes, Eminence, I'm not stupid, only want what's fair…what I *will* earn."

Bordeau left the office with financial security. Capaldo couldn't hold back a smile. In the major's position of power he could have asked for four million. Think small, ask small and get small.

Eating lunch in a private dining room, Capaldo and Wronowski discussed the major's report. Wronowski felt fortunate that he didn't have to meet with the officer. He wanted distance from the dirty work, didn't want to think about or deal with the realities. He couldn't say the words "death" or "murder" or the less ubiquitous "eliminate."

Capaldo sensed something in Wronowski's makeup didn't compute. He held a well-deserved reputation for anger and violent outbursts, not to mention doing whatever it took to gain his way, always Wronowski's way.

Yet, on this issue, Wronowski was having serious second thoughts. The whole idea of violence and murder to achieve Christian objectives was anathema. Anxiety attacks and night sweats became frequent companions. He felt this whole thing was out of control and the thought that their decision—his decision—would spawn a violent death, kept him in a state of deep depression. He didn't look his conspirator in the face. Couldn't deal with his sparkling brown eyes that exuded victory, so sure this was the right thing to do.

"That's all of it. Walter, early tomorrow you will process the requests to transfer funds into the four accounts totaling ten million U. S. dollars. When the Vatican Bank approves the transfers the funds will be in their accounts in one hour. After that you're out of it until the second cash transfer. When the contract is fulfilled, we transfer another six million into two accounts. We estimated roughly twenty million, so your slush fund is in good shape."

Capaldo knew Wronowski was on the edge and he didn't care; he had full control, pulled all the strings. "Walter, what's on your mind? What's with the glum look…you hardly touched the food."

"Ah…John. Don't you ever have second thoughts about this ah…a…thing? It's real. It's murder! This whole situation is absolutely, totally out of control. We can stop. Don't transfer the money…forget this whole thing. I know, just know, we can reason with the man."

Just once John Cardinal Capaldo wanted to pull a Wronowski and go ballistic—scream, yell, carry on like some wild man. With Wronowski near the edge he couldn't risk it. Deep inside he knew Wronowski, the chicken shit, had lost his guts. "I *am* not backing out and for your own good I *won't* let you back out. My friends expect to have this project completed as planned. It basically comes down to him or us. And it's not going to be me. Is that plain enough? Calm down. Maybe you should take a few days' rest. Everything will work out. You'll see. Go home, have a vodka, relax."

In the quiet dining room Capaldo mulled over the two million about to be transferred into his Swiss Bank account and his not too distant election to Pontifex Maximus. All he had to do was hold this together for a few days. He'd manipulated everyone so far. "A few more days…just a few more days," he muttered under his breath.

Immediately after the funds were wired into the IRG accounts, the leader met with the advisory council to discuss how to proceed with the contract. They had several choices. A bomb almost guaranteed success, although it would likely kill or at least injure members of the papal party and innocent bystanders, many of them Catholic clergy and politicians. No, a bomb would be overkill, so to speak, too messy, too impersonal. A bullet at point blank range was a sure kill but not practical. The assassin would be killed instantly or worse, captured. Who would volunteer for a suicide mission? Option three, a long distance rifle shot.

Standing in front of the Burlington Hotel in Dublin, Sergeant Michael McCoy looked at the four-story apartment building directly across the street. McCoy estimated the distance at approximately one hundred fifty meters from the hotel portico to the apartment. He tried to determine which windows had the best view of the hotel entrance. Taking the trees and telephone poles into consideration, the third floor, fifth window from the left had the best vantage-point. Checking the roster of tenants, Sergeant McCoy determined that apartment 3-F belonged to Albert and Doris Feeney. Mr. Feeney retired from the Ireland Postal Service six months prior. Perfect. As a former civil servant Mr. Feeney might feel obligated to assist the police, especially with adequate compensation for their minor inconvenience.

The sergeant paced through the parking lot, crossed the street and entered the apartment building. The estimate was slightly off; the distance much closer to one hundred and seventy-five meters. Riding the lift to the third floor, he approached the Feeney's freshly painted door. Knocking twice, he hoped the Feeney's were both at home. Albert answered with a quizzical expression, surprised to see a uniformed police officer, a sergeant no less.

Removing his aviator sunglasses, McCoy said, "Mr. Albert Feeney?"

"Yes Sergeant. How can I help ya?"

The officer handed Mr. Feeney his identification papers. "I'm Sergeant McCoy, temporarily assigned to the security team protecting the Pope on his upcoming visit. I'm sure you've heard His Holiness is schedule to visit Dublin with plans to stop at the Burlington Hotel."

"Yes Sergeant, my wife Doris is very excited about the Pope's visit and our excellent view of the event!"

"Mr. Feeney, is your wife at home? What I have to discuss concerns both of you."

"Why Sergeant, please come in and take a seat while I fetch me Doris."

Albert rushed to the bedroom, whispering, "Doris, there's a police sergeant in our parlor... he wants ta speak ta us...something bout the Pope. Hurry now, put on yer housecoat. Come...come."

Both Albert and Doris were enjoying a well-deserved retirement. It wasn't unusual for the Feeney's to begin their day at 10:00 a.m. or later. Albert was thin as a wisp, full of undirected nervous energy. Doris would be best described as rotund—equal to two Alberts, both physically and mentally. Quickly checking her appearance they moved to the parlor. The sergeant stood as they turned the corner.

"Sergeant McCoy, this is me wife Doris. Now what 'bout the Pope?"

Sergeant Mc Coy proffered a polite smile before retaking his seat. "Mrs. Feeney, how very nice to make your acquaintance. Your neighbors speak highly of you and Mr. Feeney as law abiding folk."

"Well thanks Sergeant, we do try to be good neighbors and citizens. You know...Mr. Feeney worked for the gov'nment postal his entire life...recently retired. What can we do for you?"

"Mr. and Mrs. Feeney, undoubtedly you've heard about the Pope's visit. I've assigned to the Pope's security unit and I'm here on official business. Because of this apartment's view of the hotel entrance and parking area, it's a perfect command post for the federal security forces guarding the Pontiff."

Doris spoke first. "What exactly does that mean for us?"

"As model citizens, the Irish government is asking you to vacate the apartment three days before the Pope arrives and not re-enter until after he leaves the Burlington."

This time Albert spoke without thinking, his voice full of indignation. "Impossible that! Tis' our home and we're very happy to see 'is Holiness from the comfort of this flat. Think'en of invit'en friends over, hav'en a party of sorts. Ya understand."

Undaunted, the sergeant continued. "The Irish government's willing to offer generous compensation for the inconvenience and provide an opportunity to see the Pope from a short distance, probably ten or twenty feet. Close enough to speak with him... possibly shake hands."

Doris placed her hand on Albert's knee to silence his next comment. "You've got our attention, Sergeant."

"We've reserved a suite at the Burlington for five days, all expenses paid including room, meals and refreshments during your stay. In addition, you are invited to the Pope's welcome dinner in the Burlington ballroom. The private dinner is limited to two hundred and fifty people and your table is ten feet from the raised podium where the guest of honor will address the room. If we can agree, I'm prepared to leave you with five hundred euros as a token of your government's appreciation."

The couple looked at each other in disbelief. Albert drooled for the cash; Doris had been pestering him about traveling and enjoying retirement before they were too old. This was just perfect. A paid holiday in his own neighborhood, and he could brag about helping the government and the Pope's private dinner party.

During his mental celebration, Doris replied, "Make it a thousand euros and you can have our flat on the condition that the govnment is responsible for any damage and clean the apartment 'afore we move back." Albert averted his eyes to avoid the pain of opportunity lost.

Abruptly, Sergeant McCoy stood. For a brief second, Doris was afraid she'd over-negotiated and the sergeant was about to leave and visit their neighbor in 3-H. He reached into his jacket pocket and produced ten crisp one hundred notes and handed the cash to Mr. Feeney.

"Ma'am, you drive a rough bargain."

"Anything for the Republic!"

"Mr. and Mrs. Feeney, the government thanks you. I'm sure you will enjoy the Burlington. It's a five-star hotel and the pub is six star. Just remember, you must be out of the apartment three days before the Pope arrives and under no circumstance can you enter this building or discuss this with anyone until after the Pope leaves. If you attempt to reenter this building, or I hear that you have discussed our agreement, I will be forced to place both of you in protective custody in Dublin's finest solitary confinement cell. Both confined to the same cell for days. No Burlington, restaurants or private dinner with the Holy Father, understood? Security cannot be discussed even with local police?"

Shaken out of their revelry, they mumbled "yes". They thanked the officer while escorting him to the door.

"Doris…a stroke of lok'—a holiday paid by the gov'ment."

Doris didn't want to jinx their luck, although she thought this was too good to be true. She gave Albert a big bear hug, lifted him in the air and whirled around the room until both were dizzy.

Sergeant McCoy entered the rear door of a private club, quickly changed into civilian clothes and placed his uniform in a hidden closet containing an assortment of uniforms, disguises, and assault weapons. Next he telephoned Kevin Donovan on a secure line to inform him that the Feeneys had agreed to vacate the apartment. Kevin walked into the next room and relayed the information to the IRG leader, who gave a slight nod.

Days ago when the decision was reached and the logistics settled, the leader contacted a professional assassin that the old IRA had hired for previous assignments. This professional never failed to fulfill a contract. The initial contact was via e-mail with a follow up telephone conversation over secure telephone lines. The assassin called a pre-determined number; the leader had no idea where the assassin was located. During the brief conversation the mechanic used an electronic modulator that disguised voices.

The mechanic said, "I've considered your proposal. Although I'm not a religious person, after some deep thought, I'll take the assignment. However, my fee for this job is three million in U. S. dollars. Wire-transfer two million immediately and one million upon completion…whether the mission is successful or not. If a shot's fired I receive the last million in forty-eight hours."

After a moment the leader answered. "A deal."

"Good. Give me the details of your plan: time, place, security arrangements, etc."

Long ago the leader became impervious to human emotions. He'd been hardened by years in the IRA. He talked through the plan like he was giving directions to the nearest petrol station. "The subject is scheduled to stop at the Burlington Hotel on the second day of the trip at 6:00 p.m. for a welcome-to-Dublin dinner. One hundred and seventy-five meters from the hotel entrance is a four-story apartment building. We have secured access to an apartment. It has a clear unobstructed view of the entrance and parking lot. You'll have access to the apartment three days before the subject's arrival. Plan to arrive early to avoid security checks into the building. Twenty-four hours before the visit the whole area will be locked down and under security checks and constant surveillance.

"Once inside the apartment, don't leave for any reason until the assignment is completed. Many of the local police support our cause but don't know about this contract and may inadvertently jeopardize the mission. The apartment will be amply stocked with all the necessities so there is no reason to leave. Don't use the telephone in the apartment. If calls are absolutely necessary use a cell phone. Don't use any phone during the twenty-four hours prior to the subject's arrival; the police will be scanning all communications. It won't take them very long to determine which apartment was used for the mission, so take standard precautions not to leave fingerprints or any form of DNA. I don't have to tell a professional how to conduct business; I just want to make sure all the contingencies are covered. Any questions?"

"I understand. Please continue."

"The subject is wearing body armor so the only sure spot is his head."

The mechanic immediately went on alert. "That's a difficult shot with a moving target surrounded by guards, some who might be taller than the subject."

"That's covered. You'll have a clear view of his head for at least five to eight seconds, more than enough time for a *professional*."

"If your description of the area and the subject is accurate, things will go as planned. Don't forget, I expect the final wire transfer forty-eight hours after the project is completed."

"Don't worry. We've never missed a commitment. The funds will transfer on schedule."

Brother Jacomo waited until the Holy Father had a break in his schedule before disturbing him to review the trip's agenda and attendees. He gingerly entered the office. "Holiness, do you have a moment?"

"Certainly, Brother Jacomo, come in and take a seat. What do you have for me this pleasant afternoon?" Sensing things were finally under control and beginning to go his way, Pope Alex felt relaxed, full of playful energy.

"I must confess, Holiness, it is nice to see you in a happy mood. I gather things are improving?"

"Thank you. And yes, things are getting better."

"I have a copy of the final Ireland itinerary and members of the group. As you requested, I tried to keep the group small. We have a total of nineteen people: You, five from the Vatican staff, six Swiss Guards, five Italian military and from GNN, Ms. Murphy and a photographer, Mr. D'Anella."

Reclining in his chair the Pontiff stretched back and turned down the radio volume. Brother Jacomo could see the Pope was wearing walking shorts under his white robe. "Bishop Newhart is part of the group. Who else will be joining us?"

"The Bishop's assistant, as well as Cardinal Belfonte and his assistant. His Eminence was very insistent on joining our group and of course I conceded. Including you and me, there's a total of six from the Vatican staff."

While looking at Brother Jacomo, the Holy Father's thoughts were years in the past. He thought about the lost opportunity to visit Ireland with Marie. "Brother, have you visited Ireland?"

"No, Holiness. This will be my first trip. I understand that you've visited before."

"Oh yes, many years ago, just after I was ordained. My parish sponsored a one-week trip. The pastor was ill so I was elected to shepherd the flock, so to speak. It's truly a beautiful country with wonderful people. That's why it's so disturbing that with an opportunity to start with a clean slate, after a period of calm, United Ireland has reverted to violence and hatred. We should have some time to enjoy the country and discuss the situation on the long bus rides between villages."

"As a reminder, Holiness, you are scheduled to meet with Eminence Paolino."

"Ah yes, thank you brother. I will see him immediately."

Cardinal Paolino, the Papal nuncio to Rome, held a prominent position in the Vatican. The Vatican had been a separate city-state since Mussolini's regime in 1929, the areas outside the walls controlled by Italy and the City of Rome. Therefore, the Vatican's welfare was highly dependent on continued good relations with both. Umberto Cardinal Paolino had been the Papal nuncio for over forty years and was held in high esteem.

A wizened old man shuffled into the room. After their formal greeting,

Eminence Paolino eased into the chair next to the Pontiff. Well into his late eighties, he looked old and tired.

"Holiness, thank you for seeing me on such short notice."

The Pontiff's heart skipped a beat; he knew this meeting wasn't good news. "It's always a pleasure to see you Umberto. I was very interested in your latest report on our relations with Rome. As usual, you are keeping things on an even keel."

"Thank you Holiness, but that is not what I wished to see you about." The Pope nodded and raised his hand signaling the Cardinal to continue. "With your permission, Holiness, after many years of service to the Vatican, it is time for me to retire."

The Pontiff was disappointed but not surprised. He heard rumors about Cardinal Paolino's health.

"Umberto, I am disappointed. You are one of the few Princes that I can count on. That said my friend, after so many years of service, how could I deny your request? I do, however, ask that you delay your retirement for three weeks."

"Thank you for your faith in me and the privilege to retire."

"No…thank you, Umberto, for your faithful service. As Papal Nuncio, you have known several Popes and helped them face numerous crises. I would like to ask your opinion about something that has troubled me of late. It has to do with charity, both individual giving and funding Church programs for the poor and needy. This is my quandary: Should we retain our principle assets and donate only the income, knowing we are helping but not fully eliminating hunger and human suffering, or should we make a huge donation of the principle hoping to eliminate hunger and suffering? However, once the principle has been donated, there is little in reserve for future donations." The Pontiff raised his shoulders signaling he needed guidance.

"Holiness, every Church leader has been faced with this issue. Jesus asked us to help the poor but also said the poor will be with us always. I believe there is no one right answer. Maybe…have you considered…the answer is somewhere in between."

The Holy Father brightened. "Simple words bestow great wisdom. Thank you my friend."

For security reasons and to avoid rush hour gridlock, the Papal motorcade departed from St. Peter's Square at 5:00 a.m.. The Holy Father and Brother

Jacomo traveled via helicopter, meeting the group at the airport for a 6:30 departure. Trans-Con Aviation loaned a small charter jet to the Vatican for this trip. The president of Trans-con and Cardinal Marconi were personal friends.

A number of well-wishers and two Italian journalists gathered at the private hanger to see the Holy Father off. The departure was on time and uneventful. The jet was small and compact; space at a premium. Fortunately, the flight to Shannon was a short hop and with a VIP status was immediately cleared for landing.

Shannon Airport was small by international standards. Even so, as a security precaution, the jet taxied to a private hanger some distance from the main terminal. Thousands of people anticipated this security ploy and were waiting near the hangar to greet the Pontiff. The crowd was kept behind a movable metal security fence; police in riot gear were stationed every ten feet. When the plane stopped, the cabin door opened and the Holy Father stood on the movable staircase waving with both arms, to the cheering crowd.

Stiff from the cramped quarters, he slowly descended the steps on wobbly knees, waving his right hand and holding the railing with his left. Following tradition he bent on both knees and kissed the ground. Everyone on the welcoming committee held a smile, some more earnest than others, as a row of white teeth stood shoulder-to-shoulder to welcome the Holy Man. Dignitaries approached: Bishop Gavagan from the Shannon diocese, Richard Malloy, the Vice President of United Ireland, and other local politicians. Each greeted His Holiness, shaking hands for the media photographers.

The police separated a small group of protestors, approximately forty people, from the main crowd. They were chanting but the Pope couldn't hear them over the larger crowds. Their signs clearly visible: 'Go home Yankee Pope' and 'Ireland doesn't want another Catholic Killer.' Pope Alex was surprised to see protestors this far south. Security started escorting him to the Popemobile when he said something to the Italian commander and began the long walk toward the protestors.

He didn't know exactly how to deal with the protestors, but at the same time couldn't ignore them. That would send the wrong message as to why he was in United Ireland. Security personnel immediately surrounded him, creating a human shield. He felt like a turtle protected on all sides, his head bobbing up to see across the tarmac. He wasn't afraid or concerned about his welfare. No, his greatest fear was screwing up. His first time at bat, he desperately needed a home run or even a triple. He called on the Holy Trinity and every saint he could remember during that walk inside the protective shell. Suddenly he felt calm, prepared and ready to slay the dragons named "Hate" and "Prejudice."

As Alex the Pontiff neared, the protestors were surprised and ceased shouting; they were bewildered about what to do when actually confronted by the spiritual leader. They decided to hear what he had to say, how he justified Catholics killing, the Church's neglect, and this visit.

Before he reached the front line of protestors, mostly women and old men, the surrounding area became unnaturally quiet except for the distant woosh of planes far overhead. The Pontiff projected his voice and asked, "Does anyone know why we are visiting your beautiful country?" No one responded. They worried he was baiting them in front of the news media. He continued, "To find out why hate and killing continues to shatter the fragile peace. I am here to try and stop the violence and protect the innocent, especially the Protestants fighting for justice and equality. So I thank you for demonstrating. When I leave for home, I want this whole country demonstrating for peace."

At a loss the protestors didn't move or speak, not a peep or grunt; in person no one dared question the Holy Father's integrity. The signs slowly lowered. The Pope reached out and ruffled a young lad's blond hair. The Popemobile pulled up and the Pontiff entered the vehicle already occupied by Bishop Gavagan and Vice-President Malloy. A police escort, sirens blaring, led the way followed by the Popemobile, two large tour buses, military trucks and police vehicles as the rear guard. Each bus had been retrofitted with bulletproof glass and reinforced steel.

The Vatican party split, half the group in each bus. Security planned to have the members alternate buses. Once the motorcade reached the countryside, the Bishop and local dignitaries left, returning to their daily activities. Pope Alex transferred into a bus and the motorcade picked up speed heading north. The route north was restricted to secondary roads rather than major highways. The federal security team would stay with the Vatican visitors until they reached Dublin. As the motorcade crossed county lines, a new team of local police took charge of leading the motorcade. When they neared populated areas, the Holy Father often transferred to the Popemobile, and the motorcade slowed to ten kilometers per hour so the people could see and wave to the Pope. He returned every wave, feeling the people's love and admiration.

In cities and towns with large populations that cleared security checks, the motorcade stopped to meet the mayor, local politicians and members of the ecumenical clergy. They were mostly Catholic, but Protestants and Jews were invited and encouraged to attend. During these stops, Pope Alex always spent a few minutes seeking out non-Catholics and encouraged discussion about the current political situation and escalating violence.

The motorcade traveled through Limerick, Nenagh, Tullamore, making a rest stop at Cavan, the last sizable town before crossing into the northern counties and stopping for the night.

At Cavan Castle, spectators were restricted to the parking lot while the Vatican party used the common areas to freshen up and grab quick snacks. Alex the Pontiff spent a few minutes speaking with the villagers before heading into the castle. Once inside he could see the castle had been converted to a hotel and restaurant. Making eye contact, he waved at Kate Murphy. She returned the wave as he walked over to her and a young man he didn't recognize. The journalists joined the group in Shannon and were riding in the second bus. Kate and her associate stood to greet the Pontiff, Kate knelt to kiss his ring and the Pope took her hand while kissing her lightly on the cheek.

"Holy Father, I would like to introduce Eric D'Anella, my associate from GNN and a renowned photographer."

Eric knelt to kiss the Papal ring, after which the Pope offered to shake his hand. Eric hesitated, not expecting this gesture, but quickly recovered, extending a firm grasp.

"Thank you for joining us, Mr. D'Anella. I've seen your photographs, excellent work; you manage to capture the essence of your subjects. Young man, many years ago I knew a Vincent D'Anella and you look very much like him. Are you possibly related?"

"Yes, Holy Father. I have a great uncle who knew you years ago."

"It's a very small world, Eric. Please give your uncle my best regards and of course my love to Nonni and your cousin Alicia."

Eric felt compelled to say, "I feel privileged to be a small cog in this peace mission. I especially liked the way you handled the demonstrators at the airport. My heart skipped as you approached the protestors. Amazing, after a few moments the demonstrators calmed down."

"Thank you, Eric. I hope all our endeavors work as well during this visit. The room is a bit noisy; let's walk into the courtyard to enjoy the sun and look at the statuary sprinkled about the walkway. It's also much cooler outside; this white robe is not exactly air-conditioned." Once outside he moved directly to his immediate concern, "Kate, where do we stand on the biography and interview?"

"Holiness, all of the interviews are complete, and your office received videos of each individual's unedited interview. My associates in New York are compiling and editing the final version for the Vatican's final review. You should have it early next week. At that point we can discuss any changes you wish to incorporate."

"Kate, as you can tell by my exuberant smile," he showed her a large exaggerated grin, "I'm pleased about the quality of the preliminary videos and that GNN is meeting our schedule."

Eric interrupted. "Excuse me Holiness, Brother Jacomo is signaling. The buses are boarding."

In order to save time, catered box lunches were eaten on the buses. The roads had not improved since the Pontiff's last visit twenty-odd years ago. Most roads were secondary narrow lanes that need resurfacing. Even so, the motorcade made good time, and by late afternoon crossed over into the northern counties. The bus driver expected to reach Armagh before nightfall. Once in the north, the federal security leader Inspector Black cautioned the Holy Father about stopping to greet the local citizens. Mr. Black's only concession was slowing the motorcade while Pope Alex waved from the Popemobile.

The Pope was tired and wanted to reach their destination so he didn't bother to argue with Inspector Black. Besides, the Inspector was a hulk, over six-feet four-inches tall, and broad as a boxcar. Behind smiling Irish eyes lurked a cautious man who was at the top of his profession. The Pontiff had no doubt about winning, but was also smart enough to pick his battles.

The bus driver was right on target, pulling into Armagh Castle's large courtyard as the sun set behind the towering stone wall. The group was invited to stay the night at Armagh Castle as guests of Sir James Wheelan, owner of the estate and a member of the Irish legislature. Sir James was also an elder in the Anglican Church. He and the Pontiff had a mutual friend, Donald Nedrich, the American Ambassador to England. Donald informed Sir James about the purpose behind the Pope's visit, which prompted Sir James' to offer to host the Papal group as a sign of cooperation. The gesture also sent a message to the Protestant NIA (Northern Irish Army) that while the Pope was in the north, he and his party were under Sir James' considerable protection.

Their host was waiting with a cordial welcome, holding a bouquet of shamrocks, a gesture of peace. Sir James was infamous for a hot temper, stood up for his beliefs and those of his constituents. The Pope stood eye-to-eye with Sir James although Sir James was rail thin. The Pope noticed his sharp English features seemed pronounced because of his taut porcelain complexion. Somewhere in his late sixties, Sir James was not aging well. Shortly after becoming a widower ten years ago, his health began to decline. His three children were grown and their daily lives were tied to the family estate.

Servants escorted the guests to their rooms to freshen up before dinner. Sir James planned a dinner party in their honor and invited local dignitaries, businessmen, Catholic Bishop Patrick Massey and Protestant Bishop Arthur Kilbain.

Armagh was the center of the Catholic and Anglican religions. Both have cathedrals located in Armagh and both are named after St. Patrick. Early the next day the Holy Father intended to celebrate Holy Mass at the Catholic cathedral followed by a visit to the Anglican cathedral, where he planned to participate in an ecumenical prayer session.

It was far too dark to tour the entire estate, so Sir James offered the Pope a guided tour of the castle. This was his opportunity to spend some time and get to know the Pontiff. The original castle and surrounding buildings dated back to the sixteenth century, although renovations at various periods incorporated the latest civilized amenities. The Pontiff eagerly accepted his host's kind offer. History was a hobby and, in particular, forts and castles held a fascination.

As the Irish say, the castle was "grand," huge and spacious, especially the foyer and dining room. On the top level they strolled along the high narrow battlements. Pope Alex understood the Wheelan family's ingrained connection to their home and land; the family had trusted the land to provide their livelihood for four hundred years. In return, the Wheelan's worked to preserve and replenish the estate for future generations.

While looking at the distant Armagh city lights dotting the night sky, Alex the Pontiff experienced a strange episode, a strong premonition of danger that momentarily paralyzed his speech and comprehension. His mind locked on a vague outline playing in his mind. He failed to respond to a comment from Sir James. Regaining his faculties he apologized, "Sorry, Sir James, my mind wandered to tomorrow and Belfast." The Pope never discussed these visions or episodes with anyone, even Leigh. Some things he just couldn't explain, nor wish to discuss them.

Sir James contemplated long and hard about inviting the Pope into his home. Until the last century, few Catholics other than servants were allowed to cross the threshold of this Protestant castle. Sir James knew if this trip was a bust, he was wide open to ridicule from his friends and political constituents. Reputation and pride meant everything to him and he willingly placed all of it on the line to achieve a lasting peace and prosperity for his family and people.

The lord of the castle was growing old and frail, tired of fighting, tired of hate, plain tired. Never much for small talk, Sir James openly spoke his mind. "I opened my home because you are a religious leader and a man of peace. Can you please explain what you hope or expect to accomplish from this trip?"

With the dark surrounding them, the host couldn't see the pain on his guest's face or the worry in his eyes. The Pontiff could, however, hear the doubt in Sir James' question: After four hundred years of turmoil, could anyone or anything create a lasting peace? Much depended on the next two days. Millions of lives hung in the balance. Standing on the precipice of the castle as well as his Papacy, the Pope also had serious doubts if any man could make a lasting difference; that's why he placed full faith in God. "We appreciate the welcome and generous act of friendship extended to our group," he answered.

Facing Sir James he could only make out his outline, so he continued with as much genuineness in his voice as possible. It was of utmost importance that Sir James in particular believe and support him. "I personally cannot change or alter what is happening in this wonderful country. The ultimate hard and courageous decisions that affect social change can only come from within people intent on peace and tolerance. I hope to bring the hatred, injustice and violence to the forefront. Appeal to the innate goodness of politicians and citizens to keep the peace and treat neighbors with human respect, if not caring.

"If necessary I will embarrass every Catholic into keeping the peace, pointing out their responsibilities not to ignore what is happening. Don't tolerate violence, and don't let a small faction of vengeance seekers subvert justice and equality and most important, don't violate God's law."

The voice emanating from the dark grew stronger more intent, certain of how to proceed. The Holy Spirit descended into him, guiding each thought and word. "Sir James, I am sure you know women have tremendous influence over their men. I will appeal to mothers, wives and girlfriends to take whatever steps are necessary to make sure peace is maintained. As a matter of conscience, I will advise priests not to give absolution for hate crimes until the offenders promise to repent by performing community service that clearly demonstrates their desire for peace. Without absolution for mortal sins, priests will withhold the sacraments, including confirmation, marriage or last rights. I can't even imagine the pressure women will exert on their men if they cannot receive the sacraments. Modern Popes have been reluctant to use this power; I will not hesitate for one second, not one fraction of a second!" Taking a deep breath of night air he touched Sir James shoulder. "My new friend, I pray it makes a difference."

Sir James was skeptical down to his bones, not about the Pope's genuine efforts, rather about changing Ireland's tradition of hate and violence. After hundreds of years he contemplated if violence and hatred had been embedded in Irish genes. With the smallest sprig of hope, Sir James looked out at the Armagh lights and touched the holy man's arm in wordless approval. Without further comment, the host assisted the Pontiff down the steep, uneven stone steps, through the foyer and into the dining room.

"I hope you and your traveling companions are hungry. The chef has prepared a feast."

Twenty-five guests, including the Vatican visitors were comfortably seated in the main dining room. The massive room could easily accommodate twice that many people without crowding. Every wall was constructed of solid stone block, hand laid without mortar. Heavy wood beams arching across the ceiling provided support for the upper floors. Antique tapestries depicting scenes from the 16th century lined the cold hard walls. The room had been kept in its original condition. The wood floor was so old and hard it appeared petrified. Although, a wonderful historic setting with nothing to absorb sound, the room sounded like the inside of a drum. Every sound echoed around the room returning to it original source. It was difficult to speak without shouting and shouting intensified the echo.

The host served an authentic medieval meal starting with potato soup, local greens and roast pig, hand carved in the dining room and served on pewter plates. Drinks complemented the meal with a choice of wine, ale and spring water. Melancholy Irish music played in the background. The evening festivities featured Irish dancers in traditional garb and a male soloist. By eleven o'clock, Pope Alex and most of the group were ready to turn in for the night after a long day. A few of the younger people continued to enjoy the Wheelan family hospitality into the early morning.

During dinner, Major Bordeau made his rounds checking on the security team. Making sure each guard had sleeping accommodations and a scheduled dinner break. During the tour he received a call on his cell phone from the IRG, giving him specific instructions on how and when to assist them by breaching security. He clicked the phone closed. The final plan was in motion.

The next morning everyone woke early ready to start day two. The castle's old hot water system clanged and banged. With so many people showering at the same time, only the early risers found hot water. That cold water turned out to be a blessing that energized the folks still drowsy from the late night's festivities. By 10:00, the Pope had celebrated Mass in St. Patrick's Catholic Cathedral and participated in the ecumenical prayer meeting in St. Patrick's Anglican Cathedral.

Three additional people were invited to join the group while visiting Belfast and continuing on to Dublin: Sir James, Catholic Bishop Patrick Massey and Anglican Bishop Arthur Kilbain. The three special guests and the Holy Father rode in the Popemobile from Armagh to Belfast. Starting out, the roads were virtually deserted; few vehicles and fewer people lined the highway to view the Pontiff. Belfast was going to be a difficult audience.

The previous day's GNN broadcast exposing conditions in Northern Ireland sent a chill through the Protestant community. It raised hard questions: Would this broadcast result in immediate Catholic retaliation or would the Catholics lay low until the world focused on other hot spots? Why was the Pope visiting at this time? Was he here to support the Catholics? Anticipating more trouble, would additional Army troops roll north?

Approaching Belfast's city limits, spotty groups of spectators began to line the streets. Small groups of Catholics waved the Papal flag and cheered, many asked for a Papal blessing. Much larger groups of Protestants displayed the Union Jack. Many who stood waving were there more out of curiosity than to welcome the religious leader. As a precaution, the local police made sure clusters of Catholic and Protestant spectators were kept separated. The motorcade entered Belfast from Lisburn Road, reducing speed to five kilometers per hour. Word quickly spread that Sir James Wheelan and Bishop Kilbain accompanied the Pope.

Entering the city limits, the crowds began to grow along the route through

Belfast. The motorcade proceeded through Shadsbury Square then on to Great Victoria, made a right turn onto Howard Street. Driving past City Hall, they noticed the magnificent building constructed of Portland stone. The crowds stood four and five deep. Later in the day, the motorcade was scheduled to return to City Hall for a meeting with the Lord Mayor. Metal barricades kept the crowds off the street. Police cars and motorcycle escorts led the way followed by the Popemobile, buses and security vehicles. Security personnel jogged alongside the Popemobile for added protection.

Damlier-Chrysler designed and custom built the new Popemobile. The design was based on a Mercedes stretch limo modified with a larger clear bubble top, allowing 360-degree visibility. The vehicle was bulletproof, especially the reinforced Plexiglas bubble. The bubble was high enough for riders to stand, to see and be seen. Along the route, Alex the Pontiff often signaled the motorcade to stop so he could open the bubble door to greet people. When someone caught his attention, he left the vehicle to talk with individuals in the crowd. Security frowned on this, but he stopped to meet both Catholic and Protestant spectators.

The procession moved at a slow but steady pace heading for the housing projects in West Belfast. Historically, this was the center of political and social conflict; tensions ran high and violence a daily reality. The Pontiff halted the motorcade, left his vehicle and walked to a young girl about eight years old. She sat in a wheel chair waving both Papal and Irish flags. After greeting the girl's mother, the Pope stooped down to speak with the youngster for a few moments. Leaving, he gave the young girl his blessing and a kiss on the forehead.

The group proceeded to the parking area. The security people acted jittery, the visitors quickly discerned their feeling of heightened concern. Inspector Black again warned the Holy Father not to walk through this unsecured area. The area was extremely unpredictable and the security people couldn't guarantee their safety. The Pontiff wouldn't think of reconsidering, as he explained to Mr. Black, "This is an important, if not the most critical, part of my visit."

Undaunted by fear of the unknown or of being injured, the Pope moved forward, softly humming the twenty-third psalm. If anything, his internal turmoil had festered into anger and eagerness to do battle with anyone opposed to a just and lasting peace. The wrath of God flowed through his right hand, and his words became the long sword that killed the proverbial dragons.

Before allowing the group to proceed, Inspector Black found Brother

Jacomo and verified the Holy Father wore bulletproof gear under his cassock. The Security Chief's heart rate accelerated, sweat drenched his body as he reluctantly led the group into harm's way.

Protestant leaders immediately met and welcomed the visitors and guaranteed their safety. Sir James prearranged the group's safety, not just for the Pope's sake; the Protestant cause could never withstand an accusation of violence directed at the leader of the Roman Catholic Church. It would become a perfect excuse for their enemies to escalate the violence.

The overall mood was sedate, almost somber, as the group cautiously began the tour of a typical building including the common areas and selected apartments. Seeing the Irish lace curtains the Pope had to smile, thinking, *Some things never change; then again, some things are worth keeping*. The buildings and grounds looked neat and well maintained, although densely populated like most housing projects. The residents grew friendlier as the tour progressed, where everyone in the group except the security staff freely conversed with residents.

Rounding the corner of the largest apartment building, they had a clear view of the infamous peace line, a corrugated iron fence separating the Catholic and Protestant combatants. The Pope's entire demeanor changed; he felt much like a toreador challenged by his first bull as power surged through every limb. God's invincible warrior ignored the crowd and headed directly to the metal wall, stopping ten feet from the partition. Didn't move, didn't say a word, while he collected his thoughts and harnessed a growing rage. A tingle flowed from his red ears to his fingertips. He moved next to the wall, raised his arms to chest level and leaned forward simulating a crucifixion.

The residents stood with mouths hung open, while the Catholics flinched and security people grimaced as they touched their holsters. The wall was part of the citizens' lives and heritage; it had been there for what seemed to most residents a lifetime. A symbol of protection, a line no one could cross without risking injury or death. Moving away from the wall, Pope Alex turned to face the crowd. Almost in tears, his voice strained and cracked, speaking in a different tenor, strange and eerie, albeit smooth and calming. After today there was no doubt, these were his people.

"There is an old saying: 'Good fences make good neighbors.' I say, caring people make good neighbors. This is not a peace line; it *is* a wall of segregation, a wall of Jericho that must tumble when the trumpets of peace sound. It *is* an impediment to true peace and harmony. This is the time for true peace and I *will* do everything in my power to create a lasting peace that will crumble this wall."

Walking back to the bus he knew without a shred of doubt that making this trip was the right decision. His memories wandered back to his wife Marie. Before they were married, she visited Europe, and Ireland was the highlight of her trip. They planned to visit Ireland on their twenty-fifth anniversary. They never made it to twenty-five. Whenever he missed Marie his chest felt the weight of her loss, but this day he felt the same joy she experienced so long ago. As his foot lifted to enter the bus, he thought, *It's time to deal with the politicians.*

Chapter Twenty-one

Irish television and radio stations had been broadcasting live since the motorcade entered Belfast. The recording trucks were strategically located in front and back of what became a caravan of buses, police cars, motorcycles, an assortment of media vehicles and the Popemobile. All aircraft, including media helicopters, were banned from the air space over the caravan. Reporters had to push their way through the constantly increasing crowds. The live TV and radio broadcast from the "peace line" helped turn the Papal visit into a media event that attracted people by the thousands, tripling the original spectators. Many workers left their jobs to join the crowds. Echoes rumbled through deserted stores, banks and commercial offices.

The caravan headed back to city hall to meet Lord Mayor Mark Dillard and the Belfast welcoming committee. A large number of spectators began shifting to the city hall area and the thick crowds slowed the caravan to a crawl. Separating the Catholics and Protestants wasn't possible, the crowds too large and intertwined. It didn't matter; the air was contagious with peace, obliterating everything else.

Streets were kept politely but firmly open by the police and security staff. The caravan finally reached city hall, an hour behind schedule. Belfast City Hall opened in 1906 and had been in continuous use even during the recent renovation to the Portland Stone façade and main dome. The grounds encompassed two city blocks and doubled as a park. When the caravan halted, the thick crowd stood shoulder to shoulder. The police had to clear a path through the sea of people for the Pope and his party. As they walked through the valley of human flesh a quiet reverence, and a sense of solidarity spread.

Lord Mayor Mark Dillard was the first Catholic Mayor of Belfast. Unfortunately, his personal beliefs and administration helped fuel the violence. Many like him extracted retribution for four hundred years of Protestant social and political control. The Dillards of Ireland needed to change or be replaced with public servants that worked toward peace and social acceptance.

The Pope climbed the wooden steps on to a large temporary stage greeting the Lord Mayor who bowed and kissed the Papal ring. The Pontiff proceeded to meet each member of the welcoming committee. Next the Papal party climbed onto the stage to meet and greet. Due to the circumstances, Mayor Dillard was forced to grasp hands with Bishop Kilbain and his political nemesis, Sir James Wheelan. If the Mayor had a choice, he'd ignore them or better yet, refuse to allow the Protestants on the stage. Under the circumstances, that proved impossible.

The crowd chanted "Pope Alex, Pope Alex" over and over. Mayor Dillard quickly moved to the microphones to address the citizens.

The mayor's effervescent display belied his true feelings about the Pope's interference in Irish policies. His network of informers had already relayed what transpired at the peace line. "With open arms, the City of Belfast welcomes Pope Alex IX. I am privileged—"

The chanting drowned out Mayor Dillard each time he attempted to address the audience. Finally he looked over and raised his shoulders in resignation, then walked to the Pontiff and passed the microphone.

Standing straight and tall, the Pope motioned the crowd for quiet. His heart pounded so loud he could hear it over the cheers and applause. He felt good vibes floating from the audience. This was a turning point in the peace trip and possibly his Papacy. Alex prayed for the Holy Spirit to loosen his tongue, to give him the words and courage to use them, as well as open the audience's ears and, more importantly, hearts.

The chanting suddenly changed to "Peace, peace, peace...." Eventually the audience quieted down and the Pope began.

"You are all children of God. He expects...no demands, that each of his children seek peace, work for peace and live in peace." The audience had been waiting for hours to see the Pope to eagerly express bottled-up sentiment. Cheers and chants erupted. "Pope Alex, Pope Alex—"

His arms rose like Moses in the desert held high for peace rather than death to the enemy.

When the audience exhausted their steam, he continued. "I came to see and experience first hand what's happening in this beautiful country.

Unfortunately, the whole world knows if you wish to discover what's happening to the fragile peace, visit Belfast. So here I came. What I discovered in a very short time is sad and disturbing. Belfast is a frightening place. Before reaching the peace line, I spoke with a pretty young girl confined to a wheelchair. She reminded me very much of my own great granddaughter. This innocent young child is maimed for life. With many years of physical therapy she may be able to walk with crutches. Speaking with her, I fought back tears. Not because of her physical condition, rather because of her innocence in expecting peace because it is the right thing. As I kissed her goodbye, she said, 'Mr. Pope, please pray that we have peace. My dadda died in the troubles…I am afraid for my brothers.' Hearing this young child's plea turned my sadness into doubling my resolve that all of Christ's children must work for peace. Each person here today, yes each of you, knows how to achieve a lasting peace: You only need the courage to stand up against hatred and violence.

"You all know fathers, mothers, brothers, sisters, aunts, uncles, civic leaders and especially politicians that perpetuate hatred and social unrest. It's *everyones* responsibility to speak up and say 'no.' No, you will not tolerate prejudice. No, you will not tolerate injustice, hatred or violence. Not today… not ever. I will pray each day that all Irish hearts are filled with peace and understanding. I ask you to pray that the government officials open their minds to the golden rule."

The entire Vatican community was caught up in the Papal tour, watching on TV or listening to the radio. Normal Church business came to a halt. The Pope had finally emerged as a world leader. Hundreds of visitors and Italians mingled in St. Peter's Square listening to the radio broadcast, excited about *THEIR* Pope, a man of God.

Cardinal Marconi alternated between watching the live TV broadcast and calling Brother Jacomo to get firsthand updates on the Pope's progress and health. During most phone calls they couldn't communicate; the noise was deafening. Marconi worried about the Holy Father; the trip might overtax his heart. He constantly prodded Brother Jacomo to remind the Holy Father of his doctor's advice to slow down and rest, not over exert.

Marconi also kept track of Cardinals Wronowski and Capaldo. Wronowski claimed to be ill, and stayed in his apartment for the last three days. He even stopped his staff from visiting to discuss day-to-day business. Capaldo hadn't contacted Marconi since their private dinner. Marconi half-expected the adversarial cardinals to create some troublesome diversion aimed at discrediting the Holy Father or disrupting the Papal trip, but nothing happened. The quiet added to Marconi's burden. His cousin, the mole on Capaldo's staff, claimed that Eminence was on holiday visiting his brother in Calabria. *Of all times*, Marconi wondered, *why did Capaldo leave the Vatican?*

Anna Von Helm landed in Dublin on a flight from Berlin, Germany—a stunning blond with crystal blue eyes. Just under six feet tall, her muscular frame enhanced her expensive dark blue business suit. According to her passport she was a forty-year-old German citizen. Based on the passport stamps, Anna had traveled extensively through Europe, Africa and North America. She told the immigration official that she'd be in Dublin on business for five days and was staying at the West Hotel on Grafton Street. The customs agent asked a few idle questions gaining an extra minute to appreciate the Nordic beauty. Traveling light, she had one carry on and a small-wheeled suitcase. Because Grafton Street restricted vehicles, the airport taxi dropped her at the top of the street and she walked the few short blocks to the hotel. Her employer prepaid a five-day reservation. A Federal Express box mailed from Italy and another hand delivered package waited at the hotel.

Once settled in the room she opened the two packages and checked the tools of her trade. They looked satisfactory. Obtaining a Dublin street map from the desk clerk, she walked to the end of Grafton Street and hailed a taxi to the Burlington Hotel. Anna headed directly into the hotel pub for a pint. The large windows had an excellent view of the parking lot and buildings directly in front of the hotel. After downing the dark Irish beer, she strolled to the front entrance and asked the doorman to hail a taxi. While waiting she sized up the street, hotel and parking lot from another angle.

Three blocks from the Burlington, the cabbie pulled over. Anna exited the taxi and circled back to the street running parallel to the Burlington to get a close look at the rear and sides of the apartment building directly across from the hotel. The structure stood four stories high with one main entrance, two rear entrances and one emergency exit on each side. The upper floors had fire escapes on the sides of the building. All doors were locked during the day except the main entrance where a doorman controlled access. The doorman went off duty at 6:00 p.m., and all the doors were locked. Tenants used security access cards to gain admittance. She was satisfied that the

IRG's information about the building was precise.

In route back to the hotel, Anna scoured a secondhand clothing store looking for two dresses, sizes twelve and sixteen, an old hat, umbrella and matronly walking shoes. It was imperative that her clothing was made in Ireland in case she was stopped and searched. Back at the hotel she tried on her purchases and quickly morphed into a poor old woman by including a gray wig, and severe stoop. The second disguise appeared less severe; by eliminating her make-up, she transformed into a fifty-something matron.

The Federal Express box contained an access card to enter the building, a key to the Feeneys' apartment, and identification papers for a seventy-year-old woman. The hand delivered package contained a breakdown Russian snipers rifle, compact but lethal. The box also included coded instructions to enter apartment 3-F two days in advance, before security tightened around the Burlington. That suggestion had less appeal than nails on a blackboard; it made her skin crawl with suspicion. In her profession one didn't take anything for granted. She planned to move in one day before, which gave her some time in the interim to evaluate security and enjoy Dublin, specifically the pubs. It also kept the IRG off guard.

Exactly twelve hours before the Pope's scheduled arrival, the attractive blond disguised herself as the plain fifty-year-old matron. She left the West Hotel through a rear door and briskly walked the two kilometers to apartment 3-F. The carpetbag contained false identification papers, a cell phone, a snipers rifle wrapped in old clothing and an ointment for hands and feet that prevented finger and toe prints. She entered the building with the access card key, and climbed the stairs to the third floor to avoid the closed circuit television in the elevator.

Now the hated waiting. This was the difficult part, too much time to dwell on the "what ifs." What if she missed? What if she was discovered before the subject arrived? What if the IRG tried to eliminate her after the assignment? With no witness to her pact with the IRG and a pending one million payment, that was a real issue. Her biggest concern was escaping the immediate area after the shooting. Self-preservation required avoiding the IRG and the police. That's why she entered the apartment dressed as a plain fifty-year old.

Keeping the shades down, she turned the lights off and on in normal fashion. It was time to rehearse her escape. Disguised as a hunched over demented old woman in a panic and carrying the Feeneys' cat was a good ruse.

Next Anna dismantled and cleaned the high-powered rifle, reassembled the weapon and carefully cradled it as she checked its operation. After attaching the silencer, she secured the scope that was recently calibrated for accuracy up to 500 meters. The rifle would be dismantled and discarded in pieces during her escape—a waste of good equipment, but absolutely necessary.

The rifle also had a detachable ten-inch bipod. Moving the coffee table in front of the window, she placed the rifle with bipod on the table. Sitting on the floor with the rifle mounted on the table provided perfect stability. The window had an unobstructed view of the hotel entrance. Eleven hours until the target arrived, time to rest, wait and worry some more. Although an agnostic, killing a holy man gnawed at her sensibilities. She gave the mission considerable thought before accepting the contract and had no regrets; it was a job, but something just didn't sit right. As a professional she shook it off. All things considered, building her retirement fund outweighed her conscience.

After the Holy Father finished speaking, security surrounded the stage to keep the euphoric audience from rushing the platform. When security thought the situation had stabilized, the Papal party exited the stage and moved rapidly into City Hall, down the grand hallway and out a rear entrance to the vehicles. Pope Alex, Sir James and the two bishops rode in the Popemobile. The crowd slowly disbursed while the Belfast police detoured foot and vehicle traffic to keep the main arteries open so the caravan could make its way out of Belfast. They began the last leg of their trip south to Dublin, the capitol of United Ireland. The caravan took primary roads, except for a short detour through the small village of Drogheda, the town referenced in the novel *Thornbirds*, one of the Holy Father's favorites. Reaching the Belfast city limits, the crowds thinned and the occupants of the Popemobile transferred to the buses.

Inspector Black felt half-relieved; although all the security people assigned to the Pope were professionals, they were constantly on edge, staying on top of the rapidly changing situations. The Holy Father's instant popularity as an ambassador of peace placed additional pressure on the security team. The Inspector felt, hoped, prayed in his own way that the worst was over. Dublin should be a much safer environment. Technically, at the Dublin city limits Inspector Black turned over responsibility for Papal security to the Dublin police. He planned to stay with the motorcade, although no longer in charge.

In just over two hours they'd roll into Dublin, unless spectators slowed their progress. The Dublin police knew their route and were responsible to keep the streets clear for the motorcade and if necessary, emergency vehicles.

Simultaneously exhausted and exhilarated, the rocking bus and whine of the powerful engines lulled the Pope to sleep in a matter of minutes. During the short nap, he had a vivid dream; he saw white mingled with splashes of red, followed by shouts, quick movement, hectic activity. Like most dreams, things were disjointed.

By the time the motorcade reached the main highway everyone had settled in their seats, chatted with their companions or rested. This was Brother Jacomo's first opportunity to think clearly rather than react to the hectic day. The Pope's nap was a good sign. He needed the rest for a long day that was only half over; the welcome dinner at the Burlington Hotel would last until 11:00 p.m. Cardinal Kilgannon invited Pope Alex, Cardinal Belfonte and Sir James to stay the night at his residence. It would be at least midnight before literally crashing into bed. His Holiness was scheduled to celebrate High Mass at St. Patrick's Cathedral, starting at 9:00 a.m., which meant rising at 7:00.

This quiet Pope surprised everyone—including Brother Jacomo. Who ever imagined a charismatic leader was hidden below the surface of the Pontiff's mild, almost California-laid-back demeanor?

Kate Murphy and Eric D'Anella sat rehashing the day's events and how things rapidly evolved, at times spinning out of control. They knew it only takes a small spark to ignite deeply ingrained passions.

"Kate, were you surprised at the Pope's take-charge personality?"

From the first meeting she instinctively knew the man was a born leader. "I felt he had more substance than what most people give him credit for. Look at how he handled the dignitaries and large crowds—it was riveting. My notes combined with your video and still photos will augment his biography. Eric, you must have some great pictures. I can't wait until they're developed." *Tomorrow night I must be on the flight back to New York to finalize the biography. With all the hype and exposure surrounding this visit, GNN has started advertising the biography. Audience share should be staggering.*

"I am pretty eager myself. The film is already in route to New York for developing. I can almost guarantee *Life* and *Time* magazines will pay top dollar for the photos taken at the Peace Line. They're first rate cover material."

"I tend to agree with you, Eric. However, I've been in this business long enough not to assume anything. A word to the wise, don't count your chickens until they hatch."

"I hear you. Point well taken."

In a quandary, Cardinal Belfonte contemplated his next move. He obviously chose the wrong team by joining the crusade. About time to reconsider his options. He joined this trip to document the Pope's shortcomings, and he stayed in the bus rather than ride in the Popemobile to distance himself from the Pope. There must be subtle ways to let Pope Alex know he's supporting him. Volunteering for this trip should count for something. He wondered what to do about Major Bordeau. Capaldo was insisting that Bordeau be promoted to head of the Swiss Guards. That move had to be reevaluated; Colonel Tearsue must delay his retirement for a year or so.

Major Bordeau switched buses to avoid riding with the Holy Father. His cheek twitched; the anxiety intensified as the motorcade rapidly rolled toward Dublin. He tried not to second-guess his decision to set up the Pope. The financial nest egg was wonderful, but could he live with the Judas stigma?

Just inside the city limits, the Pope and his guests transferred to the Popemobile. The major rode in the front passenger seat. During the last rest stopm Major Bordeau disabled the right rear door. Once closed, the lock jammed and the door wouldn't open. As the kilometers clicked on the odometer, he couldn't dismiss the nagging biblical stories about Judas and the thirty pieces of silver. Would he be marked for all time as a twenty-first century Judas? Was he sacrificing his soul and reputation for material wealth? He had nothing against the Pope. In fact, he'd been impressed with his fervor and genuine outpouring of love for the people. It didn't matter how distasteful his actions were; he made a commitment. He couldn't turn back without disgracing himself and his family. He started to make the sign of the cross asking for God's help, then pulled his arm down; what could be more hypocritical?

During the drive to Dublin, some TV and radio stations replayed events from the Papal visit to the Peace Line and Belfast City Hall. As soon as the motorcade reached Dublin city limits, the media switched back to live coverage. The Dublin police led the motorcade at ten kilometers per hour through barricaded streets lined with waving, cheering crowds.

Vice-President Malloy, Jon Cardinal Kilgannon, Anglican Bishop Earl Rayford and Mayor Virginia Marshall waited at the Burlington Hotel to welcome the visitors. A large portion of the parking lot in front of the hotel was roped off, reserved for the motorcade. Not far behind the welcoming committee, fifty members of St. Agnes High School band warmed up. The Irish and Papal flags flew high above the hotel on a massive flagpole partially obscured by the setting sun.

All civilian vehicles were restricted from driving in a four-block area around the hotel. Police and security personnel overlooked the entire area from the roof of every building. In addition, guards circled the hotel property. Huge crowds, waving flags and displaying banners of all shapes and descriptions, were cordoned behind metal barricades. The Dublin police strictly controlled access. Police helicopters circled three square miles preventing unauthorized aircraft above the area. A contingent of emergency vehicles, fire engines, ambulances and armored vans waited in the secured four-block area.

Security was under the command of Chief Inspector Ron O'Neil. He was quite certain his anti-terrorist team thoroughly controlled every aspect of the Pope's security. Chief Inspector O'Neil remained in constant communication with his security teams and waited confidently for the motorcade to arrive at the hotel.

About an hour before the Pope's arrival, police checked the apartment buildings across from the hotel, searched the common areas and checked residents in each apartment. An old woman holding a fluffy cat answered the knock on 3-F's door. Gradually retreating away from the doorway, she appeared eager to have visitors and invited the two officers in for tea. Her I.D. confirmed she was Mrs. Feeney, residing at that address. They quickly proceeded to the next apartment.

Anna listened to the radio commentator describe the motorcade's progress. The lead police escort approached a cross street four blocks from the Burlington. She double-checked the weapon and her getaway disguise. The Feeneys' cat was tossed in the bathroom so she could grab the animal during the few crucial seconds she had to escape. She banged the door hard to make sure the cantankerous latch held. Exiting the apartment had become second nature after numerous practices: Break down the rifle and place the pieces in a carryall, throw on a shawl, pick up the cat and walk through the door—twenty to twenty-five seconds, maximum.

Sirens blared. The lead motorcycles were just two blocks away. The apartment window shades were lifted and centered in the middle of the window. The coffee table had been set back from the window to provide a better firing angle and also to make it difficult to see into the apartment with binoculars.

The motorcade sirens blared one block from the hotel; noise from the expectant crowd increased to a dull roar. The assassin made sure the rifle was firmly planted on the coffee table and sighted the rifle toward the hotel, focusing and refocusing the scope on a police officer stationed at the entrance. Perfect visibility. Cupping the rifle bolt lever in the palm of her right hand she heard the rhythmic click, click as she lifted the lever and pulled open the bolt in one swift motion. Slowly inspecting the shiny cylindrical cartridge, Anna carefully placed the bullet into the chamber. Click, click the bolt closed and locked. Ready, now she needed those promised few seconds to fix on the target and make the kill.

The fifty-member high school band struck up the Irish national anthem amid the clamor of sirens, cheers and shouts of welcome. The police motorcycles cut their sirens as they turned left into the parking area. Following close behind, the Popemobile came to a stop directly under the two-story high portico.

Her cheek rested against the curve of the cool hard stock. Touching the long barrel felt like the caress of a familiar lover before uniting as one. The sensation eased the churning anxiety she always experienced before taking the final deadly aim. The rifle's scope knob turned in small increments, focusing and refocusing on the bubble top. Heat trapped under her wig sprinkled beads of perspiration above her brow.

Major Bordeau mumbled over and over, "I have to do this. Failure is not an option. Failure is not an option." His hands trembled. The blazer concealed the sweat-soaked armpits of his shirt and jacket. He jumped out of the front passenger seat before the Popemobile came to a full stop. Rushing to open the rear door he stumbled and almost lost his balance. His sweaty hand lingered on the rear door facing the crowded parking lot and the apartment buildings across the street. This was the moment he worried about—dreaded—his last chance to change his mind.

Inspector Black rode in a police van, four vehicles behind. From Black's vehicle, the Popemobile and Major Bordeau were clearly visible. The inspector's instincts flashed an alert, his mind screamed, *Oh Shit! Shit*! The major was about to expose the exiting passengers to the crowds and buildings across the street. Comprehending the risk, the inspector's adrenalin jumped. He couldn't allow the Pope to step out facing the crowds, and yelled into the radio, "Major, use the other door, the other door."

The radio instantly barked, "The right door's jammed. Won't open."

Major Bordeau pulled the handle and opened the left door. Standing in the vehicle doorway the Holy Father's head was clearly visible as he waved both arms to the exuberant crowd. The major reached up for the Holy Father's hand to assist him, while intentionally preventing the Pope from stepping down, providing the promised seconds. In those crucial seconds, the assassin sited the target, the scope-cross hairs dead center on the Pope's forehead. Perspiration turned to sweat that rolled along her brow and down her right cheek onto the rifle stock. Finger pressed against the trigger, she inhaled a shallow breath, and murmured, "That's it. Stay still. Okay, focus, focus, squeeze."... Pfffff! The silencer muffled the explosion as the rifle recoiled against her shoulder.

At the precise moment the trigger was pulled, Feeney's black cat leaped onto the coffee table and nudged the rifle. "Oh fuck!" yelled Anna. Traveling on a downward trajectory, the bullet exploded into the major's back, exited his chest and struck the Pontiff. The major died before the bullet ripped through his body. The vicious impact knocked Pope Alex backward into the car. Seeing blood spatter inside the bubble top, people scattered for safety.

The radio and TV reporters had a clear view and a news alert immediately hit the airway. Media commentators strained to yell above the din. Within seconds the whole area was in a furor, the crowd in complete pandemonium. Millions of stunned viewers witnessed the assassination on live T V.

Dublin police activated emergency procedures; an ambulance and armored vehicle were already en route and expected to arrive in minutes. The band and welcoming committee scattered behind vehicles or rushed into the hotel for protection. Inspector Black directed the police car to pull alongside the Popemobile, and provide protective cover. Two Italians from the anti-terrorist squad reached the Popemobile. One checked the major; his body sprawled half under the vehicle. The Italian shook his head; the major was dead. The second Italian jumped into the car and closed the door to protect the occupants.

The Pope looked disoriented, near shock, his left side numb from the impact. Blood splattered like a tie died shirt on everything in the car covering his white cassock, and the other occupants. The Italian ripped open the Pope's cassock to check the wound and excitedly yelled into his radio. "Thank God, he's alive! He's alive!"

Anna yelled, "Fuckin' cat!" over and over. She couldn't see if the shot was on target, a second shot was impossible. Following the escape plan, she picked up her pack, grabbed the snarling cat and ran out of the apartment in twenty-five seconds. Rushing through the first floor door she pushed into the panicked crowd. The police entered every building with a view of the hotel, eagerly breaking down doors or smashing windows to gain entrance. Anna barely touched the sidewalk when police bumped her as they ran into the lobby. Police also penetrated the rear doors and placed guards at the side entrances. No one was permitted to leave or enter until the police completed their investigation.

The officers tried to detain everyone in the crowd standing between the apartment and the hotel. That idea proved unworkable. Hundreds of people slipped through side streets, alleys and around barricades. There just wasn't enough manpower to contain the terrified citizens.

Pushing through the crowd, the old woman walked one block from the apartment building, confident that she managed to evade the police and IRG. Looking backward, she was startled by a police officer and a volunteer guard. Deep Irish brogues instructed her to return to the hotel block or face the magistrate. The old demented woman broke down spouting gibberish, frightened for her life. She squeezed the cat's stomach so hard it cried wildly, lurching toward the officers. Crying hysterically, the old woman whimpered about the cat, and dying. The officer's shrugged in disgust, and waved her along.

Halfway to the West Hotel, the old woman released the cat before stopping at a public toilet, where she changed disguises, transforming into a matronly fifty-year old. The rifle was discarded in various pieces and parts along her route back to the hotel.

An armored vehicle transported the Pontiff to the nearest hospital trauma unit. In the driver's haste to backup to the emergency room door, he knocked over a pole that supported the portico. One side of the portico slammed onto the armored vehicle's roof. Security surrounded in and outside the hospital, their radios traded static-filled communications.

A team of doctors tripped over each other rushing to Pope Alex's gurney. They quickly determined, with a sense of relief, the injury was painful but not life-threatening. An X-ray detected a hairline crack in his pelvic bone. His hip would be stiff, sore, and black and blue for weeks. With God's help and good doctors, Pope Alex would fully recover physically. Emotional recovery was another matter; he felt personally responsible for Major Bordeau's death by permitting his personal agenda and stubbornness to take precedence over adequate security. Although heavily sedated to relieve pain and ward off shock, he was acutely aware that his decision killed a young man in the prime of his life. Flat on the gurney he softly prayed, "Bless me Father, for I have sinned. Can you ever forgive me for placing pride and arrogance above a man's life?"

CHAPTER TWENTY-TWO

Following the failed assassination, the conspirators' emotions vacillated from anger to the depths of depression. The IRG leader's thoughts wandered in all directions; he was beside himself. In the privacy of his hideout he slipped into a self-indulgent tirade; how could a professional miss when the subject was set up for the kill? Did the assassin change her mind and back out? His watchers positively identified the assassin as a woman. "A woman, a God damned woman!" he exploded. "That bitch won't get another dime. She better retire because that bitch will never work again."

He was all too familiar with the next problem. The shit was about to hit the proverbial fan. Ireland would be under excruciating pressure to uphold the unification treaty; even the hardcore old timers would be forced to tolerate equality. Damn, damn…damn. At least the Vatican's connection to the group was silenced. *If the Vatican didn't transfer the final payment*, he thought, *they would be replacing deceased cardinals*. During negotiations the major slipped and mentioned Capaldo and Wronowski. He had names, that's all he needed.

Racked with fear, guilt and shame, Cardinal Wronowski degenerated into an emotional cripple. The confident, powerful, and self-important Vatican Secretariat of State crumbled into a mere shell of his arrogant old self. He'd been secluded for days in his darkened Vatican apartment, half murmuring, rocking as he prayed to the God he disappointed, prayed for the man he betrayed. Speaking to God, he expressed remorse. "I have sinned. Dear God, I am so sorry. I need contrition, forgiveness in the confessional. Belfonte and Capaldo are out of town. It doesn't matter. I can't confess to accomplices in my sins. Marconi is a good man; he'll help me. Hear my confession, understand and help me seek forgiveness."

The call to his assistant was barely audible, "Lucca, ah…please help me out of the chair."

"Eminence, you can't walk. Let me call for help. I'll call Doctor Bananni."

"No, no, Lucca. I must see Cardinal Marconi. Please ask the good Cardinal to come as soon as possible. Tell him it's…urgent. First help me to the bathroom. I'm dizzy, can't, can't catch my…breath."

Lucca helped the weakened Prince to stand; he was scarcely able to support the giant's frame. In lock step they slowly stumbled toward the bathroom. The Cardinal coughed, his lungs wheezed to inhale the shallowest breath. Passing out, the Cardinal's dead weight pulled Lucca to the floor with a sudden jolt. Lucca eased his crushed right leg from under the limp body, and then checked for breathing before running to the phone. The Vatican paramedics arrived within minutes and transported his Eminence to Rome's General Hospital.

Pulling himself together, Lucca notified Cardinal Marconi that before the attack, Cardinal Walter was desperate to see him. That perplexed Marconi. He knew Wronowski was ill. They were never friends, so he wondered why Wronowski wished to see him. Did he want an update on the Pontiff's condition? Something didn't quite fit. With Wronowski floating in and out of a consciousness, there was a chance the mystery might never be unraveled. Wronowski would have to wait until the Pope was out of danger.

Capaldo acted half-crazed. How could the assassin fail? He threw his notebook across the room and yelled, "That idiot major is dead!" His mood swung between dread and anger, failure and victory. He felt as low as whale shit at the bottom of the ocean. What an ugly ugly mess. No, he wouldn't allow himself to dwell on failure, on the "why" or "what ifs." Negatives only distracted from his life's goal: becoming Pontiff. So this plan failed; he still had other options, and felt there would be other opportunities. In a split second, Pope Alex became a popular world leader. Forcing the Pope to step down was shot to hell. However, members of the crusade, especially Cardinals Wronowski, Belfonte and the others, would continue to support the cause. Surely they were not defeated. They also had Wronowski's slush fund. All that money available to make things happen and he knew how to make things happen, he always did!

He needed time to unravel this mess, and decided to postpone his return to the Vatican for a few more days. Time to contemplate and there was no better place than his family homestead.

Cardinal Marconi found the incident bizarre. The entire world saw the assassination attempt on live TV, it happened so quickly the stations couldn't edit out the broadcast. The TV interrupted his thoughts.

NEWS UPDATE... Henry Cardinal Belfonte, Vatican spokesperson at the Dublin Hospital is making an announcement: "Ladies and Gentlemen. I am relieved to announce to the world that the Holy Father's injuries are minor and we expect a full and total recovery. We anticipate his release from the hospital tonight or early tomorrow. More details will be released as they become available. His Holiness and the entire Vatican community mourn the tragic loss of Franz Bordeau, Major in the Swiss Guard. We ask the world to pray for him and his family."

Marconi pushed the intercom button. "Brother Bruno, did you see the news flash? The Holy Father's injuries are minor. He's okay!"

"Yes Eminence, wonderful news."

"Yes it is, brother. I'm sure most of the Vatican heard the news. I want to make sure, so please broadcast the information on the voice mail system. I will make an announcement on the public address system for the visitors in St. Peter's Square."

Marconi's private line rang. Brother Jacomo confirmed that the Holy Father was not seriously injured and in good spirits, all things considered. In an hour or so, the group planned to move to Cardinal Kilgannon's residence for the night.

Marconi looked for his emergency telephone list and called the Holy Father's daughter Gina. The phone answered on the first ring. "Gina, this is Cardinal Marconi. I'm sure you and your family are very upset about your father. I'm calling with very good news. Your father is out of danger and not seriously injured. In fact, he's leaving the hospital in about one hour. You should be able to reach him at this number in about two hours."

Gina nervously thanked the Cardinal while writing down the telephone number in Ireland.

His hip and surrounding muscle tissue throbbed incessantly during the night. Painkillers helped to a degree, but the pain was persistent enough to interrupt the Pontiff's sleep several times. At 6:30 a.m. Brother Jacomo tapped lightly, and gingerly entered the darkened bedroom.

"Holy Father, I hate to disturb you. How are you feeling this morning?"

"Tired, brother. I slept on and off. The hip is extremely sore, still throbbing. Please help me out of bed. Let's see if this leg can hold any weight."

The Pontiff stood without much additional pain, and with Brother's aid he shuffled into the bathroom.

"Holiness, do you wish to cancel celebrating High Mass? You could sit beside the altar while Cardinal Kilgannon celebrates Mass."

"I intend to celebrate Mass as promised. I'll need a sturdy cane and a chair near the altar in case the hip gives me trouble. I also want to attend the Irish Assembly. We've made great strides on this trip, one long day to go. I can rest when we get home." For a second he was taken back by his own comment, then realized the Vatican finally did feel like home.

After the previous day's attack, security was placed on high alert. The Papal group staying at the Burlington arrived at the cathedral and cleared security before the Pope left the Cardinal's residence. This freed up police and security personnel who shifted duties to protect the Pontiff. Pope Alex sat in the Popemobile for the short ride to the cathedral. Inspector Black, technically off duty, insisted on riding in the front seat. Overnight, the lock on the right rear door had been repaired.

As early as 3:00 a.m., people began to assemble waiting for St. Patrick's Cathedral doors to open. Everyone passed through a metal detector and IDs were checked. Every precaution double-checked. The Dublin polices' reputation couldn't withstand another blow. The massive cathedral was standing room only.

The High Mass was a blend of joyful song, praising God and the solemnity of consecrating bread and wine into the body and blood of Jesus Christ. The congregation looked forward to hearing the Holy Father speak. The injury left him weak and unsteady. Without prompting, Jon Cardinal Kilgannon tried to save the Pope from speaking and gave a short sermon about the prodigal son and the need for brotherly love.

When the Cardinal concluded, it was very obvious the congregation expected the Holy Father to speak, so he acquiesced, and motioned for the microphone. Leaning on the cane he slowly stood up. "Brothers and sisters in Christ. Your wonderful Cardinal gave a moving sermon about brotherly love. I ask each of you to remember we are all brothers. Every day, *we must* all live in peace and harmony. Every day, Irish citizens must send an overwhelming message that Ireland wants peace. The violence is over because you, the citizens want it to be over!"

For a brief moment the quiet seemed eerie. Suddenly, the silence broke, a monsoon starting in the rear spread through the pews as the assembly clapped, embracing the reality of peace.

Mass took longer than expected. Fortunately, the Irish Assembly was not far from the Cathedral. Well-wishers lined the streets three and four deep, cheering as the motorcade passed by. After the motorcade drove by, the crowds quieted in anticipation of their legislators handling the growing crisis and grassroots movement toward peace.

Entering the courtyard, the visitors were immediately greeted by President Edward Staquet and Vice President Richard Malloy. The house majority leader, Bill Touey, was conspicuously absent. Pope Alex speculated if Touey was tending to business or signaling his disapproval of the Pope's interference in Irish matters.

The presidential introductions were cordial, although cold and perfunctory. The Staquet administration had come under intense pressure since the GNN human rights broadcast, made worse by the Pope's visit. The President felt cornered and didn't like the scrutiny. Wealthy and influential people with ties to the old IRA exerted pressure to retain their power and the status quo, while the vast majority of citizens, including respected religious leaders, both Catholic and Protestant, demanded reform and equality. By the close of the day's session the whole of Ireland would have a clear idea which direction the country was headed.

Pope Alex, Bishop Rayford, Cardinals Killgannon and Belfonte were quickly ushered to the second row of seats, an area reserved for visiting dignitaries. Sir James Wheelan occupied his normal assembly seat. The other members of the Papal party and media representatives were escorted to the balcony.

Before making this trip, the Pontiff reached out to Interpol for intelligence reports on the conditions in Ireland, including how influential politicians aligned themselves in this struggle. President Staquet had no personal feelings or agenda; he simply wanted to retain the office of president. In that regard, he would bend to the will of the majority. House Majority leader Bill Touey was a hard line right wing advocate of the old IRA brotherhood and the new IRG. The House Minority leader, Ervin O'Hara, leaned toward a liberal position, supporting laws necessary to secure a lasting peace. Below those leaders, many legislators, although not all, generally followed their consciences, not party politics. Legislators with a moral spine were encouraged by their constituents' ferocious ground swell for peace.

Bill Touey opened the meeting with the Irish National Anthem, followed by a prayer offered by the chaplain, an intentional slight to the visiting religious leaders. Mr. Touey did acknowledge the special visitors by name. The mention of Pope Alex created a spontaneous ovation. A bit huffy, Mr. Touey moved on to business and opened a debate on additional security measures needed in Northern Ireland.

He turned the floor over to one of his cronies who spoke for well over an hour, followed by a succession of Touey supporters. They managed to control the assembly floor for three hours. An usher delivered a note to Brother Jacomo. After reading the note he hand carried the message to Pope Alex. The note read:

> Dear Pope Alex,
> Touey is trying to filibuster the meeting to delay a vote on upholding the unification agreement. This can last for days as long as his people hold the floor.
> Follow my lead. If we can manage to have you address the assembly, when you are finished, turn the floor over to me.
> Sir James.

A few minutes later, the speaker sipped a drink of water and a group of legislators took this opportunity to start a ground swell, yelling, "Pope Alex speech, speech Pope Alex, speech Pope Alex." The balcony spectators joined in. They escalated the chanting and added foot stomping. The speaker could not continue with the noise level. He looked at Bill Touey for some signal on how to proceed. Touey shrugged his shoulders, and attempted to signal hold your ground. The speaker interpreted the motion as an acceptance of the audience's request, so he put his arms high into the air, and carried the microphone to the Pope, "I give you Pope Alex IX."

Outraged, Bill Touey jumped up to protest, but he was too late. The assembly eagerly wanted to hear Pope Alex speak. He chose to remain at his seat rather than walking up the stairs to the speaker's podium. Live television or any type of video recording was forbidden during legislative sessions. Radio broadcast was allowed, although restricted to a public broadcast radio station funded and controlled by the government.

Clearing his throat, the Pope looked left then right across the audience. "President Staquet, Vice-president Malloy, ladies and gentlemen of the legislature, visitors and most importantly, people of Ireland. Thank you for the gracious invitation to visit your wonderful country. This is my second visit in twenty years. During the first visit, I was impressed with the beauty of the people and the countryside. I believe every visitor leaves your country feeling touched by this magical land you call home.

"When I heard about the growing turmoil and violence, I was drawn to return. I didn't plan to address this assembly. Rather, I was hoping to witness legislators, people of good will, acting to reset Ireland on a path to true equality and non-violence. A wonderful human being, Pope John Paul II, expressed his thoughts at the dawn of the new millennium. His words were so inspiring I carry them with me as a constant reminder."

Steadying the cane, he reached into his pocket for a folded over and dog-eared piece of paper. "I would like to read his words because they are and will continue to be relevant until mankind learns to love God and neighbors. Quoting Pope John Paul II: 'When we are dead through sin (cf. Eph 2:5), the Son of God wished to unite himself to human nature, ransoming it from the slavery of sin and death. This is a slavery which man experiences every day, as he perceives its deep root in his own heart (cf. Mt 7:11). Sometimes it shows itself in dramatic and unusual ways, as happened in the course of the great tragedies of the twentieth century, which deeply marked the lives of countless communities and individuals, the victims of cruel violence. Forced deportations, the systematic elimination of peoples, contempt for the fundamental rights of the person: These are the tragedies that even today humiliate humanity. In daily life too, we see all sorts of forms of fraud, hatred, the destruction of others, and lies of which man is both the victim and the source.... Through the virtue of hope, Christians bear witness to the fact that, beyond all evil and beyond every limit, history bears within itself a seed of good which the Lord will cause to germinate in its fullness.'"

Alex the Pontiff raised his eyes and searched their faces, made eye contact to see if the speech had any impact on the men and women entrusted with protecting all the citizens of United Ireland. "I pray that the seeds you germinate will bloom into a lasting peace for Ireland and all of its citizens."

The full assembly gave him a standing ovation. His outstretched arms accepted their enthusiasm. After a few moments he bowed and waved, requesting quiet.

"Your enthusiasm is warming, thank you all. Now, I would like to turn over the floor to Sir James Wheelan."

Sir James jumped up and trotted to the speaker's podium. Bill Touey, in a deep brogue yelled, "Foul," and ran down the aisle to challenge Sir James' right to hold the floor. Bill Touey was pissed, mad enough to start a fistfight at the speaker's podium. The assembly was in an uproar over who was entitled to take control of the speaker's floor. Bill Touey and Sir James stood eye to eye, neither willing to budge or negotiate. Each had a hand on the precious podium. Sheer willpower kept them from physical contact, both eager to engage in the latest clash in their prolonged political struggle. Touey gritted his oversized teeth and trembled as hate and disgust coursed through his limbs. Red blotches filled the white spaces between his brown freckles.

Sir James held his hard fought ground. He counted to ten, holding back the urge to kill the bloody bastard.

After a sustained ruckus, the assembly finally fell silent in order to hear their arguments. Bill Touey asked for an immediate ruling. Normally the speaker of the assembly made the final decisions on parliamentary protocol; however, Mr. McNally was home recovering from a heart attack. Next in line, Vice President Richard Malloy. This might prove to be the most important decision of his career.

Vice President Malloy would have liked nothing better than a recess to cool off tempers and confer with President Staquet. At the same time, he couldn't afford to appear indecisive. He bought some precious time waiting for the assembly to fully come to order. Glancing sideways he looked to the president seated beside him for guidance, some sign on which way to rule. While the Vice President slowly raised his microphone, President Staquet judged the political mood and whispered, "Sir James."

Vice President Malloy appeared calm, in control; inside his stomach churned, the bile erupted into his throat. The old guard would not forget or forgive today's decision. "Ladies and gentlemen, although this situation is highly unusual, the original speaker specifically relinquished the floor to Pope Alex. In so doing, Pope Alex can relinquish the floor as he sees fit. Therefore, Sir James is entitled to the floor."

The hall rocked, engulfed with cheers and applause. In a show of victory, Sir James' arms shot toward the ceiling as he accepted the floor. With the process in capable hands, the Holy Father signaled their departure. The group gathered in the courtyard waiting for security to clear the parking area. Pope Alex looked for Inspector Black; he wanted to speak with him in private. It didn't take long to find the inspector, who was usually near by.

"Inspector Black, I want to personally thank you for all your hard work and concern. You and each member of your team will receive a personal thank you letter when I return to the Vatican. I also plan on sending a letter to your superior, commending your team and your personal dedication."

The inspector gave a slight nod. "Thank you, Holy Father. It's been a privilege to be part of this peace mission. I know the men will appreciate receiving your letter of commendation."

"Inspector Black, did I hear correctly that you are a well known rugby player and your nickname is Biggie?"

"In my young days I did play a wee bit of the sport."

"I have a friend, Steve Hardeski, an avid fan, played in his younger days. Can you help me get two tickets for the rugby championship game?"

"My pleasure, consider it done. On a more serious matter, the investigation into your attack has already produced some vital information. We know the shot came from an apartment across from the hotel. The residents, a Mr. and Mrs. Feeney, were convinced to vacate the apartment by a phony police sergeant. All indications point to a professional assassin. The question of course is who and why. It may take some time, but we will crack this case. Rest assured!"

Without further conversation they clasped hands. Pope Alex liked this rock of a man whose mere presence gave people a sense of security. After proffering his Papal blessing, the group boarded the buses and the police escort started toward the Dublin Airport.

The main roadway to the airport was temporarily blocked, allowing the motorcade free access. One taxi driver didn't mind waiting in traffic. His mirror had a perfect view of his back seat that was occupied by a gorgeous blond with blue eyes. The taxi driver thought his passenger was not only attractive but very polite, a real lady. Not harboring a grudge over her failure, Anna waved farewell as the motorcade passed within a few feet of the cab.

A chartered jet waited at a secure hangar some distance from the main terminal. The military C-150 was flight listed to deliver Mrs. Bordeau and the major's casket to Switzerland before returning to Rome with the Popemobile and Italian security team. Mrs. Bordeau wanted to bury her husband in his hometown, and planned to move back to Switzerland as soon as arrangements could be made.

This was the Pope's first opportunity to speak with Mrs. Bordeau since her husband's death. She acted cordial but cool, an unmistakable strain in her composure. Her emotions wavered between tears, frustration and deep rage. The widow's eye sockets looked darker than her long black dress. Pope Alex tried to console her, without much success. Her speech barely audible, more a mumble, words coming out disjointed. He couldn't tell if she was in borderline shock or so irate she had difficulty controlling angry eruptions that might spew any moment, at anyone and everyone. Following the short, strained conversation, Mrs. Bordeau proceeded to board the C-150 warming up for departure.

The Pontiff gave Brother Jacomo specific instructions about making sure that Mrs. Bordeau was well taken care of in Switzerland. Considering the circumstance, he felt responsible for her welfare. If only he hadn't pushed for a quick departure date. Life is a series of "if only." He knew first hand life goes on; you shouldn't look back or second-guess.

A strong cooling breeze tossed their hair and clothes while huddling on the warm tarmac waiting to board the aircraft. In his own shy way, Pope Alex thanked each person for his or her assistance during the trip, and especially the indispensable Brother Jacomo.

Kate and Eric quickly said their goodbyes and half ran to the main terminal to catch a flight to New York City. During the flight they hoped to work on incorporating the Ireland trip into the Pope's biography. Late next week Kate was due at the Vatican for the dress rehearsal.

The flight back to Rome was short and thankfully uneventful. Somehow Inspector Black managed to arrange NATO jet fighters to escort the charter plane all the way to Rome. The entire group appreciated home after the stressful trip. Media hoards invaded the airport for photos and, if fortunate, some comment from the Pontiff. As a security precaution, Pope Alex, Cardinal Belfonte and Brother Jacomo were whisked passed the media to a waiting helicopter. The Pontiff usually preferred the scenic drive; on this day, near exhaustion and in pain, he couldn't wait to land on Vatican soil.

The Pope noticed Belfonte insisted on taking the helicopter. That started his mind churning, wondering if Belfonte was choosing him over his friend Wronowski. The helicopter lifted off, spun 90 degrees and headed home.

Overcome with relief, Brother Jacomo released a sigh from the recesses of his soul. In a few short minutes they'd be back, and he'd no longer bear full responsibility for the Holy Father's welfare.

The deafening noise was compounded by rhythmic rotor vibration. Brother

Jacomo had to shout above the din, "Holiness how are you feeling? Is the wound causing you much pain?"

"Right now it's throbbing. Mostly...I'm tired. I guess it'll be impossible to avoid a brief a brief session with Eminence Marconi. He's been checking on me every half-hour. Afterward I want a light dinner, then straight to bed. And brother, make yourself scarce...you deserve some time off."

"Thank you, Holiness. May I suggest a few things?"

The Pope thought, *Here we go, worse than a wife.* "I just said you're off duty."

"Yes Holiness, but not until we land." They chuckled as the Pope patted Brother Jacomo's knee, each sensed the barrier between them was gone. "You should see Dr. Bananni for a quick check up.

"I'll think about the good doctor. Anyway, he always manages to show up."

Pope Alex also made a mental note to call Leigh as soon as possible. She must be glued to the news reports and probably climbing the walls with worry.

Sister Martha and a squad of Swiss Guards waited for the 'copter. Sister fidgeted until they landed and she saw the Holy Father first hand. Losing her normal reserve, Sister kissed the Papal ring then hugged the Pontiff with all her might, a single tear formed in the crook of her eye. While he sincerely welcomed the genuine affection, he felt a bit awkward even under the most platonic circumstances.

Golf carts shuttled everyone to their quarters. The Pope barely entered his library when Marconi arrived, bursting to discuss the trip, especially the huge spike in the Pontiff's public image. However, he understood the Holy Father well enough to know that he would be reluctant to discuss these issues in depth until tomorrow or possibly the next day. Marconi didn't care. Later was too late. He couldn't control the compulsion to be with his friend, if only to welcome him home.

Already exhausted, Pope Alex managed a full smile when he saw the map of joy across Marconi's Italian face. With the Pope's entire domestic staff present, Marconi's greeting remained formal. Shaking both of the Pope's hands, he offered a wide grin and reassuring wink. Understanding Marconi's fixation, Pope Alex thanked everyone for his or her concern, assured them he was on the mend, and proffered his blessing. Before hobbling to his desk, Pope Alex took Sister Martha aside. "Sister, I may need help. If this meeting lasts longer than an hour, please interrupt and save me. Also, would you be good enough to order a light supper?"

Sister tried unsuccessfully to suppress a smile. Now that the Pope had returned safely, she felt responsible to make sure that he took care of himself, and had no qualms about reminding and if need be, badgering him as often as necessary.

Marconi literarily erupted, bouncing on the soles of his feet. "Holiness...how is your hip?"

"Much better, my friend...it's fine, sore but healing quickly for an old goat. You can stop worrying. I'm back home under your watchful eye."

"Holiness, you can't even imagine how worried we were. Not just your immediate staff, the whole Vatican, even people who acted ambivalent just days ago are truly concerned about their Pontiff. Not the Pontiff, *their* Pontiff, a significant distinction, no? The staff's been inundated with telephone calls, faxes, e-mails and get well cards. The vast majority concerned about your health as well as congratulations on your peace efforts."

Standing behind an armchair, Marconi continued to bounce on the soles of his feet. The Pontiff didn't ask him to sit, hoping the conversation would be short. "I'm very touched Dominic. I truly am, and would like to read some of the cards and e-mails. This could be a turning point in public confidence. Please include some of the negative comments as well."

"These communications are not from just the Vatican community or the Catholic community. After the last few days you caught the attention of the entire world." Marconi didn't want to leave but felt obligated to ask, "Oh...forgive me Holiness, you must be exhausted. Ah, would you rather rest? I can come back later. Let me know when you're rested and can spare a few minutes for a quick update on the media and information about our cardinal friends."

"Okay, Dominic, I know you're beside yourself to tell me about everything that's happened. Go ahead. But...keep it brief." Inside the Pope had to laugh. His friend certainly knew the right buttons to push and he recognized the Marconi smirk as his friend sat.

"First, Wronowski's gravely ill...had a massive stroke. Coincidentally, it was just minutes after the news report about the assassination. He's paralyzed and in a vegetative state, not expected to survive."

Startled, the Pontiff hesitated before he replied, "He has served the Church...I'm sorry to hear this. He'll be in my prayers."

"The other one, Capaldo, is missing in action. His staff hasn't heard from him since you left for Ireland. Word is he's down south visiting his brother. I was surprised that the group didn't try to cause some type of ruckus before your trip. This is totally contrary to their mode of operation. When anticipated problems don't happen, I really begin to wonder what's going on."

"Try not to overanalyze every event or non-event; life's too short. Speaking of which, I wonder if Capaldo knows about his partner's illness, also when he plans to return?"

"I wish I knew, Holiness. Now, for some good news...my mole in Capaldo's office finally obtained the names of the other cardinals."

The Pontiff had been waiting for their names. Now that the information was at hand, he worried that the group of conspirators may be far too powerful for him to out maneuver. He reminded himself that God sat on his bench. "Who are they?"

"I'll give you the names, but I want you to sleep on the list before making any rash decisions. With your current popularity they are toothless tigers. In the short run no action may be the best action. Do you agree to think about this?"

"You know I'm not impulsive. Now, the names please."

Before Dominic revealed the names, the Holy Father could tell by his dower expression the names he was about to hear were a litany of who's who in the Church. "Cardinals Francis Pasquale, Kurt Breckhold, Daniel MacRay, Raj Patel, Timothy Hildabrand, Frank Gonzalez, and the biggest shock, your travel companion, Henry Belfonte."

The Pope was not quite stunned, but taken back by the diverse demographics and number of faithful these cardinals controlled. "My God, that's a powerful list. They control important and influential segments of the Holy Church. It's inconceivable that they joined forces against a Pontiff. They must be deathly afraid of the reforms we're contemplating. Belfonte is not powerful, but he's too close to our day-to-day operations, especially security. It explains why he insisted on joining the trip. Is that the entire list?"

Dominic thought about the Pope's comment, "reforms we are contemplating...." He always supported the Holy Father, firmly believing the Pope was God's chosen one. He never considered his personal opinion about the reforms; always followed the Pope's lead. The comment "we" meant the Pope thinks he fully supports the changes for the betterment of the Church. Marconi realized he better look beyond friendship and loyalty, into the core of the issues and decide if he fully agreed with all the reforms. If not, he better express his opinion quickly.

"Yes and no, Holiness. That's the list of active members. There's also a group that won't take overt action against the Papacy but committed to support the crusade when they're in control. I don't have their names nor do I expect we will ever know who they are. At this point they are not important. We shouldn't waste any time on them."

"The crusade?"

"Oh, didn't I mention…they consider this a crusade to save the Church!"

The Pope wiggled in his chair. "This whole thing is getting more bizarre by the hour. Can you imagine considering these terrible un-Christian actions a crusade?"

"Holiness, if you recall history, during the Crusades, Christians were desperate, and desperate men take despicable actions."

"I will follow your advice and sleep on this. Anything else you wish to discuss?"

"Yes, one last item, the news media. Since your trip they've been like rabid dogs pestering the Vatican media staff for information. It seems the public's appetite for news about the Vatican is insatiable, at least for now. A short broadcast from you on the Vatican radio station would help."

"Good idea! Please make arrangements for a radio broadcast. But tomorrow, not today!"

As Dominic smiled with a sense of pride, Sister Martha knocked and sprinted across the room to turn on the television. "Excuse me, the BBC just announced a special news bulletin about Ireland." Sister stepped back from the screen, but stayed in the room.

"Hello, I am Cary Schwartz, reporting for the BBC. We are broadcasting live from the Irish legislature in Dublin. Today, the legislature made great strides in passing the first in a series of bills designed to uphold the civil rights of all Irishmen, including the citizens of northern Ireland previously protected under the terms of the unification agreement. The legislators have adjourned for the evening. Mr. Bill Touey, the ultra conservative leader, is walking toward me. His opposition to the new civil rights bills was thoroughly defeated. Mr. Touey, can you spare a moment to discuss today's startling events?"

Raising his hand to block the camera he snarled with large bared teeth, "I've no comment for the news media, especially the BBC. Go home, Englishmen! You've no business in Ireland!"

"Well, you saw and unfortunately heard Mr. Touey's reaction. He's not taking today's events very well. I hoped to have a few words with Sir James

Wheelan, the well-known legislator from Northern Ireland and the sponsor of what has become known as the 'peace bills.' Unfortunately, Sir James, amidst a crowd of supporters, left by a side entrance. For those who have not been following the events of the last few days in Ireland, I will give you a quick update. The peace movement accelerated when Pope Alex IX made a historic trip to…"

The Holy Father clicked the remote control turning off the TV. "We don't need a rehash of recent events."

"Excuse me Holiness, dinner is ready and Dr. Bananni called to say he will stop by to see you in a half hour or so."

"Thank you, Sister. You can serve the soup I'll be finished in a few moments. Well, it's good to be home. You heard the boss, unless you have other urgent business, dinner is ready. Would you care to join me for a light meal?"

"No thanks. I'm sure you will appreciate some time alone." His friend knew him oh so well.

Pope Alex was sipping coffee when Dr. Bananni strolled in wearing a three button dark blue suit with his trademark vest and green bow tie. When he placed reading glasses on the edge of his Roman nose, the Pope knew it was time for a Bananni lecture.

"Doctor, what an unexpected pleasure. Somehow you always manage to visit just before dessert. Would you care to partake of the chef's homemade dessert or would you rather make me feel guilty while I enjoy the treat?"

Dr. Bananni threw up his arms. "Oh well, the old Pope is back. I thought, God knows why, you'd come back a new man. Ireland's been known to do that; I hear it's their women. If not exactly new, at least watch your health, considering everything you've been through!"

"Actually, Doctor, it did help me to reconfirm what I've known for a long time: Life is uncertain and you should eat dessert first. That said…it's good to see you again. Sister is preparing your cinnamon espresso."

The doctor sat next to his friend and reached across to feel his pulse. "Seriously Holiness… I know health is low on your list of priorities but I am concerned. You look tired and more than a bit pale. After the espresso—and by the way, you forgot to mention my favorite biscotties—I want to check your vitals. Even before checking them, my prescription is at least three solid days of rest. Do we understand each other?"

The Pontiff begrudgingly nodded, and placed his left hand on his friend's shoulder.

"Now, Holiness, give me the real inside scoop on your trip!"

Chapter Twenty-three

The second payment was due to the IRG forty-eight hours after the assassination. The late wire transfer agitated the IRG leader. He called the Swiss bank several times in four hours. Each time they verified no cash was transferred.

Initially the leader was not going to pay the assassin her final payment. She failed and he didn't accept failure. Reconsidering, he thought it best to uphold his end of the deal and make the final payment, but only after the IRG received their cash.

The leader had no way of knowing the man responsible to approve the transfer, Cardinal Wronowski, lay in the hospital hanging on to life. His partner Cardinal Capaldo was on holiday and didn't have the slightest inkling that Wronowski was ill or that the funds hadn't been transferred. Major Bordeau was the point man and the IRG leader's direct contact with the Vatican.

One hour before the bank closed the leader decided to contact the third partner in their venture. He wasn't sure who in the crime organization approved the guarantee but he had to be someone high up in the organization. He decided to call his old contact for smuggling illegal weapons, Sergio Cellucci, capo in Messina, Sicily. They hadn't spoken in two years. In the new United Ireland, the IRG had free access to all the weapons they needed.

Sitting in a dimly lit back corner of a warehouse, a man answered the telephone on the second ring. "Pronto."

"Is Sergio there? This is an old friend that buys used medical equipment."

"Hold while I check."

Sergio had answered the call and from the Irish brogue, immediately recognized the caller. The call smelled like trouble. As a security precaution, he took a few moments to verify the call was originating from Ireland on a secure line.

"Hello, my old friend, it has been some time since we last spoke."

"My Italian friend, you have a very good memory. How are you and more importantly how is business?"

"I am *molto bene*, and my business is always good. What can I do for you, my friend?"

"Today, I only need your help with information about contacting a medical associate. Recently, two partners arranged a surgical procedure. Doctors from Rome contacted my hospital and recommended surgery. Regrettably, the surgery was not successful. However, my hospital is waiting for the final payment that's due today. I can't contact the doctors in Rome, but I was told that your company recommended the surgery and provided insurance on the payment."

"That's strange, most surgical referrals come through my office and I don't recognize this patient. When did the operation take place?"

"Two days ago."

"Interesting. I'll inquire and get back to you. Are you still at the same number?"

"Yes, and please hurry. I've yet to pay the surgeon."

"I understand my friend. This may take a day or two, so be patient."

Cardinal Capaldo repeatedly tried contacting Cardinal Wronowski, leaving urgent messages on his cell phone and pager, all with no response. At 8:00 p.m. he again called Wronowski's apartment. The phone finally answered. "Pronto, Cardinal Wronowski's residence, Lucca speaking."

With a sense of relief he thought, *It's about time.* "This is Cardinal Capaldo. May I speak with his Eminence?"

"Eminence, I am very sorry. Apparently you haven't heard the news. Eminence Wronowski had a massive stroke and is gravely ill. Most of his body is paralyzed and he can't speak. The prognosis is not good. If he recovers, which is unlikely, he will be...I'm sure you understand. His cousin and sister are arriving from Poland this evening."

"That's terrible! When did this happen?"

"Ironically, it was right after the attack on his Holiness. His Eminence had been ailing for days. He asked to see Eminence Marconi, then without warning collapsed. The attack was over quickly."

Hesitating, Capaldo considered the timing of the stroke and realized the final payment hadn't been transferred. This could turn into a disaster. His hands began to shake as he thought about the implications. The IRG lost their connection to the Vatican. If they get impatient and call the Mafia, it would lead directly to his doorstep. Shit! He had to contact the Vatican Bank first thing tomorrow and expedite the funds.

"Eminence, are you still on the line?"

"Yes, yes…just thinking. I'll return to the Vatican early tomorrow and visit His Eminence as soon as I can. Meanwhile, please watch over him and his family. If he receives any urgent or unusual telephone calls, notify me immediately. Please take down my cell phone number."

Late that evening, Sergio Cellucci and his bodyguard drove back roads to reach Don Petruzzi's villa before he retired for the night. Sergio attended the special meeting when the council discussed Cardinal Capaldo's request and understood this tied into the Irishman's telephone call.

Sergio had been nicknamed "the Arab," simply because he looked like an Arab from Semitic genes inherited centuries ago when the Moors invaded and governed Sicily. He hated the nickname with a passion, and few men were brave enough to call him "Arab" to his face.

He called the Don for an appointment, declining to discuss details over the telephone. They couldn't risk any breach of security on a momentous issue. It was common practice to discuss special issues in private, nothing can replace face-to-face discussions. No place in Sicily had more security than the Petruzzi Villa. Many of his overnight guards were off-duty police officers. The local mayor paid weekly homage to the man who was more influential than the governor of Sicily.

Cellucci's BMW pulled up to the Villa gates at 10:00 p.m., perfect timing; the Don had finished supper and it was a civilized hour to discuss business. The guards checked the occupants as well as the vehicle. Once satisfied, the gates opened and the BMW proceeded the quarter mile to the country villa, perched on a cliff with an unobstructed view of the Mediterranean Sea. Three guards greeted the visitors at the front steps. One man accompanied the bodyguard to the guesthouse. Another searched Sergio, and once satisfied, they escorted him to the vestibule, where he was turned over to the Don's houseman.

"Don Petruzzi is expecting you. Follow me."

This wasn't the first time Sergio had the privilege of visiting the Don's treasured Villa, his sanctuary from the tremendous responsibilities of his position. During each visit, Sergio noticed another room that he previously missed or saw an expensive work of art or a unique flower imported from an exotic land. The Don personally supervised every aspect of his beloved villa. The villa smelled fresh and clean from the sea mist wafting through the open windows. They headed for the study, a magnificent room designed around a two-story atrium. Half of the roof and one exterior wall was solid glass tinted light green. At the end of the room a double set of French doors led outside to a ten by ten meter veranda overhanging the rocky coastline. Crossing the threshold the capo's feet sank into a plush Oriental carpet, while his mood dipped far lower. No one liked to deliver bad news, especially to the Don. Sergio's role was to smooth out the rough spots, not make the boss's life more complicated. The waxing moon shined through the glass ceiling like a beacon, while all he could dwell on was spelling out the bad news.

Don Ricardo stood and welcomed his capo with a firm handshake and a Sicilian hug. The Don offered a seat directly across from where he sat. The bodyguard nodded hello, and took two steps back.

Sergio stroked back thick unruly hair. "*Patrone*, thank you for seeing me on such short notice."

"It's always an honor to have you as a guest in my home. I can see you've had a long day. Can I offer you some cake and coffee or a drink of some kind?"

"No, thank you. Hopefully after our talk you can enjoy the remainder of the evening."

The formalities concluded, the Don raised his hand to proceed; Sergio the messenger was eager to get the news out. The bodyguard moved to the farthest corner of the room, giving them privacy, while remaining near enough in case his services were needed.

Sergio wasn't nervous meeting with the Don but cautious about what he said and ever conscious of showing respect, always the proper respect. "A few weeks ago, I was privileged to attend a council meeting where you presented a request to assist a Vatican official on a very delicate issue."

Those few words piqued the Don's attention and his upper body leaned forward.

"This afternoon, I received a telephone call from a former Irish customer, who claims he hasn't received final payment on a contract that was executed in Dublin."

The Don's face looked bewildered. "What does this have to do with our business?"

Sergio leaned forward placing both elbows on his knees, his hushed voice millimeters from Don Ricardo. "This man is highly placed in the IRG. We've done business with him for years...a good customer, never a problem. Claims he was assured our Family approved the contract and guaranteed payment. The negotiator was a Vatican employee and the deposit was paid on time, so he didn't question the connection between our Family and the Vatican."

Frowning, Don Ricardo sat back sinking into the soft cushion. He placed a soft hand under his chin while mulling over the far-reaching complications. Capaldo ignored his warning about implicating the Family in his scheme. If the Cardinal acted on his own initiative, the Don would be obligated to present the facts to the council. The issue could be cloudy because he didn't tell Capaldo not to take action against the Pope; he told him not to involve the Family. With this information, he didn't contemplate a council meeting. Their edict was crystal clear, and violators must be punished.

"I'm sure you understand the unpleasant business ahead of us. First our Irish friend, will he accept that we are not a party to this, and we won't pay? Or do we have to eliminate a potential Irish problem?"

Sergio sensed trouble if the Family ordered a hit outside their sphere of control. He tactfully related his concerns. "I'll talk to him. Even if we remove the leader, other members in his group may think the Family's involved. Without their names, eliminating the leader doesn't do us any good and we will be open for retaliation. Let me work on the him."

Nodding approval, the Don looked angry. "That fuck Capaldo is a stickier problem. His brother Roberto will go crazy, his blood hot for vengeance. After cooling down, Roberto will have to accept the council's decision...what are his options. Roberto attended the council meeting and knows I made a special trip to Rome to personally give his brother the final decision. The idiot intentionally ignored the warning and he'll pay the price, Cardinal or no! He's visiting Roberto in Calabria. I hear he's leaving tomorrow.

"Some eliminations are also warnings to other violators. This is not one of those occasions. The contract has to look like an accident with no possible link to us. I want you to personally handle the arrangements. He can't be allowed to reach the Vatican."

"I'll personally handle it."

"Go with my blessing. And don't worry about Roberto… I'll handle that one."

The next morning Sergio called the IRG leader. Before he could begin to explain the Family's position, the leader thanked Sergio for his cooperation. The Swiss bank just verified transfer of the funds. Sergio loathed discussing Family business with outsiders. At the same time he was reluctant to allow the IRG to believe the Family was involved. This was an exception, so he told the leader that the wire transfer was simply a coincidence. They were never involved. The leader didn't believe the story. No matter, the message was clear: Keep silent. As far as the leader was concerned, everyone should forget the whole ugly mess.

Transferring four million dollars required approval from a Vatican Bank officer and the account holder. Without Cardinal Wronowski approval, Capaldo was in a bind and had to transfer his personal funds before the IRG caused a stink with Palermo. The funds could easily be replaced once he gained access to Wronowski's bank records and hidden slush funds. A few minutes after the bank opened, Capaldo telephoned and arranged a transfer of funds. The second call was to Giorgio, asking his driver to prepare to leave for Rome in two hours.

Roberto was the only member of his family at home; his wife was out shopping for the evening meal. Roberto's children were grown with their own families. The brothers often discussed the twists and turns of life's journey, how each set out on opposite paths yet in the end both worked for the Family. The difference between them was vast. Roberto had never been a phony, would never hide behind a priest's cassock. He loved his younger brother John and was proud of his position as Prince of the Church, although disappointed that John used his exalted position to further his personal wealth. If their lives had been reversed, Roberto would not compromise his beliefs for personal gain, especially at the expense of the Holy Mother Church.

"Well my brother, thank you for the hospitality. I enjoyed our time together and visiting old friends, especially the cousins I haven't seen in so many years. Unfortunately, I have been notified of urgent business. I'm leaving in a few minutes."

He hugged his older brother and patted him on the back. "Give my love to Philomena. It's a shame she is out on errands. I wanted to say goodbye in person. Please thank her for the home cooking…the best veal in all of Italy."

"I know the American Pope cannot run the Vatican without your assistance. We will miss you my brother. God speed and be careful."

The scene was reminiscent of the day the brothers embraced in the old family kitchen before John left for the seminary. Just then Giorgio pulled up at the front door. The travel bags sat at the doorstep so Giorgio placed them into the trunk of the Cardinal's new toy; a Mercedes S-class sedan, a powerful and comfortable driving machine. Standing at the kitchen window, Cardinal John slowly looked around the old house and orchard, part of the family heritage for well over a hundred years. Involuntarily reaching back a half century, he recalled as a young boy, working the fields and orchard with his father after school and on Saturdays. Their father, Roberto Sr., although short in stature, worked like a bull. A quiet man who spoke very little, but when he did, people listened because they were usually words worth listening too.

Josephine, his wife and soul mate, always had something to say. After a long day at school and later in the fields, the smell of homemade supper drew her men to the warm and comfortable kitchen where Momma insisted on talking about the day's events. Some evenings John felt so tired he only wanted to grunt. Momma insisted on proper social graces at the supper table, which always included conversation. John thought his father was happiest with children around the house, because his wife would talk to them, and give the old man some peace. When his parents did have long conversations, it evolved around the farm or more likely the children's education or careers.

His father finally prevailed in his argument that Roberto, the oldest son, should inherit the farm. With that settled, the next child was Patricia, leaving them not much to discuss. She'd finish high school and find an acceptable husband and raise grandchildren. Next came John, Momma insisted John receive an education and become a priest. Her pregnancy with John was difficult and she almost lost the baby. Momma told everyone that her prayers to the Blessed Mother included a promise that one of her children would do God's work. It was proper that John fulfill that promise.

As a young man, John was determined to go into business, the religious life virtually last on his list of possibilities. Finally, after many months of supper discussions, his father unexpectedly broke the stalemate, conceding to his wife's wishes. John would become a priest and was enrolled in seminary. Naturally, John pretended to be upset and wouldn't discuss the decision all summer.

However, the men in the family knew he had no choice. After he and his friend robbed and vandalized a mob warehouse, the local capo offered to spare John's life, but only if he became a priest. On those rare occasions when he thought about deceiving the only women in his life, bile uncontrollably invaded his esophagus. He could feel the gagging taste, and the putrid smell overcome his taste buds. It was time to leave, to move on, time to put the disappointment entirely and forever behind him.

The only thing that made those days more tolerable was his Momma, a not-so-simple farmer's wife intent on shaping his entire life. There were moments when he missed the farmer's hard physical labor and less complicated way of life. *At this juncture*, he thought, *it's far too late to change a thing: I am what I am, the Church my life, the Vatican my home*. Although he loved returning to his roots, it was time to return home.

Standing at the rear door, Giorgio waited to assist His Eminence. Capaldo glanced around one last time before sliding into the rear white leather seat. He waved out the side window as Giorgio pulled away toward the main road.

Giorgio had worked for the Capaldo family long before he became a tour bus driver. At fifty-five he was forced to retire, so he offered his services to the Capaldo's as a freelance driver. The local mountain roads with steep climbs and deep ravines were familiar territory. An experienced driver, Giorgio traversed the entire area with ease. In some remote sections the roads had been neglected, wasted away to one lane. The closest entrance to a modern highway normally took thirty minutes, depending on road conditions and the number of farm animals slowing traffic.

Motoring east the orange morning sun hovered midway in the sky, radiating a strong glare into the driver's eyes. On better stretches of road their speed exceeded 50 kilometers, the max speed he could safely maneuver without risking an accident or damage to the Mercedes. The Cardinal attempted to use his cell phone without success; the lack of towers and the high mountain peaks mired wireless communication. He hated being out of contact, especially with his plans in turmoil.

"Your Eminence, cell reception will be available in about twenty minutes when we reach the main highway. I left your briefcase in the back seat in case you wish to read."

"Thanks. How was your holiday? Do anything exciting?"

"Yes, I struck up with an old girlfriend who became a widow last year. Marriage turned her into a much better cook."

"It's not a good sign when you talk about a woman's cooking."
"Excellency, I save the juicy bits for confession."

Capos normally assign dirty work to trusted lieutenants. In this instance, Sergio promised Don Ricardo he would personally handle the arrangements. Logically, he was reluctant to contact men from the Calabria region because they might be loyal to Roberto and warn him about the contract before it was completed. Before dawn broke, things were settled and in motion. The capo explained the assignment, clearly indicated it must appear to all investigators as an accident and must happen long before the target reached Rome.

The increased fee, not to mention the goodwill forged with Sergio and his superiors, easily overcame the mechanic's slight hesitation about the target. The mechanic didn't bother to mention that his secondary reason for accepting the assignment was to settle an old grudge with Roberto. Sergio told the mechanic where the target was located and his expected departure for Rome later that morning.

The mechanic and his partner were familiar with Calabria. They had performed specialty work in and around the area. There were only two roads that led to the main highway from Roberto's farm and one was nearly impassable. Choosing the most likely route, they arrived early to wait for the Cardinal's vehicle. An associate staked out the unlikely route to make sure their query didn't slip through.

The mechanics drove a large Volvo dump truck half loaded with gravel. They parked near the top of a steep hill with a clear view of the approach for at least a kilometer. The road ascending the mountain toward their position was just over one lane wide. The right side was solid rock, the left a sheer drop of fifty meters or more into a ravine.

About two hours into the wait the mechanic nudged his partner and pointed to billowing dust one kilometer out. At half a kilometer the white Mercedes was clearly visible picking up speed as it prepared to tackle the steep incline. A spotter radioed, "It's the Cardinal." The mechanic nodded and the driver put the truck in reverse and backed the truck onto the road stopping just below the crest of the hill, the solid metal rear bed blocked the narrow roadway.

As the Mercedes crested the knoll, the truck sat in the middle of the road. Giorgio jammed on the anti-lock brakes. The front end dove forward a second before crashing into the truck's solid metal. The front end crumbled, the exploding airbag pinned Giorgio against the seat. He punched away the deflating airbag, and reflexively turned to check the back seat. The Cardinal looked shaken, his wild eyes begged for an answer. Giorgio erupted in disgust, ready to rip out the truck driver's throat.

Before he could lift the door handle, the dump truck shifted into reverse, the rear wheels spun spraying dirt, gravel, and dust over the windshield as the truck slammed the Mercedes against the stone wall. Giorgio laid on the horn, savagely ripped at the door handle, while he shouted at the metal monster, "What the fuck is going on! STOP! STOP the fuckin' truck!"

To his left he saw a steep cliff. To his right, the passenger side twisted and crumbled as the Mercedes compressed against the wall of rock. The truck driver popped the clutch and floored the gas pedal; the Mercedes bounced off the wall. Metal scraping rock echoed through the valley as the Mercedes angled toward the steep cliff. They both panicked, trapped, helpless to halt the truck's relentless assault.

Cardinal John braced one arm against the front seat and clutched his gold pectoral cross. His gut screamed this was the end. He screwed up! "Oh God! Oh God, I am sorry for—" Before he could finish the sign of the cross he was jolted sideways, the crumpled car toppled over the edge, flipped in mid air, tumbling down into the rocky canyon. The crushed and twisted metal was obscured by a blinding red and orange fireball.

One mechanic hopped out of the truck to check the road for any type of evidence. He touched the deep gouges in the stone wall. It appeared as though the car lost control and side swiped the wall then veered into the canyon. The dump truck had no visible damage other than scratches from normal construction work.

A farmer cultivating his fields saw thick black smoke in the distance and called the fire department. By the time they arrived the blaze was all but extinguished, the car a hulk of twisted smoldering metal. The fire department notified the police that two charred bodies were visible and the vehicle had a Vatican diplomatic license plate. The police obtained the owner's name from the license plate number and notified the Vatican police. News of the accident spread faster than an echo through the Vatican corridors.

The police chief drove to Roberto's farm and personally delivered the ugly news. The Capaldo family felt ripped and shaken by the untimely loss. Roberto silently vowed to discover what happened, no matter how long it took. Giorgio, a professional driver, knew every inch of the local back roads. How could this happen? Inconceivable! The investigation would have to wait until after the funeral. He needed time to grieve and console his family.

After soul-searching, Roberto decided to bury his brother in the local church cemetery rather than at the Vatican. His decision to keep his brother John close to the family was secondary. The motive for internment in St. Francis Cemetery was quite simple: John would be the most prominent resident. Roberto also took some comfort in knowing his brother the Cardinal would be pleased with this decision. After all, humility wasn't one of the Cardinal's virtues.

Marconi and the Holy Father were surprised when they heard about Cardinal Capaldo, especially the way he died. To the outside world, Capaldo remained a respected member of the Curia. The Capaldo family made a special request, asking the Holy Father to celebrate the funeral mass. The Pope's health and his work schedule prevented his attendance. He did promise to send a cardinal. The question was who? The Pope considered Belfonte and asked Marconi into his study to discuss his choice.

"As a member of the Curia, it's appropriate that a Cardinal officiate at the funeral. I'm considering Belfonte. Assigning him sends a message about his past loyalty to the crusade. In fact, I would like to personally give him this assignment. Your thoughts?"

"I agree, Holiness. I'll schedule a meeting for later today. One other matter, if I may? Our media people completed their review of the GNN biography and they have no major objections. Did you have a chance to review the tape?"

"Yes, early this morning. I'm very pleased. You can tell GNN it's all right to begin broadcasting. It's certainly strange to view your whole life on a one-hour video. They achieved the main goal of capturing Anthony Pavelli, the man."

Marconi was delighted that this media thing was almost finalized. It had become a distraction. Although at the time it was a brilliant idea, the Vatican needed to get back to basics. "I expect GNN will begin broadcasting in a few days and Ms. Murphy is scheduled to arrive the day after tomorrow. She's ready for a dress rehearsal for the live interview. Can we rearrange your schedule to meet with her?"

The Holy Father's dark eyes sparkled as he thumbed through his activity calendar. "Since she arrives on Sunday, let's schedule the rehearsal on Tuesday. That gives everyone some time to prepare."

Following doctor's orders but never to the letter, the Holy Father still worked short days. His hip was gradually mending, but his lack of stamina bothered him. For once he listened to medical advice. Before taking an afternoon nap, he meditated and prayed for guidance on the changes he was about to initiate, prayed for guidance to follow God's will and not superimpose his own ideals. Why else was such an unworthy man elected Pope? It had to be God's intervention. He asked God the Father, Son and Holy Spirit to direct him.

Early Sunday afternoon, after celebrating High Mass and repeating his homily on the Vatican radio, His Holiness met with Bishop William Weber. The Bishop was an expert theologian specializing in original translations of the Bible, both Old and New Testaments. The Papal encyclicals announcing the Church reforms had been drafted; all they required was his signature and subsequent announcement to the Catholic world. Before taking this huge step he wanted to check with yet another expert on these changes relative to the Bible's original text before it was translated a number of times and potentially corrupted from its original intent.

Bishop Weber waited in the dining room while the Pontiff removed his liturgical vestments. The Bishop was nervous about his first face-to-face meeting, as well as the nature of the pending discussion. He silently recited a Hail Mary to build confidence and settle the weakness distressing his intestinal tract; he hoped the medication would work. Meanwhile, Sister Martha tried to be sociable and kept interrupting his meditation.

The Holy Father smiled and offered the American Bishop a jovial greeting. After Bishop Weber kissed the Papal ring, the Holy Father sat right next to his guest at the dining room table.

The Bishop's anxiety doubled. His palms felt moist, mouth dry and intestines constricted. He couldn't help wonder why the Pope sat right next to him when the table comfortably sat twelve.

"Well Bishop, I imagine with your theological background this is not your first visit to the Vatican?"

"You're correct, Holiness. Unfortunately it's been some years since I spent time in the Vatican library. It's good to be back."

"How are your living accommodations? Are they satisfactory?"

"Just fine, Holiness. I have guest quarters in San Giovanni towers."

"Good. I took the liberty of ordering lunch, garden salads and sandwiches or would you prefer something else?"

"No Holiness. That will be fine. I'm not really hungry at the moment."

"Before the food arrives, I would like to discuss the confidential papers I sent you last week. Did you have an opportunity to read the information?"

"Yes, Holiness. I spent the last four days studying the information and how it relates to the Testaments."

During the two-hour meeting, the Pope ate a hearty lunch while the Bishop's stomach was so tied in knots that he could barely look at the food. They discussed in detail each of the proposed changes in Church doctrine and policy and how they related to Church dogma, Canon law, tradition and the Bible. The Bishop's unqualified opinion was that none of the changes conflicted with the Bible but he continually stressed, "This is my opinion." Other theologians may disagree with him on any number of issues. Every change, however, was in fact contrary to longstanding Church tradition. The Holy Father wasn't worried about tradition because life is a journey of constant change, and therefore, change becomes a tradition.

Towards the end of their conversation Bishop Weber began to relax, discussed his thoughts and the correlation of information and historical facts flowed. By the end of the meeting each man had a better appreciation of the other.

Before the Bishop left, the Pope's voice became emphatic for the first time during their meeting. "Bishop, this conversation and the pending changes must not be discussed with anyone and the copies of the encyclical drafts must be immediately destroyed. Confidentiality is paramount."

"I fully understand, Holiness."

He offered Bishop Weber a gift of sorts, suggesting he spend as much time as he wished in the Vatican Library. Pope Alex thanked the Bishop and excused himself. Before leaving the dining room the Pontiff turned back to the Bishop and said, "*Che Dio ti protegga*, may God protect you!"

The smiling Bishop prepared to indulge in his favorite pastime, while the Pope wondered how Catholics would accept his monumental changes.

Chapter Twenty-four

Early Sunday morning Kate Murphy landed, hoping this was her last trip to Rome for many months. Although her favorite European city, things with Matt had only improved slightly and they needed to spend more time together. Plus, she promised that after the Papal assignment they'd seriously deal with their future. That time rapidly approached. Kate suspected that Matt was contemplating marriage and shopping for a diamond engagement ring. His heart blossomed with love but she didn't know if he could fully understand and accept her need to excel in her chosen profession. Every day turned into a tug of war between home life and career. Somehow she dreamed love could find a compromise that still allowed her to be the journalist she needed to be. Love and career are not mutually exclusive; other people pulled it off.

After a short delay she cleared immigration; some English tourist caused a fuss and held up the line. The suitcases had not surfaced on the carousel. Looking for Giorgio, she scanned the crowd waiting beyond the security gates. Instead, she saw an unfamiliar driver holding a sign with her name. Securing the bags, she wheeled them to customs, and cleared immediately. Hustling the bags she entered the main terminal.

"I'm Kate Murphy."

"Welcome to Rome, Miss Murphy. My name is Bruno."

"Hello, Bruno. I was expecting Giorgio."

"Miss, I was asked to pick you up. I don't know Giorgio. If you're ready, the car is just outside in the loading zone."

She nodded, and Bruno wheeled the bags to the curb and loaded them into the trunk. Disappointed, Kate hoped this wasn't a prelude for the remainder of the trip and remained silent until arriving at the Hotel Michaelangelo. She thanked Bruno and asked for a pickup at 9:00 the next morning.

Eric D'Anella was scheduled to arrive from France Monday morning to meet Kate at the GNN office in Rome. They planned to spend the better part of the day with Aldo Fumo reviewing plans for the live interview. Aldo designated himself the on-site producer and Eric was in charge of cinematography. GNN accelerated the schedule for Pope Alex's biography; the first broadcast was aired about the same time Kate's plane departed from New York. With only moderate advance advertising, the broadcast became a ripping success. GNN's ratings spiked due north. The program was scheduled to air twice each day for a week in an effort to reach Christians around the globe.

GNN planned to increase advertising for the biography and announce the live interview for next Sunday. Kate counted on the ratings shooting off the chart. GNN provided a pay-per-minute telephone number for viewers to ask questions and provide comments about the Pontiff's biography. GNN administrators reviewed the questions to decide which would be presented to Pope Alex during the interview. So far the early responses were positive, exceeding all of their expectations.

Aldo Fumo conducted the meeting in which the team focused on how the interview should flow, starting with a panoramic view of Vatican City, then a wide angle shot of Saint Peter's Square. Next they'd meet the Pontiff and tour his living quarters. Mr. Fumo previously met with the Vatican staff and decided that the library, while an ideal setting, wasn't large enough for the people and the equipment. If they restricted the interview to the Pope's quarters the dining room was the only setting that worked.

During a break, Kate remembered to ask Aldo about Giorgio and saw his expression sour. "Did you hear about the cardinal that died in a car accident?" Kate nodded. "Well, I have some...bad news. Giorgio was his driver."

Kate remained silent for a long moment, controlling the trembling that surged through her torso. She rose and headed for the restroom to deal with the loss in private. Although a business associate, she felt a hard-to-describe closeness. Returning to the meeting she asked Aldo's secretary for Giorgio's address so she could send her condolence.

The meeting turned into a late dinner with Aldo and Eric. The men were determined to show Kate the nightlife in Rome. In the evenings she normally sequestered herself in the hotel and they wanted her to lighten up, especially before the dress rehearsal. It worked a little too well. The down side was that 7:00 a.m. came quickly when you didn't call it a night until 3:00. Kate still felt groggy after a long hot shower. Room service delivered a pitcher of tomato juice; the old hangover remedy didn't help.

Meeting in the hotel lobby, Eric appeared crisp and fresh. She wondered how he could party all night then look and act fresh the next morning. Heredity or conditioning? She hoped that after a few nights on the town she'd learn the secret or at least have fun trying.

Bruno was a capable and efficient driver, but not as gregariously earthy like Giorgio; he had always made her feel special. For a Tuesday morning, traffic was unusually light and they entered the Vatican a half-hour early. Kate used the extra time to give Eric a quick tour of the gardens near the Papal quarters. She hoped to see Giorgio's cousin, Vito the gardener, so she could offer condolences. Vito saw Kate first, dropped his rake and walked over. Vito said hello and offered his hand, was then taken off guard when Kate hugged him.

Holding him at arm's length, Kate choked up. With a halting voice she said, "I'm so sorry…about Giorgio. We'll all miss him so much. Your family…how are they holding up?"

"We are doing the best we can. Thank you, Signorina. Yes, he will be missed. Our greatest consolation is that he was doing God's service by driving Eminence Capaldo."

"Although I never met his family, please offer my sympathies and prayers."

Vito couldn't speak. He held her hand, his eyes moist; no words could lift his pain. After gently squeezing Kate's hand he returned to his greatest joy.

The camera crew and grips had arrived an hour earlier, and the equipment assembled. Most of the video depicting the Vatican would be selected from GNN's library footage. Eric wanted video footage of the private garden and walkways leading to the Papal Palace, so he asked the camera crew to video that area as they moved toward the entrance door with close up shots of the Swiss Guards.

When they entered the Papal quarters the Pontiff sat in the makeup chair, fussing about not needing makeup. Aldo calmly interceded, explaining that the intense lights and close up shots were very revealing; everyone needed some touch up because of the camera's scrutiny. The Pontiff finally conceded.

While they waited, Sister Martha gave Kate and Eric a guided tour while Eric filmed the various rooms, testing the light quality. This footage would be reviewed prior to the broadcast to determine which rooms they should focus on during the live tour.

The reality of a live broadcast to billions of people finally hit home. Pope Alex began to get jittery, his body acted like he drank a pot of espresso. He looked for Kate and Eric, trying to find familiar faces. Kate commented to Eric that Alex epitomized the Papal image, dressed in white from the top of his snowy hair to his shoes; robes so stark they almost reflected light. Eric wanted the cameras to capture what he saw with his naked eyes, and he intended to perform his magic to make sure the cameras cooperated.

Aldo suggested a dry run of Pope Alex giving Kate a tour of the Papal apartment, rooms in the Vatican the viewing public never had access to. The cameras captured the Pontiff as he moved through each room while reciting a brief history. The tour ended in the dining room where the actual interview would take place.

"This is the last room on our tour and the one with the most significance. I'm certainly not an expert on the Vatican's artistic treasures. However, I can easily spend hours discussing the antiques and art in this dining room. The real importance is not the furnishings, rather the history of people and events that took place within these walls. Just imagine the number of Popes who lived and ate at this mahogany table. Like most households, the dinner table is the center of activity where people talk, laugh and cry over a lifetime. Consider the secrets discussed within these walls. Pope Pius struggling with atrocities during World War II, secrets of Fatima, Benito Mussolini establishing Vatican City as an independent state, struggles to feed world hunger and spreading Jesus Christ's Gospels; hundreds of years and thousands of stories. That's one of the reasons this room was chosen for our conversation."

Realizing it was time to begin the interview, the Pope abruptly stopped speaking and stared at Kate. Off guard, she faltered for a second before recovering. "Holy Father, thank you so much for showing us your magnificent home. I'm sure the viewers are fascinated and you will receive e-mails and letters asking endless questions about the history and art work."

"My pleasure, Miss Murphy. However, this is not my home. It belongs to the Catholic world congregation. I'm just fortunate to occupy the rooms for whatever period of time God permits. A little later I hope to discuss the less obvious significance of Vatican art."

"You know this conversation is being broadcast to the world and GNN has been airing your biography." The Pope acknowledged her question with a smile.

"Since the broadcast, telephone calls, e-mails and faxes have flooded the GNN offices around the globe. Most are positive responses, I might add. Many viewers have questions about the Catholic religion and Pope Alex. After spending a good deal of time working on your biography, I also have some questions.

"Holiness, you contacted the news media months ago to discuss an interview, an unusual request from a religious leader. Previous Popes shied away from direct media attention at all costs. Can you tell us the reason for this highly unusual request?"

"Certainly. It's the same reason that I authorized the biography. My election as Pope came as a shock to many in the religious sector. I became a priest late in life. Many religious and laity wonder if I'm Papal material. Some even questioned why I became a priest or how I was permitted to become a priest." He paused for effect.

"I firmly believe God called me to the priesthood precisely because of my background. I lived fifty years as a Catholic parishioner. I know the laughs and aches of life's experiences, and when the Church helps or hurts individual parishioners.

"I also believe God chooses Popes, and I was selected to make changes in the Church in order to preserve and improve His Holy institution. What else could explain my progression from priest to Pope in a short period? The Catholic religion must continue to meet its destiny to spread the word of Jesus Christ and assist the needy through good works. Jesus taught us over two thousand years ago they go hand in hand. When information spread that I was prepared to make radical changes to the status quo, some people began a campaign of rumors and half-truths to discredit me, thereby discrediting any actions that I sponsor. I felt that if people learned the truth about their Pope, they would better understand the actions necessary to continue the Lord's instruction."

"Wow, that's a lot for the audience to digest."

"Yes it is Miss Murphy, but I am not here to pull any punches. During your research I am sure you heard the rumors and distortions."

"Unfortunately I have, Holy Father." Kate waited for a reaction. Pope Alex didn't continue on that path. He simply sat continuing to look at her with a faint smile. "Can I ask you some of the interesting questions or observations from the biography viewers, plus a few of my own?"

"Please do!"

"The most frequently asked question is: How can a divorced man who remarried and has children and grandchildren become a priest?"

The Pope's tension began to ease, his hands no longer clenched the arms of the chair, his posture slouched a bit. "A very appropriate question. My first marriage, although it produced a child, was annulled. My second marriage ended when my wife Marie passed into God's hands. Even though I had three children and two grandchildren at that time, I was technically eligible to become a priest, as long as I passed the physiological testing and graduated from the seminary. Incidentally, the church turned me down when I first applied, due to my age. Only with persistence did they concede and grant admission to the seminary program."

Kate's confidence grew, willing and ready to ask the tough questions that both the audience and Pontiff wanted addressed. "Holy Father, this question has crossed my mind and I am sure many viewers are wondering. Do you believe twenty years as a priest qualifies you to be Pontiff of the Roman Catholic Church? Even your former mentor questions your qualifications."

"I consider the Bishop a personal friend, a member of my extended family, so to speak. He is certainly entitled to his opinion. I know life's experience conditioned me for the priesthood. When parishioners seek a pastor's help about family problems, as an example, difficulty with disobedient children, do they want advice from a bachelor or someone whom has raised children? If a marriage is in trouble, is it best to seek council from a never married person? Functioning as a Church leader and especially the Pope requires a broad range of skills. In my opinion, relating to God's people is the most important element."

"I am sure the viewers can certainly understand your thoughts on that." Kate crossed her legs and leaned slightly forward toward the Holy Father. "Many people are also curious as to how you became a Cardinal in less than twenty years?"

Following her lead, the Pontiff crossed his legs, looked directly into the camera, offering a sheepish grin. "It wasn't just my sparkling personality, I can assure you! I brought years of business and management experience to the priesthood. I did have mentors, a bishop and later a Cardinal. Ability and mentors alone cannot propel a fifty-something priest through the Church ranks. No, I firmly believe my being here is part of His overall plan."

As usual, Marconi had arrived early to make sure things were in order and the Vatican properly represented. His behind-the-scene direction actually helped; decisions were quick and efficient. Even though only a dress rehearsal the Cardinal felt on edge, although any questions or issues that were out of line could be eliminated prior to the actual interview. Marconi's emotions ran in tandem with the Pope's; as Alex relaxed, so did his chief of staff.

Marconi studied Kate. She wore a modest but charming yellow spring dress with a faint floral print, a perfect choice epitomizing the proverbial girl next door. He drifted back to the conversation when Pope Alex first discussed the idea of a media interview, an idea that seemed far fetched, way out of the box. He questioned the Pope's decision to voluntarily expose himself and the Vatican to a microscopic review. It could backfire. Today that gamble appeared to be paying off; the biography telling his story certainly attracted record audiences.

The interview was expected to garner an even larger audience share.

Mr. Fumo looked pleased, often signaling encouragement to Kate. He held a optimism about the entire project thus far. As production director, Fumo imagined the viewers on Sunday evening, relaxing at home and warming first to Kate then the Holy Father. Pope Alex held quite a media presence, but more importantly he shouted creditability. This was not a glitzy politician, rather a man exposing his life so that he could accomplish good works.

In her peripheral vision, Kate watched Mr. Fumo for any signs or subtle guidance; so far everything was a go. Encouraged by his nonverbal responses, she felt even more confident and assured as the interview rolled forward. "How were you appointed Pontiff? How does the whole voting secret conclave process work?"

He uncrossed his legs and sat up straight, knowing the most difficult questions were about to begin. He hated every second of sitting in front of the camera's eyeball. He pondered, is this what the Pontiff's office has been degraded to—divulging his private life to an inanimate object not even capable of providing immediate human feedback? No body language or facial expressions to judge the viewer's reaction. Although a test of his patience and perseverance, he vowed to see this through to the end. "The College of Cardinals elects the Pope using secret ballots. Election requires at least a two-thirds plus one majority. If a vote is unsuccessful, black smoke rises from the voting room chimney. When white smoke rises, a new Pope has been elected."

"Most people believe it is a very secretive thing. Your explanation is easy to understand. Earlier you mentioned your election process was quite lengthy."

"You have a very good memory, Miss Murphy. The election did take a number of days. Early in the process, each Cardinal vies for his favorite candidate. The candidates are weeded out and ultimately God makes his choice known."

"Holy Father, something tells me this abbreviated version of the Papal conclave is all you are about to disclose." He offered a sheepish grin.

"Holiness, while researching your biography I couldn't help thinking how difficult it must be to be separated from family."

"The physical separation is probably one of the hardest sacrifices that religious life requires. Knowing that going in doesn't make it any easier. God's work has other rewards; it permits the religious to collect extended family wherever they are stationed, and I believe we will be with our loved ones and friends in eternity."

"How often do you see your family?"

"As often as we can. The problem, as with all families, is time."

As the questions flowed, his confidence continued to increase. He became animated, often gesturing with his hands. His spontaneous laugh and warm facial expressions made him appear human and likable.

"Much like political world leaders, a Pope lives in the public's eye twenty-four hours a day. Every move scrutinized. Do you miss freedom and privacy?"

"Until inviting GNN and the world into these quarters, this apartment was my resting place away from the hectic world. To answer the question, 'yes.' I often miss being an average citizen. The first months as Pope were the worst: Do this. Go there. Tradition requires this or that…it seemed that's all I heard for months. But I've reached an agreement with the staff, some things are necessary and I'll follow decorum. On less important items I take the lead and do what I think is correct for the Church first, then for my personal preference. I would like to tell a little secret." An impish grin revealed his true nature. "Not long ago, just before the trip to Ireland, I had cabin fever and snuck out of the Vatican for a night. I spent the whole evening enjoying Rome as a tourist. So in the future when in Rome, watch out; the old guy next to you may just be the Pope!" He paused for effect, again playing to the camera.

Feeling confident, assured, at his pinnacle, he decided to continue with whatever flashed into mind. "When I was a kid, which is hard to remember, I always pictured the Pope in full white robes every moment of the day. I wondered if he slept in those white robes. Anyway, another secret is that at the end of the day I change into sandals, cargo shorts and a T-shirt. At first the staff was surprised——well, actually shocked—but they've gotten use to seeing me in civilian clothes tooling around the apartment."

This comment surprised Kate. She faltered for a second then looked at Mr. Fumo for guidance. He rolled his hands to go with it. "I'm sure the audience has some difficulty picturing you in shorts."

"Miss Murphy, what can I say?" The bit of levity further relaxed both of them and brought a humanistic element to the interview. He wanted the audience to comprehend above all else he was human, a person like everyone else.

"Many viewers wondered because you joined the priesthood so late in life, if you ever had any regrets about leaving the secular life?"

"No matter what profession or walk of life we choose, there are bad days, but I deal with the specific issues. Some days we win; others are lose or draw. But I've never second guessed my decision to accept God's calling or the direction He's led me."

"Do you think being the first American Pope contributed to your initial difficulties—let's call it low ratings—as Pontiff?"

"I'd say to some degree. Many people and countries have a love/hate relationship with the United States of America and always will. My birth country has made its share of mistakes; however, I recall we have also saved the free world a number of times. Judgments should never be based solely by a person's country. Look at Stalin and Hitler—their magnificent countries were home to monsters. The real issue is Pope Alex, the individual. My background provided raw fuel for rumors and speculation. Also, I don't have ah… shall we call it an outgoing personality. In fact I'm usually quite shy, which often comes across as aloof. I love people; it just takes me some time to warm up."

"How interesting, thanks for sharing that. Recently you personally experienced a terrible, I'm sure traumatic incident…um, the attempted assassination. The world stood still, in shock watching the live broadcast. The sane people of our global community were outraged by terrorist action against a religious leader. Do you know why you were targeted and who might have planned such a cruel violent act?"

"I wish…with all my heart I knew who or what prompted the attack that killed Major Bordeau. The incident is still under investigation. Some day justice will be served, if not in this world then in the next. I have forgiven the culprit or culprits, but it's not my forgiveness that counts!"

Kate's head bowed as she paused to remember the major. "GNN has received numerous questions of a personal nature regarding your relationship with Leigh Stevens. I'm sure based on the rumor, some of them titillating, that you are anticipating our viewers' curiosity. Do you mind if we move into that area of your personal life?"

The Pontiff scratched his white eyebrow, looked at Kate then back to the camera thinking, *Here it comes, both barrels.* His hands formed a steeple, while he took deep breaths to ward off any temptation to tell them to go to hell. After all, he asked for this. "Yes Miss Murphy, I anticipated questions regarding my long-term relationship with Miss Stevens. It's unfortunate that people, even good Christians, tend to dwell on or speculate about sexual issues; it's a weaker element of human nature. I am prepared for a frank discussion about our relationship. These rumors in particular were what prompted me to ask for the interview with GNN. Before proceeding, let me remind everyone of an old adage mothers tell their children: Don't believe half of the gossip you read or hear!"

Kate squirmed, her face stone serious and slightly flushed, palms turned moist. Her stomach suddenly craved food to handle the stinging acid. After months of work and research, the entire outcome of this live interview hinged on the next personal questions. "Your Holiness, was Miss Stevens your significant other, and did you live together?"

"Yes, while I was single and before I joined the seminary we were lovers and lived together."

"What is your present relationship with Miss Stevens?"

The warm geniality so evident moments ago had vanished. His whole demeanor turned pure business. "It's fairly common knowledge that we are close personal friends. Miss Stevens' business requires frequent trips to Rome and we have dinner once a month. In fact members of my staff are very fond of her visits. I respect her advice and opinion."

"Do you still love Miss Stevens?" Kate held her hot bitter breath, waiting for an answer.

The Pontiff cleared his throat. He knew this question was impossible to answer with absolute honesty. No one would ever be able to understand how he truly felt about Leigh. At times he was still uncertain. He decided to whitewash the reply with a politically correct answer. "Yes, Miss Murphy... I love all of God's creations, especially my family and close friends. But I am no longer *in love* with Miss Stevens."

"Holy Father, I'll ask this as delicately as possible." She paused allowing the Holy Father a few seconds to prepare himself for the most personal question, "Do you have an intimate physical relationship with Miss Stevens or any other person?" Her face turn beet red. She reached for a sip of water to moisten her parched mouth, cool water to wash the bitter taste that lingered in her mouth.

From the beginning he knew that the questions would be sharp, probing and personal. He objected in particular to this extremely pointed question. He pinched his leg to regain control and as a reminder that he asked for this chance to tell his story, and was determined to follow through without displaying the slightest trace of irritation. The meekest of smiles crossed his face. Only those closest to the Pope understood this smile signaled his embarrassment.

"I have a very intimate but platonic relationship with Miss Stevens; she is my best female friend and confidant. Clarifying our relationship might help. We were lovers and are now very dear friends. She has a standing invitation for lunch, dinner, or a casual visit at any time. I have a similar invitation when I'm in her hometown. It's the same relationship people around the world have with close friends. To answer the last part of the question...I have been celibate since I joined the seminary and dedicated my life to Jesus Christ."

"Thank you Holy Father for putting those questions to rest."

"I certainly hope so. Miss Murphy, one question that you didn't ask, that needs to be clarified."

Kate looked at the Pontiff and wondered what the question was. She knew the signs: He was pissed, very near the breaking point, and could call this off at any moment. "Certainly, please present the question."

Anyone watching the interview could see the determination flash across his countenance, eyes set hard, opened wide. "I want the entire audience to understand, in order to rectify this rumor. No, let's call it what it is—this lie. All my children and grandchildren are legitimate offspring. I don't have illegitimate children."

She quietly sighed and released the arms of the chair. They made it through the last huge barrier. "Thank you for the clarity. Now, for a current topic; rumor has it you are about to celebrate a birthday."

His eyes softened and he faked a smile while working to regain the easy flow they shared before the personal issues surfaced. "Yes, in a few days I will be one year older, but I never divulge my age," he said winking, since his age was very public information. "Now young lady, I have an answer to a question you asked me at the end of our first meeting. Do you remember the question?"

"As a matter of fact I do. I wondered about the changes you were contemplating for the Catholic Church."

"Well, I am prepared to provide an answer." Reaching toward the chair to his left, he picked up a dog-eared legal size manila folder, and placed it on the dining room table. "For many months my trusted advisors and I have been drafting these encyclicals announcing and clarifying monumental changes in the Roman Catholic Church. I won't labor through all the details but I do wish to summarize the most important items. Before I begin, I must tell you they are extremely controversial. I believe they are sorely needed to solidify the Catholic religion, and continue its existence in order to spread the Holy Word of God.

"Some Catholics will believe it's about time. Others will consider the changes a death knell for Roman Catholicism. Everyone will have an opinion. As previously stated, I have no doubts that these changes are necessary to energize and refocus Catholics on God's substance. Before judging, I encourage everyone to think about the Church's stated goal and its purpose for existence. I ask that each of you keep an open mind."

He opened the manila folder and spread the papers across the table. "So with that preamble, I am immediately convening Vatican Council III to focus on and resolve the monumental issues we face as Catholics and members of the Global Christian community. The issues: 1) Bringing Catholics back to actively practicing in their faith. 2) Increasing the number of missionaries working to spread Christ's Holy Gospel. 3) Defeating world hunger by helping people to feed themselves. A major part of the hunger issue is a reexamination of the Church's position on artificial birth control. 4) Allowing divorced Catholics to receive the sacraments."

Once the cork popped, he was determined to move forward and outline the most relevant issues. He internalized the compulsion for speed, to get it all out, to barrel ahead at 100 kilometers per hour. It was critical to present the information slowly, in a controlled manner. He needed a drink of water to help calm the anxiety that he knew was assaulting his aging body. Feeling a brief heart flutter, he counted to ten, caught the camera's lens and began again. "All of God's work requires prayer, dedicated people and funds for education, training and supplies. In order to provide the funds necessary to implement these programs, I have authorized the way and means. Until sufficient priests are available, we will continue to consolidate churches into cluster parishes. The vacant buildings and land will be sold. Half of the proceeds will be used to pay down local parish and diocesan debt, and the other half used to fund the world programs.

"Earlier today I spoke about the artwork in this room…magnificent paintings, almost priceless. Over the next two years, half of all Vatican treasures and works of art will be sold to fund the world mission and hunger program. Many people will agree that it is about time. Others will argue that the Vatican is a sacred repository for keeping ancient priceless art safe from the ravages of man and nature. Some of the program detractors will quote Jesus when he said: 'The poor will be with us always.'"

The Pontiff again lingered so the audience could assimilate what he was telling them. He relied on single-minded concentration to slow his presentation and maintain full control. His composure and presentation were impeccable, while inside his stomach churned and his chest pounded, close to a full angina attack. The naturally placid Pope had learned to control his emotions. During his long life there were rare instances when his emotional Richter scale elevated above two. At that precise moment his body quaked with a magnitude that jolted the needle above eight.

"As a parishioner and later as a priest, I cringed when sermons involved donations. Although, I must be frank: Catholics have been spoiled. Many other religions practice tithing, that is donating 10% of a member's income to the Church. Today, I am asking Catholics to meet less than half that amount, and begin donating 5% of after tax earnings to your Church."

As the Pontiff outlined his programs, the producer and every spectator comprehended the vastness of his pronouncements. Aldo Fumo quickly instructed the camera crew to slowly narrow the picture and focus a close up on the Pope, filling the entire screen with his head and torso. The picture so detailed the audience could see the slightest bit of perspiration forming along his hairline, and a small vein pulse on his forehead. Earnest enthusiasm radiated through the picture tube.

"The third Vatican council will be a monumental undertaking. I encourage leaders from Protestant sects and especially Russian and Greek Orthodox Churches to actively participate. The Vatican Council will require a strong leader to manage daily activities and no individual is more capable than Dominic Cardinal Marconi.

"To assist the Vatican council in their mission, I am also issuing encyclicals that will bring new life and blood into the Roman Catholic Religion, they are:

"Religious Sisters (nuns) and Brothers will be permitted to marry but only before taking their vows.

"Gay Catholics will be openly accepted into religious life as long as they remain celibate.

"Priests will be permitted to marry; however, married priests cannot rise above monsignor.

"Women will be permitted as deacons and priests. They also will be permitted to marry.

"These directives are not up for discussion or debate. I am speaking ex-cathedra, thereby pronouncing infallibility on these issues."

The Pontiff looked down at his notes for a quick second, then immediately refocused into the camera. When he continued, his voice reached a much higher pitch and he finally lost control as emotion overpowered logic. "Roman Catholics around the globe will be divided, as we were when the Latin Mass changed, altars where reversed to face the congregation and eating meat was permitted on Friday. Fifty years from now it will not matter. What's important is that the Christian faith will not just survive but grow and prosper; billions will continue to hear and accept the salvation of Jesus, our Christ."

Visibly drained, his color changed from mildly flushed to pale. His right hand raised, he managed a slight smile and proffered his Papal blessing. The cameras panned to Miss Murphy who quickly thanked the Holy Father and said goodbye to the viewers.

The GNN crew, Vatican staff and Cardinal Marconi were speechless. Marconi never expected him to release all the encyclicals at the same time. He felt they should be gradually released during Vatican III sessions, making them appear as recommendations from the council. The GNN crew began to clap, followed by Vatican staffers. No one was quite sure if they applauded the changes, the courage to initiate the changes, or the Pope's presentation. Most likely a combination.

When Pope Alex rose, the manila folder slipped from his hand and the encyclicals scattered under the table. Kate knelt to help scoop up the papers and handed him the folder. Wishing to leave the room, he didn't want to deal with Marconi's probing as to why he released all the encyclicals at once. He was not quite sure himself. He thanked everyone as quickly as possible. The last and most appreciative thank you was saved for Kate. "You made the interview feel so natural. You are a wonderful journalist. Thank you so very much. Now if we can only duplicate this during the actual interview."

"Our conversation was open, informative and your sudden disclosure certainly held everyone's attention. If Sunday is half as good it will be a huge success."

"Until Sunday. God bless you, Kate."

Sister Martha accompanied the Pontiff into the kitchen; she couldn't wait to give him the birthday gift package sent by his family. He wanted to hold off until his birthday but the birthday package read: "Perishable, open immediately." That was all the prompting he needed. While he wondered what people give a Pope who has everything at his fingertips, the sister unwrapped the heavy brown shipping paper. Looking at he contents he had to grin. What a great gift! *Who thought of it,* he wondered, *certainly one of his women.*

Enclosed were Philadelphia food treats: A sampling of Tasty cupcakes, soft pretzels, cheese steaks, chicken cheese steaks and an Italian hoagie. The food he loved so much from his hometown.

"Sister, you won't completely understand this, but this is the best gift anyone can receive if they ever lived in the Philadelphia area. Please put these away for later." His shoulders sagged as he moved the box toward Sister. "I'm tired and want to rest for a while. If I fall asleep don't disturb me for dinner. It will be a good excuse to eat my gifts."

"Holy Father, do you feel ill? Can I get you something?"

"Just tired Sister, but I would use a cold drink."

"I just happen to have a Diet Coke in the fridge."

He laughed to himself while slowly shuffling to his bedroom with the drink. Disrobing, he turned back the bed covers and gently lay on his side of the bed. Even after all these years, the left was his side, while the right had been occupied by the loves of his life. He reached for his prayer book and opened it at the marked page. His eyesight blurred; so blurry that reading was a strain. He made a mental note to schedule an eye appointment for new reading glasses. Dropping the book on the night table he began to say afternoon prayers from memory. Halfway through the first verse sleep overcame him.

After hours of dreamless sleep, Pope Alex woke in a pitch-black room. Feeling weak and listless, his body needed food to replenish his blood sugar. Remembering the Philadelphia treats, he groaned, straining to lift out of bed. He threw on casual clothes and headed into the kitchen. Un-wrapping a cheese steak, he placed it in the oven and began picking at a chocolate cup cake. It didn't taste right without a cold glass of milk. As the refrigerator swung open he felt an intense pain, so sharp he envisioned a knife penetrating his chest. The pain traveled down his right arm, a second excruciating stab in the middle of his back. The force pushed him against the open door. Alex the Pontiff slid down the refrigerator, collapsing on the cool marble floor. Desperate to raise himself, he heard his name softly spoken. Marie's voice radiated from a blinding light.

The loud and instant ringing echoed in his head. He glanced at the clock; it was four in the morning. He grumbled about a call to his private number at that hour. Barely awake, he sat up and lifted the receiver, rubbed the sleep from his eyes and ran fingers through mussed hair. "Pronto."

The voice on the other end was weak and sobbing. Irritated, he said, "Pronto, this is Cardinal Marconi, who is calling?"

Trying to catch her breath she said, "Forgive me Eminence, this is Sister Martha. It's terrible, so terrible…."

"Sister, has something happened to the Holy Father?"

"*Si*, Eminence. I just found the His Holiness on the kitchen floor. The Pope…Pope Alex is dead. He must have died a few hours ago. I just now found him."

He slumped back in bed, trying to collect his thoughts. "Sister, call Dr. Bananni. We'll need an official death certificate. I'll be there in a few minutes."

"Eminence, please hurry."

While dressing he mulled over the loss of his friend and, more importantly, a good man. His friend's untimely death turned everything upside down. *God certainly has his own agenda and is truly, what's the popular term…oh yes, an agent of change*, he thought. His personal grief would have to wait. There was much to do, starting with summoning all the cardinals to Rome for the funeral and the Papal election. Notify the media, ring the Vatican bells and lower the flag to half-mast. Invite world dignitaries to the funeral, and arrange a public viewing. Oh God, he had to make the dreaded call to the Pope's family before the media broadcasts the news.

The various preparations were made and the funeral scheduled for Saturday morning. Time for Marconi to deal with GNN.

Still in Rome, Kate was assigned to cover the funeral and subsequent Papal election. She patiently waited with Mr. Fumo in the reception area. They'd been summoned to meet with Cardinal Marconi. This was GNN's first official conversation with anyone in the Vatican since the Pope passed. The journalists were escorted to a covered patio overlooking a garden area.

Marconi rose to greet them. Kate noticed he didn't offer his hand, clearly a bad sign. "Miss Murphy and Mr. Fumo, please have a seat. May I offer you refreshments? Possibly, some tea, coffee or mineral water?"

Both thanked the Cardinal and declined. They selected chairs next to each other and across the small table from Marconi. Both offered condolences personally and from GNN. Kate also mentioned that the Pavelli family was staying at her hotel. Naturally, the family was in deep mourning.

Marconi started. "I look forward to meeting with the entire family later in the day." With the formalities completed, Marconi occupied the driver's seat and didn't waste any time coming directly to the reason for their meeting. "I'm sure GNN is eager to broadcast the Papal interview or incorporate the interview into Pope Alex's biography. It's natural to strike while the iron's hot. I have asked you here to discuss how GNN can accomplish that while meeting the Vatican's requirements. We all agree that the Vatican has final approval on all segments of the biography and Papal interview, no?" He looked closely at their reaction. Both visitors sat stone faced, not sure where the conversation was headed.

Aldo Fumo nodded. "Yes Eminence, however, we know that Pope Alex would not wish the Vatican to unreasonably withhold the interview conducted just hours before his death."

"I agree. Pope Alex was a very fair and reasonable man. Remember, however, his first interest was always the Catholic Church, represented by the Vatican. Until a new Pope is elected, I'm responsible for approving media releases. GNN can air the interview or incorporate the interview into the biography, except for the portions or segments about the pending third Vatican Council and the encyclicals."

After all her effort and untold hours, Kate approached the point of no return and totally losing it. Only Aldo's presence held her back from blasting Marconi, but only in the most respectful way. Trying to rein in a flash of self-defeating anger, she squeezed her leg with enough brute strength to form a black and blue mark. "Eminence, that's one of the reasons why Pope Alex conducted the interview, a global forum to announce the changes."

"Miss Murphy and Mr. Fumo, I fully understand his intent. There is another compelling issue—the encyclicals are in draft form and never signed. Therefore, they cannot be announced. The entire process will be placed in the hands of the new Pope, whenever he is elected." Marconi's piercing blue eyes left no impression of any compromise. "GNN must understand a premature announcement would become an embarrassment if the new Pontiff chooses not to support the reforms!"

Again Kate's control teetered neared the shattering point. Her thoughts pushed away all logic and decorum. *How dare they interfere with GNN and me? This is ours; we made this happen. The holier-than-thou bastards can't take this opportunity away, not after all the time, the work.*

She leaned across the patio table, adamant in her response. "Eminence, I could swear! Excuse me." Her voice was high pitched with angst. "I mean…I'm sure I saw signatures on the encyclicals."

Losing patience with this young woman, Marconi gripped the arms of the chair and straightened his posture. He felt his eyelids flutter just before responding, and realized a trained journalist would pick up on the body language, that his reply was a bold-faced lie. Marconi responded in the softest possible voice, "No doubt you are mistaken. Those documents are merely draft copies."

Kate was ready to scream. Damn, she was right. The Pope had executed the documents, but the Church, especially this bastard Marconi, held all the aces. It was time to change tactics and see if she could work around the issue. "Eminence, I completely understand why you are taking this position on the encyclicals!" She gave him a challenging stare before continuing. "Rumor has it that you will most likely be elected the next Pope. If you are chosen, will you move forward and sign the encyclicals and convene Vatican III?"

"Miss Murphy, Miss Murphy, always the journalist. I can see why Pope Alex chose you for the interview. I should emulate some Americans and take the 5th. Instead, be assured I will personally make any new Pontiff aware of Pope Alex's dreams and aspirations for the Church. If God chooses me to lead the Roman Catholics, I will give these documents the utmost consideration, because I deeply respected Pope Alex and his belief that God selected him specifically to make these difficult decisions."

Before Aldo could respond, Kate reverted back to her less-than-diplomatic sarcasm. "Your Eminence, we respect your candor. However, as the Pope's trusted adviser you had advance knowledge of the changes he openly discussed on camera and must have tried to persuade him in one direction or another; therefore, you must know how you intend to react if elected Pope."

Extremely annoyed, he'd reached his limit with Kate's attitude, and had no qualms about abruptly ending the meeting if things turned into an ugly scene. "Well spoken. However, there is a distinct difference between advising and making the actual decision. I will ask the new Pope to give this his primary consideration."

Mr. Fumo tried to contain Kate by nudging her foot while saying, "Thank you, Eminence. We know you have a full schedule, one last question if we may?"

Marconi gave an affirmative nod. Kate scowled at Aldo and kicked his leg, letting him know they shouldn't terminate the meeting without some concession from Marconi. Kate could scowl all she wanted, but Aldo controlled GNN's final decision.

"When will the College of Cardinals convene the conclave?" asked Aldo.

"The Novemdials is the traditional fifteen-day mourning period. The College of Cardinals will commence the locking in with a key on the sixteenth day. It's unsettling not having a Pontiff in office."

His interest and patience waned, and the Cardinal terminated the meeting. Crossing his legs he looked beyond his guests and focused on the blossoming trees. "As you mentioned, I do have a busy schedule. I think we are finished, so please excuse me." Kate and Aldo pushed their chairs back to stand and Cardinal Marconi escorted his visitors to the reception area.

Almost as an afterthought the Cardinal added, "Please give thanks to everyone in GNN for the exceptional work." Kate didn't bother to respond. She felt betrayed; after helping them, the Vatican tossed her out in the street without a second thought.

Walking to the car, Kate felt aggravated and more than a bit belligerent. "Why did you let him, that pompous little Napoleon, off the hook so easily?"

Aldo took the hand of a young woman experiencing the unpredictable events that when dealt with properly build character. "My dear Kate, Marconi is the gate keeper and in total control. *Roma locuta est; causa finita est*. In other words, Rome has spoken; the matter is settled. Let's play his game and see where it leads us. We may need his help in the future and at least we have permission to use part of the Pope's interview."

Freeing her hand, she was not about to give up that easily. "The Pope's trusted friend is not being totally honest. He said the documents were a draft and not signed. Aldo, the Pope dropped his folder and when I help pick up the scattered papers, the encyclicals were absolutely signed and dated. Why is he holding back that information?"

"Based on the Marconi's reputation, I suspect he's protecting the Church. What if he allowed the documents to be published and the new Pope immediately rescinded them, stating that Pope Alex was in poor health and not in control of his faculties? It could result in a nasty scandal and tarnish the concept of Papal infallibility."

"Okay, I understand that. There's nothing that says we can't some time in the future broadcast the entire interview, do you agree?"

He turned and touched her shoulder. "Unless you are discussing twenty years from now, that ploy could return to haunt GNN. We gave our word and the Vatican has total approval concerning the interview content."

Her head sagged. "Again you are right, Aldo."

"That's why they pay me the big euros! Chin up. You have plenty of work ahead covering the funeral and election."

Her thoughts returned to what she'd been mulling over the past few days. Hating to admit she had underestimated how hard knocks or the unexpected could alter her charmed life. Her finger was on the brass ring when fate rocked the carousel and it slipped away, beyond her control, out of her reach. Yes, she still wanted fame, recognition and financial security, but she finally realized other things were just as important if not more important.

Fame and fortune were fleeting. Family and loved ones counted the most. Mrs. Pavelli's comment rumbled through her mind, "Don't be fifty years old and have regrets." She swore, *From this day forward Matt comes first!* The decision actually helped ease losing the live Papal interview and dealing with Marconi's bull.

Kate found temporary office space in GNN's Rome headquarters. She thought about flying home but would have to return in a matter of days. Her extra time in Rome was spent gathering information on rumors about the leading Papal candidates. Although the favored candidates made good copy, they are not always elected. Prime example: Anthony Pavelli.

Gathering her notes in a neat pile, Kate looked up to find Matt standing in the office doorway. She brightened, yelling, "Matt!" She dropped the papers and ran into his solid arms. They kissed passionately while he raised his left leg to kick the door closed.

"What a great surprise! Welcome to Roma. How long can you stay?"

"How long do you want me, woman?"

"A week would be perfect. I will show you the whole city and with your birthday around the corner I will bring you to see a huge Italian cake."

Matt reached one hand into his pants pocket. "Kate, for your answer to my question, I hoped you'd say, 'For the rest of my life.'" He uncurled his hand holding a small dark blue box. He watched her expression as she opened the lid. Spellbound, she didn't know whether to laugh, cry or scream with joy.

"Oh my God. Matt…YES! Yes, yes. I will marry you!"

After the third vote, the white smoke signaled an election. The Papal election was a foregone conclusion. In retrospect, most Princes of the Church believed Dominic Cardinal Marconi should have been elected as the last Pope. He was highly respected, Italian, and knew the intricacies of the Vatican administration. A man of honor, he always placed the Church above all else. The important question the College of Cardinals never asked was: Does Dominic revere the Church as an institution or simply a vessel to serve Jesus Christ? It was an important distinction that separated ordinary Popes from truly great ones, like Pope Alex IX.

Eminence Marconi, the newly elected Pontiff, made his first appearance on the Papal balcony and waved to the crowd in St. Peter's Square. It was clear to Marconi that Miss Murphy could be a true friend or obstinate foe. The relentless young journalist would push the envelope to find the truth, regardless of effort or cost. Every time he stepped onto the balcony the spirit of Pope Alex and the shadow of Ms. Murphy would be present. As he told Kate Murphy and Mr. Fumo, the leap from adviser to decision-maker is monumental. Starting from the moment of his election, the tough decisions stopped at his desk.

He never doubted his friend was on a mission from God. Now it was his turn to carry the banner. Would God test his fortitude to complete the work Pope Alex started? He'd do what needed to be done, he always did. In the mean time, he was about to send his first message to the Roman Catholic Community.

Cardinal Tornetta, the next chief of staff, walked onto the balcony overlooking St. Peter's Square eager to introduce the new Pontiff. "The College of Cardinals wishes to announce that Eminence Dominic Marconi has been elected Pontifex Maximus of the Roman Catholic Church. The new Pontiff wishes to speak to the Christians of the world." Cardinal Tornetta bowed slightly before turning over the microphone.

"Today, God has spoken through the College of Cardinals and chosen a Pontiff to lead the Roman Catholic Church. My first act as Pontiff is choosing the name Alex X, in honor of a great visionary. The next years will test our faith…."

Standing directly in the center of St. Peter's Square, Kate witnessed the white smoke so reminiscent of past Papal elections. She scanned the crowded square, and watched ordinary devot people waiting for the Pontiff elect to make his appearance. She wondered why deep down she was pleased with Marconi's election. Especially since she was positive that Pope Alex had signed the encyclicals, and Marconi hid this vital information. Marconi was capable and would be readily accepted by the laity and clergy; however, his dishonesty about the encyclicals still disturbed her. She was prepared and determined to dog the encyclical issue until completely satisfied. The Pontiff knew she was in the crowd, the one person who understood the whole unvarnished truth.

When the Pope elect announced his chosen name, all her questions were answered. God's plan came rushing together. The visionary Alex IX had the metal to fight the entrenched officials. The new Pope, Alex X, would assure their universal acceptance through his diplomatic skills and reputation.

Chapter Twenty-five

A month after the Papal funeral, two wooden crates with Vatican seals were delivered to Tom and Beth's house. The larger wooden crate contained Pope Alex's books, manuscripts and personal journals. The family had already decided to donate these items to St. Charles Seminary. The west wing in the library would be named after Pope Alex, and the donated possessions placed on display.

The smaller crate contained the Pope's other personal items, like the remnants of his coin collection. The majority of his coins were previously gifted to his children. It also included his beloved fountain pens, shoes, belts, and clothing. Removing items from the crate, Beth noticed envelopes held together by a plain rubber band. The handwritten envelopes were addressed to each of his children and Leigh.

She called Leigh at work to see how she was holding up and to tell her that a letter arrived from Anthony. Living a few miles from Beth and Tom, Leigh said she would stop by on her way home from work for a short visit.

It was difficult to concentrate on work. Leigh's mind slipped back to memories of Anthony. Her thoughts sifted through bittersweet emotions that she experienced when Anthony swiftly moved through the ranks of the Church, not to mention her joy about the good works that he spread along his journey. Leaving work early was her goal, but as usual it didn't happen. Employees and clients absorbed her time right up to the end of the day. Finally, time to return home, the one safe and comfortable place, her personal cocoon.

When Leigh and Anthony moved into their dream house, her drive to work was twenty-five minutes; twenty years later, with the increase in vehicles and only minor road improvements, the drive time had stretched to just under an hour. That day she was more eager than usual to stop by Tom and Beth's before heading directly home.

Beth opened the front door and greeted Leigh with a big hug, literally surrounded Leigh with arms and body. She felt the flow of warmth and comfort in the bear hug.

Guiding Leigh to arm's length, Beth spoke softly with honest concern. "How are you holding up?"

Leigh hadn't really laughed since the funeral. "A bit better, not quite back to normal. Each day gets a little easier."

"It takes time, Leigh! When you can think about your happy times together and smile, you're making progress."

The women walked into the kitchen and Beth quickly transformed into her animated congenial self. "Can you join us for dinner? Tom will be late but I expect Ashley any minute. We're having my famous lasagna. What do you say?"

"Thanks for the invite. I'd love to any other night...I'm beat, can't wait to get home, and into comfy pajamas."

"At least take some food home. We have plenty and you won't have to cook."

"Deal. I'd like that."

While Beth wrapped the food Ashley came whirling through the door and ran upstairs, leaping two steps at a time. Within seconds, packages were dropped, shoes kicked off and she jumped back down the stairs to hug her Leigh. They had a special bond. Ashley loved to spend time with Leigh. Leigh loved Ashley like a favorite grandchild. They hugged and kissed. Ashley said hi to her mother, and gave Beth a quick peck on the cheek.

"Lee Lee. You're staying for dinner, right?"

"I'd love to honey, but I'm tired and want to get home and relax. Had a tough day."

"When will I see you again?" asked Ashley.

"Come over Sunday afternoon. Let's have a cookout. How does that sound?"

Ashley leaned close and whispered, "Good. Unless I have a last minute date with you know who."

"Sloppy seconds again," she gave Ashley a quick wink. "Thanks kids, have to run. I'll call you Beth. Kiddo, help your mother clean up."

During the short drive home, Leigh was tempted to pull over and read the letter but forced herself to wait. Like many people, Leigh had a nightly routine: pick up the mail, pet the cat, check the cat's food and water, and play new messages on the answering machine. Without a second thought she abandoned the routine, walked directly to her bedroom, kicked off shoes and sat in an oversized reading chair. Her treasured chair, the worn fabric no longer matched the room's décor. No matter, the room and chair were one of her favorite pleasures, a comfort zone.

She stared at the sealed envelope for what seemed like hours, deciding if she wanted to read the letter tonight, tomorrow, next week or possibly never. Leigh found Anthony's funeral draining, physically and emotionally, and this letter would reopen those still tender feelings. The handwritten envelope continued to beckon. Resistance to this man proved impossible, even after death.

Trying to preserve the Vatican waxed seal she slowly sliced through the envelope. Inside she found a letter dated six months before, written in Anthony's erratic handwriting.

> My Dearest Leigh:
> If you are reading this letter it means that I have passed on to a better life, joining family and loved ones. Don't mourn for me.
> There are things that I couldn't express in person because once said, there was no turning back. Since I committed to God's path, I savored my thoughts and feeling until reaching the end of my earthly journey. Leigh, you're a strong, capable woman but that's not your greatest attribute. Your ability to love and care about people around you is what makes you so special and what compels, yes compels people to remain part of your life. You once told me that no one stops being a part of your life until you are ready to let go. I thank God that day never came.
> I hurt you more than anyone, yet you continued to give me unconditional support and friendship. We have remained dearest friends. You are my confidant and advisor in all areas of my life.
> During our time together, you took a man that focused on materialism and self-absorption and through kindness, caring, and example taught me what is truly important in life. Your example helped open my heart to God's calling. HE spoke for many years

but I didn't recognize or accept his message until you pried open my mind and heart.

The decision to become a priest was a difficult one. Once made I never second guessed; however, there wasn't a day that I didn't love you, think about and care about you. Each day I missed you next to me falling asleep at night and waking in the morning. I loved you and still love you very much as a woman and a human being. If I were granted a second life on earth, I would spend it with you.

When God calls you, I will be waiting on the other side, finally together and for eternity!

Loved you always,
Anthony

Misty eyes made it impossible to read the letter again. She carefully folded the letter and inserted it into the Papal envelope, placing the precious note on her nightstand. Leigh would re-read the letter for many nights to come, hoping to dream of their past and future days together.

THE END